TIMELESS LOVE

Kat stared at her painting. "And so it all hinges on your conference," she said. "If we can save that, we can save Europe. Or can we?" She looked up at him.

The horror in her expression sent a wrenching ache through him. "We can," he said with more conviction than he felt.

She shook her head. "Won't Louis Napoleon try something else? Graeme, what if it never ends? What if I'm stuck here for the rest of my life, painting these horrible predictions so we can keep history following the right path?"

He cupped her face between his hands, allowing his cane to slide to the chair behind him. His fingers stroked her cheek as he tried to calm her growing agitation. "Who's to say what history should become? Kat, it doesn't all lie on your shoulders. This one incident, yes, but that's enough for any person to deal with. You are here, with me now, and we can prevent this one thing from happening. But that is all there is. All."

Somehow, it seemed reasonable to kiss her forehead—just to soothe her—and when she turned her face toward his, he closed her eyes with the gentle caress of his lips . . .

JANICE BENNETT

Across Forever

PINNACLE BOOKS
WINDSOR PUBLISHING CORP.

PINNACLE BOOKS are published by

Windsor Publishing Corp.
850 Third Avenue
New York, NY 10022

First Printing: June, 1994

Printed in the United States of America

For Roberta

Chapter One

Her eyes played tricks on her. That could be the only explanation. At least the only sensible and logical explanation. She closed them, counted to ten with deliberation, then looked once more. Nothing had changed.

Kittyhawk Sayre sprang up from her folding lawn chair and paced away from the canvas and easel on which she'd been working. Deep breaths, she told herself. Deep, calming breaths. She shoved the curling lock of copper-brown bangs from her forehead and returned to stare at her painting.

At a casual glance, everything appeared normal. She should have stopped at that. But no, she'd had to give her work the critical eye. That was when the impossible image emerged from the precise arrangement of colors and patterns she had created.

Her fingers tightened on her brush, and she thrust it into the jar of paint thinner that stood at an angle on the grass. Above her, twenty-one multihued hot-air balloons drifted with the air currents against a sky of brilliant cerulean. Beneath them, dotted with walnut and elm trees, rolled the gentle green hills of the Essex countryside. She'd used a softened viridian, shadowed with ultramarine and highlighted with pale cadmium yellow. She had captured the scene in the perfect detail of photo-realism.

Except for that eerie tracery that somehow had crept onto the canvas.

Only it couldn't have. She took too much care with her work, planned the composition and balance, experienced every brush stroke. If she had painted that image, she would know it.

Yet there it was, defying all logic.

Weird. In fact, it was the strangest occurrence she could recall. And living for twenty-seven years with a father like Adam Sayre, she'd had plenty of strange adventures.

She stirred the brush to clean it, all the while studying those impossible lines. No random image, this. It took none of her artist's imagination to recognize an outline map of Europe, all the way from England in the painted renditions of the clouds down to Italy in the shrubs and grass. And in the center, emerging from the overlap of three of the colorful balloons, hung a French flag.

Her subconscious must have devised an elaborate practical joke for her. She contemplated the breakfast she had consumed of bangers and grilled tomatoes, but it had been surprisingly good. Probably not indigestion.

But perhaps she should have allowed herself just one of those pastries, after all.

She wouldn't mind one, now—even if it did defy the perpetual diet.

Maybe that was her problem—low blood sugar. Perhaps she'd been sitting here too long, engrossed in her work. She needed exercise—preferable to a bag of shortbread cookies—to give her a boost.

Her gaze slid back to the canvas. Shivering, she looked away at once. Not now. Unlike the Red Queen, she wasn't into seven impossible things, either before or after breakfast.

Oh, rats. A good, brisk walk, she reminded herself. She could leave her things where they lay and come back for them later. Maybe when her father returned he would have some reasonable explanation for that uncanny map.

She glanced up, seeking the blue, purple and green of his balloon. She should probably have gone up with him and not tried to finish the painting. Maybe that was the problem: she would much rather have been flying free than stuck here on the ground. Well, she would go tomorrow. Three more days still remained of the week-long One Hundred Fortieth Annual Graeme Warwick Balloon Ascension.

In spite of the painting, she was glad she'd accompanied her father to England. It would have been even more fun, of course, if her brothers and sister could have come, too. Being an artist had its advantages— she'd been able to pack and leave on a moment's notice, which was all her father ever gave any of them before departing for one of his madcap, aeronautic-related adventures. This one had seemed tame compared to last year's biplane flight across Canada.

Far more comfortable, too. Her gaze strayed over her shoulder to the venerable Tudor mansion which presided in haughty grandeur over the fifty-acre Durham estate. A fountain at the center of the graveled drive danced and sparkled in the sunlight. Except for necessary upkeep and security, the trustee managers had made no changes in the hundred and sixteen years since the last owner's death.

With her rapid, swinging stride, she set off toward the lake where she could glimpse swans basking in the warmth of the early May morning. She'd walk its perimeter twice—it looked to cover about three acres—then return to her canvas. If she still saw things that couldn't possibly be there—No, she'd wait to deal with that *if* it happened.

Thrusting her hands into the pockets of her jeans, she crossed the drive, the gravel scrunching beneath her tennis shoes. She'd already removed the down jacket she'd worn for the dawn ascension, leaving her with only the T-shirt with its rainbow-hued balloon and the name and date of the event emblazoned across both front and back.

A groundskeeper looked up from the border he weeded and nodded to her. Behind him, another started the engine on his riding lawn mower and headed it toward the makeshift compound where the balloonists camped. It certainly looked an odd assemblage, with gear ranging from the dome tents Kittyhawk and her father sported to twenty-four foot RVs. She could only be glad meals were provided with the event and served in the great state dining room in the elegant old Durham Court. The trustees, in accordance with the will of the last owner, the redoubtable Victorian balloonist Lady Clementina Durham, really laid on a spread. The buffet line, with its hollandaises, *au gratins* and *crèmes,* proved sheer torture to her willpower.

A small gazebo stood at the far side of the lake. Kat started toward it, keeping her stride brisk. She'd paint here this afternoon, she decided—this time an impressionistic scene *à la* Monet, capturing the beautiful pattern of the white swans and the pinks, yellows and greens of the water lilies, and perhaps the reflection of that little Greek temple.

She regarded it with loving consideration, then came to an abrupt halt as the image blurred. Now a black swan stood on the steps, accepting bread from the hand of a middle-aged woman in an old-fashioned straw bonnet and a long purple dress with a bell skirt. Kat blinked, and the image vanished.

She drew in a deep breath. What *had* been in that banger, anyway? Hallucinogenic mushrooms? Or maybe it had been the coffee. Or too many paint thinner fumes. Her father always told her they'd get to her if she weren't careful. She risked another glance at the gazebo, but its steps remained reassuringly empty.

After a moment, she continued, keeping a watchful eye on the graceful Grecian lines of the little building. She passed it without anything else weird happening. Relaxing a bit, she quickened her pace. She'd gone on this walk to refresh herself in the first place. She'd gain nothing by dawdling around the lake.

Halfway back along the gravel path, the house and drive shimmered before her eyes. A horse-drawn carriage, with a top-hatted driver perched on the box, rounded the corner into view, and a flush of irritation—somehow not her own—swept through her. She felt herself increase her stride, yet with every step her left leg ached, and she found herself limping, leaning to that one side as if she held a cane to support her weight. A hand rose from her side—not her own, but a larger, roughened hand, a *man's* hand, with a large gold ring set with an emerald on the little finger. . . .

She stopped short, swallowing the scream that rose to her throat. Her frantic gaze flew to her arm—no, that was *her* hand, with the pale pink polish on the nails, the gold watch on her wrist and her fingers devoid of jewelry.

What was happening? She hugged herself, her hands rubbing her upper arms. Was the place haunted? Her father hadn't said anything about it, and if there'd been even a hint of ghosts at Durham Court, he'd have regaled her with every tidbit of hearsay he could glean.

She shivered. She could be packed and back safe in some London hotel in about an hour. Durham Court was only twenty minutes away by train.

She glanced up again, to where small dots against the brilliant sky were all that remained to be seen of the drifting balloons. They wouldn't land for hours yet, then it would take still longer for the chase vehicles to return with the tired aeronauts and their equipment. No, she wouldn't run. She'd wait to hear her father's opinion. He'd probably advise her to switch to pastels or water colors and throw away the paint thinner and varnishes.

Squaring her shoulders, she marched back to where her easel and chair remained undisturbed. She faced the canvas without focusing on it, closed her eyes and counted to ten, then gazed fully at it.

No mistake. The tracery outline of the map remained. She hadn't imagined it.

She put her paints, brushes and palette in her paint box, folded the easel and tucked it all under one arm, then picked up the canvas and headed toward the side entrance of the great house that the Ascension attendees always used.

Walking into the library gave her an uncanny sense of having stepped back through time. Mahogany bookcases extended floor to ceiling, filled with ancient leatherbound volumes; a wheeled ladder leaned in the corner, ready to provide access to any of these. In the middle of the room, two Chesterfield sofas in tones of red and gold stood on opposite sides of an oriental rug, with an oval marble-topped table between them. Carved occasional tables, located at regular intervals about the room, held gas lamps topped with rounded glass shades. The lingering odor of mildew mingled with that of lemon oil and beeswax. Aside from the elaborate brass fittings on the fireplace and a number of growling lions carved or cast on a number of protrusions, she found the place less fussy than the pictures she'd seen of other Victorian interiors.

She laid everything but the canvas on the long table near the door, then let herself out into the hall beyond.

A wizened little man in a neat brown suit sat behind a huge cherrywood desk in the spacious entry hall. A ruff of silvery hair encircled his bald pate, and a little mustache of darker gray adorned his upper lip. A hat—a very proper Homburg—hung from one of the many brass arms of the claw-footed hat rack at his side.

He looked up as she approached, adjusted his bifocals, and peered at her. "Miss—Sayre?" His tenor voice rose on a note of pleasure. "You've been painting again, I see." He rose and came around to join her.

"Good morning, Mr. Jameson." She held out the canvas for his inspection. "Is there somewhere I can store this until it's dry?"

A beam of pleasure lit his face. "Beautiful, my dear. Beautiful."

"You don't see anything . . . odd . . . about it?" She held her breath.

"Odd? Certainly not." He fixed his earnest gaze on her face. "A delightful work. Quite delightful."

And if it weren't, would the little man be too sweet to say otherwise? Where was her father when she needed him? Adam would be blunt as always in his comments, but at least she'd learn the truth—if she, alone, saw things in her painting.

With a silent sigh, she waited while Mr. Jameson collected several sheets of the previous day's newspaper, then followed him across the marble-tiled hall and into a small sitting room that looked out over the drive. Here, several of the other balloonists had already left possessions they did not want outside in their camp. Mr. Jameson laid the sheets of newsprint over the oak parqueted floor, and Kat set the canvas on it, balancing the top edge against the arm of a chair.

"Beautiful," the man repeated, still gazing at the scene. "So very true-to-life. I like that in a painting, don't you? Will you start another, now?"

"Not for a while." Not, at least, until she'd gotten over the effects of those paint thinner fumes. "I'll take my pastels out, instead. Just a few quick sketches."

He beamed at her. He was barely taller than her own five-foot-four, she realized. A nice little man, who seemed perfectly suited to his role of trustee for the

Durham estate. She smiled as she preceded him into the hall, then headed back toward the library where she collected her things and returned outside.

In her tent, she packed away her oils and produced instead a selection of pencils, a box of pastels, a spray can of fixative and her sketch pad. The box lunch she'd been given along with the balloonists that morning remained on the end of her air mattress, and she pounced on it. Probably jam-packed with sugar and fats. She'd share the forbidden items in it with the swans down by the lake.

But *not* with any black ones. Nor with any women in long purple dresses.

As she left the encampment, she saw that someone had brought out another balloon. It stood in position on the sloped lawn, its cream-colored bag filled, straining at its ropes. Its basket . . . she stared at the creation in awe, a rush of exultation sweeping through her. A wicker dragon perched on four clawed feet, its pointed wings folded back, forming the basket. At the rear, a great tail looped up then down, so that its spiked tip rested on a back claw. At the front, a long, slender neck curved backward, the flared head pointed straight up into the balloon.

The whole assemblage shimmered, then vanished.

Kat sank to her knees on the newly mown grass and stared at the spot where the dragon basket no longer stood. It hadn't risen—a quick survey of the sky assured her of that. It had simply disappeared. Like the swan and the woman—and the horse-drawn carriage and the man's hand.

She drew in a deep breath; the memory of what she

had seen remained vivid. She opened her sketch pad and began drawing with quick, rapid strokes.

Three hours later she sat cross-legged on the floor of the little Greek temple, staring at the water. About her on the tiled floor were scattered four sketches: the dragon basket, the black swan, the woman in purple and a close-up of the woman's face. The last had appeared to her again while she had been sitting in the temple, scanning the lake and surrounding shrubs for any non-white water fowl. She hadn't spotted a single one. What she had seen was a fleeting image of the woman's fine-boned, weathered face with the prim, determined mouth and a challenging expression in her wide-set gray eyes. Her blonde hair, faded and flecked with gray, swept down over her ears, then up to the top of her head, where a lace scarf covered it.

Frowning, Kat opened her box lunch, resisted the packet of barbecued potato chips and instead unwrapped her chicken salad sandwich. At the first rustle of the plastic film, the squawking started at the lake, and three ungainly birds waddled toward her, wings flapping to keep their balance.

They weren't going to be satisfied with mere crumbs. She scooped up her drawings to the safety of a wooden bench, broke open the package of crisps and sailed a few out like frisbees. The birds turned in midstride and ran honking after the treat. Kat took a couple of hasty bites of the sandwich, regarded it wistfully, then allowed the swans to have the rest of the bread.

This they finished in moments, then turned back to her, their attitude expectant. She had only a banana and a packet of carrot and celery sticks left, none of which were likely to placate the birds. She grabbed up her sketching supplies and set off along the path around the lake to escape their importunings. For several hundred yards they followed her, then lost interest when she supplied no further handouts. With a last, admonishing honk, they waddled off.

Kat continued until she found a grassy knoll over-looking a shaded watery nook filled with lilies. Peace reigned here; only an occasional ripple broke the still surface. She settled down with the sun full on her back, ate the remainder of her meal and selected her pastels.

The rumbling of the first chase vehicle as it turned onto the gravel drive roused her from her concentration. She snatched up her things and ran to greet the returning aeronauts, driven by an urgent need to see her father, to hear his opinion—no matter how unflattering to herself. At least it would be honest—and as close to sane as Adam Sayre ever got.

Not much to her surprise, she found him in the last vehicle, lounging in the open back of the truck, a natty Alpine hat covering his unruly salt-and-pepper hair. He leaned against one basket, his feet propped against another. A release valve and a camera lay in his lap, clasped under protective hands.

"Kat!" His luxuriant mustache twitched as his lined face broke into an ecstatic grin, his enthusiasm and energy only enhanced by his fifty-three years. "You should have come."

"I know," she called back. The truck pulled into the ancient stone stable yard. She had to stand aside to allow a now-empty van to pull out of the arched gateway, then she hurried within.

The vehicle in which her father rode had drawn to

a halt before the half-timbered carriage house. Several of the balloonists carried baskets into the waiting stalls, where they could be kept dry from any mist or dew. More waited on the flagged paving.

Two pre-teen sons of one of the couples pushed past Kat, grabbed another basket, and with the help of two girls in their mid-twenties—French, by their accents—stowed it away. Kat cut through the bustle and made her way to the truck, grabbing one side of the tailgate as a middle-aged man released it, and together they let it down.

Adam Sayre unfolded his wiry frame and sprang to the gravel. His gaze rested on her face, and his eyebrows lowered. "Yes. Hmmm. I think one of the hooks is loosening on Bertram, here." He patted his wicker basket as helping hands dragged it from the truck bed. "Want to go over it with me?"

The words weren't an invitation. With a jerk of his head, he signaled for Kat to take one corner of Bertram. She dropped her drawing supplies inside the basket and complied. He grabbed another side, and with the help of a bashful teenager with thick glasses, they carried it into the carriage house.

"Here." Adam stopped before a long wooden tool bench and dropped his end.

Kat did likewise, thanked the kid who had helped and busied herself examining the hooks.

"Kat." Her father's voice held a note of command, demanding that she look up. "Out with it. What happened today?"

She shook her head. "I want you to see something, first. Without any priming."

His weathered face frowned, then he nodded. "Fair enough. Hand me that wrench, will you?"

After that, the only words he spoke were directions, until he at last stood back to admire his handiwork. When they'd carried Bertram to its assigned stall, which it shared with two other baskets, Kat collected her sketch pad and drawing supplies, and they started toward the house. Only a few people remained in the yard, fussing with their balloons or propane tanks.

Adam Sayre waved a cheery farewell to them and draped his arm about Kat's shoulders. "Now, what do you want me to see?"

"It's in the Court."

The lawn, so very much her own that morning, now boasted upwards of a dozen loungers or strollers. More would join them, as soon as tents and RVs had been visited. Kat glanced at her watch. Only half an hour until Mr. Jameson would preside over afternoon tea.

She led the way through the library into the hall, then to the front parlor. Her painting stood where she had set it, now flooded with the afternoon sunlight that shone through the paned window. The smell of her oils surrounded her, overpowering the faint mustiness of the old leathers and wools of the furnishings.

"You finished it." Adam leaned forward, studying the delicate lines and vivid hues. "Not bad," he said after another minute—his usual form of high praise. "Why'd it upset you?"

Kat folded her arms, forcing herself to breathe normally. "Look again. Try standing back a bit."

He did, his head nodding in approval. Abruptly, it stilled. "Playing 'connect-the-dots?' And why a

French flag? Been hanging around that du Brec character? He's too much of a ham for you, Kat."

"Du Brec's a pain." She dismissed the debonair Frenchman who had hovered at her side after dinner the night before. "I didn't paint that on purpose. It was just there."

Adam transferred his frowning gaze from the canvas to her face. "What else?"

Her lips twitched. Her father had an uncanny knack for sensing her moods. It had totally destroyed her few attempts at being a rebellious teenager. "I've been seeing things. Things that aren't there." Briefly, she described the black swan, the woman in purple, the carriage and the dragon basket.

Adam leaned back against the padded arm of a chair. "I'll give you one thing, Kat. At least you don't see boring, mundane things. I like that dragon. That's got a touch of real creativity behind it."

"Dad—"

He held up his hand. "See anything now?"

"Not since everyone got back." She offered him her sketch pad.

He took it in silence, studying each of her drawings, lingering the longest over the graceful wicker dragon. "Now that," he murmured, "is a beauty. What do you think, Kat, if we weave—"

"This wasn't meant for a plan," she snapped.

He inclined his head in acknowledgment, but his expression held the hint of a mischievous grin. "Wouldn't you give anything to fly that?"

"At the moment I'd give more for some explanations."

Adam rubbed his chin, but his covetous gaze returned to the dragon. "If we—"

The door opened, and a husky young man, all good-natured expression beneath a mop of brown hair, looked in. "Seen Jameson anywhere? It's been a long time since lunch."

Kat directed a reproachful look at her father, reclaimed her sketch pad and left the two men to talk. She might have remained herself if the newcomer hadn't been married. Funny how every man she met was either already committed or a royal pain. Or maybe she was just too much of an idealist, or too demanding in her tastes. Her relationships rarely went beyond the superficial, and always left her with a sense that something important had been missing. They left her lonely. And then Wilbur or Orville—every inch Adam's sons—would call her out of the blue with some harebrained scheme they'd concocted, and she'd be swept up into family fun and adventure.

A sudden wave of longing for her older brothers swept over her. For Clementina, too. She hadn't seen her elder sister since Tina married last January. Their annual reunion this Christmas would be that much more enjoyable.

She dropped everything off at her tent, but hesitated before going back to the Court. Everyone else seemed to have gone inside already, leaving the lawn once more to her sole enjoyment. She strolled across it, relishing the smell of the grass, the freshness of the air. Somewhere in the yews lining the drive a lark sang. She closed her eyes, breathing deeply, experiencing the moment.

The next vision flickered across her mind, gone in an

instant. Her eyelids flew wide. A *train?* She retained the haziest impression of an antique steam engine. She swallowed, trying to recapture the image, but it had vanished.

She turned her steps toward the library doors. Why had she experienced that wave of released impatience, as if she had waited for that train, annoyed by its tardiness then relieved that it finally arrived? First a carriage, then a balloon, now a train. What would she see next? Spanish galleons on the lake?

The two drawing rooms on the opposite side of the front hall from the parlor had been thrown into one, providing comfortable seating for the fifty-two attendees of the Balloon Ascension. Kat ducked away from du Brec, whose too-handsome countenance took on a predatory gleam as he spotted her. She didn't feel up to a game of keeping track of his hands.

Adam stood by the window, conversing with three other middle-aged men. Their wives sat on nearby chairs, each holding a delicate china cup and saucer. A plate of cookies and sliced cakes rested on a low oval table before them. Rats, sticky buns, too. Her favorites. Kat turned her back on them and made her way to where Mr. Jameson presided over a silver coffee urn. He handed her a cup; she thanked him, then wandered among the milling people.

How could she be in the midst of so much humanity, yet feel so alone? Only she *didn't* feel alone. What—or rather, who—touched her mind? The sensation persisted, not quite hers, yet part of her. She groped to get a hold on it, but it faded, vanishing at last into the merest memory.

Unsettled, she strode over to join her father.

* * *

Kat awoke, trembling, staring with wide eyes into the darkness of her dome tent. She sat up in her sleeping bag, found her flashlight and switched it on, listening. Silence engulfed her, broken by a gentle snore some distance away. The entire encampment must be asleep.

So what had disturbed her? A dream? She eased the zipper on her tent open and stuck her head outside. A few feet away she could see the dim outline of her father's tent, and beyond it several more, then a line of trailers and RVs. She looked the other way, seeing only the stillness of the night. Nothing.

She sank back on her air mattress, then slid under the nylon-enshrouded down as the chill penetrated. She must be the only one awake. She flicked off the light and closed her eyes once more.

In her mind, unbidden, formed the image of the dragon basket, beautiful in its design, lifting free from the confining ground. She wanted to go with it, to fly in that beautiful creation. She wanted . . .

Something nudged at her mind, a presence, as if another person were with her.

Probably that woman, complete with her swan, Kat told herself in disgust. Except that hand she'd seen had been a man's. She squeezed her lids tight and fought off a pang of unwarranted low spirits. Again, not her own.

Someone, some *man,* invaded her mind.

Chapter Two

Her father's voice, calling her name, awakened Kat. She opened her eyes to see the green glow of sunlight flooding through the nylon of her tent.

"Come on, sleepyhead." A hand shook the top poles, setting the fabric shimmering. "I thought you were the early riser in the family."

She fought back a yawn. "I'll see you at breakfast."

"Promises, promises." He laughed as he gave the tent a final pat.

His cheerful whistle drifted back to her as she unzipped the sleeping bag and groped through her duffel for her jeans and a sweater. She must have gone back to sleep in the early hours of the morning. She yawned again and dragged a brush through her hair, grateful it was no more than shoulder length, though its thickness seemed to invite snarls. She untangled a knot at the nape of her neck, gave her hair one last lick with the brush, then fastened it with a bow-covered barrette. Today, she promised herself, she would ignore any peculiar images that tried to haunt her. She grabbed up her sketch pad and a selection of pencils and set forth.

A few other stragglers made their way across the lawn to the library doors of the graceful Tudor mansion. Kat slowed her steps, allowing them to get ahead of her. She didn't feel like company. She felt . . .

She *felt*.

She stopped in her tracks, trying to analyze the transient sensations. Frustration, dejection, determination, followed by—longing? Yet none of these emotions had anything to do with *her*.

The longing took hold until she ached with a need for she knew not what. She closed her eyes, and almost at once the image of the dragon basket filled her mind. A glorious release built within her as she felt herself rising beneath that cream-colored envelope. Her fingers clenched wicker, and the pain of her leg faded into insignificance compared to the freedom of flying . . .

The sensations vanished, along with the image, leaving her standing on the grass, arms spread to hold the absent dragon's side. Now all she felt was . . . alone. Terribly alone. Shaken, she strode across the lawn, almost running to join the others.

The Ascension Committee, chaired by the trustee Mr. Jameson, considered breakfast to be an informal, "drop-in" affair. Most of the participants had already been and gone, off on their early morning flight. Kat made selections from the chafing dishes on the sideboard, then had a serious and almost losing argument with herself over a fat-laden, sugar-drenched Danish pastry. The memory of the tug it had taken to fasten her jeans helped. Nobly, but not without regrets, she took a slice of oatmeal bread instead. She joined her father where he sat beside a couple of Canadian men, both in their late twenties.

Only meager scraps remained on all three plates— the sugary remains of sweet rolls, she noted. The men still held steaming cups in their hands, and the aroma of strong coffee surrounded her. Neither of the two Canadians spared her more than a glance, but her father waved and gestured with his head for her to take the seat beside him.

The two young men took their leave, and Adam Sayre turned his scrutiny on Kat. After a moment's consideration, he said, "You look like hell."

Kat dropped a light kiss on his unruly hair. "Thank you." She seated herself, then picked up her tea.

"Been seeing dragons, again?" Adam kept his voice low.

"On the way in here." She kept her gaze on her cup. "Dad, it's crazy, but I'm *feeling* things, too. Like I'm intruding into someone else's mind. And whoever he is, he isn't happy."

"He?" Adam's eyebrows rose. "Not the woman with the swan?"

Kat lowered her cup to the table. "No." She shook her head, perplexed. "I don't know what's going on." She brought out her sketch pad, closed her eyes a moment, then sketched the dragon once more, this time in three-quarter profile. Adam took it from her, his eyes gleaming, as if he analyzed the design.

Rapid footsteps sounded behind them, and Mr. Jameson's beaming face appeared over Adam Sayre's shoulder. "You'll be late for the sightseeing—" He broke off. "What a truly remarkable likeness that is.

Really, Miss Sayre, you are quite talented, quite talented indeed."

"Likeness?" Her throat felt dry.

"Captain Warwick's basket. Remarkable, isn't it? I've always thought we should bring it out and display it during the annual Ascension, but the lady's will was quite specific about keeping it hidden away until—" Again, he broke off.

"Until what?" Kat demanded. Her father's foot came down on her arch, and she cast him an indignant glance.

He ignored her. "Captain Warwick's, is it? The original Warwick?"

Mr. Jameson paid him no heed. He regarded Kat with an intensity unexpected in him. "Did you see a painting of it, Miss Sayre? I don't remember one in any of the ground floor rooms."

"I haven't. I thought I made it up. There really is a basket like this? Here? On the estate? May I see it?" Already she stood, excitement racing through her.

Mr. Jameson's eyes narrowed. "Could you be—" he murmured, then blinked. "Excuse me, Miss Sayre. Mr. Sayre. I'll be right back."

Kat sank once more onto her chair. Her father handed her the cup of tea, and she sipped from it.

"What is all that about?" he asked.

"I wonder if Captain Warwick ever felt depressed or in pain?" Kat whispered.

Adam's walrus-mustache twitched. "What are you planning, a seance? The fellow's been dead for—"

"For well over a hundred years." Kat shivered. "I want to see that dragon basket."

She had finished her eggs and bread before the prim

little man returned. He held his handkerchief between his hands, pleating it with his fingers in short, nervous movements. "Would you come with me, please? This is most extraordinary. Most extraordinary, indeed. To think—but then of course—but how should I expect—and in *my* time—"

"What on earth are you blathering about, man?" Adam followed them from the room.

Mr. Jameson jumped and turned wide eyes on them, peering through his bifocals. "To be sure, it must seem quite odd—but then it *is* odd, isn't it? Most peculiar, in fact."

"What is?" Adam demanded.

"I—I'm not supposed to say. That is, there are instructions for this happening, only no one has ever taken them seriously, though I've read them, of course, since it seemed such a very odd thing to include—but I mustn't run on."

"No, Dad." Kat caught her father's arm, warding off his exasperated tirade. "Let's just look at the basket, since apparently that's allowed. Maybe we'll be able to figure a few things out for ourselves."

Adam glowered at her, but made no further comment as they exited the house through the library doors and crossed the drive that led to the stableyard. Instead of entering the cobbled area, they circled around to where a low stone building formed one of the sides. Mr. Jameson swung the huge door wide, then flipped the light switch set into the wall on the left. Fluorescent tubes flickered to life, illuminating the inside of the vast building, throwing shadows from the various trucks and cars that filled the ground floor.

"Up here." Mr. Jameson led the way to a flight of wooden stairs set along the left side of the barn.

Easy, Kat ordered herself. Her heart pounded erratically as she mounted the steps, and she clutched the railing for support.

An incredible number of shrouded shapes filled the loft above. Kat advanced with care, following the nimble Mr. Jameson as he eased between barrels, crates and sheet-covered objects. Dust filled her nose and mouth, and she could see the motes swirling in the beams of light.

At the far end Mr. Jameson stopped. "Mr. Sayre?" Adam stepped forward, and together the two men dragged an aged sheet from its position.

Kat caught her breath.

Before her stood the wicker dragon with its gracefully curving tail and neck, exactly as she had seen it—except now fire had blackened and scorched the wicker. Thin metal plates, rusted with time, bolted the fragile corners together. She reached out, her hand hovering, not quite daring to touch.

"Made by Captain Warwick himself, about a hundred and fifty years ago." Mr. Jameson looked from the dragon to Kat. "Just like your drawing, isn't it? Haven't been up here myself to look at it since just after I took over this job. I—" He broke off again.

Kat forced her trembling hand to just rest on the wicker. Raw emotion surged through her, love, longing—desperation. Almost of their own volition, her fingers ran along the dragon's head with its flared nostrils.

She had to fly in this basket.

There lay her only hope of ever understanding the

visions that plagued her. She knew that as a certainty. But it was more than that. She *needed* to fly it, just as she needed to breathe.

"What a remarkable creation," murmured Adam.

Mr. Jameson removed the sketch pad from Kat's clenched hand and examined her drawing. "You've done it exactly, except for the fire damage." He shook his head. "It's remarkable." He looked up, fixing his expectant gaze on her.

She ran her fingers along the tail, experiencing an indescribable joy in the grace of the curves. No one in their right mind would let strangers—or anyone, for that matter—take out anything so fragile and beautiful. It would need repairs just to make it safe, and how could a trustee allow that? Yet she *had* to fly in this. Longing, now all her own, swept through her, and tears stung her eyes. She blinked them back.

"Well?" Mr. Jameson watched her with growing anxiety.

Kat clenched her fingers on the wicker side, unwilling to let it go. "It's exactly—" Exactly what? Like she'd seen it in her visions? She could hardly say that; the poor man must already think her crazy.

Mr. Jameson looked from the drawing to the basket, then to her face. "But don't you want—I mean—"

A shaky laugh escaped her. "What I want is impossible."

"Is it?" Hope filled the man's face.

Kat glanced at her father, but he had squatted down on his heels, his attention wholly fixed on one of the rusted plates. She swallowed. "I'd give anything to be able to fly in this." There, she'd said it. Now he'd have to tell her . . .

He smiled, relief in every line of his slender build. "I *knew* you would. I just knew it." He beamed at her. "When?"

Her breath caught in her throat. "You mean you'd *let* me?"

"Oh, yes." An enigmatic smile played at the corners of his mouth. "Oh, yes, indeed. In fact, I am quite anxious for you to do so."

"It'll need some work." Adam's gaze remained riveted on the basket. "I wouldn't trust this to support its own weight, let alone ours."

Mr. Jameson squatted beside him. "How long do you think repairs will take?"

Adam turned to study him. "You really want us to take it up, don't you? Why?"

Mr. Jameson drew back. "Well, as to that, who wouldn't want to see this fly? Why don't we carry it down where you can get a better look at it?"

Kat stepped forward at once, grasping the dragon about the neck. She knew all about proverbial gift horses, yet she was afraid if she hesitated for as much as a moment, her chance would be snatched away. Flying this dragon meant everything to her. She wouldn't question why she was being permitted to do so, she would simply do it.

They struggled down the stairs with the aged wicker, taking care not to bump it against the wall. Keeping it carefully balanced between the three of them, they carried it across the empty cobbled stones to the carriage house that had been converted into a work room. The sightseeing expedition, it appeared, had already departed. Good. That left them to work in peace. Even the groundskeepers were about their duties.

Mr. Jameson remained with them while Kat and Adam went over every inch of the basket, assessing the damage and extent of repairs needed. The little man almost danced in his excitement, Kat noted, jarred out of her preoccupation with the dragon by his compulsive movements. He could barely contain his glee. Why should it matter so much to him?

At last, as if unable to control his emotions a moment longer, he excused himself and ran toward the house. Kat glanced at her father, but his attention remained focused on trying to loosen the bolts from the metal plates. She grabbed a wrench and helped.

When the first rusted piece came free, the damaged wicker separated. Kat caught a falling fragment, then laid the bolt aside, following it soon with another.

"This was a good job." Adam said at last. "Just the way I'd have fixed it. See? The supported metal takes all the stress."

Kat turned over the metal plate. "It's light, isn't it? Are we going to be able to find anything like it to make the repairs?"

Adam, already at work on the next corner, grunted in response. "Should be able to make anything we can't find. Or maybe Jack or Vince will have something. Did you get a look at that repair kit they hauled with them? Pass me the WD-40, will you?"

When the first of the chase vehicles rolled into the yard some three hours later, Adam looked up from his work. "Damn, I've missed my lunch. Kat, be a good girl and fetch me a sandwich, will you?"

For the first time, she became aware of the hunger that must have been gnawing at her for some time. Still, she left with reluctance. Halfway across the lawn she encountered Mr. Jameson, bearing two boxed lunches, hurrying to meet her.

"My dear," he exclaimed. "I'm so terribly sorry not to have remembered these earlier."

"Why should you? We should have come back." She eyed the boxes and fought off a yearning desire to discover if any chocolate chip cookies lurked within.

"How do you go on?" His watery blue eyes glittered behind their thick lenses, avid. "I didn't want to disturb you, and it all seems so impossible, I wanted to check—" He broke off. "But there, I mustn't say, must I?" He thrust the cardboard containers at her and hurried away before she could demand any answers.

Thoughtful, she returned to the barn where several people now gathered about the dragon basket, watching her father at work. In silence she held out his lunch. Adam wiped his hands on a rust-streaked rag and dove with gusto into the container.

Kat perched on an open tailgate and foraged through her own lunch. Rats—or rather, good. No cookies. Only an apple and packet of potato chips, and not a swan in sight. She fought the impulse to taste one of the salty—*greasy*—crisps, thrust the package out of sight beneath her napkin and concentrated instead on her sandwich.

One of the teen-aged sons of an American couple toed a wicker corner and regarded it with all the lofty superiority of his sixteen years. "You wouldn't catch me taking that thing up."

"No one with sense would," remarked his mother. "It'd probably fall apart on you."

The father shook his head. "Impractical. No instrumentation. Or are you just going to tether it? That'd be best."

"We're going to fly it." Kat surprised even herself with the vehemence in her voice.

A middle-aged man squinted through his glasses and snorted. "Better you than me."

Another chase vehicle pulled into the yard, and the balloonists deserted the dragon basket, going to offer assistance to their returning comrades.

"Good." Adam set aside the rest of his meal. "Let's get on with it before we have any more interruptions." He picked up a rusted metal plate, tapped it with a considering finger, then made a bee-line for the well-supplied workbench.

Shortly after nine o'clock that evening, under the flood lights that illuminated the stableyard, Adam pronounced the basket fit for flight. Kat walked around it, studying each of the new supports that reinforced the burned fragments, urgency welling within her as her more cautious, rational self acknowledged the truth of her father's words. In spite of all odds—in spite, perhaps, even of common sense—the wicker held together.

In a few short hours the dragon would fly once more.

The two Canadians, who had strolled out after dinner to offer unrequested advice, helped Adam and Kat carry the basket under shelter, where Kat lovingly draped a sheet over it. "Tomorrow," she whispered, and didn't know to whom she made that promise—to herself, to the dragon . . . or to the mysterious presence that haunted her.

Only he hadn't, today. While she'd helped her father, not once had she seen any unsettling visions, or even experienced those foreign emotions. Had the basket protected her from them? Or had it been the constant presence of someone else? She'd always been alone when those strange occurrences had come to haunt her.

Alone. She shivered and hurried to join the few remaining spectators as they strolled toward their various accommodations for the night.

Chapter Three

Kat woke before dawn, amazed that her anticipation had permitted her any sleep at all. She dressed quickly in jeans, thick woolen socks and two layers of sweaters before adding her down parka on top. She crammed a knitted hat over the coppery waves of her hair, then went to call softly into her father's tent.

He groaned in response. "It's not morning, yet."

"Stick your head out," came her unfeeling response. "Not a star left in the sky. We haven't fitted our balloon to the basket, yet, remember? And you know how long it takes to fill it."

The sound of a cavernous yawn emitted from within the nylon dome. "Coffee, Kat. Lots of it."

"Strong and sweet," she promised. She collected her thermos from her own tent and strode off toward the manor house.

Well-being flooded her as she crossed the expanse of lawn. Whatever they did this day, it was right. Inevitable. And necessary.

Something touched her mind, a gentle caress, and she slowed her steps, opening herself to this uncanny yet increasingly familiar experience. No, the feeling vanished, as softly as it had come. She had missed it yesterday, she realized. Had she been too absorbed in the restoration work to notice it? When the sensation came, she felt less alone, less cut off. Yet it scared the life out of her, too.

To her surprise, she found Mr. Jameson, already awake, dressed and at his desk as she started to cross the dimly lit hall. He looked up from the yellowed papers he perused by the glow of the painted glass lamp at his side. An unopened envelope, also yellowed with age, lay before him.

Hastily he shoved both papers and envelope into a drawer of his massive desk, then rose, coming to meet her and taking her hand. "Well, Miss Sayre?" Eagerness suffused his words.

"Well, Mr. Jameson?" She fought off her uneasiness at the repressed excitement of his manner and forced a teasing note into her voice. Why did he want so much for her to take the dragon aloft? Curiosity got the better of her. "What do those mysterious papers of yours say?" she demanded.

"When you come back, I can tell you. Yes, Miss Sayre, I promise. When you come back from this flight. I really don't know everything myself, yet, you see. There are more instructions . . ." His voice trailed off.

"*Whose* instructions?" Kat tried, but merely got an apologetic shake of the head for an answer.

When they got back. Well, that wouldn't be long. She doubted they'd take the dragon basket far—

Again, longing surged through her to take the basket and fly, escape, drift through the heavens, never to come down . . .

"Coffee." She jerked herself out of that dreamy mood. A good aeronaut kept her head about her, watched her instruments to make sure nothing went wrong. Only the dragon possessed no elaborate altimeter or rate of climb indicator. Not even a compass. They'd have to keep alert.

"Of course there's coffee, Miss Sayre. In the breakfast room."

He led the way to the familiar apartment, where as yet no food had been brought out. Mr. Jameson pressed the bell as they entered. "There will be muffins along presently, I shouldn't wonder. Do you wish this filled?"

He took the thermos from her hands and held it under the urn's spout while the steaming, fragrant liquid poured inside. Kat added a dollop of cream and enough sugar to sweeten ten cups instead of the sixteen ounces the container held, then fixed a less syrupy cup for herself to drink before going back outside. Mr. Jameson remained in the room with her the whole time, holding coffee of his own that he never touched. His curious gaze remained fixed on her until she felt like a performing seal. Uncomfortable, she drained the cup and left to take sustenance to her father.

She found him dressed, shaved and where she'd expected him—giving the dragon basket one more inspection. She paused in the stableyard behind him, studying the wicker creation with a love that startled her. The elegance of the lines, the whimsy of the design. Suddenly, she longed to see flames shoot from that up-flung snout, to see the ground drop away from beneath those wicker clawed feet. She wanted to *fly*.

"It's about time." Adam held out an imperious hand for the thermos, then unscrewed the lid and swallowed a scalding mouthful. "That's better. Nice to feel human again. Nothing like a good shot of caffeine, is there?"

Kat's gaze never left the dragon. "Mr. Jameson is practically panting for us to take off."

Adam cast her an assessing glance. "So are you, I see. Well, the sooner we get the envelope spread, the sooner it gets filled. Come on."

Together they fetched their blue, purple and green nylon balloon and carried it to the grass where they stretched it out. By the time they returned for the dragon, the first few aeronauts had straggled in from their tents and RVs and lent willing hands. Within minutes, the connections had been made.

One of the Canadians—Vince—started up the gas-powered fan and Adam aimed it into the balloon. The nylon rippled in response to the caressing air, billowing outward. Nothing for her to do except wait . . .

Before her, for a fleeting second, a very different balloon filled, cream-colored . . .

She blinked, and once more her father's striated nylon undulated on the ground as air streamed inside. Kat backed away a pace, her hands clenching together. What visions would she experience when she actually *rode* in that dragon?

Memory of her painting rushed back, of the tracery of the united Europe under the French flag. She hadn't been aware of painting that. Was she receiving other visions, below her level of awareness, that would only come out through her painting? When better to test that possibility than while actually riding inside that dragon?

She left the others watching the balloon fill and raced to her tent. She wouldn't need much—yes, she'd need a lot. An easel, a canvas or two, her paints and brushes, a palette, the paint thinner. She'd never painted aloft, before. The ride was usually smooth—until the landing, or unless they hit turbulence. She'd keep lids on everything—especially the paint thinner jar.

She grabbed the wooden box that held her supplies from where it sat just inside her tent, located two canvases and the folding easel, then collected her sketch pad and pencils as well. Never hurt to be prepared. She returned more slowly under the added weight to where the crowd increased about the dragon basket.

Several more baskets now rested on the lawn, scattered about forty feet apart, their envelopes spread, fans blowing. General attention, though, remained fixed on the dragon. Several of the wealthier aeronauts might soon be placing orders with basket companies, Kat reflected.

Adam glanced up as Kat approached and his brow shot down. "What the—" he began, then broke off, his expression one of dawning enlightenment. "Good idea." He helped her place the equipment inside, then returned to monitoring the filling process.

Why couldn't it hurry, just this once? Why couldn't the envelope be filled, pulling at its tethers, ready to lift her away from the dreary, pain-filled reality to the freedom of the skies? Why couldn't the hydrogen already strain against the oiled silk and the—

She broke off the thought, isolating herself from the mental intrusion, and the unbearable longing faded. *He* was there, *he* had invaded her mind again, and with more subtlety this time, as if it became easier for him with practice.

She cast an uneasy glance over her shoulder. She must have stirred up his ghost, somehow. The ghost of Captain Graeme Warwick. With caution, she probed her mind, no more than a tentative touch, but could detect no alien presence. At the moment. Had she frightened him off?

A ghost. She sank onto the grass, her down-clad arms wrapped about her knees. Poor Captain Warwick must have died with something weighing heavily on his mind, and his spirit lingered, unable to find peace.

She considered that, and frowned. On the whole, she wasn't sure whether she believed in ghosts or not. Yet *something* sure invaded her mind. Maybe not a ghost, though. The brain operated rather like a radio, didn't it? Perhaps his broadcast on a wavelength similar to hers, and she picked up lingering emanations from him. That could explain everything.

Yet reaching that conclusion didn't bring her the satisfaction she expected. She still longed to fly in the dragon with a desperation that superseded any casual picking up of someone else's emotions.

"Kat?" Adam's voice held a note of encouragement, as if he had called more than once.

She looked up to see him standing in the dragon, his propane tank in position, the flame shooting into the envelope which already rose toward the sky. He must have been heating it for some time already.

One of the teenagers offered her a hand and pulled her to her feet. She brushed the lingering grass from her jeans, discovering in the process the lawn had been damp. Oh, well, no time to change now. She clambered over the side and shoved her gear out of her way with her foot. Taking up a position opposite her father, she stretched her arms along the dragon's sides. At once, the sensation of warm sunshine washed over her, as if she floated through the air on a hot August day, leaving her worries behind . . .

Not *her* worries, but *his*.

With a wrench, she reclaimed her mind, and again stood in the chill early light of the May morning, surrounded by about forty spectators, several of whom ignored their own filling balloons in favor of watching the dragon take once more to the air.

Mr. Jameson elbowed his way through the throng, stopping inches from them. He reached a tentative hand toward the wicker side, then pulled it back as if repelled by an electric current. He opened his mouth, then closed it as if uncertain what to say. "Be careful," he managed at last. "Don't go too far. We'll have the van trailing you, of course, but—"

Adam fixed him with an exasperated look. "I've flown without instruments before. The wicker is sound and the rest of the equipment is my own. What can go wrong?"

Oh, boy, if those weren't famous last words. Kat stifled a giggle which she recognized as a rising hysteria. Stop this talking and *fly!*

Her gaze rested on the propane tank, the head of

which her father had inserted into the dragon's hollow, metal-lined neck and up-flung head. Flames shot upward from the dragon's mouth into the bag's opening, heating the air. Any minute now . . .

As if in answer to her silent urgings, the faces near her drifted downward, and as always it took her a moment to realize the basket no longer rested on the ground. Airborne, lifting skyward, toward the lowering clouds. Her heart soared with it. They could go on like this forever—or at least until the fog enveloped them.

Kat blinked, once more herself, surprised at the haze surrounding them. She'd swear it hadn't been there a moment before. Or had she lost all track of time again? She glanced over the side, but they were only a few feet above the heads of the watchers— watchers whose legs vanished within a swirling mist. It closed about them from all sides, even above. She could barely see her father, less than a yard from her.

"We'd better go down," she said, her words sounding muffled by their misty shroud.

"Valve's stuck," came Adam's succinct response.

She started to protest, then closed her mouth. She'd checked it before they started. For that matter, he must have, too.

Without waiting to be asked, she groped through their emergency tool kit and produced the necessary wrench and placed it into his extended hand. It was eerie, suspended in space, unable to see or hear much besides her father's muttered abuse at the recalcitrant valve. His words broke off abruptly with a satisfied sigh, and as the flame diminished to almost nothing, he handed back the wrench.

"Down in a couple minutes," he told her with his usual cheerfulness. "We'll let this blow over, then try again."

Now she could scarcely see anything, and her father's voice came thin and hollow, as if from a great distance. A wave of disorienting dizziness swept over her, and she gripped the sides of the basket. Not her mind-sharer this time, she realized hazily. Legitimate light-headedness. Her stomach roiled, then the nausea passed, leaving her perspiring and shaken. Her fingers tightened their hold on the wicker.

"Kat?" Adam's voice quavered. "Strangest ride I've ever had. Did you just feel sick, too?"

She nodded, then managed a shaky grin. "What, just have your first bout of airsickness?" She sobered. "Weird timing."

"Ummm." He stood up.

Kat realized they both had been sitting on the floor of the basket. She had no memory of that. They'd been standing . . .

"It's clearing," he announced with relief.

Kat blinked. That was one emotion she'd never expect from her indomitable father. She didn't blame him. This whole thing was spooky beyond words. Weakness sapped her muscles, leaving them unresponsive. She had to pull herself up to look over the edge, only to see more grayness below.

It took her a second to realize she stared at water, not mist. "We're over the lake," she announced. The effort it took to speak surprised her. "Pretty low, too. No more than ten feet, I should think."

Adam grunted, glanced over the side, and nodded in satisfaction. "How big is it, remember? I don't think

Mr. Jameson would appreciate our taking the dragon for a swim."

"No worry. I think it only covers a few acres. In fact—" She broke off, peering into the evaporating mist, wishing she didn't feel so shaky. "Yes, there's the bank. And the fog is lifting, it should be clear in a few more minutes. Want to go back up?"

Adam considered. "After I check the equipment again," he said at last.

He pulled the release valve and they skimmed barely three feet above the water, sinking lower and lower. Then they were over land, and a startled swan took off at an awkward run, wings flapping, and the basket collided with a low shrub and settled to the ground with a lurch.

Kat closed her eyes and drew in a deep breath. "Haven't lost your touch at landings, I see."

Adam regarded her with a pained expression. "My dear Kittyhawk, I'll have you know I could set a balloon down on any specified spot in worse fogs than that. And as for that slight bump—"

'We're bumping again." Kat lunged over her father's shoulder and pulled the release valve, draining away more of the hot air, and the dragon came to rest.

And vanished.

Instinct took over through the shock, and Kat caught one of the loosened lines, running with it as the balloon, free of part of its load, sailed with the breeze once more. Adam dragged on the release valve with one hand and with the other caught another line, and followed perforce. For several minutes they struggled, then the bag ceased to pull at them. In another minute it sagged, and they were able to begin drawing it down.

With the striated nylon at last touching the ground, continuing its slow collapse, Adam sat back on his heels and wiped his forehead with the back of one hand. "Correct me if I'm wrong, Kat," he said in a deliberate tone, "but didn't we have a wicker dragon with us when we started?"

Kat gazed back the way they had come from the lake, to where the tanks and valves and ballast and even her painting supplies lay scattered on the grass. But no basket. Where—? Her mind refused to cope with one more eerie occurrence. The dragon must have succumbed to old age and disintegrated with the impact of landing. Yet shouldn't there be debris?

"Nope," she said with steady determination. "No dragons. Must have been an illusion."

"That's what I thought." Adam nodded, but he didn't appear convinced.

Kat rose and brushed herself off. "So where's the rescue party? The least they could do would be to bring a wheelbarrow to help us cart this stuff back."

"Mr. Jameson," Adam said as he stood, "is going to be livid."

"It's his own fault." Kat folded her arms in front of her, trying to keep from shivering. "He shouldn't have insisted we take it up."

Where *had* the dragon gone? She carefully refrained from asking. Someone might tell her, and she had the sneakiest feeling she didn't want to know.

"I think we're about to get some explanations," Adam said.

Kat glanced at him, and he inclined his head toward the lake. Kat turned and saw a four-wheeled carriage, pulled by a single horse, trotting toward them along the graveled path that followed the edge of the lake. "So that's his game. Mr. Jameson just wanted an excuse to dress up, and we played right into his hands," she declared, disgusted. "Do you suppose they'll try to do the rest of the event in Victorian outfits? Oh, rats, you don't suppose they'll expect *us* to wear costumes, too, do you?"

Adam harummphed. "If they think—" He broke off, peering at the approaching vehicle. "That's not Jameson, it's a woman driving."

"Oh, great, he's got support, then. But I'm warning you, Dad, I am *not* wearing a bustle and button shoes, or whatever they wore in Captain Warwick's time. And that's final."

The open carriage pulled closer and the driver transferred her reins to one hand and waved the other. "Are you having trouble?" Her voice, deep and vibrant, carried easily.

"Her outfit looks early Victorian," Adam muttered to Kat. "Dammit, if Jameson wanted this to be a fancy dress affair, why didn't he just say so up front? Or do you suppose it's just in honor of our taking out the dragon basket?"

"Then he's going to be a bit disappointed, isn't he? Since we went and lost it, I mean."

"How *could* we have—" Adam began, then closed his mouth as the carriage pulled up abreast of their gear, which remained where it had fallen on the grass.

A woman of medium height and comfortable build, garbed in a purple silk gown with sloping shoulders and huge sleeves, eyed them with interest from beneath a high poke bonnet that concealed her hair and most of her face.

She turned her head, and her gaze settled on the multihued bag. "Thought I saw a balloon from the stable," she announced, sounding satisfied. "But where is your basket?"

Adam stepped forward with all the appearance of one playing along under protest. "It seems to have disappeared."

"Into the lake? Bad luck, that." The woman hitched her reins to the side and jumped down, her broad skirts swinging with the movement. "I brought the phaeton in case you needed help getting back." She gestured down the length of the two-seated vehicle.

"Madam," Adam intoned with a sweeping bow, apparently getting into the spirit of things, "you are most welcome. Kat, want to throw your gear in the back? I'll grab the balloon."

The woman turned, facing Kat fully for the first time, and a good-humored smile lit her countenance. A very pleasant, but all-too familiar countenance. Kat's knees gave way, and she sank to the damp grass, her bewildered gaze fixed on the woman's face.

She'd seen it before—but never in the flesh. This woman shouldn't be here, she belonged to the realm of Kat's visions.

Chapter Four

The woman's expression showed sudden concern as she watched Kat. "Are you not feeling quite the thing? It's no wonder, if you've just had a close escape. Here," she strode forward, offering her hand. "Why don't you—" She broke off. "How very brave of you, my dear. Really, I'm quite impressed. How often I have longed to wear men's garments while flying, but I have never quite had the nerve. I can see I am going to enjoy this acquaintance immeasurably. Now, do come sit in my phaeton and I'll help the gentleman collect your things."

"But—" Kat started to protest, but a wave of dizziness made it impossible to speak. The woman assisted her to her feet and ushered her toward the waiting carriage. Kat went without protest.

"Now, do not be alarmed, my dear. You'll feel more the thing in a trice."

"But you're—" Kat's voice failed her.

The woman inclined her head. "Lady Clementina Durham. You've landed at Durham Court—about sixteen miles from London."

"Lady Clementina," Kat repeated, still sorting through her personal fog. The next moment, her mind cleared. "That's the name of the woman who ballooned across the Channel ten times. Were you named for her?"

"Not named for her. I *am* her. How could I be named for someone my own age?" Amusement tinged with skepticism filled her voice. "And I've only flown across the Channel seven times. Not that I wouldn't mind trying it again, of course."

Kat climbed into the backseat of the carriage, holding onto the edge as it settled on its springs with her added weight. Lady Clementina Durham. Kat had grown up on her father's tales of that daring Victorian-era lady's aeronautical exploits. He'd even named his first child after her—much to Tina's irritation.

So all this must be part of some sort of re-enactment. Kat probably really *had* seen the woman about the grounds in costume. And as for her "visions" of the dragon basket, that could have been done with mirrors, or even a holographic projection. Clever, but awfully complex.

That didn't explain the mysterious feeling of having her mind invaded. Or could that be due to some hypnotic suggestion? Perhaps she'd been the only one in the group susceptible, and everyone else would now be in on the joke.

Gullible, that was her. The Ascension Committee wanted to stage a re-enactment of the first annual ascension from 1852, and chose her for their fall-guy.

Resentment swelled in her, which she fought down. No, she'd be a good sport about it and play along. She didn't have much choice; she'd only look a complete fool if she lost her temper. Better to lead the laughter any day.

She accepted the painting box "Lady Clementina" handed her. Let the woman help Adam with the heavy work. She deserved it for being part of the joke.

Kat leaned against the single rail that formed the back of her seat and examined the carriage. A phaeton, the woman had called it. It looked old, but certainly nowhere near a hundred and fifty years. More like twenty. It must be a modern replica of one of Lady Clementina's own vehicles. Kat admired it, as she knew she ought, then helped haul up the propane tanks and their fittings. The striated envelope itself, rolled as small as possible to avoid spooking the horse, came last, almost burying Kat.

"Okay under there?" Adam's voice held a cheerful note.

"Mmmmph," Kat responded, though she could have spoken perfectly well.

Adam laughed. "Good girl." He lowered his voice. "Woman's keeping herself perfectly in the role. Wonder what we'll find at the Court?"

"They couldn't have done too much," Kat murmured back. "We've been gone not much more than half an hour. It'll be interesting to see."

Lady Clementina unhooked the reins from where she'd knotted them, and Adam, with another sweeping bow, handed her into the carriage, then climbed onto the seat at her side. The phaeton lurched, then jolted forward. It had springs, Kat could tell, but she doubted their real value.

The path was too narrow to allow them to negotiate a turn, so they continued around the huge lake. Kat watched the swans—two black ones had joined the three white ones—and absorbed the jolts as best she could.

"Where did you start from?" The woman's hearty voice broke the silence.

"Not far from here." Adam's held a wealth of amusement.

A twinge of unease set Kat on her guard. She never quite trusted her father when one of his Moods, as the family called them, struck him. The next thing she knew, he'd probably have the whole Ascension party rigged out in Victorian gear, ballooning across the Channel with equipment the *real* Lady Clementina might have used. She'd have to keep an eye on him.

Rats, why couldn't Orville or Wilbur have gotten off work to chaperon him this time? To think she'd actually thought this would be fun!

A little voice in the back of her mind whispered it was, but she tried to ignore it.

Then dizziness engulfed her once more, and she clung to the nylon, hugging it to her. Through the haze that surrounded her, her father's voice reached her, though his words sounded strange. She forced herself to concentrate, to make sense, to understand. Horses. He talked about a corral, a gunfight, fast draw—She straightened, suddenly alert. He told an outrageous and wholly fictional tale of life in the American west in 1850, as if he and Kat actually lived at that time.

Her father was incorrigible. The woman listened with an air of absolute awe, as if she swallowed the old goat's line. Ten more minutes of his company, and she'd probably be begging the Ascension Committee to put him in charge of next year's event. He'd do it with flair, she had to admit that.

As they rounded the curve behind the gazebo, the carriage shimmered, and suddenly she sat in the front, not behind a single black mare but with a pair of grays before her. The one on the right tilted its head to deliver a sharp nip to the neck of its companion, and a sensation of amusement rippled through her as she caught the colt's mouth with a deft move of her hand. Only she held nothing but nylon.

Another carriage came toward her, a large, lumbering conveyance pulled by four horses of various shades of brown and bay. They weren't on the gravel path by the lake, but a wide road lined with trees on one side and a field on the other. Dust swirled in the air, then vanished as the scene dissolved back into Durham Court.

What had set that off, the swans? Or the gazebo, perhaps? Shouldn't her visions have ended now that the Ascension Committee had launched their charade? She wanted out of this. She wanted her mind to herself, not invaded by these ridiculous images of a time long past. She hated being manipulated this way.

Leave me alone! Her silent scream filled her mind, followed at once by a wave of startled surprise. Embarrassed, she glanced at the two in the front seat, but they paid her no heed, Adam intent on some tale of ballooning recounted by Lady Clementina.

Kat's teeth clenched. When would everything return to normal? They'd be back at the Court soon, and she'd have to laugh and pretend to enjoy it. She probably would, too, once she could call her mind her own again. That, she realized, was all she resented. She didn't mind in the least the joke they played.

They rounded the last curve and headed, still at a steady trot, toward the west lawn where the Ascension attendees had set up their encampment. She blinked. Only an expanse of grass, dotted by an occasional hawthorn or oak, met her startled gaze.

Oh, no. This was carrying things too far. Where had they moved all the tents and RVs—or for that matter, *how* had they moved them so quickly? She couldn't even see any traces of the outdoor restrooms and showers, and surely they had cement foundations. Unless they rolled out a grass-colored lawn—astroturf, perhaps?—to cover the tell-tale signs of modern improvements. Mr. Jameson and his committee must have gone to considerable lengths to make this recreation as realistic as possible.

Her father, she noted, studied the lawn as well. Kat leaned forward and touched his arm, and the look he directed at her would have been comical had the whole not disturbed her so much. His expression comforted her, though; at least she wasn't going crazy, not if bewilderment assailed her father as well. Accept it and enjoy it, she told herself. So much effort . . . *So much insanity* . . .

She stifled that thought. At least the old manor house appeared the same as ever. It reassured her that no one had tried to alter the beautiful mullioned windows or the huge oak door. But the spring flower beds no longer showed displays of hollyhocks and pansies as they had this morning; now they boasted old and well-established rose bushes.

"Those are remarkable roses." Adam's voice held a note of determined calm.

Quite uncharacteristic for him. Kat held her breath, waiting for the woman's response.

Lady Clementina threw a beaming smile at Adam. "My mother planted them. Bloom for the better part of the year."

Kat found herself believing it as they swept past the vigorous shrubs covered in large blooms of yellows, pinks and reds. That sort of growth took time to develop, not the scant hour or so since she had last walked across the front drive.

They turned onto the path leading to the stableyard and passed between a line of freshly planted yews. Hadn't they been taller—at least ten feet taller? Her stomach lurched. A logical explanation evaded her. Yet there had to be one. She'd have to congratulate the special effects person.

They pulled through the arched gateway into the cobbled yard where three diminutive men pitchforked soiled straw from the stalls that only hours before had held nothing but wicker gondolas and ballooning equipment. Now three equine heads regarded them from over the ropes looped across their stall doors. A blue roan pricked its ears forward and nickered a greeting, and the black between the shafts of their phaeton answered.

Had she hit her head when the balloon landed and knocked herself out? Dreams could be weird. But were they as vivid as this?

One of the grooms leaned his tool against the stone wall and ran forward to take their horse's reins. His bright eyes rested on the passengers, and his mouth dropped open as Kat hopped down and steadied herself against the side of the carriage.

"I was right," Lady Clementina announced, "and they had an accident. Their basket smashed up and landed in the lake."

By now the other two men joined the first, and cast awed glances at Kat as they unloaded the equipment from the back of the carriage. The tanks and regulator valves appeared to fascinate them, and they turned them over, examining them from all sides. One, the youngest, nudged his companion and rolled his eyes.

"Get on with it, then." An older man emerged from the carriage house and glared at his subordinates from beneath bushy brows. He nodded to Lady Clementina with the ease of long service, looked toward Kat, then Adam, and blinked. He strode forward, cuffed the second of the lads who still gawked at the equipment, and with a jerk of his head sent him running to stow his burden. He himself set about unhitching the horse.

"Good man, Norbert." Lady Clementina patted the horse's neck, then turned to Kat and Adam. Her lips pursed, then twisted into an easy smile. "Ummm, yes. I can't say I blame them, I suppose. Well, we'd better get you inside until we can arrange to get you home."

Yes, home. Or at least her tent. Kat took an unsteady step forward and caught her father's arm as he reached to help her. Together they followed the woman from the yard.

Where had the Ascension people moved everything? A glance around the drive showed not so much as a single RV anywhere in sight. Someone could have driven them into the wood, she supposed, but it looked too thick to allow the large vehicles entrance, yet not thick enough to conceal them completely from sight like this.

Curiouser and curiouser, to quote Alice. She was beginning to think she knew how the poor girl felt. Only Kat and her father hadn't fallen down a rabbit hole. They'd gone up in a balloon.

And come down without the dragon basket.

What was Mr. Jameson going to say about that? For that matter, where was he?

She studied the house as they approached the library doors. Someone had removed the spotlight that illuminated the terrace and entrance for the convenience of the balloonists. Pots of geraniums now decorated the flagstones. Rather attractive.

Now for inside. Bracing herself, she entered the vast bookroom. And came to an abrupt halt.

Subtle changes had occurred here, also. Nothing drastic, just the rearrangement of furniture, a few more candelabra, different glass globes for the gas lamps. Kat shivered, caught her father's frozen expression, and his resemblance to a stuffed trout—with a mustache—almost made her burst out laughing.

Except she didn't want to laugh. Frustration washed over her, an impatience that had nothing to do with her current circumstances, an irritation aimed at a frailty she didn't possess. It vanished the next moment. Sobered, Kat followed Lady Clementina toward the door.

In the corridor beyond, the changes leapt at her. Green and gold wall paper covered the walls instead of the white and blue she remembered. An intricately woven runner ran the length of the polished oak parquet. Mr. Jameson's desk no longer stood in the main hall, nor did his lamp or telephone. She couldn't even see where the phone jack or the electric switches and plugs had been.

Her throat constricted, uncomfortably dry. She'd called Orville from that nonexistent phone only a couple of nights ago. And he'd answered and talked to her.

A hand clutched her elbow and she jumped, then turned to see Adam's uneasy expression. She managed an uncertain smile, which he tried to return.

"Did I fall asleep watching old reruns of *Twilight Zone?*" he muttered.

"Nope. *Time Tunnel.* Or maybe *Quantum Leap.* That's the only possible explanation."

At that, his usual grin flashed. "Do you know, if it weren't impossible, I could almost believe we *had* gone back in time?" They crossed to the front salon where Kat had stored her painting only the day before. "She looks so much like the photos of Lady Clementina it's uncanny."

"I—" Kat broke off. This room had changed completely, and not a trace of the belongings of the balloonists remained. Her painting . . . "Where—?" Kat began.

Lady Clementina tugged the bell pull, then gestured toward the chairs. "Refreshments will be here in a moment. Now, you must tell me how I may help you. Will there be someone along shortly searching for you? I could send a groom out to lead them here."

Her gaze once more settled on Kat, and an expression of amused envy lit her countenance. "Really, my dear Miss Sayre, I'm ashamed of myself for not taking a similar stand on practical ballooning clothing myself. But I admit I am surprised to see you do so. Your Papa must be quite permissive."

"That's one way to put it." Kat managed a polite smile, though her inner turmoil increased. Nothing made sense. Nothing seemed right. And nothing could—nothing *would!*—go wrong with the conference. The need to prove her usefulness flooded through her as her vision blurred, and once more she sat in the front seat of a carriage behind those two grays, feeling their strength as she controlled the reins. They swept around a corner, onto a gravel drive, then through an iron gate. Ahead of her, in the full beauty of the spring morning, stood Durham Court . . .

Only she sat inside a front parlor, she couldn't possibly be seeing the place from the gate. Relief touched her mind, both as of coming to the end of a tedious journey and of coming home. Home? Was *he* outside?

She rose and ran from the room, barely noting her father's sharp question or Lady Clementina's startled exclamation. Outside . . . she crossed the hall and dragged open the great oak door, then burst through it onto the bricked entry porch with its shallow stairs.

Less than fifty yards separated her from the grays and their carriage. And the driver and passenger. Her throat closed with a surge of longing that this time came from within herself. He came . . .

"Graeme." Lady Clementina's voice sounded beside her, her pleasure patent. The woman hurried past, coming to a stop on the gravel drive, allowing the carriage to come abreast of her.

Kat folded her arms before her, forcing herself to remain where she stood, not to give way to the dizziness that left her weak-kneed and trembling. The driver seemed a tall man; his voluminous cloak covered him so she could tell little of his build. His high-crowned hat threw his features into shadow, hiding them from her. The passenger appeared to her as only a blur, a small man, portly, insignificant beside the other. She tensed, waiting.

As the carriage pulled to a stop, Lady Clementina hurried to it and laid her hand on the driver's wrist. He bent to kiss her cheek. She said something, too soft for Kat to hear, and his head jerked up. His gaze came to rest on her. Kat swallowed as an alien curiosity pricked at her mind.

From around the corner the youngest of the grooms appeared at the run. He had just taken the reins of the pair when from within the house appeared a majestic individual, a suit of solemn black garbing his impressive proportions. Beneath a receding hairline, sharp eyes viewed the arrival, and the faintest of smiles appeared beneath the beak-like nose. A second, younger, man emerged in his wake, also clad in black. This one ran to the rear of the carriage where he unstrapped the single large suitcase fastened there.

Only it wasn't really a suitcase, more like a small leather trunk. One more period detail to add to all the others in this crazy montage.

The passenger jumped down, took the case, and himself conveyed it past her into the house. The others—apparently enacting the roles of servants—followed. Bit players, Kat assured herself.

Adam strolled forward, and Kat gathered her wits and followed. The committee had certainly found a striking man to play this new part of the driver, whoever he might turn out to be. Rugged. Very attractive in a chiseled, outdoorsy sort of way. She quite liked the bushy red-gold sideburns that extended toward his squared chin. The firm mouth showed character, and his prominent cheekbones set off eyes of a smoky gray.

Kat found their gaze locked on her, and to her surprise she lowered her own, not quite daring to stare into their depths. His presence wrapped about her, compelling. It would be too easy to lose herself to the sensations that crept through her. She peeked up and saw his eyes widen, puzzled.

"Graeme, allow me to introduce our visitors. Mr. Adam Sayre, from America, and his daughter Miss—" She faltered over the name.

"Kittyhawk," supplied Adam. "Kittyhawk Sayre."

"Americans," murmured Lady Clementina. "Miss Sayre, Mr. Sayre, permit me to present to you my nephew, Captain Graeme Warwick."

Of course you are. Kat barely prevented herself from speaking the words aloud. Or did she want to laugh and laugh—and keep on laughing? Of course there would have to be a "Captain Warwick" at any re-enactment of the First Annual Ascension. After all, the event was named after him. He must have started it.

He raised his hat, revealing a mass of thick, waving blond hair. "My aunt tells me you are balloonists, and your basket disintegrated." He collected an ebony cane from the floor and, leaning on it, climbed down from the carriage. He started for the house, his left leg not quite bending so that it dragged with each step.

Sensations of pain and frustration assaulted Kat, and in dawning wonder she stared at the man who passed her with his uneven gait. Yes, pain with each step. Frustration hovering beneath the surface. He, she realized, was the source. No posthypnotic suggestions. No tricks or mirrors. This man.

What was happening?

He paused at her side, and an image flashed in her mind of a young woman with bright brown hair tumbling about her shoulders and a puzzled, wary expression in her green eyes. Herself, in fact, as *he* saw her. For the briefest moment, awareness sparked in the depths of his eyes, awareness and flat disapproval. Abruptly, he turned from her, and a wave of cold seemed to emanate from him, as of utter rejection.

Kat glanced down at her jeans, her heavy knit sweater and leather running shoes, but could see nothing amiss. Certainly nothing worthy of that complete disapproval she had just experienced. Yet Lady Clementina had been fascinated by her clothes, as well. What insane madness had happened to them?

This man, this supposed Captain Warwick, caused those uncanny visions and emotions that assailed her, of that she was certain. And from him, she suddenly realized, she might be able to get some answers—even to those questions she didn't know how to voice.

She studied his profile, concentrating, for the first time consciously opening her mind to whatever might come. Nothing. Then . . .

Only hazy impressions reached her at first, merely flickerings, feelings. Then came a more fixed knowledge of the man and his world. Her knees wobbled, and she extended a hand to balance herself, fortunately encountering her father's coat sleeve, which she gripped. She'd received what she wanted, all right.

But now she had it, she wished like anything she could be rid of the knowledge again.

As far as this man was concerned, he *was* Captain Graeme Warwick, and he—they—existed in the year 1851.

She swept the front of Durham Court with her gaze, noting once more each of the little differences between now and an hour or so ago—or did she mean a hundred and forty years or so ago? As impossible as it might be, *could* she and her father actually have traveled back in time?

Things like that just didn't happen!

But if they did, a little voice whispered in her mind, there would be one damned good reason for it. Which left her, she realized with a sinking sensation in the pit of her stomach, to discover *why*.

Chapter Five

Kat roused from her daze, aware of a pressure on her arm. She looked up into her father's worried face and managed a brief nod. He gestured toward the front door, toward which Captain Warwick and Lady Clementina headed. She still found it difficult to believe they were the *real* people, and not a couple of actors.

She drew back, waving her father on with the others, then turned away. She couldn't face company just now. She needed to think. No, she needed to accept the impossible. But it *was* impossible, and therefore it couldn't have happened, and therefore there was nothing for her to accept.

Pleased with that bit of logic, she glanced around to see if everything had returned to normal. It hadn't.

Lady Clementina appeared in the doorway with a soft rustle of her silk skirts, her expression puzzled. "Ah, there you are, Miss Sayre. Will you not join us?"

Might as well, Kat reflected, and mounted the shallow steps. She re-entered the spacious front parlor to find her father seated in a comfortable armchair set before the hearth. Captain Warwick—

Again, the captain's presence hit her like a tangible force, stopping her in her tracks, filling her mind, numbing her to anything and everyone else. He leaned against the mantel, a blond, rugged giant, his stance not as casual as it appeared. The pain he held in check touched her, as did the strength of will with which he denied it. A man who didn't play on his injuries for sympathy.

He made a striking figure in the fawn-colored trousers that strapped beneath his gleaming black boots, a double-breasted coat of forest green that fell to just above his knees, and a cream-colored waistcoat embroidered in a pattern of gold and green leaves. He regarded her through gray eyes that clouded, a brooding stare that seemed to penetrate right through her. Awareness of him forced itself into her consciousness, followed at once by a recognition of her own physical attractions, of his appraisal—and of his flat disapproval. He turned back to her father, leaving her with vague sensations of emptiness and rejection.

Her father gestured for her to take the seat beside him, and she did so. A plate of cakes rested on the table before him. Oh, rats, she needed one; the diet could just lump it for once. She selected a piece filled with poppy seeds and took a bite, then another. That helped. It would also wreak havoc with her willpower for the rest of the week. Her gaze strayed once more to Captain Warwick's rough-hewn features, but he ignored her; she could feel the barrier he raised against her, as solid as if it were made of plate armor.

"The captain has just been to view the Crystal Palace Exhibition," Adam said. His toe prodded her instep in a purposeful manner.

She managed a polite smile. "How very nice."

She received a slight kick in the foot, and realized she'd made the wrong answer. What on earth was the Crystal Palace Exhibition? Or better yet, *where* was it? In France, maybe? Should she make a comment about Paris? She focused her mind on the tall, broad-shouldered figure before the hearth, seeking a clue, and again his sense of his own world washed over her.

Oh, lord, not where. *When.* The Crystal Palace Exhibition of 1851. That fit with everything else she picked up about Captain Warwick.

That gentleman's gaze narrowed on her face. "You seem dismayed, Miss Sayre. Do you not approve of the Exhibition?"

"No. I just—" She caught her father's mischievous glance, and a shaky laugh burst from her. "It would just be a real kick to get to see it, that's all. I—I can honestly say I never thought I'd get the chance."

Lady Clementina directed a searching stare at her. "You must take the opportunity to do so before you return to America."

Adam winked at Kat, then turned once more to the captain. "I understand you are a balloonist, yourself. Do you go aloft often?"

A gleam lit Warwick's smokey eyes. "Not as often as I should like."

Wistfulness brushed across Kat's mind, tinged with regret and chagrin. *His* longing, she realized, to float above the land where his damaged leg made no difference, to experience real freedom. . . . She roused from her reverie to hear her father speaking.

"I'd like to have a look at your equipment. See if it's different from our American things, you know."

Kat shot him a piercing look. "I think we'd better concentrate on how to get home."

"We just got here!" Mischief danced in his green eyes, teasing her.

"Dad—"

"Come on, now, Kat. We're in a—a place we never thought we'd be. Don't you want to explore? There's a whole world out there just waiting for us."

She swallowed. Yes, she wanted to explore. Yes, if they really *had* wound up in 1851, she wanted to see everything, experience everything, *enjoy* the miracle and make the most of it. But—"*Someone* has to be practical, Dad."

His easy grin flashed. "You just rely on your old father."

"I've known better than that since I was a baby! I wish we'd brought Wilbur or Orville. They have some sway over you."

Lady Clementina laughed with hearty enjoyment. "Where are you staying?"

"We—" Kat began, but Adam cut her off with a quick stomp on her instep again.

"Nowhere at the moment, I fear. Along with our basket, we lost everything, even our luggage."

Kat rolled her eyes, caught Captain Warwick watching her, and gave an unconvincing cough.

"What were you about, going aloft in an unsafe basket?" he demanded.

"An experiment," Adam declared. "We were testing equipment, and I assure you, I went over every inch of the wicker and even attached metal plates. Nothing should have gone wrong."

But it had, dreadfully wrong. Or had it? She realized

the others spoke, but she didn't hear. She gazed at Captain Warwick, experiencing a wave of exasperation and distrust emanating from him, directed at her and her father. She *felt* it, experienced his emotions, even saw through his eyes. She couldn't deny the reality of this link with him.

Nor could she deny the reality of the fact they were here, in 1851, almost a hundred and twenty years before she was even born. Things like this just didn't happen by chance, did they? Had her mental link with this man crossed the barriers of time, drawing her to him? Or was it more than that?

She'd come back in time, complete with her father; Captain Warwick hadn't been brought forward. Did that mean in the great cosmological scheme of things she was supposed to be here? That sounded like a lot of nonsense—but no more nonsensical than sitting in the room where in approximately a hundred and forty years she would store a painting . . .

Her painting. Blood drained from her face, leaving her clammy and chilled. Her painting, with its outline of Europe with one flag.

Was that the answer? Did history, at this moment, stand at a crossroad, with one path the timeline she knew, the other the united Europe of her painting?

But what had that to do with her and her father?

She didn't know anything about history, she was no great political mind, nor was her father! It would make sense if one of them were a diplomat or taught European economic or political history. But they didn't. She was an artist, her father an escapee from a NASA think tank, and they were both balloonists. She couldn't think of two people less qualified to deal with the potential situation. And right now, she only wanted to go home.

With a sinking sensation, she realized she wasn't likely to get her wish. She was here, something was about to happen, and the odds were very much against her getting away until she completed her role in whatever drama lay ahead. If she could leave even then . . .

She cut off that thought; it only distressed her. She *would* get home, back where she belonged. As for right now—

Right now, thinking was beyond her. She needed to readjust, accept the unacceptable, believe in the unbelievable. She would get nowhere if she spent all her time fighting this new reality.

The key must be Captain Warwick. Only half-listening to the animated discussion of ballooning involving the other three, she studied him, opening her mind once more to impressions. His injured leg—an image flashed in her mind of a rocky mountain pass, of soldiers in scarlet coats on horseback, then boulders pounding down on them, of turbaned figures leaping from cover with rifles blazing, making the most of their ambush. The vision faded, leaving her filled with his pain and dejection. So he'd seen service in India, been injured so badly his military career had ended, and now he felt useless.

She checked the sympathy that welled in her; for all she knew, her thoughts and emotions might assail him in the same manner his did her. That thought she found appalling. A man—a *stranger,* at that—privy to her innermost feelings? Not if she had anything to say about it! And he, if he were aware of it, would undoubtedly feel the same.

Definitely, she needed to get to the bottom of this weird mental link. Perhaps it would provide answers to her questions, reasons for her presence here. And most importantly, a way to get back to her own time.

Captain Graeme Warwick eased his knee into a position that hurt a little less, all the while keeping his features frozen into those of a genial host. Who the devil were these people? The young lady, Miss Kat Sayre—not Katherine, which was a proper name, but something outlandish. Kittyhawk, that was it. Did it come from one of those red Indian tribes that were all over America?

His Aunt Clementina picked up the plate of biscuits and the young lady sprang to her feet, taking it from her to pass to the others. Impulsive creature. She disturbed him, though he couldn't place why. Disquieting thoughts had filled his mind ever since she came into his vicinity. He eyed her askance as she held out the plate to him, and shook his head in a curt refusal. She certainly wore the most peculiar garments.

"You are looking at my daughter's—er—denims?" Mr. Sayre watched him, one corner of his mouth quirked upward.

Graeme inclined his head. "I have certainly never seen anything like them before."

"Not on a woman, he means." The young lady grinned, eyes sparkling an unspoken challenge.

Very attractive eyes, too. Deep green, surrounded

by a fringe of thick dark lashes. He cut off that line of thought. "Not on anyone," he corrected.

"They're very popular out in California." The old man threw his daughter a mischievous look.

California. The mad rush for gold that began a couple of years back. Were they prospectors? Any number of eccentrics had struck rich veins, he had heard, and now traveled the world trying to acquire a little culture and breeding to accompany their new-found wealth. These two certainly seemed out of place. Yet aside from their outlandish garments, they did not seem vulgar.

"Gold mining!" Lady Clementina turned her fascinated gaze on Mr. Sayre. "Have you truly been to California? One hears such tales of the dreadful deprivations one must endure." She gave an exquisite shiver.

Mr. Sayre smiled, as one seized by a delightful prospect. A flicker of alarm crossed his daughter's face, then she rolled her eyes as if resigned to the inevitable. Interesting little by-play, that. Graeme's suspicions rose once more.

Mr. Sayre beamed at Lady Clementina. "Madam, the tales I could spin for you."

"Yarns, you mean," his daughter muttered.

Mr. Sayre directed a disdainful glance at her, then returned his attention to Lady Clementina. "I remember one morning out by the river . . ."

"Later, Dad. Or maybe you should write a book. You could call it 'Tales I learned at Knott's Berry Farm.' Or maybe 'Paint Your Wagon Revisited.' "

Mr. Sayre's grin, Graeme decided, acknowledged a hit. But over what? He looked from one to the other of them, seeing the amusement on Mr. Sayre's face, the strain on his daughter's. Tiny lines etched about her eyes, and he could almost feel her unease.

Lady Clementina set her china cup on its saucer. "Do you make a long stay in England?"

"I wish I knew." Miss Sayre strode to the window and stared out over the lawn.

Mr. Sayre selected another biscuit. "Our plans are somewhat indefinite at the moment."

"We've lost our basket." Miss Sayre's voice sounded bleak.

Her father looked up, a slight frown creasing his brow. "We'll find a way back, Kat."

Lady Clementina looked from one to the other of them. "Is no one searching for you?"

"Even if they were, I doubt they'd find us." Miss Sayre managed a shaky laugh.

Her father cleared his throat. "We appear to have gotten ourselves into a spot of difficulty, and we have no one but ourselves to get us out of this. We are adrift, as it were, in your . . . country."

The devil they were. Graeme's eyes narrowed.

Lady Clementina nodded to herself, as if coming to a decision. "Why do you not remain as our guests until you know what you're doing?"

Graeme's head came up with a jerk. "Aunt Clem—"

She waved his protest aside. "They're balloonists in distress, Graeme. There, it is settled." She beamed on the two visitors. "I shall order rooms prepared for you at once. No," she held up her hand, stopping Miss Sayre's protest, "you will be doing me the greatest favor by staying. It is so very seldom I am able to enjoy the company of fellow aeronauts. It is different for

Graeme, with his government work, but he forgets that I am buried here in the country—"

"So terribly far from London," Graeme murmured.

"—and see so very few interesting people," his aunt went on, ignoring his interruption.

His hand clenched on the polished mahogany mantel, and he forced his fingers to relax. He didn't want these strangers around. Or did he? The alarming possibility flickered on the fringes of his mind. He didn't know enough about them, only that the old gentleman had a charming manner, to which Aunt Clementina had succumbed.

As for his daughter—such an impulsive creature, life vibrated from her. He couldn't let it upset his carefully controlled world. There could be no place in the life of a cripple for the daring and spontaneity he sensed in her lovely face and laughter-lined eyes. Prudence, caution, logic—indeed, every attribute of an intelligent gentleman—warned him to shun her company.

His gaze rested on her as her sudden smile flashed at something her father said, and he grasped at another line of defense. No such loving, vivacious woman could ever be interested in a battered wreck of a man.

The timing of the arrival of this Miss Kat Sayre and her father disturbed him, too. Why now, of all times? Unless . . .

It seemed too preposterous to consider, that they might in some way be connected with the conference. Still, he'd be a fool, with an event so momentous in the balance, to take this couple at face value. He'd worked too hard.

He closed his eyes, reviewing—as he did so often of

late—the arrangements he had made to ensure the secrecy and safety of the meeting of the financial ministers of the majority of European nations. The Crystal Palace Exhibition made an excellent cover for their various journeys to England; no suspicions should arise from that point. As for the rest . . .

He drew a steadying breath as the weight of his responsibility bore down on him. It was an honor, he reminded himself, not just a horrendous undertaking, that he had been placed in charge of organizing the conference. And that included its security.

He pushed away from the hearth, steadied himself with his cane, and bowed to his aunt and Miss Sayre. "You must excuse me."

"Why?" Dismayed, his aunt looked up.

He fought a sudden smile. He already had one impulsive, outspoken female in his life. That was more than enough.

"You only just got here, Graeme," she went on. "Surely you may sit for an hour over tea without feeling guilty. The conference will in no way be blighted by your attention to your duties as host."

"On the contrary, dear Aunt. It is with those duties I am currently concerned. I go to order the searching of the lake, to see what might be recovered of our guests' belongings."

The young lady glanced at her father, and a wave of uneasiness so palpable he could feel it emanated from her. So, he was right to distrust them. Regret tinged his satisfaction—regret at the potential danger to the conference.

And, he admitted with reluctance, regret that the

intriguing creature might well prove to be a spy or saboteur.

Irritated with himself, he went in search of the gardener, gave his orders, then retired to the quiet of the library. A small fire had been kindled in the hearth against the chill that lingered in the great house even on a fine May morning, and he settled in an overstuffed chair before it. Drawing a handful of papers from his satchel, he set to work. After ten minutes of studying the one uppermost, he realized he had a more vivid image in his mind of Miss Kittyhawk Sayre than of the preparations he supposedly planned.

With a muttered exclamation, he laid his work aside and, leaning on his cane, set forth to see how the workers progressed at the lake. Halfway across the lawn, an image flashed into his mind of a black swan swimming away from the rowboat in which sat the gardener and two grooms, all three wielding fishing nets in search of any floating debris. He blinked, and the vision vanished, leaving him facing nothing but an expanse of grass and shrubs and the row of hedges beyond that masked the lake from his view. Yet it had seemed as if he actually *saw* it.

Forcing the incident from his mind, he proceeded to the gravel lane which led around the water. There, just as he'd pictured it, lay the boat on water stirred by the strokes of the oars and the searching of the net poles. Eerie. A touch of the sun, perhaps? Yet he was not one to suffer from such indispositions. His service in India would have ended much sooner if he had been so afflicted.

Still puzzled, he headed toward the folly, which he regarded with a touch of tolerant amusement. He could only be glad that his ancestor had designed no more Grecian temples on the property. He found one to be more than sufficient.

As he drew closer, he realized someone sat in the shadows, leaning against one of the fluted columns. The unconventional Miss Kittyhawk Sayre, sitting on the steps and sketching. She seemed engrossed in her occupation, looking up to stare fixedly at the men in the rowboat, then back to her pad as her pencil moved with rapid, precise strokes. She must have heard his approach—one did not move in silence on gravel, especially when one needed a cane—but she did not acknowledge his presence.

He mounted the steps, irritated by her ignoring him. Then she looked up, staring fully into his face, and tension seemed to explode within him. She opened her mouth only to shut it tight again—he could see the whiteness about her lips. She looked back at her drawing.

Graeme positioned himself just behind her where he could see the detailed sketch of the lake, the rowboat, and the black swan. She possessed considerable ability, he acknowledged. He could find no fault with her execution—certainly nothing to make her frown so as she studied it.

"Have they found anything, yet?" His gaze shifted to the furious concentration of her expression.

"No." She stared at the sketch, then cast the pad down to the step beside her. "And neither have I." At that she looked up at him over her shoulder and smiled. "I don't know why I thought I might."

He raised polite eyebrows and drew forth the high-backed wicker chair from its position just behind the pillars and placed it near her side. "I would have expected parts of the basket, at least, to float."

She outlined a shrub on the back of her page as if she hadn't heard. "I like things that make sense," she said at last.

He had a shrewd notion that she had not meant that comment as idly as it sounded. He stretched his legs before him, easing the ache in his knee, and considered. "I myself prefer an ordered, logical existence."

She turned at that, her slow gaze traveling the length of his long form, resting at last on his face. "Do you? You have all the earmarks of a risk-taker."

He stiffened with resentment. Once, he had been. Once, he could afford that luxury. Now, he could not.

"I'm sorry." At once, she was all contrition. "That was a stupid thing for me to say. We're all bound by restrictions in one way or another, aren't we?"

"Are *you?*" he asked before he could stop himself.

Her lightning-fast mood shifted, and laughter sparkled in the depths of her green eyes. "It's finding our boundaries—and the rules of our games—that makes life such a challenge. Just when you're sailing along, convinced you know what you're up against, bam, someone goes and alters the parameters and leaves you all adrift."

Like he felt at the moment. He found her words a trifle incomprehensible, but he understood their import with no trouble. In fact, he found himself experiencing a frustration and uncertainty that with a sense of shock he recognized as hers.

He straightened up in the chair, blocking out the sensations. The next moment he realized he must have imagined the whole, for the young woman sat before him, her puzzled gaze resting on his face. He looked away, over the lake. "They may yet find something," he said simply to break the silence, to give his mind another direction.

"I hope they do." Her voice held an odd note in it.

He decided it would be safer to ignore it, and groped instead for another topic of conversation. He found one readily at hand. "Do many women wear such garments where you come from?"

She smiled again. "Everyone does. For the mining, you know." Again, her eyes danced as if at some secret joke. "Would *you* like to try anything active in long skirts?"

He wasn't likely to try anything active at all with his knee, but he kept that thought to himself. "It seems a trifle unusual, that is all."

She shook her head, setting her soft coppery-brown waves bouncing about her shoulders. "It's all perspective, you see. Where I come from, a dress like Lady Clementina's would be unusual."

His gaze traveled along her—what had her father called them? Denims? Yes, along her denim-clad limbs. Those trousers hugged her shape in a manner he found most improper—and more than a little provocative. They left little to the imagination—and at once he had to curb his thoughts from filling in the enticing details. He directed his gaze instead at the little boat, which had turned about and now headed toward the far shore. He would not look at her denims again until he mastered his unruly—and highly improper—reactions.

"I can see where they might be less hampering than skirts in a balloon," he managed. He rose. "If you will excuse me, I will return to the house. I have a great deal of work to do."

Without waiting for her reply, he descended the shallow steps, then struck off along the gravel, setting his cane with care. It would have been far too easy to remain at her side for the next hour, basking in the warm sunshine, listening to her melodic voice, appreciating the picture she made. She was a lovely woman—but a mysterious one, as well. He had best overcome his ridiculous partiality for her company and regard her with the distrust she deserved.

He returned to the library, found it dark and cool, and refused to think of the sunlit lake and the compelling young woman he had left in the folly. Now was not the time for him to take chances. He went at once to his desk, drew out a sheet of writing paper, selected a quill, and dipped it into the inkwell. Thomas, Lord Uxbridge—assistant to England's Foreign Minister viscount Palmerston—might be very interested to learn of this strange invasion of the home of Graeme's aunt, of this acquaintance that had been thrust upon the conference's organizer.

Graeme penned the missive, read it through, then sealed it and rang for a servant. A groom could deliver it in Whitehall before two hours passed.

Once he had sped letter and carrier on their way, he paced about the apartment until his knee made that occupation too painful, forcing him to once more seek a chair. He could think of no more precautions he should take. Or did he overreact? What harm could this rather odd couple do?

Still restless, he rose and poured himself a glass of Madeira from the decanter on the pier table. Did his worry create hobgoblins where none existed? Or perhaps not his worry, but his shattered sense of his own self-worth. That, though, was ridiculous. Even if he had been forced to sell out of the army because of his injuries, he could still serve his country in other ways.

His fingers tightened on the crystal stem as he swirled the ruby liquid. Damnation, he didn't need to prove that to everyone every single minute of the day! And he certainly didn't need to prove it to himself. He would quit being an alarmist and proceed by the most expedient course of simply observing these two unexpected visitors, keeping their movements under surveillance.

It therefore behooved him to search out Miss Kittyhawk Sayre. At once.

Chapter Six

Graeme emerged from the library onto the terrace and circled toward the lawn and the gravel path beyond. As he rounded the corner of the great old house, he saw Miss Sayre seated on the edge of the fountain in the drive, once more busily at work with her sketch pad. She looked up, studied the ivy-covered facade, then shook her head. Her shoulders heaved with a sigh, and she wriggled off her perch and dusted the seat of her deplorable denim trousers.

"Is there something the matter with your drawing?" He held out his hand in a peremptory manner. After a moment's hesitation, she gave it to him.

He beheld a beautiful sketch, rich with detail, certainly nothing to cause the troubled expression that still lingered. He studied her face for a moment, seeking answers that eluded him. "You have considerable talent," he said after a moment.

A very becoming blush tinged her cheeks, highlighting her large, green eyes. No artist could do her loveliness justice, he decided. How could anyone capture that vibrant spirit, that effervescence that radiated from her even now, when weighed down by concern?

The sound of a carriage on the drive diverted his attention, and he realized with a flash of irritation he must have been gazing at her for no little time. Her color had deepened even more, and her lips parted. Such very tempting lips. But he was no foolish, callow youth to be ensnared by a voluptuous siren.

Glad of the intervention, annoyed with himself, he turned away from her as a bay, harness-bell jingling, drew a cabriolet around the curve of the fountain. The burly young driver drew his horse to a halt beside them and doffed his high-crowned silk hat in a sweeping gesture, revealing a shock of curling black hair just touched with gray. Bright hazel eyes regarded Graeme from a round, ruddy face.

"Devilish glad to have found you, Warwick. I say!" His gaze settled on the young lady in men's trousers.

Graeme stiffened. "May I present you to Miss Sayre? This is Sir Francis Matlock, my assistant."

Miss Sayre held out her hand, and Sir Francis caught her fingers, carrying them to his lips in an elaborate, old-fashioned gesture that sat oddly with his bluff manner. She smiled, as if delighted by it.

Graeme frowned at his assistant, and found himself wishing him at the devil. "What brings you here?" he demanded, more sharply than he'd intended.

Sir Francis stepped down from his vehicle and handed the ribbons to a groom who ran up from the stable. "Business, my dear fellow, what else?" He stripped off his driving gloves. "Uxbridge most urgently desires I give you every assistance. And so you see me come to place myself at your complete disposal."

Complete disposal was exactly what Graeme felt like doing with the man's assistance, but he resisted the temptation to tell him so. He didn't like the way Sir Francis eyed Miss Sayre. He glanced at her and found her watching them.

"Am I in the way?" she asked.

Her forthright manner took him aback. Before he could respond, a guffaw of laughter burst from Sir Francis.

"Couldn't possibly be," that gentleman assured her with a sweeping bow.

Graeme clenched his jaw. Damn the fellow, he seemed forever in the way—and never more so than now. "Join me in the library," he said shortly. "You must excuse us, Miss Sayre." He started away, but not before he noticed her balancing her sketch pad in her left arm and making rapid gestures with her pencil. Did she seek to capture Sir Francis Matlock's energetic stance and untrammeled stride? May she have much joy of them.

He led the way to his own sanctuary, aware of the foulness of his mood. Once inside, he poured Matlock a glass of wine, then refilled his own glass. "What brings you to the Court?"

The man strode to the French window and peered along the terrace, as if hoping to see Miss Sayre once more. "Charming young woman. Acquaintance of your aunt's?"

"She is here with her father. Balloonists."

Matlock's bushy brows descended and his glass checked. "Intrepid of 'em. Explains her garments, I suppose. Unusual. Well." He took a mouthful of wine. "Everything progressing as you'd wish for the conference?" The man kept his tone light, but his fingers twirled his glass with uneasy speed. "No hint of any trouble or sabotage?"

"Have you heard anything?" Graeme countered.

Matlock puffed out his ruddy cheeks. "Nothing, dear fellow. Nothing at all. One just worries. Conspiracies can—But that's neither here nor there, is it?" He tugged at his collar, then offered an expansive smile. "You've heard nothing. Well, nothing to hear, is there?"

"So one should hope." Graeme's gaze lingered on him. What the devil ailed the man? If he'd heard rumors of a conspiracy, why didn't he say so?

"Need me to do anything? No? Fine, fine." Sir Francis drained his glass. "Well. Best be getting back, then. Won't be returning to town tonight, will you? Not with your guests. I'll just be going, then."

Graeme strolled with him to the stable and saw him off, but they exchanged nothing more than the merest pleasantries. So why the devil had the man come at all? To make sure Graeme *hadn't* heard any rumors? Lost in thought, he made his way back toward the library, then changed his mind and went once more in search of Miss Sayre.

He found her on the east lawn, her sketch pad abandoned in favor of a square of stretched canvas on an easel, her pencil replaced by a brush and an assortment of paints on a palette. Paints, and outside. How could she have mixed them without the powders blowing away? Several pieces of crumpled paper lay scattered about her feet. "You didn't like your drawing of Sir Francis?" he inquired.

"You saw that?" She shrugged. "It's down there." She gestured with her brush to the discarded sheets.

He stooped, balancing with his cane, and collected two—both representations of the Court's facade. The third showed the robust countenance of Sir Francis, the drooping of the full lips, the jutting, broad nose and the bushy black side whiskers. Realistic. Not at all complimentary. Insensibly, Graeme's temper improved. He crumpled the sketch once more and dropped it among the others. The one of the Court which he'd examined before he retained. "Might I have this one?"

She glanced at it. "Sure, if you like."

"I do like." He folded it and placed it in his pocket. "It's very good. They all are."

"Thank you." She sounded indifferent rather than pleased at his praise. Yet it wasn't an exaggerated sense of her abilities but complete preoccupation with her present pursuit. She painted as if frantic, the same way she sketched.

A sense of odd urgency filled him, and he moved away, leaving her to her labors. The conference must be getting on his nerves, and Miss Kittyhawk Sayre's presence seemed to intensify it. When he was near her, he experienced the strangest sensations—almost as if he could feel her emotions.

That was nonsense, though. Still, he felt uncomfortable. Vulnerable. He needed control, logic. He needed to protect himself.

And right now, he needed to remain far away from a certain young woman whose eyes seemed to look directly into his soul.

* * *

Kat returned to the house, looking for a place to set her painting to dry. So far, she detected nothing of interest in her rendition of Durham Court's facade. Maybe she had to wait for the details to be added. After all, she was almost finished with the balloons when she first discovered that weird tracery and the flag. She'd make sure to include plenty of ivy and bushes in the next session.

As she hesitated in the hall, unsure where to take the canvas, measured footsteps approached from the back premises. She turned to see the butler, his portly figure approaching in solemn state. He reached her and stopped, his expression remaining impassive as his gaze no more than flickered over her.

He cleared his throat and focused on a point several inches above her head. "Does Miss require something?"

"A safe place for this to dry." She held out the painting.

He lowered his gaze, and for the briefest moment interest registered on his countenance, to be masked again at once. "Certainly, Miss." He took it from her. "There is a sitting room that faces west that is seldom in use at this time of year."

He led the way. A few minutes of walking along several corridors—with a stop at the library to pick up a section of the previous day's *London Times*, brought them to the sunny room. Kat arranged the sheets on the floor and the butler positioned her canvas with extreme care, balancing it against the side of a table.

He stepped back and nodded in satisfaction. "I will see that no one disturbs it, Miss."

"No one will want to," she assured him. "This whole room will smell of the paint in a very short time." She exited to the hall, then turned back. "Do you know where my father is?"

"Mr. Sayre is in the parlor, Miss, where you partook of tea earlier." With a slight bow, he left her.

She actually found him in the hall, still in the company of their hostess. Lady Clementina was in conference with a thin woman of indeterminate age, whose hawk-like features gave her an austere, disapproving appearance. A servant, Kat realized; she wore a gray dress covered with a freshly pressed white apron. The piercing gaze of the woman's beady eyes came to rest on Kat, and the thin lips tightened. Her sudden silence spoke volumes.

Lady Clementina looked up. "Ah, Miss Sayre, you're back. I was just about to send out a search party for you. This is Mrs. Erling, my housekeeper. She has just come to tell me that rooms have been prepared for you both. Go along, now, and I'll see you when you have had a chance to refresh yourselves. Dinner will be at six—unfashionable, I know, but I always get too hungry to wait longer." With that she excused herself, leaving Kat to eye the housekeeper with uncertainty.

"This way, Miss, Sir." Mrs. Erling's voice, deep and melodious, betrayed none of her feelings. "Such a dreadful experience as you've had."

She led the way up the great staircase that Kat had been dying to explore—since her own time. Portraits hung against the oak paneled wall at evenly spaced intervals, climbing with the dark oak steps. A loomed runner of deep burgundy covered the treads, then joined into a matching carpet running the length of the portrait gallery that looked down on the hall below.

Kat slowed her steps, gazing at the Durham ancestors. Regency, Georgian, Jacobean, Tudor—representatives of every era met her wondering gaze, generation upon generation of wealthy aristocrats. Yet it all stopped here, with Lady Clementina, who possessed no heirs and left the estate in trust for posterity.

Why didn't she leave it to her nephew? Then the obvious reason struck her. He must die before his aunt. That could still leave him a long life, but it was sad he didn't leave any heirs. This was a house to be lived in, where laughter should echo through the rooms. It shouldn't become a shrine.

Sobered, she followed her father and Mrs. Erling around a corner and into the South Wing. They stopped at the first door, and the housekeeper swung it wide and stepped back to permit Adam to enter. Massive furniture in gleaming mahogany set against white walls and green draperies greeted Kat's curious gaze. A comfortable chamber, spacious and warm, filled with light and fresh, rose-scented air from the open windows.

Mrs. Erling withdrew to the door. "Ring when you are ready, Sir, and the captain's own valet—Walters, his name is—will assist you in finding something more suitable to wear."

Adam raised his eyebrows and winked at Kat before she exited once more to the hall. He would manage perfectly well for himself, she knew. He always did, no matter how peculiar the situation in which his antics landed them. But this time they had gone beyond the realm of anything they had known before. It still didn't seem possible.

Mrs. Erling led the way to a chamber two doors farther along the hall and on the opposite side. Kat stepped inside and looked about with approval. A giant mahogany bed, enshrouded with blue and white floral print hangings, dominated the airy apartment. Thick tasseled cords tied back matching draperies on either side of a bay window, and a thick carpet in tones of blue and gray covered the center of the hardwood floor. The mahogany fireplace mantel, on the wall opposite the bed, boasted a clock, a vase, and two china figurines.

A middle-aged maid, dressed in the servants' gray dress and white apron, stood before an open wardrobe of the early Victorian period. Wisps of fiery red hair escaped from beneath her cap, and the face she turned on them showed scattered freckles on the fair skin. The woman stared at Kat, and her blue eyes widened.

"This is Middens," Mrs. Erling said. "Lady Clementina's own maid. She will help you with your clothes."

"If you please, Miss?" Middens crossed to the bed and gestured toward an array of garments that lay across the coverlet, everything from white muslin undergarments to yards and yards of colorful skirting.

Kat regarded the pile in dismay. "I'm no clothes horse," she protested. "Look, it's very kind of you, but really, there's no need."

Mrs. Erling and Middens exchanged horrified glances. "You surely cannot *wish* to come down to dinner as you are," the housekeeper protested. "Her ladyship always dresses. I shall leave you to do what you can, Middens." Her tone held little hope of a happy outcome.

Better not protest, Kat decided—though she found her jeans perfectly suitable for dining at home. But she wasn't home. She was thousands of miles—and about a hundred and forty years—away from everything she knew. She caught the waver of panic and squelched it before it could grasp her firmly in its clutches.

If it weren't for her father's presence, she would write this all down to hallucinations started two days before, when those weird images began appearing. It might still all be hallucinations, she reminded herself. She might only *think* her father was with her.

"Miss?" Middens stood before her, offering a glass of water.

Kat took it, then glanced about the room for the source. No faucets—at least, not in here. A pitcher stood on a marble-topped table in which a blue and white china basin rested. She swallowed a large mouthful, but it did little to settle her reeling world. If only she could hop back into that dragon basket, take off, and find herself once more in her own time, where the world had seemed to make sense.

She took a smaller sip and felt herself steadying. As impossible as it might be, she really seemed to be here, in the past.

The past. Like a gigantic living history museum, only better. And all hers to explore until she found her way home. What an incredible opportunity. With a sense of rising delight and wonder, she rounded on Middens. "What do you have there? I want to see everything."

The maid selected the top gown, a confection of pale green silk edged in lace. "We may need to make some alterations before you can wear this tonight, Miss."

"Tonight?" Kat held it up before her and examined her reflection in the cheval glass that stood in the corner. It would be beautiful—but the waist looked so baggy and the skirt so voluminous. . . . Her gaze flew to the bed where she saw a stiff-looking corset which very fortunately flared out over the hips. She already carried a little too much cushioning in that area. The prospect of adding a bustle—yes, that padded half mini-skirt with the waist-ties was probably one—made her cringe. No more of those poppy seed cakes, she supposed.

Well, she might as well get on with it. When in Rome and all that. With the sensation of embarking on an adventure, she laid the gown aside, then hesitated. The presence of the maid bothered her innate modesty, but the woman showed no signs of removing herself. Chalk it all up to experience, she told herself. She kicked off her tennies and dragged off her jeans.

Middens gasped. "Oh, Miss!" She came forward a tentative step, a hand held out in awe.

Kat glanced down at her floral print bikinis in shades of beige and rose, trimmed with matching lace, and fought back a giggle. Underwear. What on earth did they wear at this time? She was likely to find out, and in pretty short order.

"Oh, Miss, where did you ever get anything so— so—" Middens broke off, at a loss for words.

"California." And if she weren't careful, she'd start weaving tales as fanciful as her father's about that legendary land. "A lady has to have something pretty to make up for wearing these denims all day."

"Oh, yes, Miss. But they're so—so very *little.*"

"How could you get anything bulky under jeans?" With mischievous abandon, Kat dragged off her sweater, revealing the bra that matched her bikinis.

A reverential intaking of breath was the maid's only audible response; her enraptured gaze said the rest.

Kat grinned. "Help me look respectable by your standards here, and I'll try to make a copy of these for you."

The woman's mouth formed an ecstatic "O." Eyes shining, she busied herself among the cotton and muslin underthings on the bed. "This is what we wears, Miss." She held up what looked like a pair of very baggy cotton pants with a drawstring at the waist, several decorative tucks along the legs, and an edging of embroidery and lace at the hems.

Kat fought back a laugh. She'd feel ridiculous in them—but if it meant getting to wear that pale green silk gown—it was worth it. She held out her hand for them. At least they didn't feel too rough, and she'd need something to wear, anyway, while she washed her bikinis. And after they wore out . . .

How long would she be here, in this time period? No, best not think about that now. Best cope one step at a time, not torment herself with fear beyond the simple need to survive, to fit in. If she *were* here for some specific reason, perhaps she could go home as soon as she completed whatever task awaited her.

Or perhaps she couldn't . . .

If she were stuck in this era for any length of time, she vowed, she'd get herself some silk or satin and sew up more bikinis and bras. Did they have elastic, yet? If not, she'd figure out how to manage with drawstrings.

After the pantaloons came a chemise made of a soft, light material, square-cut in the neckline, with a drawstring that allowed it to be extended to the points of Kat's shoulders. Short, full sleeves gathered onto narrow cuff bands above the elbows. The front, to her surprise, was fitted, with gussets sewn in to accommodate her generous curves. The whole garment hung almost to her knees.

"And now the petticoats." Middens selected one, then tossed it over Kat's head.

The maid fastened its waistband at the back with strings. Another, made of horsehair, followed, which came only to Kat's knees. A third, of the same lightweight cloth as the first, came next, and at last a beautifully decorated one bordered in lace and embroidery.

"And this here is the very latest in corsets, Miss," Middens assured her. "Hardly any whalebone at all, you see? Just this elastic thread."

Now this, Kat decided as she adjusted the stays, was more like it. Instant figure. Add a little black lace to its edges, and it would be downright sexy. Just the sort of thing for dance hall girls in the old western "B" movies.

A camisole came next, covering the corset. Kat twisted gently at the waist, and was relieved to find she could still move. She could also breathe.

"You just need a dress improver, Miss, and we're almost done." Middens picked up the padded half skirt and draped it about Kat's waist.

"Bustle," Kat pronounced, and fingered it, somewhat disappointed. She'd hoped for one from an even earlier period, one that would resemble a bolster with ties. She couldn't bounce this one.

"Now we can fit the gown, Miss." Middens gathered up the armload of pale green silk.

Obligingly, Kat held up her arms. The maid gave an expert toss, settling the endless yards of material over Kat's head, then twitched and smoothed the fabric into place. The neckline fell in a low "V" in the front, then swept to the points of Kat's shoulders from which lace fell almost to her elbows.

Eager, Kat turned to the mirror, then regarded her shapeless reflection with a frown. "It's rather loose," she said at last.

"And short," Middens agreed. "Well, Miss, it was made for her ladyship, and it might be worse." She pinched the material in back on one side and inserted several pins, then repeated the procedure on the other side.

At once, the front of the gown took on a definition that pleased Kat considerably. She turned a little, feeling the heavy, full skirts swirl about her in an intriguing manner. "It's not that bad!" She spun around, enjoying the unfamiliar sensation of the material swinging about her ankles. Thank heavens she didn't have to deal with hoops.

"Goodness, Miss, haven't you never worn a dress before?" The maid regarded her wide-eyed.

Kat stopped. "Not anything like this," she admitted. "At least, not for awhile. One forgets, in the wilds of the mountains, you know." Her father would be proud of her improvisation—no, he'd opt for adding outrageous embellishments.

"It must be ever so difficult, Miss," the woman

breathed. "Here now, I'll just take this and make the alterations, and—"

"Alterations! But it's Lady Clementina's gown. I thought I was just going to borrow it."

"She wants you to have it, Miss. And I'd be ever so grateful if you took it. This gown just doesn't become her, not to my way of thinking. On you it looks a treat."

With that last plea, Kat acquiesced. Would Captain Warwick still regard her with disapproval when she came down the stairs in this? Well, maybe she'd have to restyle her hair, as well. She found she looked forward to the prospect.

They tried another gown on her, a striped muslin printed all over with small, multicolored flowers. This one fit quite well, needing only the tiniest of tucks about the waist and back and a ruffle about the bottom to add the needed length.

Middens disappeared with the two dresses, and Kat, still in her voluminous borrowed undergarments, stood in the middle of her chamber. She stared at her antiquated surroundings and felt the now-familiar rise of panic as reality again struck home. She was actually here, in an alien time, without so much as a toothbrush or comb to her name! Why hadn't someone warned her she was going time-hopping? She'd have packed a suitcase!

She shivered and hugged herself, chocking back an impulse to laugh which she feared would turn hysterical. *Why* had this happened to her, of all unlikely people? Why—She turned to the bed, discovered a light wrap similar to a bathrobe, dragged it on, and went in search of her father.

She found him preening before his own cheval glass mirror, dressed in black trousers with loops beneath his feet, a white waistcoat with a subtle pattern in blue woven through, and a black frock coat that fastened with a button just above his waist, then tapered toward the back where it ended just above the knee. Kat sat on the end of his bed. "You look like their butler."

Adam twisted, trying to get a glimpse of his back view. "Actually, their first footman supplied these. It seems we're much the same size. This is his stand-in uniform." He gave his neckcloth a final pat and turned his attention to Kat, and at once frowned. "What on earth have you got on under that thing?"

"More slips and petticoats and chemises than I've ever owned in my life. And they wear them all at once!"

He grinned. "Look upon it as a challenge."

"Easy for you to say. You've got the best of it."

"What, walking around looking like a butler?"

"Beats those old Forty-Niner denims," she shot back.

"Yes, and that reminds me, what was that derogatory crack about Knott's Berry Farm? The gold rush stories I learned there were very entertaining. Pure family fun. Nothing the least bit off-color."

She pulled her feet up and sat cross-legged, fixing him with a steady regard. "I've been thinking, Dad."

"Heaven help us," he murmured. "Is the strain making you feverish?"

She ignored him. "We came here in *his* dragon basket."

He arranged his features in a suitably solemn expression. "That we did, my girl."

"Then it makes sense that that's the way we'll have to leave, doesn't it? *If* we can, I mean."

He sighed, rolling his eyes heavenward. "In case it escaped your notice, we arrived here without it. No basket. Not so much as a hint of a dragon."

"Oh, do be serious a minute, Dad. If that's possible. I think it disappeared because it couldn't exist in two places at the same time."

Adam shook his head. "Advanced physics, girl. Sure you're up to it? You were an art major, remember."

"The basket *is* here. Wherever Captain Warwick keeps it. All we have to do is borrow it, and . . ." Her voice trailed off.

Adam seated himself beside her and took her hand in his. "Even art majors must know time travel isn't a normal sort of occurrence," he said, serious for once. "We *might* make it back in his dragon basket. But if we're here for a specific reason—?"

Kat nodded. "I keep trying to forget that. Oh, Dad, what kind of mess have we landed ourselves in?"

"I don't know, Kitten." He twitched one of her curls. "Have you had any more 'insights?' "

"Too many. And they're from him, all right. Do you know, I actually *saw* myself through his eyes? It was the eeriest thing. He doesn't trust us. It's something to do with this conference he's working on. He's been thinking absolutely murderous thoughts about me."

Adam's gaze strayed once more to the mirror. "Don't suppose you can read Lady Clementina's mind, can you?"

"No. And I can't really *read* his mind. It's just impressions and images." She watched her father's faint smile for a moment. "What do you think of the real Lady Clementina? Pity Tina couldn't have come with you instead, to meet her."

Adam shook his head. "Tina's too scatter-brained, though I daresay they'd like each other. Introductions might be awkward. Tina'd blurt right out that she'd been named for her."

"Better than being named for a town."

Adam chuckled and ruffled her hair, leaving it disordered. "That's what you get for being born so soon after the twins."

"And don't think Wilbur and Orville are any too fond of their names, either." She rose and straightened her dressing gown. "You're a pain, Dad. Have we ever told you that?"

"Frequently. Now, off with you, girl. I want to go find my hostess—to see if I can learn anything about why we're here."

They parted at the door, he to go downstairs, she to return to her room and wait.

She didn't have to for long. Less than twenty minutes later, a breathless Middens hurried into the room, the green silk cascading from her arms. She positioned Kat well away from any furniture, tossed the folds of cloth over her head again with an expert flick, then smoothed it down with loving hands.

"Yes, that will do," the maid announced, pleased. She began fastening buttons. "You look much more the thing, Miss—if I may take the liberty to say so."

"I'm glad to hear it." Kat regarded her reflection with a surge of pleasure. There was something about a gown that slipped just off the shoulders, and yards of wide lace circling a low neckline that made her feel absurdly feminine.

Would Captain Warwick like it? She'd know, she realized; he wouldn't be able to keep his reaction from her. She wasn't certain whether to be glad or regretful at this enforced honesty.

Shoes were harder to come by than clothes, but at last she slid her feet into a pair borrowed from an under housemaid. Not the height of fashion, perhaps, but far better than her own tennies. They'd look absurd beneath the silk and lace of her gown.

Her hair, at least, proved simple. Middens brushed it out, parted it in the middle, then swept it back over her ears and fastened it in a chignon at the nape of her neck. A garland of artificial roses nestled amongst the coppery-brown waves. Kat inspected it with uncertainty, knowing it looked well, yet feeling silly, as if she alone dressed up in a costume while everyone else remained in their everyday clothes.

"Now these, Miss." Middens held out a pair of gloves. "I'll have a pair of mittens ready for you in the morning."

Kat took them with misgivings. "I don't need any for daytime."

The maid stared at her, shocked. "Everyone wears them, Miss. Every lady, leastways. Even her ladyship."

Even Lady Clementina, huh? Well, mittens it would be, it seemed. With a sigh, she pulled on the gloves.

The maid draped a lace shawl about Kat's elbows, then gave her one last, thorough inspection. Abruptly, she nodded. "You'll do, Miss," she announced, and sent Kat downstairs.

Kat reached the main hall and stopped, looking about for some clue where to go next. As if by magic a footman appeared, a young lad somewhat nervous but eager to please. He directed her to the salon and admitted, blushing, that the butler had directed him to wait for her.

She entered the room, and Captain Warwick's presence hit her as a tangible force. With an effort she avoided looking at him. Instead she concentrated on Lady Clementina, who sat with her back to her on the blue brocade sofa. Adam, who lounged on the opposite side facing Kat, looked surprisingly debonair in his borrowed butler suit. His eyebrows rose as he studied her, and he gave her a quick nod and wink of approval.

Collecting her courage, she turned to face Captain Warwick, who stood before the fireplace staring into the flames, a cut crystal glass in one hand. He, like Adam, wore somber black—but there was nothing of the servitor about his appearance. He stood erect, his garments outlining his muscular form, elegance in their every line. A single gold chain crossed the deep green velvet of his waistcoat, and the emerald, set in its heavy gold band, sparkled on his finger.

Kat caught her breath. His dark blonde hair curled back from his forehead in thick waves, and his thick sideburns—what did they call them at this time, side whiskers?—gleamed red in the firelight. The tight set of his squared jaw betrayed the pain which seemed to be his constant companion.

He looked up, directly at her, and an awareness not her own washed over her, a surge of hunger and yearning. At once, he controlled it. She turned away, awash in swirling emotions, aware of desire, longing—and at the same time utter rejection.

"There." Lady Clementina faced her over the back of the sofa. "I knew that gown would become you, Miss Sayre. She looks quite delightful, does she not, Graeme?"

A grunt, that might be taken for acquiescence, was his only response.

Chagrined, Kat approached her hostess. A cloud of silver and lavender silk surrounded the lady. She had swept back her graying blonde hair in a style similar to Kat's, but covered it with a lace cap decorated with clusters of lavender ribbons. The delicate scent of the herb hung about her, as well. Very different she appeared from the purely practical figure of the morning.

Kat cast a suspicious glance at her father, who merely smiled at her in feigned innocence. Foreboding gripped her—though at the moment it seemed hard to imagine he could sink them into any deeper trouble. With a wry smile playing about her lips, she turned back to her hostess. "You've been too kind. Really too kind. I don't know how I can repay you. But I certainly appreciate it."

Lady Clementina waved her hand. "Middy loves to work with gowns. She is regarding the alterations as a rare treat, I assure you. Now, you look quite delightful, not at all the ragamuffin of earlier. Your father has been telling me about the rest of your party's going on to France."

Friends going to France. Kat filed that improvised fact for later reference.

"For your sakes," Lady Clementina went on, "I hope they return soon, but not for mine. I shall quite enjoy your company. But you must tell me what you would care to do tomorrow."

Unexpectedly, Captain Warwick said, "I find I need to return to the Crystal Palace Exhibition." He hadn't moved his position from the hearth, but his narrowed gaze rested on Kat. "Do you care to accompany me, Miss Sayre?"

Kat blinked, trying to read his intent, but gleaned only the veriest jumble from his mind. Yet she knew he suggested this for a purpose, for she detected no trace of idleness—or even pleasure.

"The very thing!" Delighted, Lady Clementina looked from one to the other of them. "We will all go. I have only visited it once, myself, so far. You will like it very well indeed, I make no doubt. Fascinating exhibitions. And from so many different countries. It's a splendid idea."

Kat wracked her memory, searching for any information that might lie buried there about the Exhibition. She'd heard it mentioned—where, on a British television show? Hadn't it been rather like a world's fair? And might it have anything to do with that unexpected outline map in her painting?

"Many countries?" she asked, catching her father's eye. "Most of Europe, perhaps?"

"It will keep you entertained for hours," Lady Clementina assured her. "We must set off early, to be in good time and to escape the dreadful crowds. That's settled then."

Maybe the Exhibition would provide some clue about what she was doing here. But would she understand it? She didn't know *anything* about this era. If she saw something out of place or potentially history-changing, she probably wouldn't be able to identify it.

Would Captain Warwick? Perhaps this mental tie they shared was meant to alert her to whatever would go wrong. She'd supposed her paintings would do that, but so far—based on today's efforts—she had learned nothing.

A sense of distrust filled her. Captain Warwick. She glanced up and caught him watching her, his expression thoughtful. A slow, disquieting smile touched his lips as their gazes met, and a wave of determination slammed into her mind. It left her shaken—and more than a little afraid.

Chapter Seven

This, Graeme decided the following afternoon as they entered their fifth hour of touring the Crystal Palace Exhibition, had not been as bad an idea as he'd feared when he first suggested it. In fact, he enjoyed himself more at this moment than at any time in recent remembrance, certainly since India . . .

That memory clouded his pleasure, clutching at him with its familiar pain, but for once it failed to sink him into depression. He had no room for such feelings, not when this unfamiliar excitement seeped through him. That mystified him. He'd seen the Exhibition before; why should it fill him with wonder and delight now?

The vivacious creature at his side gasped and darted forward, stopping before a display of gemstones. "The colors," Miss Sayre breathed. "Oh, rats, if only I had my paints!"

"You said that about the locomotives in their great hall." He joined her, smiling in spite of his determination to distrust her. Her enthusiasm knew no bounds, and it infected him.

The slightest dimple showed in her left cheek. "I

didn't mean to keep us there so long. But I'd never seen anything like it before."

"Nor the mill machinery?"

"Well, not fully operating like that." She moved on to a display of finely wrought jewelry. She regarded it, her expression pensive.

He studied it also, and experienced a sensation of mild disapproval, as if it were all too fussy. He'd never thought much about jewelry before. Perhaps that was why.

She glanced at the delicate little watch that fastened about her wrist into a bracelet. "I wonder what happened to my father and your aunt? It's been over an hour since we saw them."

"They are probably still among the carriages, arguing over design. If I know anything of my aunt's stamina, they'll remain in that exhibit until forcibly ejected."

"Unless some other display has caught their eyes."

"Your father is—" He hesitated over a choice of words.

"Outrageous?" suggested his not-so-dutiful daughter.

"An original, certainly," he amended.

Miss Sayre laughed. "You can say that again. This is the last time I take off on an adventure with him without having at least one of my brothers along to ride herd on him."

"To—" Yet in spite of the unfamiliar term, he realized he understood her meaning quite well. He could deplore her want of filial respect, yet in this case he found it fully justified.

His gaze rested on the coppery waves that peeped

out from beneath her borrowed bonnet, and enjoyment filled him. For the first time since—yes, for the first time since his injuries forced him to sell out of the army, the prospect of living through another day did not loom as a dreaded chore. She brought life back to him. She stimulated his senses, she—

She stimulated *him,* damn her. He drew back, retreating into himself, seeking the familiar ground of detached safety. It should come as no surprise to him that someone so vivacious and impulsive would stir his desires. His crippling disability made him no less a man. But she could never be attracted by someone like him.

They continued their erratic progress about the great hall, weaving among the throngs, he with his ungainly limp, she with her darting eagerness. If he didn't keep a close watch on his companion, he might lose her in the crowd. In fact, it might be best if he offered her his arm.

He did so, and to his mingled pleasure and consternation, her face brightened as she took it. The devil! The chit made him feel as if he indulged in some quaint habit. Yet he could not stay annoyed, not when her expression became rapt and a long, breathless "ohhh" escaped her.

She eased her way between two gentlemen and stood before a long display case. "Look at all the anti—all the guns."

Graeme managed to join her, and his eyebrows rose. "Do you shoot, Miss Sayre?"

She shook her head with patent regret. "That's something I haven't tried, yet. They're beautiful, aren't they? Look at all that detailing in the metal. They're so elegant."

"And so deadly," he reminded her with gentle reproof.

"These are meant to show off more than shoot. This one, though—" she gestured to the plain Colt Repeating Pistol "—this one's meant to kill."

Disapproval touched his mind. Odd, he'd never questioned the occasional necessity before. As an officer, he'd known it to be his duty. Had he changed so much since selling out?

"There's no elegance there," she went on. "It's all utilitarian. It's meant for a particular job, and it's not making any bones about it."

She moved on, and he sensed her anxiousness to distance herself from a distasteful object.

The next moment, she stopped. "It's a bomb!" She leaned toward the case, reading the printed sign, and shuddered. "Explosives."

"You don't approve?"

She shook her head. "They can do too much damage. Oh, I know they're useful for mining and—"

"Warwick?" A deep voice sounded behind them.

Graeme turned to see the familiar bushy eyebrows set in the narrow, lined face of approaching middle years. Quiet elegance wrapped the lean frame of Thomas, Lord Uxbridge, though a distracted frown increased the severity of his expression.

"What the devil are you doing here?" The man strode over to join them. "Should be hard at work. Only days left. Can't leave anything to chance, you know. Terrible business if anything should go wrong."

Graeme's jaw clenched. "Everything is under control, my lord."

The bushy brows bunched together. "Sure of that? I received your note. Entertaining houseguests! Now, of all times."

Graeme drew himself a little straighter, and forced his fingers to loosen their vise grip on the head of his cane. He wished he hadn't informed his superior of the Sayres' presence. "My aunt's—friends. May I present Miss Sayre? This—" he bit back the term "pompous windbag," and wondered what put it in his mind. He had never thought of the man in so disrespectful a term. "This is Lord Uxbridge, assistant to viscount Palmerston. Our Foreign Secretary," he added at Miss Sayre's obvious lack of comprehension of the significance of the viscount's name.

Miss Sayre extended her hand as if bestowing a favor upon the man. "How do you do?"

Uxbridge took it, and allowed his quick, assessing gaze to travel over her. Apparently he found nothing amiss in the young lady's borrowed gown of flowered muslin, for he acknowledged the introduction with a short nod.

She peeped up at him through surprisingly long lashes. "You must forgive me for taking Captain Warwick from his work, though I'm certain he isn't neglecting anything."

Uxbridge's gaze narrowed. "You're American. And a guest of Lady Clementina Durham?"

"My father and I."

"How delightful." Uxbridge rubbed his jaw. "Warwick, a word with you? If you will excuse us a moment, Miss Sayre?" He caught Graeme's arm and pulled him through the milling crowd, leaving the lady standing alone.

Graeme caught his balance with his cane. "Do you hope to be private in this mad house?" he demanded.

"Only from her. Listen, Warwick, I took a chance, giving such an important assignment to you."

Graeme's jaw jutted forward. "I am aware of that, my lord. However—"

"No," Uxbridge waved his explanations aside. "Not accusing you of negligence. Just not sure you understand the seriousness of what's at stake here."

"I believe I know better than most men what disastrous results can occur when plans go awry."

"Well, well, I'm not saying you don't." His expression softened. "I'm not reprimanding you, mind. Just mean this as a little reminder."

"You may inspect my preparations at any time, my lord. You will find nothing amiss."

Uxbridge nodded and patted him on the shoulder. "Glad to hear it. Now, if Matlock isn't enough help, be sure to let me know. I've found a promising young man, destined to rise high in government circles. Just the one to take charge of this matter if it gets too much for you."

"It won't."

Uxbridge regarded him with a dubious eye. "Ummm. Just so. I'll expect a progress report on my desk tomorrow morning." With a dismissive nod, and every inch the assistant to the Foreign Secretary, Uxbridge about-faced on his heel and strode off.

For a long moment, Graeme remained where he stood, until a gentle touch on his arm recalled him.

"What was eating him?" Miss Sayre's murmured words barely reached him.

He turned, forcing back his ill-humor as her concern touched him. "He wants *another* report."

"He doubts your abilities," she declared as a statement of fact. "He doesn't know you very well, does he?" She gazed off in the direction where Uxbridge had disappeared amid the throngs of people.

"He's a dedicated man." Yet even in his own ears, Graeme could hear his resentment. He didn't need anyone doubting his abilities. He did enough of that on his own.

Miss Sayre tugged at his arm. "Come on, let's go find our errant chaperons. It sounds like you've got work to do this afternoon."

For a moment, his fingers covered hers where they rested in the crook of his elbow. It wasn't easy to remain depressed in her company. Resolution solidified within him, a renewed determination that nothing would be permitted to go wrong with the conference. He would prove to Uxbridge he was no old warhorse to be put out to pasture.

And he would prove it to himself.

Graeme stood on the gravel, warmed by the morning sun, watching his messenger ride for London. In an hour, Uxbridge would have his precious report. It had taken Graeme a good portion of the night to complete it, but he felt reasonably certain he had included every detail, no matter how small. And if that didn't satisfy Uxbridge, he thought with savage force, nothing would.

He turned away as the groom disappeared through the iron gates of the Court. Perhaps he should visit Sevington House himself this morning. Yet he had gone over every inch of the luxurious townhouse in Grosvenor Square, assured himself all was in readiness. What else could he do?

A week—a full seven days—remained before the conference. He already had arranged for trusted servants of government officials to wait on the foreign dignitaries, he'd overseen menus—with his aunt's help—and arranged for sufficient cooks, potboys, and footmen to serve at meals. Fresh linens would be aired and waiting for those few who would actually stay in the house rather than at hotels. He'd ordered workmen to inspect the gas piping to ensure nothing would go wrong with the lighting and that hot water flowed from the taps in each of the bedrooms. He'd enumerated it all in his report.

He dragged a hand across his tired eyes. An image of roses flashed before him, of neatly raked and weeded paths among his aunt's prize blossoms. Miss Sayre would be there. He didn't know how he knew that, but he felt certain of it. And right now, he wanted company. Leaning heavily on his cane, he worked his way around the side of the house.

There, as he'd expected, he saw Miss Sayre seated on the marble bench near the center of the formal garden, sketch book in hand. He slowed his pace, but she looked up, directly at him, and stood in a flounce of yellow muslin skirts. The gown hung a trifle loose on her, accentuating her rounded curves, and a rather fetching confection of lace and ribbons perched in the drawn-back waves of her hair.

"You finished," she called.

A statement, again. She always seemed to know what he was about. He found it satisfying, at a fundamental level. Comfortable.

He shied from that, recognizing the inherent danger. "I've just dispatched the messenger." He reached her and picked up her pad from where it lay upside down on the bench. The heady scent of the roses surrounded him, stirring memories of moonlit gardens and flirtatious young misses—before he journeyed to India.

His fingers gripped her pad and he turned it over. Balloons met his surprised gaze, seven of them filling a cloudless sky, floating above rolling hills dotted with trees and a tilled field. Instinctively he glanced upward, but the azure sky revealed only a dotting of fluffy white clouds.

"Why aren't you happy with it?" He didn't know how he knew, but he did.

She pursed her full lips. "I'm trying to portray something—I guess you might call it the *essence* of something. It's not coming through."

He studied the sketch, unable to see anything wrong with the delicate rendition. The patterns on the balloons intrigued him. So many different styles, yet all utilizing stripes and bands. Nothing really fanciful, not like the one he'd just designed for himself with orange and red swirls curling across the cream-colored silk, making the effect of flames hovering above his dragon. Suddenly, he wanted to go up in it now, to soar through the sky with his lady . . .

She was *not* his lady.

She looked up. "We have company."

He turned, glad of the interruption to his thoughts,

and saw Adam Sayre approaching with another gentleman—Sir Francis Matlock, he realized. He handed
Miss Sayre her sketch pad. "In case you wish to capture his likeness again," he informed her.

She wrinkled her nose. "Once was quite enough."

Feeling out of all proportion pleased, he waited for
his assistant to reach them. Bustling with self-impor-
tance as always, Graeme noted—Matlock probably
thought himself the perfect image of a minor official of
the government. He watched the free, swinging stride
of him as he approached, and for once experienced a
touch of amusement instead of irritation.

An expression of pleasure lit Matlock's eyes as his
gaze came to rest on Miss Sayre. He greeted Graeme,
then turned at once to bow over her hand. To Graeme's further satisfaction, she extricated herself at
once.

Matlock's mouth tightened, and he faced Graeme.
"Seems our work is to begin at once, Captain." A
touch of smugness crept into the words.

Graeme tapped his cane on the gravel. "How obtuse
of me. I thought I had been working for months past."

Matlock waved that aside. "The first of our—guest-
s—arrived this morning. They're desirous of rest, and
have no wish to remain amid the bustle and crowds of
London. Lord Uxbridge feels they'll best be accom-
modated here, as visitors to your aunt."

"He does, does he?" Graeme murmured, *sotto voce*.

Matlock didn't appear to hear. "He will bring them
down himself this afternoon. I trust all can be in readiness?"

Graeme raised an amused eyebrow. *"You* trust?"

The ruddy tone of the man's complexion deepened.

"His lordship trusts, as I am sure we all do. I believe Lord Uxbridge has the greatest respect for Lady Clementina's abilities as a hostess, and the Court, of course, is capable of entertaining a great many house-guests."

Pomposity, conceit—why had Graeme never before realized how entertaining these faults could be? "My aunt," he pointed out with an air of apology, "never mentioned Lord Uxbridge's asking her."

Matlock blinked, then laughed. "My dear fellow, there hasn't been time! Only carried his request to her myself, just now."

"Ah, I see. A pity you were unable to find me first—as would have been proper."

"No need, no need." Matlock smiled, apparently oblivious of having committed any *faux pas.* "Your aunt was gracious as always, only too happy to be of assistance. But then, Uxbridge knew we could count on her. Such a relief to him to know the—guests—will be in the charge of someone so capable. Now," he went on, apparently oblivious to the subtle insult he had delivered to Graeme, "he also charged me with ascertaining whether or not you feel in need of more assistance. Worries you're over-taxed, you know."

"Does he?" Graeme regarded his assistant with fascination. "I suppose that depends upon whom his lordship has deigned to invite to visit my home."

Matlock's gaze strayed toward Adam Sayre. "Henri-Phillipe de Loire and his wife."

Graeme stiffened. "The de Loires? Of course they should not remain in London. And Uxbridge will bring them himself, you said?" His frowning gaze roved over the grounds, searching out potential dangers to the French delegate. Only serene gardens stretched as far as he could see. He turned back to Matlock, and his amusement returned. "Have you also seen to the ordering of their rooms?" he inquired with mock innocence.

Matlock laughed. "I feel certain Lady Clementina will have done so by now. Admirable woman. One need feel no qualms about leaving difficult matters in *her* hands." Only the slightest emphasis sounded on the pronoun. "Must make certain nothing goes wrong. And now," he inclined his head, "must be on my way if I'm to reach town before our honored visitors depart." With a last nod for Graeme, he strode off toward the stable.

A soft laugh escaped Miss Sayre. "He's priceless! You did say that man is *your* assistant, didn't you?"

He inclined his head. "We all suffer for our sins."

She grinned. "Repent," she advised, then sobered. "He's after your job."

"Two-faced back-stabber," Mr. Sayre added.

Miss Sayre touched Graeme's arm, allowing her fingers to rest a moment on the sleeve of his coat. "Don't trust him."

"My only concern is the success of this conference. Whatever stratagems he might entertain about his personal advancement are of no interest to me."

Miss Sayre's brow furrowed, and her expression became pensive. "Watch out," she advised.

Her father snorted. "Wouldn't be surprised if this Uxbridge already knows him for a conniver. Well." He puffed out his cheeks. "Think I'll go see if your aunt needs any help."

Graeme watched his departure, then turned to find

Miss Sayre watching him, her brow still wrinkled. "And you, Miss Sayre?"

"It doesn't sound as if your Sir Francis has left much for anyone else to do."

"I should enjoy it while I can. Usually his efforts go wrong and only increase my workload." Was it due to Miss Sayre's influence that he viewed Matlock in a new and more tolerant light? Normally he'd be furious with the man's innuendoes.

But had Lord Uxbridge been listening to them? That would explain his sudden doubts and concerns about Graeme's abilities. Of course, considering the importance of the conference, Graeme couldn't blame Uxbridge for being plagued with fears.

There was nothing for it but to prove them wrong.

And to do that, the conference must succeed without so much as a single problem.

Chapter Eight

Shortly before three o'clock, two carriages pulled up at the top of the curve in the wide, circular drive. Graeme paused in his pacing of the length of the salon and looked out the window. "They are here."

"Is that fool Sir Francis with them?" Lady Clementina demanded.

Miss Sayre leaned on the back of a chair, peering out. "No. That man we met at the Exhibition—Lord Uxbridge—he's just climbed out. And now he's helping a woman—oh, my." A soft laugh escaped her.

Graeme directed a warning glance at her. "Do you find something amusing?"

"What is it?" Lady Clementina rose to join them.

Miss Sayre threw him an impish grin. "Nothing at all. I suppose that is the height of French fashion?"

Graeme looked back to study the slight figure of the French delegate's wife, and became aware of an immense number of drooping flounces and ruffles, a shawl that seemed to be all hanging lace and fringe, and a bonnet topped by exotic plumes and clusters of ribbons, all of which curled downward about the woman's pointed chin. "I realize it is a far cry from those—those denims in which *you* chose to arrive," he informed her, "but—"

"Oh, don't worry, I won't say anything to embarrass anyone. At least," she added judiciously, "I'll try not to. And Dad, you are *not* to flirt with her. Is that understood?"

Mr. Sayre looked up with interest from the gentleman's magazine he perused. "Why? Will I want to?"

A man now descended from the carriage, a solidly built figure moving with determined energy in spite of his advancing age. His clothing, as somber as his wife's were frivolous, nevertheless bespoke elegance and a staggering tailor's bill. *Madame* de Loire took his arm, hanging upon it, and together they followed Uxbridge.

Graeme met them in the hall, his swift gaze assessing the couple. Thirty years must stand between the two, he realized, noting the woman's youthful countenance and mass of dusky hair swept back from her face. Large blue eyes appraised him in return as she extended a languid hand. He took it, awarding her a bow, then turned to her husband.

At least thirty years, he decided. Henri-Phillipe de Loire would not see his sixtieth summer again. Lines of exhaustion from their travels etched deeply into his rounded face. Bushy side whiskers, with a few brown hairs amid the gray to show what color they once had been, blended into a wild mane of gray hair, revealed as he released his hat into the hands of the butler.

A footman staggered into the hall under the weight of three cases, and Uxbridge followed in his wake. He paused, a harassed frown just touching his thin mouth.

"Ah, Warwick. *Monsieur, Madame,* may I present to you your host, Captain Warwick?"

Madame de Loire directed a long, sideways gaze at Graeme that held an invitation difficult to ignore. Graeme managed, merely bestowing on her a polite smile before turning back to her husband.

"I cannot remain for long," Uxbridge went on. "I must return almost at once to London."

"Then, *monsieur,*" de Loire said in a deep voice that still held strength, "I must thank you for your so very kind escort, and you, *monsieur Capitaine,* for your so great kindness in inviting us to stay."

Graeme, with a twisted smile, said: "I am honored," and ushered them into the salon to meet his aunt.

Uxbridge stopped short in the doorway, his gaze resting first on Miss Sayre, then on her father. His mouth tightened, but he merely approached Lady Clementina and performed the introductions. While Lady Clementina murmured polite phrases of welcome, Uxbridge retreated to Graeme's side. "Warwick, a word with you," he demanded.

Graeme followed him into the hall, where two footmen now sorted the bags under the watchful eyes of a strange maid and valet. Uxbridge waited with exaggerated patience until the servants took themselves off bearing the various valises and trunks, then rounded on Graeme. "Who the devil are those people? No, you've told me their names, but what are they still doing here? I sent Matlock this morning specifically to make certain you would have all in readiness."

Graeme's jaw set. "And it is."

"Why are they still here?"

"They are guests of my aunt. Americans. You knew they made an extended stay with us."

Uxbridge's countenance took on a florid hue. "I gave you warning so they might be removed."

"You have a very odd notion of the duties of a host," Graeme said with a mildness he did not feel.

Uxbridge waved that aside. "You have a very odd notion of the duties involved in this conference. Warwick," he laid his hand on his arm, "can you not realize the immense importance of what we hope to accomplish? If anything should go wrong—"

"There will be no harm to the conference from that quarter, I assure you." And to his surprise, at that moment he believed it to be true. That thought startled him, but he did his best to cover his reaction. "They are no saboteurs."

Uxbridge studied him for a long moment, his expression grave. "For your sake—for all our sakes—I must hope you are right." Without another word, he turned on his heel and left.

Graeme straightened his shoulders, acknowledging himself the winner of that round. But had he committed the greatest folly imaginable? What did he really know of Mr. Adam Sayre and his unusual daughter?

Only that he liked them, he realized.

And what if he were wrong? It would be wisest, he knew, to remove them from the vicinity of the delegates. Did he endanger the conference in order to indulge his desire to remain in that young lady's company a little longer? Disgusted with his uncertainty, he made one definite decision—to keep a closer watch on them. He strode into the salon where he could put his resolve into action.

Neither Miss Sayre nor her father appeared to be behaving in a manner that could be called the least bit suspicious. Mr. Sayre sat beside M. de Loire, discussing the beauties of the English countryside. Mme. de Loire sat between Lady Clementina and Miss Sayre, showing off her shawl with every appearance of delight.

The lovely French woman looked up as he entered and directed a dazzling smile at him. "But your aunt and your guest, they are of the most delightful!" she exclaimed. "We shall have a stay of the most enjoyable, *sans doute.*"

"It is our sincere hope."

The drooping eyelids lowered over pupils of a vivid blue, their invitation once more unmistakable. Graeme made a rapid calculation on the risks of offending the wife or the husband, and chose to mistake it.

Irritation played at the corners of his mind, settling into a dislike for blatant flirtation. Odd, he'd always rather enjoyed it, before. Now—

Now, he had a sudden unprecedented urge for ... for a pastry, stuffed with apples and cinnamon and dripping icing. That really did surprise him. He rarely ate sweets. Yet right now, he could hardly wait for Newcombe to bring in a refreshment tray for the visitors.

Uxbridge returned that evening, arriving just as the party gathered in the salon before dinner. He strode into the room, closely followed by a young gentleman with a Grecian countenance and supercilious air. An otherwise unexceptional costume was made a shade too dashing by a silk waistcoat of a startling shade of puce shot through with gold thread.

"May I present viscount Ellesmere?" Uxbridge led the man to Lady Clementina, then left him there while he himself joined Graeme.

Graeme watched as the fellow acknowledged his hostess, nodding rather than bowing and taking her hand as if he conferred a great honor upon her.

"We have been much exercised upon your behalf at Whitehall." Uxbridge kept his voice low, so that only Graeme might hear.

"And this is the result?" Graeme raised derisive eyebrows.

Uxbridge didn't appear to notice. "An excellent man in a houseparty. Unmarried, of course, which makes him a most welcome addition. He delights in dancing, and can be counted upon to take charge of the most cantankerous dowager or the shiest wall-flower, and he is a dab hand at cards. He will serve you well in entertaining the de Loires." With a dismissive nod, he went to take the viscount about the room, performing introductions.

"I get the impression he's staying," Miss Sayre's soft voice murmured at Graeme's shoulder.

He acknowledged her comment with a short nod.

"He's very . . . decorative," she hazarded.

Graeme studied the gentleman under discussion, trying to gauge his rather old-fashioned Byron-esque looks. "I suppose females might find him so. He is here because he can dance and play cards and entertain the de Loires." *Better than I can,* he added silently.

"Mmmm. Where I come from, that sort of man's called a gigolo. When we're being polite. Another good term is Lounge Lizard."

A rumble of amusement shook him, breaking forth

in a soft chuckle. "What? Are you impervious to his charms?"

"Shall we find out?" She moved forward as Uxbridge presented his charge before her.

A gleam lit the viscount's eyes as they rested on Miss Sayre. "A very great pleasure," he murmured, retaining her hand in his.

Graeme caught the devil of laughter in her face and threw her a forbidding glare. She met it, hesitated perceptibly, then murmured nothing more than a polite rejoinder. Graeme welcomed him in his turn, then Ellesmere and Uxbridge moved on.

"What were you going to say to him?" he demanded when the two men were out of ear shot.

"Nothing that would have made your aunt uncomfortable," she assured him.

He snorted. "That leaves a very wide range."

She threw him a glance brimming with laughter, and suddenly Ellesmere didn't seem so bad after all. He would be entertaining. In fact, Graeme found himself looking forward with amused speculation to the next couple of days.

Lady Clementina approached Uxbridge. "You will join us for dinner, of course?" Dry cynicism just touched her words.

Uxbridge inclined his head, as one bestowing a great honor upon his hostess. "I shall be delighted," he pronounced.

"Then you must excuse me. I fear I have a few arrangements to make." She crossed to the bell and rang.

When the butler entered a minute later, she sent him for the housekeeper and, when Mrs. Erling arrived, engaged her in a low-voiced conversation. Graeme strolled over in time to overhear the ordering of another bedchamber to be prepared.

Lady Clementina hesitated, her frowning gaze resting on the unexpected addition to the houseparty. "The Red Room, I think, Mrs. Erling."

She'd placed Ellesmere as far as possible from the Sayres, Graeme noted, with the de Loires in between. The arrangement pleased him; he hadn't liked the way the viscount had been eyeing Miss Sayre. Not that he could blame him, he admitted with reluctant fairness. Miss Sayre was lovely in her borrowed gown—damn it, she was lovely in her deplorable denims. It was her vivacity, those huge, sparkling eyes and the mouth normally curved for laughter. She brightened any gathering just by walking through the door.

He glared at Ellesmere. He'd put him to good—and busy—use by having the man tend to Vivienne de Loire. That should relieve him of both problems.

Newcombe returned, and with the somber formality due to the importance of their visitors, announced dinner. With a measure of reluctance, Graeme took his place as host to lead in Vivienne de Loire. His aunt, ever the perfect hostess, went to M. de Loire, and Lord Uxbridge narrowly beat out Ellesmere to take Miss Sayre.

Graeme feigned interest in the coquettish comment of the woman at his side, while his attention focused on Miss Sayre and Uxbridge behind him. He couldn't hear what his superior said, but he did hear Miss Sayre's soft laugh, and was surprised at the phoniness of it. Uxbridge, to Graeme's surprise, didn't seem to notice. Graeme's brow furrowed. He seemed to be a little too perceptive where Miss Sayre was concerned.

Dinner, he could admit with all honesty, did not bore him tonight as so many diplomatic functions usually did. On the contrary, he found himself on edge the entire meal, studying each of his guests. It had never been his intention—or desire—to host a houseparty. He had too much work still remaining for the conference, he needed to spend his time at Sevington House checking preparations and details. Viscount Ellesmere might entertain in his absence, but he could not replace the host.

Vivienne de Loire leaned toward him, her laugh a touch shriller than it had been two glasses of wine before. *"Mon Capitaine,* do you not agree?"

He brought his attention back to her. "I beg your pardon?"

She laughed again. *"Tiens,* it is these gentlemen who are diplomats. They are of the most dreary, *n'est-ce pas?* So few who are young. Me, I so much prefer a livelier sort of companion." Her gaze fluttered first to Graeme, then to Ellesmere, and her slow, inviting smile curved her rouged lips.

Ellesmere leaned forward, waving his wine. Was that his fifth glass? Graeme's eyes narrowed. There could be no mistaking the man's state of inebriation. Graeme shot a glance at Uxbridge, who listened to something Lady Clementina said, apparently oblivious to his latest protege's slip from decorum.

"I trust," Graeme remarked, turning back to Mme. de Loire, "you will not find the Crystal Palace to be dull."

"Mais non, how could one, *enfin?"* Vivienne ex-

claimed. *"Voyons,* but will I be able to see it?" She pouted.

Rather prettily, too, Graeme noted, and attributed it to practice. It surprised him it moved him not in the least. "I have arranged for those traveling with the delegates to have coaches at their disposal. You may certainly visit the Exhibition—and any of the other sights of London and the surrounding area that you might wish."

"Vraiment? But how kind, *monsieur.* I shall enjoy it of the utmost. And if I might but have a delightful companion—?"

"It is my loss I shall not be able to fulfill that role myself, *madame."* Graeme hoped he didn't sound too insincere. "I believe Ellesmere is free. Are you not?" He turned to the viscount.

Ellesmere gestured with his wine glass. "I shall be delighted to be at your service, fair lady."

"Then all is settled," Graeme said, and could only hope it was.

Ellesmere's gaze strayed to Miss Sayre. "I shall be delighted to escort as many fair ladies as you might wish." His words took on a slight slur.

The viscount didn't hold his drink well, Graeme noted; he'd have to keep a close eye on the man. He tilted his head ever so slightly, catching the attention of the butler who stood by the door, overseeing the meal. He gave the slightest shake of his head in Ellesmere's direction. Newcombe's expression remained impassive except for the slightest fluttering of one eyelid that Graeme accepted for the man's acknowledgment. Ellesmere's supply would be rigidly curtailed. The footmen brought in another course, Newcombe caught the young man who carried the wine bottle, and Ellesmere received no more than a splash.

"Are you perhaps, sir, a balloonist?" Adam Sayre's voice sounded loud in a momentary lull as he addressed Henri-Phillipe de Loire.

"Mais non." The French delegate shook his head. "But often I have admired their so great gracefulness."

Mr. Sayre sighed. "It is an experience not to be missed, my dear sir. To drift with the clouds, at peace with all the world—"

"You never told me," Graeme interrupted. "Is ballooning something you did often in California?"

Mr. Sayre met his gaze with a bland smile. "Of course."

Miss Sayre, though, flashed Graeme a quick, searching look, which further confirmed his suspicions. There was something very false about their California story. He would find out what.

He glanced down the table and saw that Uxbridge still listened with a bored expression to Lady Clementina. From the determined light in his aunt's eyes, he guessed she had some purpose in mind. He supposed he would find out soon enough.

He turned back to his dinner companion, and watched with a measure of disapproval as Mme. de Loire brought her long lashes into play as she looked at Ellesmere. Then her gaze moved back to Graeme, and he received the exact same ploy. She eyed them both as if trying to make her choice from a buffet table. He didn't like that feeling of being viewed as a plum ripe for her picking—if the whimsy took her.

De Loire's displeased gaze rested on his flirtatious wife, and deftly Graeme reclaimed her attention from

Ellesmere, who leaned on the table as if considering crawling across it to join that lady. "Perhaps," Graeme suggested, "Miss Sayre might be interested in the latest French fashions."

Miss Sayre threw him a comprehending glance and at once, in spite of the fact it involved speaking across the table, begged the woman to "tell all."

"Mais non, mademoiselle," Vivienne protested. "It is you who must tell me of the gowns to be found in this California of yours."

"Oh, the hardships we are forced to endure!" Miss Sayre fluttered her long lashes in feigned dismay—and in fair imitation of the French woman. *"Madame,* you would be horrified at what we are reduced to." Her green eyes sparkled with mischief.

Her father hummed a few bars of a sprightly tune, and Graeme noted the difficulty with which Miss Sayre kept from laughing. Obviously, that tune held meaning—and it had something to do with their tales of California. He would learn more of their supposed adventures there.

Mme. de Loire, though, did not seem to notice this little by-play. She regarded Miss Sayre with curiosity. *"Tiens,* do not your *modistes* receive the latest fashion plates?"

"We have no *modistes,*" Miss Sayre assured her in tragic accents belied by the twinkle in her eyes. "So please tell me all that I have been missing."

With this, Mme. de Loire, nothing loathe, complied. In relief, Graeme turned his attention from them. He could count on Miss Sayre to occupy the French woman's attention—though how he knew he could, and how Miss Sayre knew he needed help, he didn't quite know.

Ellesmere glowered at the two ladies, then leaned forward to join their conversation. Vexed, Graeme looked up and caught his aunt's eye. She met his gaze, and with the slightest of nods acknowledged his unspoken request.

She brought her one-sided conversation with Uxbridge to a conclusion and rose. Mme. de Loire and Miss Sayre followed suit. "If you gentlemen will excuse us?" Lady Clementina smiled upon the men, who hastily stood. "We will await you in the drawing room." She led the way out the door.

Uxbridge resumed his seat and lounged back, making no attempt to disguise his relief. "So many details," he said. "Your aunt has been telling me of all the preparations that have been made." Acute boredom sounded in his voice. "Warwick, a word with you."

Another? Graeme repressed a sigh of resignation.

Adam Sayre collected the port, glanced at the viscount, then replaced the decanter on the table at some distance. "Ellesmere." He took the man's arm and urged him to his feet. "Shall we join the ladies? We might be able to interest them in a game of cards. *Monsieur?* Would you perhaps care for a game?"

The diplomat rose, and Ellesmere, who apparently had been mulling over the suggestion, brightened. He slipped his arm companionably through Adam Sayre's and accompanied him quite jovially from the room with de Loire in their wake.

Graeme noted with interest this masterly handling

of the young man, then turned to Uxbridge. "What did you wish to say?"

Uxbridge rose, paced the length of the room, then turned back, his expression troubled. "This is a difficult situation," he said.

Graeme let that pass. The whole situation had been extremely difficult.

Uxbridge poured himself a glass of brandy, then stared into the deep amber liquid as he swirled it slowly in his glass. "The de Loires," he said at last. "How do they strike you?"

Graeme leaned back against the sideboard, watching his superior. "In what way?"

"Do you think they are as they would have us believe?" Uxbridge pursued.

Graeme raised speculative eyebrows. "Do you think they are not?"

Uxbridge sipped his brandy and stared thoughtfully into his glass. "There is a rumor—no more than that, just a rumor—that *Madame* de Loire has been and might still be the mistress of Louis Napoleon."

Graeme's gaze narrowed. "How reliable is this rumor?"

"Let us say I have no reason to doubt it," Uxbridge temporized.

"Louis Napoleon," Graeme said slowly. "Is he likely to receive the power he seeks in France?"

Uxbridge paced a few more steps. "I don't know. Nor does Palmerston."

"But Palmerston supports him," Graeme said quickly.

Uxbridge remained quiet for a very long minute.

"Palmerston may be seen to do one thing while in actuality he does another."

"Do you think *Madame* de Loire might have more interest in the conference than her husband suspects?"

"Rumors!" Uxbridge slammed his empty glass on the table. "There is no way of knowing for certain. It is even possible *Monsieur* de Loire uses his wife for his own ends with Louis Napoleon."

"And you want me to find out?" Graeme asked.

"I want you to . . ." Uxbridge's voice trailed off. "I want you to make very certain that nothing goes wrong, even if it means spending a great deal of time in the de Loires' company."

Graeme inclined his head. "And Ellesmere? I thought that was what he was here for."

"He is here to entertain for you, to free you for more important . . . observations."

Graeme acknowledged this, and the amused anticipation he had experienced earlier deserted him completely. Now, only foreboding remained.

Chapter Nine

The early morning sunlight sparkled on the lake, dancing across the ripples caused by the swans as they paddled on their stately way. Kat sketched quickly, trying to catch a pattern in the reflections in the water, freeing her mind, allowing her pencil to flow. She added a swan, played with the pattern of its feathers, then studied it in despair. If only her drawing might reveal something, anything to give her a clue why she was here. It was getting uncomfortable.

All because of Capt. Graeme Warwick. He entered her mind; she'd sensed his moods shifting in response to hers, the enthusiasm that bubbled within her transferring to him, then bouncing back to her, intensified. She felt invaded, violated—and guilty for doing the same to him. Captain Warwick—

As if the mere thought conjured him, awareness of him filled her mind, feelings of worry, of long-familiar pain. An image flickered before her eyes of gravel surrounded by low shrubs. He was coming.

She looked across the lake and saw him approach along the path with his uneasy, dragging gait. Yet there was nothing about him that allowed pity. Admiration flooded her, for the strength she detected within him, for his quiet determination, for the powerful will that drove him.

She waited, knowing there was no need to go to him. He would come. He came expressly to see her. Yet she knew better than to be flattered by his attention. This was no idle stroll to check on the well-being of one of his guests. He sought her for a reason; she could sense the purpose within him. He wanted something from her.

And what he wanted, she guessed, he usually got. Few people would be able to deny him for long. Which meant she might well come to a battle of wills with him in a very short time.

She watched him, her uneasiness growing. She couldn't deny his rugged good looks—or their appeal to her. She'd never been partial to fair men before, but there was something about him. It went beyond mere physical attributes.

He checked for a moment; she felt a wave of self-consciousness. He must have become aware of her watching him. When he started forward once more, he stood more erect, using his cane with practiced care, dragging his left leg as little as possible.

Kat experienced his strain as he tried to maintain this macho facade. If he only realized she experienced what he did, felt his pain . . . no, best he didn't guess. He would be mortified. His injuries were bad enough without his having to endure others being aware of his inner struggles. To know oneself pitied—Yet that was one emotion she didn't feel for him. She couldn't. Rather, she should fear his strength of mind.

He didn't stop again until he reached the base of the shallow steps to the folly. From there he gazed up at her, that slight crease she was coming to know forming in his high brow. "You are sketching again."

She looked down at the pad in her lap—away from his delightful bushy side whiskers. "So I am. I was wondering what I did."

"Why?" he demanded. "You make use of your pad and pencil every chance you get."

"I like to remember things." She smiled at him, but could sense his growing irritation.

"You have reason behind what you do." He spoke slowly, as if testing the words. He mounted the first few shallow steps and held out his hand. "Let me see."

She offered him the pad. "I like swans." His hands, she noted as he took it, were strong. He was a man of action, reduced to this life of physical idleness. It wasn't fair.

He turned to gaze out over the lake, comparing her drawing with the scene before them. "You wish to remember ripples?"

"Allow me some creativity, please. Are your other guests not yet up?"

"Not yet. *Monsieur* de Loire's valet has assured me his master is not likely to rise before ten."

"And *madame?*"

"She breakfasts in her room. And then young Ellesmere has requested the privilege of exploring the grounds with her."

"What? You didn't reserve that honor for yourself?" Kat grinned up at him. "She's rather beautiful— if you hadn't noticed."

"She's rather a flirt—if *you* hadn't noticed. No,

thank you. Ellesmere can earn his keep by entertaining her."

"And you are to entertain her husband? Or is Lord Uxbridge coming back again?"

"We are—not to be so fortunate."

Kat narrowed her gaze on him, sensing his real meaning—that they were to be spared. He'd changed the words just in time.

"I thought," he went on, studying her face, "since I had a free hour, you might tell me more about California."

Kat didn't need the slight emphasis he put on his words to detect his suspicions. She leaned back in her chair, recalling images to mind of postcards she'd seen of the coastline, of Ansel Adams photographs of Yosemite and the Sierras. With an effort, she blocked out thoughts of Los Angeles traffic. Why had her father invented that ridiculous gold rush story to explain their clothes? Why couldn't he have picked their home state of Virginia, or at least a place she had visited?

"Are your memories painful?" His voice—gentle, for once—interrupted her thoughts.

She looked up to find him studying her, the corners of his eyes wrinkled in puzzlement—and concern. He experienced her emotions, she realized, though he probably didn't understand the sensations she caused. She played to it, allowing a shuddering sigh to escape her. "It's something I prefer not to think about," she said with complete honesty. "I miss my brothers and sister. Do you have any family?" His sadness filled her, and at once she was sorry she'd brought something so painful to his mind.

Before she could speak, he said shortly, "Dead."

She touched his arm. "So is my mother. In a ca— carriage accident." She tried to block the rush of memories.

"You were with her," he said, sounding surprised.

"So were my brothers and sister. She'd come to pick us up from school."

"But the rest of you survived your injuries." He frowned, honest concern struggling with something.

He was struggling to comprehend the emotional tumult that filled his mind, she realized. How could she have thought him cold? For a fleeting moment, she sensed the enthusiasm, the idealism that had been destroyed on that mountain pass in India.

He drew away abruptly, his expression uncertain, distrustful once more. "I must be getting back." Without waiting for her response, he turned on his heel and, with the aid of his cane, descended the steps and strode away.

Kat watched his retreating back, wishing she could say something to ease his confusion and pain. She closed her eyes, mentally reaching out to him with a wave of comfort and—and caring? Startled, her eyes opened.

He had stopped about forty paces from her and turned, staring back. She did care, she realized—but how could she help that? She practically inhabited the man's mind. And he, hers, though he didn't realize it yet.

He nodded to her in an unspoken goodbye and resumed his walk. Kat rose abruptly, shoved her pencils in their box, stowed her pad under her arm, and strode off in the opposite direction.

What did she know about the man? Everything, she

realized—and almost nothing. She knew his torment. She recognized what he once had been, before an ambusher's bullet destroyed his career—and life. She sensed his uncertainties, his frustration, his determination. She knew who he was, where he belonged—and that he must be important to her purpose here in the past.

She halted, then slowly about-faced to stare back the way she had come, to where she had last seen him. *Why* did she share this link with him? Up to now, she'd been too overwhelmed about why she and her father had been snatched through time, what momentous historical events they faced. But what about her momentous *personal* involvement? Why her? And why him? Had it been this link with him that brought her back? And might her presence here cause the change to history her painting predicted? Or was it her presence here in that past that made history the way she knew it?

She set forth once more with long, swinging strides to relieve the tension building within her. Should she confront him about this link they shared? He couldn't experience it as strongly as did she—unless his stubbornness blocked it.

She wished she didn't care. She wished none of this had ever happened, that she was still home in Virginia, had never crossed the Atlantic, had never heard of Capt. Graeme Warwick—

No. Meeting him had been like—like meeting the other half of herself.

She walked on, her pace slowing, as the wonder of that realization crept through her. But why here? And why *now?* Why not someone in her own time?

Because she shared this link with Capt. Graeme Warwick, *not* with someone in her own time, came the obvious answer.

It must have been this bond that brought her through time to join him—but that didn't explain the strange tracery in her painting, she reminded herself. There was nothing simple about any of this.

As she neared the great house, two people emerged from around back, a man dressed in somber black and a woman in a purple gown that swayed with her determined stride: her father and Lady Clementina. Kat quickened her pace to join them. Lady Clementina said something to Adam; he looked up and hailed Kat.

"Drawn anything interesting?" he called.

"Nothing." She stopped before them, eyeing them with no little speculation. "Where are you off to?"

"Oh, just around the grounds." Adam waved an airy hand.

"Been sketching, Miss Sayre? May I see?" Lady Clementina asked.

Obligingly, Kat held out her pad, allowing her hostess to leaf through the collection of sketches, from those done the day before to those representing the morning's work.

The woman's gaze narrowed as she studied each one, then looked up at Kat. "I'm impressed. You would find a large number of people willing to sponsor you if you were a man."

Kat's mouth tightened. There were, of course, very few professional female artists of any note at this time. Later, of course, when the invention of tube paints allowed outdoor work and the Impressionists came into their own, women, too, would make their mark.

But not yet. She forced a smile to her lips. "I support myself with my work at home."

Lady Clementina's eyes widened. "Do you, indeed? Good for you. A woman should use her talents. I'll tell you what. I've never had a portrait done of myself. I'd like to engage your services. Let the men go begging."

"You'd—" Kat broke off, swallowed, then continued. "Would you? Really? I'd love to do something to help repay you for all you've done."

"Nonsense." Lady Clementina waved that aside. "This way I get the pleasure of your company *and* a portrait I'll be proud of. It's settled. When do you want to begin?"

Kat hesitated. She'd only brought two canvases, neither big enough for this sort of work. It would take time to locate a place to buy supplies, then she'd have to stretch the canvas and prime it and then . . .

Lady Clementina settled the difficulties. Without further ado, she led them inside where she dispatched a footman to London with a list of everything it seemed possible an artist might need. Then she turned to Kat, beaming. "What setting shall we use?"

"Balloons," said Adam, who had been trailing after them. "It's the only possible setting for you."

To Kat's surprise, a slight tinge of color crept up the woman's neck and highlighted her cheeks.

"The very thing," Lady Clementina announced, perhaps a shade too heartily. She looked away from Adam and cleared her throat. "Shall we inflate it on the south lawn, perhaps?"

"Why don't we go look at your balloon, now?" Adam suggested. Over the woman's shoulder he winked at Kat.

"I'd love to see it," Kat said at once, picking up her cue. "Is it the same one you used to cross the Channel? Then of course that's what we need to use in the painting."

And while they were at it, perhaps they could get a look at Captain Warwick's basket.

A frisson of excitement set her shivering. She could hardly wait to see the dragon's graceful lines, its arched neck and thrown-back head, even its wicker claws.

Her father grasped her arm just above the elbow and propelled her after Lady Clementina, who had started toward the library. "Pull together," he muttered in her ear.

"Do you think this is safe?" she shot back.

For a moment, his steps slowed. "What could happen?" he asked at last. "If we see the dragon, I mean. We saw it in our own time and nothing happened, remember."

"We have to fly in it," she agreed. "Do you think—?"

"Wish I knew," he muttered back. "But Warwick's flown in it any number of times and never gone time-hopping."

"No." She studied her hands, in which she clutched her sketching supplies. "Dad, I—I don't really think his dragon caused it. It might have been the vehicle, because it was *his*, but—"

"His," Adam repeated. "You and Warwick, huh? Next time you decide to go on a long-distance date, leave me home, okay?" But his gaze strayed to the elegant figure of Lady Clementina where she awaited them just inside the library door.

"Dad—" Kat began, threatening, but broke off, not wanting to risk being overheard. It looked, though, like he was considering a little cross-time dating of his own. Where would this all lead?

They let themselves out onto the terrace, then started down the gravel path leading to the stable. In the distance, just crossing the south lawn, she could see two people strolling. Kat narrowed her eyes, and made out a pink ruffled gown on a slight figure topped by a preposterous hat bristling with drooping plumes. That could only be Vivienne de Loire. Her companion possessed neither her husband's determined gait nor Captain Warwick's dragging step. That meant it must be young viscount Ellesmere, conducting the lady on the promised tour. From the way he bent his head toward her, he seemed to be enjoying his assignment.

To where had their host vanished? Almost at once, an image formed in her mind of papers—charts, mostly—spread across a cluttered desk, and a desire filled her to escape, to clamber into the wicker dragon and sail from this earthbound prison.

We're going to look at it, Kat thought before she could stop herself.

Surprise exploded into her mind, a brief moment of utter confusion, which faded as if with deliberate effort. She'd actually reached him, contacted him! But how? In words? In images? Or in feelings? She'd seen through his eyes before, but never—at least, not that she knew of—sent a message back to him. From the chaos that still flickered through her consciousness, she realized he wouldn't accept what had happened if she tried to tell him. He'd blame it on anything and everything else rather than accept the possibility of this mind link.

That was probably for the best.

They reached the barn, and one of the grooms came running. Lady Clementina gave her instructions, and the young man led the way to one of the closed stalls. He dragged open both halves of the heavy door and there, to Kat's immense disappointment, stood only one wicker basket, a strictly conventional one. Lady Clementina stepped inside to run a loving hand over the side, and Kat pulled herself together and spoke properly admiring words.

"And the balloon?" Adam asked. "Kat will need to know the color."

"Many colors." For a moment, Lady Clementina looked somewhat embarrassed. "I had a new one made recently, with a rainbow sewn into it."

"A rainbow. How beautiful! Is the rest of the balloon sky blue?" Kat asked.

Lady Clementina's sheepish smile flashed. "With white clouds."

"This I've got to see—though I suppose we ought to wait to inflate it until I'm ready to do the sketches." Still, she felt a measure of regret at the delay. Somehow, a rainbow didn't seem to be quite Lady Clementina's style. But was a dragon Captain Warwick's? The same touch of the fanciful, the unexpected, marked that choice.

Adam went to the next stall and laid a hand on the hasp. "What's in here?"

"My nephew's basket. I think he should show it to you himself, though. He's very particular about it."

"I doubt they'd be interested," Captain Warwick called from across the yard.

Kat turned slowly, allowing her longing to see the dragon fill her. He'd know.

For a long minute he remained where he stood, then he crossed the cobbles, the tip of his cane clacking with his every dragging step. He cast a considering look toward the stall, then his gaze drifted to Kat, her father, his aunt, then back to Kat. "If you'd really like to—" Shyness crept into his expression, mingling with a boyish eagerness, his desire to show off his favorite toy tinged with the fear that it might be scorned.

Kat found it completely disarming, another side of this complex, often grim man. He nodded to the groom, who still stood nearby, and the lad dragged back the heavy door.

Kat tensed, catching her breath, as she stared at the dragon, so familiar and yet so very different. The dark wicker showed no signs of great age, had no metal plates. The wild beast crouched in the straw, head thrown back, as if ready to spring into the sky.

"You like it." His deep voice sounded just behind her.

Kat blinked, but didn't look over her shoulder at him. "It's exactly—"

No, it wasn't. This was the nineteenth century version, complete, not yet damaged—and not yet repaired. She swallowed, suddenly feeling weak. Somewhere, in the back of her mind, she'd held the unexpressed hope that once they'd settled whatever business had brought them into this time, she and her father could simply commandeer the dragon basket for the journey home. A round trip.

But that wouldn't work. This wasn't the basket of her time. It belonged here, where it would be damaged, repaired, and stored for over a century.

Was she stuck here, in this era, for the rest of her natural life?

Chapter Ten

Miss Kat Sayre worked on a painting, and one that really mattered to her. Graeme didn't know how he knew that fact; he just did. Ever since yesterday—when he'd shown her and her father his dragon basket—she had grown more withdrawn, to the point where he could feel her tension.

Yet she had loved his dragon. He *felt* her reverence for it, a sensation he shared. He stood in the stall staring at it, wondering about the onslaught of sensations that had all but overwhelmed him as they'd gazed at his wicker creation. Why, after only a few moments, had she suddenly seemed so devastated?

He exited the stall, closed the heavy door behind him, and stared thoughtfully at the house. She wasn't working on his aunt's portrait; she'd made her canvas, prepared the surface, then left it to dry. No, she worked on something else, something that mattered a great deal to her. And she worked with a desperation that at one level he shared without understanding in the least.

He found the situation intolerable.

If he wanted to talk to her, he'd find her in the conservatory. That was something else he knew, without understanding how. In fact, at this moment, she was totally involved in . . . in *what?* She was desperate, driven, frantic to . . . to *what?* Maybe if he confronted her, demanded to see this painting, he'd discover . . . discover *what?*

He'd go, now, and get to the bottom of the mystery she represented. With a sense of purpose that surprised him, that had evaded him ever since that bleak morning on that mountain pass three years ago—that had been lacking even throughout the planning of the conference—he set forth.

He experienced no surprise at all to see her as soon as he opened the door of the huge multiwindowed chamber. Warmth surrounded him, along with the pungent, earthy smell of the numerous plants in their massive pots. Everywhere leafy green greeted him, along with the sunlight amplified by the pale yellow walls. Miss Sayre stood near the long line of windows, her easel before her—and her canvas covered. He frowned, noting her brushes thrust into a jar, her palette multihued with its globs of unused paint.

She tugged the last corner of the concealing cloth into place, then turned to him and smiled. "What a surprise. I was just finishing here."

Only she hadn't finished—he felt certain of that. He'd interrupted her. But that meant she had to have known he—or someone, at least—was coming. And she certainly wasn't surprised.

He folded his arms before him. "May I see your work?"

"Not yet." She sounded airy, as if no more than a whim prevented her from flinging back the covering.

Her manner didn't fool him for a moment. She would fight to prevent him from seeing what lay beneath that cloth. Again, he didn't know how he knew; he just did. "You've let me see your other work," he pointed out.

"Those were just sketches, nothing important." She swished her brushes in the vile smelling liquid, then wiped them briskly on a clean corner of her painting rag. "What may I do for you?"

A slow smile tugged at his lips. "I believe I am the one who should say that. You are my guest, after all."

"Whether you wish it or not?" Her sudden, infectious grin flashed.

Graeme caught his breath as the full impact of it hit him.

"You're bored!" she announced as if making a discovery. "Everyone else has gone out, haven't they? Even your aunt and my father. You should have gone along as a chaperon. They'd certainly show you a livelier time than you're having here."

He stiffened. "I have been about business for the conference."

"Of course you have, and been finding it deadly dull—I wager. Let me just take this to my room—" she hefted the canvas "—then we'll go exploring."

"You can leave your painting here. No one will disturb it."

She wrinkled her nose. "No, thanks. I might get inspired in the middle of the night. You never know. Grab my workbox?" She started from the room.

He'd certainly never met such an unorthodox young

woman, he reflected as he gathered her things and followed her from the conservatory. Knowing her was likely to prove a fascinating experience. He studied her back, the way her bright brown hair swung against her shoulders, the way the flowered muslin of her skirts swayed about her full hips. A fluffy, bouncing kitten . . .

She stopped abruptly in front of him and turned an astonished face toward him, her large green eyes alight with surprised laughter, her cheeks flushed. For an instant he experienced an almost uncontrollable urge to gather her into his arms and swing her about, then kiss that—He broke off the thought abruptly, for her color had deepened, and she regarded him with a curious stare.

Lord, had she read his mind? His own face burned at the possibility. She always seemed to know what he thought—was he that transparent to her? And was she to him? Memory filled him of the odd sensations he'd experienced, of his inexplicable knowing where she was, what she did.

On impulse, he concentrated, reaching out to her with his mind, a tentative, searching touch. . . . Before him stood not Miss Sayre, but himself, as if he stared into a mirror—as if he saw himself through her eyes. The image vanished, and he stared into the face that had begun to haunt him, filled now with comprehension—and a touch of unease.

He backed away a step, too stunned to think. It made no sense. . . . No, it hadn't happened. He'd imagined it. He'd tried too hard to envision what was in her mind, and he'd provided the obvious vision.

"It takes a bit of getting used to," she said. Her

voice sounded gentle, encouraging. As if she knew what had happened. Only she couldn't know, because nothing *had* happened.

"What does?" he demanded, then realized he must have sounded antagonistic.

She didn't appear to notice. Her eyes widened in a look of innocence. "Why, carrying an artist's work-box, of course. What else?"

"What else, indeed?" he muttered, and followed her down the corridor to the main hall.

She moved with her usual springing stride, but made less than her normal forward progress. She kept pace for him, he realized—and in such a manner that he probably shouldn't have noticed. Yet he had. With an effort, he turned his thoughts from the all-too enchanting picture she presented and concentrated instead on what he might offer her in the way of entertainment.

"I wish we might go back to the Crystal Palace," she said as if reading his mind.

He stiffened. Coincidence, he assured himself. And not so remarkable as all that, either. Not remarkable at all. "I can certainly arrange it," he said, though he experienced a touch of disappointment that he could not accompany her. Seeing the exhibit with her had been a delight, filling him with a sense of joy and discovery he experienced only in her presence. It was as if she brought him alive again and—He cut off that thought, and realized she had spoken.

She smiled over her shoulder. "I said we could go some other time when you aren't so busy. That goes for exploring London, too. Right now—" She broke off, her brow puckering.

Images of hiking through the wood, of dancing, of

running across the grass lawns, of playing shuttlecock and battledore, all flashed through his mind. Of course, Miss Kat Sayre would want to do something—anything—active. Things he couldn't do.

"Would you take me for a drive?" she asked, interrupting his morose thoughts. "I—I've never actually handled a carriage before. I'd love a lesson."

Her sincerity invaded his mind even before he read it in her expressive countenance. "It would be my pleasure," he said, and realized he meant it.

They left her painting things in her chamber and she rejoined him where he awaited her in the hall. "Will you not wear a hat?" he demanded, surprised.

Her expression vexed, she turned back, grabbed up a straw bonnet borrowed from his aunt, and hurried out, dangling it by its ribbons. A most unusual lady—and one far more intriguing than the usual milk-and-water misses or blatant flirts he had encountered before. She knew her own mind, he realized—and his, as well, or so it seemed. He moved a cautious pace away from her as they descended the stairs.

She cast him a mischievous glance. "Do you have a carriage that needs only one horse? I don't think I could manage more."

He doubted there was much she couldn't manage, but held his tongue.

Fresh morning air filled his lungs as they set forth from the stable in a gig. He tooled the single black along the drive, then out onto the lane beyond where the pungent odor of the hedgerows overpowered the smell of the dusty road. The well-oiled leather of the harness added a subtle and pleasing counterpoint.

They continued thus for a little way while Graeme

explained to his companion the principles of handling the horse, stressing the necessity for a light touch on the bit. She listened attentively, a slight frown on features normally given over to laughter, and it pleased him she took the matter seriously. At last, he pronounced her ready to try.

She took the reins from him as if afraid they might break. The horse continued its plodding walk, and after a few moments some of the tension eased from the set of her shoulders and her fingers relaxed their grip. Her face brightened. "It's not that different from riding, is it? Except you're so far from the horse and you don't need your legs. How do I make him trot?"

As he showed her, he realized he hadn't enjoyed an outing like this so much in a very long while. Was it just her obvious delight? A soft laugh escaped her, and he found himself echoing it. Exhilaration surged through him, as if massive straps that had been binding his chest—his soul—snapped, freeing him.

He'd known such freedom before, when he'd been whole. Now—? Now he only experienced it in Miss Sayre's presence.

That thought brought him back to sanity. He ventured too far from his safe world. This wasn't for him, not for a man with his restrictions. When she left, she'd take his joy with her, and leave him in a deeper depression than ever. He had best hold back from her.

They reached the end of the quiet lane, and without hesitation Miss Sayre turned them onto the main road. Graeme tensed, prepared to spring to her aid. He slid closer to her, then stopped, all too aware of her, of her vibrance, of her physical charms. Discretion, he reminded himself, and eased back to his original position. She could proceed on her own at this steady trot.

Around the bend ahead of them swung a heavy coach drawn by four cantering horses. Miss Sayre stiffened, grasping her lower lip between her teeth. Her hands remained steady—or had she simply frozen? Then they'd passed, and delighted laughter broke from her. Again he experienced it also, that relief of stress, the rush of excitement, the sheer enjoyment of being alive.

No, not at all safe for him. "Back to the stables, I think," he said.

She glanced at him. "How?"

She hadn't asked "why so soon." He took the ribbons and pulled onto the grassy verge. The horse, docile as ever, made neat work of the maneuver, and in another minute they trotted back the way they had come. He relinquished the reins to her once more, and did not reclaim them until they reached the narrower turn between the wrought iron gates and proceeded up the drive.

They pulled into the stable to see the four-passenger open carriage standing in the middle of the cobbled yard. The coachman stood beside his equipage, deep in conversation with the groom. Viscount Ellesmere, dashing in his gray frock coat over plaid trousers, stood a little distance away with the de Loires.

"We aren't the only ones just returning," Miss Sayre murmured.

Another groom ran forth from the carriage house to take charge of their horse, and Graeme eased himself down. Miss Sayre jumped lightly to the ground before he could reach her and went at once to join the other three.

"Miss Sayre, what a delightful surprise." Ellesmere directed an appreciative glance over her.

Graeme fought an overwhelming desire to land him a facer. Miss Sayre wanted to do much the same, he realized in surprise. She didn't like the way he looked at her, as if she were a morsel for his delectation. Good lord, did he, himself, look at her like that? He meant no offense when he admired her. The sensation filled his mind that he gave none, that his looks were very different.

What placed that thought into his head? What—

Miss Sayre smiled warmly at Mme. de Loire. "What a lovely gown."

The Frenchwoman responded, preening under the attention, but Graeme, stricken with a rush of realization, didn't hear. Miss Sayre didn't like Mme. de Loire. He *knew* that, despite the fact nothing in her manner betrayed it. Did he know her so well, already? Why should she attempt a friendliness she was far from feeling . . . just to help him?

He gave himself a mental shake. His preoccupation with the damned woman interfered with his work. He was forgetting Uxbridge's request to learn more of the de Loires, especially the lovely Vivienne's intentions.

They started back toward the house, and Graeme offered that lady his arm. She took it with alacrity and directed a speculative, inviting glance up at him through thick lashes. A dimple peeped in one cheek as she gave his arm a surreptitious squeeze.

Now seemed a good time to try. Her responses to a few questions might prove very interesting. *"Madame,"* he began, "why do you not remain here, with my aunt, when the rest of us must depart for the conference?"

She laughed—did it sound just a touch artificial? *"Mais non! Voyons,* but how can you ask me to be separated from the gentlemen of the party? I go, *cela va sans dire."*

"Once the conference begins, there will be little time for pleasures," he reminded her. "The delegates must accomplish a great deal in a very short time. There will be no parties."

"Voilà tout! Where I am, there is always a party." Her eyes sparkled, then turned serious. *"Mais je vous assure,* I will not be parted from my beloved husband."

Graeme inclined his head and turned to address M. de Loire, who followed with Miss Sayre and Ellesmere. "And you, sir, if there is any way in which we can help you achieve your purpose in this conference—"

"Now is not the time to talk politics, *eh, bien?"* he said with surprising curtness.

"Let them be." Ellesmere winked at Miss Sayre. "They have no need to think of work yet, let them enjoy themselves. You are far too serious, Warwick. A drink, that's what we all need. Come." He increased his pace, neatly sweeping Mme. de Loire along with him.

Henri-Phillipe de Loire curled his lip, fixing a look of extreme distaste on Ellesmere's back, but he followed his wife.

"I thought he was here to help you," Miss Sayre murmured, joining Graeme.

His mouth tightened. "So did I."

"I don't trust those two," she added. "I keep getting the feeling they're hiding something."

With that, Graeme found himself in complete agreement. He refrained from speaking that sentiment aloud—yet he had the distinct impression Miss Sayre understood. Damn the woman! She never seemed to be out of his mind. He strode ahead as fast as his bad leg allowed. "Ellesmere!" he called, returning to the issue at hand.

The viscount looked back, his expression surly.

"A word with you in my study. In five minutes."

"I—" Ellesmere began to protest.

"Five," Graeme repeated. "You may bring your drink with you. You must hold him excused," he added to the de Loires. "Pressing conference business, with which we have no desire to bore you."

"Good dig." Miss Sayre grinned at him. "No, don't worry about me, I had a great time, and thank you. Now get on with your work. I'll take a walk." She set off.

She had her good points, he admitted, albeit grudgingly. She proved to be surprisingly supportive of what he had to do. Still filled with thoughts of her, he made his way to his study, where he waited not five minutes, but just over thirty.

Ellesmere swaggered in at last, an empty glass dangling in his hand, an owlish expression on his face. "Leave 'em alone," he advised without preamble. "Delightful people, the de Loires."

"Lord Uxbridge," Graeme informed him through gritted teeth, "has particularly requested that more be learned about them—particularly their political inclinations."

Ellesmere blinked. "Why?"

"He fears there might be trouble involving them."

For a long moment the viscount stared at him, then burst out laughing. "Nonsense. Beautiful woman. Bound to get a shady reputation with those looks. And they're more than looks, I'll have you know. A cuddly armful." He gave Graeme a broad, lewd wink and weaved his way to the marble-topped table where a silver tray held a decanter and glasses. He refilled his empty one without asking and downed half the contents in one swallow.

With deliberation, Graeme crossed to join him, removed the decanter, replaced the stopper, then carried it to his desk and set it at his side. "The de Loires must be sounded, carefully, to discover their real feelings about the conference. If that isn't possible, then they must be watched."

Ellesmere flung himself down in an armchair. "I'll watch the delectable Vivienne any time."

"You will behave yourself like a gentleman."

Ellesmere preened. "I am placing myself totally at the lady's disposal, and will obey her every wish or whim." He leaned forward, reaching for the decanter.

Graeme removed it to well beyond his reach. "I will thank you to remain sober, or you may pack your things and go back to London at once."

Ellesmere tilted his head to one side. "Rather like the sound of that second suggestion. I'll be off in a trice. Don't wait up for me, I'll probably dine with friends, then go on for a convivial evening—if you know what I mean." He lurched to his feet and careened out the door.

Graeme opened his mouth, then shut it again. At

least he was rid of him. Graeme replaced the decanter on the tray and rubbed a hand over his eyes. He'd talk with Uxbridge about a replacement for that useless— no, more than that, potentially damaging—assistant.

Mindful of his instructions concerning the French couple, he passed the rest of the afternoon in a game of chess with Henri-Phillipe de Loire. He would rather be anywhere else, he realized, as his repressed energy tried to break loose. If only he could go for a long tramp through the wood, as he did when he was younger—before India.

Frustrated, he made a careless move, placing his knight in jeopardy. M. de Loire didn't seem to notice. The man worked from a plan, Graeme realized, suddenly alert to his opponent. Every move the French delegate made was intended to maneuver him into one particular position. When Graeme made a move contradictory to that plan, M. de Loire ignored it and continued with his purpose.

Did that imply a narrow thinker, one who could only focus on a single goal? Graeme sat back in his padded chair, contemplating the elderly statesman. If he could figure out M. de Loire's intent, he could concentrate on sabotaging it to see how the man responded. It would be interesting to discover whether the French delegate could formulate a new strategy and campaign to fit a changing situation, or if he'd have to try to bring the situation back under his control.

A sensation of annoyance struck him, at variance with the intrigue he'd just been feeling. Something going wrong, a vexation . . . Miss Sayre, he realized. She was coming—and not alone. She didn't want to come, did not want to interrupt him when he tried to discover something.

The door flung open and in danced the vivacious Vivienne de Loire in a cloud of filmy pink muslin, a shawl trailing in her wake. Miss Sayre strode in the next moment, her countenance becomingly flushed, her hands clutching her skirts as if she found them in her way.

Vivienne burst out laughing. *"Voyons,* but you are right, *mademoiselle,* they are here, and oh, how my Henri-Phillipe detests to be disturbed when he plays this so silly game." She fluttered up behind her husband and draped her arms about his neck. *"Tiens,* but this is too bad of you. *Mademoiselle* Sayre and I are left without a gentleman to bear us company. You must leave your so tedious game and play at cards with us."

Graeme read Miss Sayre's mute apology in her expressive countenance—and felt it at a much deeper level within himself. She'd tried to entertain the Frenchwoman—but Vivienne would never be content with mere feminine companionship. She wanted men.

Henri-Phillipe patted his wife's arm. "Very well, *ma cherie.* I cannot allow you to be bored." He added something else, softly in French, that didn't carry.

Vivienne dimpled prettily and swept the chess pieces from the board. *"Eh, bien.* We shall play something of the most entertaining, *enfin."*

Miss Sayre, Graeme discovered, was not familiar with whist. Instead, she offered to teach them a game she called Crazy Eights—simple to learn, she assured them, yet intricate strategies for winning could be worked out. She dealt, they played their hands, and

Graeme found it insufferably simplistic—until Miss Sayre won, leaving him with a handful of cards.

He met her gaze, then suddenly laughed. "I see what you mean about strategy. Come, we must have another hand and see if we have learned anything."

With this the de Loires agreed. Miss Sayre shuffled and dealt again, but before they had played more than a few cards, her father entered the room. He examined her hand and nodded.

"Want something, Dad? Or did you just come to kibitz?"

"What? Oh, Lady Clementina's balloon is almost filled. Do you want to start your sketching, Kitten?"

Miss Sayre sprang to her feet at once, tossing her cards on the table, then hesitated. "I'm sorry," she said, her expression contrite. "I'm just anxious to get to work."

"And we to see this balloon," Henri-Phillipe declared. "You will permit?"

"Just let me get my things." She ran for the door.

She returned a few minutes later with her sketching materials, and they all trooped out to the lawn near the stable, stopping abruptly as the full glory of the oiled silk envelope greeted them. Awe and wonder filled Graeme, though he'd seen it often before. The sensations intensified as Miss Sayre took another step forward, gazing upward at the intricate pattern covered by the rope mesh netting that supported the basket. It didn't yet lift from the ground or strain at the ropes— but that would come soon.

His aunt stood by the tethered basket. Her normal, determined stance seemed even more defiant than usual. It was something about the way she held her head, as if she issued a challenge. Graeme's eyes narrowed as he studied her. She wore her customary ballooning gown, the skirts—

He stopped dead. Her skirts didn't bell out the way they should, they gathered about her ankles. An awful suspicion filling his mind, he strode forward. "Aunt Clementina."

Her chin thrust out farther; she didn't wait for him to comment. "Yes," she said simply. "I'm going to have my portrait painted in this."

"It's wonderful!" Miss Sayre hurried up to join them, her gaze fixed on the baggy makeshift trousers which were gathered onto narrow bands at the ankles.

It was shocking—not to mention absurd—but typical of his aunt and eminently practical. He struggled against the amusement welling within him and fixed the blame squarely where it belonged. He rounded on Miss Sayre. "I suppose this was your idea."

Delight sparkled in her green eyes. "For once, I'm innocent."

"She only provided the inspiration," Clementina informed him. "The design is mine. And my maid's." She awarded him a bland smile. "Middy is a marvel with a needle. She is copying something else of Miss Sayre's, as well. Something," she added with significance, "in silk."

A choke of laughter escaped Miss Sayre. "Good for her." She glanced at Graeme and made an effort to recover her countenance. "Let's get you posed. We've got to immortalize your split skirt. Shall we call the portrait 'Independence?' "

She stepped back, circling the balloon, staring into the sky where the sun would be in the morning. At last she nodded and paced the distance to the small building that housed the hydrogen generator, considered, then moved a few feet to the right and dropped her sketching pad to mark her place. At last, she positioned his aunt beside the wicker basket, reaching up as if to adjust the valves at the neck of the balloon. Miss Sayre examined the result, nodded, and set to work at once.

"Remarkable woman, your aunt." Adam Sayre tugged at one end of his drooping mustache. "Not many women of this time would dare to be so different."

"Outrageous, you mean." Odd, how the man had phrased the bit about "this time." Graeme let it pass. "I doubt she'd have tried this latest if she hadn't seen your daughter in her denims."

Adam Sayre chuckled. "As well she hasn't seen what else Kat wears. Unless that explains the comment about the silk—" He broke off, grinning. "Have to ask Kat about that."

What the devil did the man mean by that? On the whole, Graeme decided, it would be safer not to know. Instead, he should find out just what Miss Sayre had in mind for this portrait. He could sense her concentration. He strolled behind her, suspicious, but only the roughest of sketches greeted him, little more than shapes taking their positions.

The need not to disturb her filled him, almost as if she erected a mental barrier to keep intruders at bay. He backed away.

Henri-Phillipe, he noted, appeared fascinated by the balloon. As Adam Sayre strolled over to check the hydrogen generator, the French delegate followed and inquired about the process of making the gas. Graeme frowned, remembering a story that had circulated through Whitehall only a couple of years ago, when bombs had been attached to balloons and set adrift to float over the enemy—only to return to their makers when the wind shifted. Did de Loire have some such object in mind?

Mr. Sayre turned to de Loire, obviously delighted with his interest. He showed how the iron and zinc filings were stirred into the diluted sulfuric acid, how the resulting gas was dried to remove lingering moisture, then how it was carried to the balloon in a series of pipes. Did the man unwittingly present Henri-Phillipe with dangerous information? The Frenchman, he remembered, didn't seem to think in devious patterns, but in a direct line with a single plan. To what use might he put a balloon?

The lovely Vivienne flounced over to her husband, tugged at his arm, and drew him back toward the house. Graeme, after one last look at the images taking shape on Miss Sayre's sketch pad, accompanied them. He would rather stay—damn it, he would rather jump into the basket, free the tethers and rise into the late afternoon sky, drifting away from everything . . .

He was no coward or shirker, though. He would stay here and do his duty, no matter how boring. That his duty might be improved immensely by Miss Sayre's returning inside, he tried to ignore.

He saw nothing of her again until dinner that night, when she arrived late, flushed and smiling to dazzling effect. He stood by the table, the decanter arrested in mid-pour, gazing at the laughing, vibrant picture she made in her borrowed green gown.

"Please excuse me." Her step almost danced as she crossed to Lady Clementina. "I've been transferring the sketch. First thing in the morning we should check for colors and shadows."

"*This* painting doesn't worry you," Graeme said before he could stop himself.

Miss Sayre opened her mouth, hesitated, then said, with the ring of complete honesty, "This one I want to do."

Then if she didn't want to do it, what drove her so hard on that painting she kept hidden? Perhaps he should try to see it—or would she know his intent by that mysterious means of hers and prevent him? A great deal about Miss Kat Sayre troubled him.

They went in to the meal, and Miss Sayre at once drew Mme. de Loire into a discussion of the de Loire estate and the entertaining she must do. He listened for a moment, appreciating Miss Sayre's tact, then joined a discussion of ballooning with Adam and M. de Loire. He was jarred out of this some time later at the sound of the name Louis Napoleon, spoken in Miss Sayre's awed voice.

Stillness engulfed the table, broken the next moment by Miss Sayre. "We gather in America that France goes on well with him as—"

She broke off a moment, staring at Graeme. *President,* he thought. *He's France's president.*

"—in power," she went on, though a trifle uncertainly. "Since your husband is in such an important position with the government, and you entertain so many important people, I only wondered . . ." She let the sentence trail off.

Madame de Loire gave an artificial laugh. *"Tiens,* we have indeed met him—oh, often. A most charming and witty man. He depends, *c'est entendu,* upon the counsel of my husband. For myself—" She gave an elaborate shrug. "And you, do you visit your capital of Washington?"

Miss Sayre at once launched into a description of the countryside surrounding it, and the tension in the room eased.

Graeme found the exchange very interesting—if not as enlightening as he might hope. Mme. de Loire certainly reacted to the Napoleon name, lending some credence to Uxbridge's rumors. What, though, had possessed Miss Sayre to bring up the subject?

She hadn't understood his message about Louis Napoleon being president. So she couldn't read his mind, after all. He was glad—or was he just a little disappointed? How did she know so much else, then? The mystery she represented remained. No, it increased.

The evening passed in cards, then an early retiring to bed. Graeme lay in his great four-poster, staring at the canopied top, his mind inevitably drifting to Miss Kat Sayre. It would be better if he could put the damned woman from his thoughts, but she persisted on returning, on tantalizing him, on inching her way into his being until she seemed to belong there.

He rejected that last as naught but whimsical nonsense, and concentrated instead on thoughts of unhitching his aunt's basket from her balloon and attaching his own dragon. If he were up before the others, he could slip away, lift into the gray sky before sunrise, float free of his earthbound troubles. . . . A vision imprinted itself over this of a very different balloon, of flames shooting dangerously into an open neck, yet the silk didn't spark or burn. Instead, the balloon rose higher.

Hot air, he realized. Images of an unfamiliar coastline beneath him drifted through his thoughts, soothing, beautiful, the crashing of the waves against rocks clear as he seemed to hang motionless in the air watching a tableau unfold beneath him . . .

He must have drifted into sleep, for the opening of his door brought him fully awake. Light flooded the room from the hall, silhouetting a man's figure hesitating just over the threshold. Graeme rolled, reaching for the lamp that burned low by his bed, and brought it to full flame.

"Warwick?" Sir Francis's voice, unusually shaky, sounded. Gone was the overconfident manner, the cocky intonation of his words. His black hair curled in wild disorder, his ruddy features held a look of wild alarm.

"What is it?" Graeme shoved his nightcap aright and reached for his dressing gown.

"The Crystal Palace. Rode down straight away." He broke off, gasping as if out of breath. "Uxbridge thought you should know at once, though why—"

"Steady yourself, man, and tell me." Graeme threw back the covers and eased himself from the bed. He donned the brocade robe, belted it about himself, then grabbed his cane. "Sit down."

Sir Francis advanced uncertainly into the room. Graeme lit a lamp on the table near the hearth and gestured his assistant into one of the chairs. From the

dresser he collected the brandy decanter and two
glasses. He filled one and shoved it into Matlock's
hand. "What made Uxbridge send you? What happened at the Exhibition?"

"Robbery." Sir Francis swallowed a large gulp.
When he could speak again, he continued, "Weapons.
New ones, innovative. A Colt Repeating Pistol and a
display of bombs." He took another drink, and it
seemed to revive him.

"Good God," muttered Graeme. A repeating pistol.
Bombs. Someone planned to do a great deal of damage to something. The conference . . .

"They're going to get him, with all that." Sir Francis
twisted the crystal stem.

"Get whom? What are you talking about?" Graeme
demanded. His thoughts flew over his expected delegates. Any one of them would be important enough to
be the target of some saboteur's attack.

Sir Francis looked up briefly into Graeme's face,
then down again, his expression haggard. "Maybe I
shouldn't say anything. Only a rumor, y'know, but if
it's true . . ."

"You damned well better say it. What, exactly, is
this rumor? And where did it come from?"

Matlock straightened. "Circulating Whitehall," he
said, answering the last question first. "Whispers only,
of course, but the *fear* it's causing—"

"What is?" Graeme demanded. He gripped the back
of a chair to keep himself from shaking his assistant.

"Revolutionary group." Sir Francis drained his
glass, then clung to it.

"We've had rumors of those before," Graeme said

slowly. "Such groups have never been well-enough organized to cause any serious threat."

Sir Francis shook his head. "You know how Her Highness dotes on him. She'd do anything—"

"Dotes upon whom?" Graeme demanded.

"Prince Albert. Rumors say this group plans to abduct Prince Albert."

Chapter Eleven

Late the following morning Graeme descended the stairs, his mind still groggy from lack of sleep. He entered the breakfast parlor to find only the butler standing by the sideboard, replenishing the contents of one of the chafing dishes. He rubbed a hand across his gritty eyes. "Where is everyone, Newcombe?"

"Mister and Miss Sayre have already eaten, sir." The butler replaced the lid and checked the flame beneath it. "I believe they are outside with the balloon."

"They're lucky." Graeme took a plate, but found he had little appetite. A repeating pistol, he reminded himself, could shoot over and over and over, killing or wounding several men. Damn, why were such destructive weapons ever invented?

Sir Francis dragged into the room, looking considerably the worse for his nocturnal ride. He glanced about the parlor and his lip curled in his usual, cocky manner. "Should have kept Ellesmere down here," he announced.

Graeme turned from the coffee pot. "You knew he had gone back to town?"

"Saw him there yesterday evening, drinking his way through a bottle with a very peculiar man. They left before I could reach them, and I lost them in the crowd."

"He needs to go." Graeme added sugar and stirred his cup. "A drunkard does me no good."

Sir Francis inspected the contents of the first covered dish and scooped out a large helping. "He can fulfill his role here. Up to you to keep him in line."

"He has offended de Loire—"

"Not *madame*, I'll wager." Matlock raised a suggestive eyebrow. "No, you keep him in line, and he'll do."

"I'm going to have him replaced."

Sir Francis straightened. "Seem to think we've an unlimited supply of trustworthy men at Whitehall, don't you? No one else we can spare."

Matlock, Graeme reflected, was an arrogant idiot. How he was blessed in his assistants. "We'll do without him, then," he said mildly.

Sir Francis snorted. "Doubt Uxbridge will agree to that. Knows how Ellesmere can charm the ladies. He wants the beauteous Vivienne letting all her secrets slip. And until Ellesmere is once more at his post, I shall take his place."

Graeme choked back a bark of laughter. "She'll know in a trice what you're about. You've no subtlety."

Color flamed, deepening the already ruddy hue of Sir Francis's face. "You underestimate me, Warwick. I told you exactly what—" He broke off.

"What did you tell me?" Graeme asked with feigned politeness.

"What I was supposed to," the man declared, though he sounded a trifle uncertain.

"You were supposed to tell me something?" Graeme pursued, enjoying the man's discomfiture.

"Of course I was. Demmed silly thing to ask." He puffed out his rounded cheeks, setting his side whiskers bristling. "Your assistant, aren't I? My job to bring you information from Uxbridge. Do a devilish good job of it, too."

So why did the man look so uneasy? Had he revealed more than Uxbridge had ever told him? But about what? Or did Graeme simply make too much of the man's irritating manner?

They ate their meal in silence, then Sir Francis excused himself to seek out the de Loires. Graeme made his way to the study, where he sat for some time over the list of servants engaged for the duration of the conference, studying every name and the information provided on each by Whitehall. From this he was disturbed some time later by the sound of voices outside the door. The door burst open without ceremony and in strode Lord Uxbridge. Behind him, and looking considerably abashed, came Ellesmere.

Graeme set down the pen he held and waited.

The viscount eased himself into a chair, propped one elbow on a padded arm, and rested his forehead in his hand.

"Jug-bitten?" Graeme regarded him without sympathy. "What have you been about?"

"Can't remember," Ellesmere muttered. "Must have been drugged." He looked up, all defiance. "Only possible explanation."

Graeme raised questioning eyebrows toward Uxbridge, who paced about the room.

"He was found," Uxbridge said shortly, "asleep on a sidewalk in the early hours of the morning by the local constable. He has no memory of his activities since arriving in London yesterday afternoon."

"He might ask the friends he dined with." Graeme regarded the young man in distaste.

Ellesmere shook his head with care. "Don't remember them. Don't remember anything. Oh, my head." He leaned back in the chair, his hand covering his eyes. "What I'd give to know who did this to me."

"Ask Sir Francis," Graeme said shortly. "He saw you. My lord," he turned to Uxbridge, "if—"

"Matlock?" Ellesmere sat up, his gaze surprisingly sharp. "Think I'll have a word with him. No one can do that to me and get away with it. Drugged, robbed, left in the street," he added in disgust. He heaved himself to his feet and staggered out.

Graeme turned once more to Uxbridge.

"Someone," his lordship said, "apparently took the liberty of relieving him of his purse."

Graeme snorted. "I want him out of here."

"We need him." Uxbridge rubbed his chin. "Don't worry, I combed his hair with a joint stool for him. He'll stop claiming he was drugged once he's certain we're giving him another chance. I brought you someone else, too. He's out at the stable."

Graeme bit back a retort about not needing any other incompetents. This one just might be a pleasant surprise. He felt about due for one. He set forth across the lawn with considerable curiosity.

As they reached the cobbled yard, he saw two men

beside the barn where the gardener stored his tools. One, a young lad of wiry build and violent red hair, Graeme recognized as the undergroom whom the gardener commandeered any time weeds sprouted amid the roses. He held a pitchfork, regarding it with his habitual air of uncertainty. The other man towered over him, a great burly individual whose grizzled brown hair had been cut with a military precision that sat oddly with the coarseness of his garments. A bulbous nose dominated the face weathered by years of outdoor living. Intelligence shone in the dark eyes that took rapid survey of Graeme.

"Sergeant Bartholomew Reed," Uxbridge announced by way of introduction. "Late of the Forty-Third Light."

Reed snapped to attention and saluted. "Captain."

Graeme acknowledged it. "Your position here?"

"Security, sir. Nasty business, that robbery at the Crystal Palace. I'll be pretending to be a gardener. Good way to keep an eye on things."

A wry smile tugged at Graeme's mouth. "Such as making sure no one steals the de Loires?"

Uxbridge frowned. "No need for flippancy, Warwick. This is only a precaution."

"You're taking the rumor about His Highness seriously then?" Graeme shot back.

Uxbridge stiffened. "What rumor?"

Graeme's gaze narrowed. "The plot to abduct Prince Albert. Matlock told me about it."

"Of course." Uxbridge drew in a deep breath. "No one but Sir Francis is taking it seriously, I assure you. It has nothing to do with the conference, either. Prince Albert is not scheduled to visit it."

Sir Francis strode across the lawn toward them, his bearing purposeful. "Good thing you brought Reed," he announced as he reached them. "Been looking the place over, and all I can say is, good thing the conference isn't being held here."

Reed nodded. "Never a truer word spoke, sir. Only been 'ere a few minutes, meself, but it's obvious. If'n anyone wanted to sneak in and do some 'arm, it would be the easiest thing in the world, it would."

"Sevington House would require more ingenuity." Sir Francis rocked back on his heels, smug.

Graeme fought a smile. "You are to be congratulated, then, for selecting it."

Sir Francis's color deepened. "You make fun of it. Don't you realize how serious all this is? There is so very much at stake, the future of Europe—" He broke off and swallowed.

"We must, of course, hope for economic accord," Uxbridge said mildly.

"Of course we must," Matlock muttered.

Uxbridge looked at him steadily for a moment, then turned to Graeme. "I have gone over your schedule for the meetings. I cannot emphasize to you the importance of making certain everything moves according to plan."

"Timing!" Sir Francis exclaimed, then subsided, flushed, under Uxbridge's darting look.

"As your *assistant* reminds us," Uxbridge went on, "to have everything run smoothly, we must follow the schedule to the minute. I leave the details to you, but see that everyone is kept busy. And now, will you convey my regrets to the de Loires? I must be back at Whitehall within the hour."

Graeme saw Uxbridge to his carriage, then returned to his study with Matlock trailing after him. Ellesmere, Graeme noted, was nowhere in sight. Probably just as well for him; Graeme was in a far less tolerant mood than Uxbridge had been.

"We should go over the charts of meeting lengths and topics again," Sir Francis muttered. He drew out a watch, then pulled a small notebook from his pocket and jotted something down. He paced to the window and looked out.

Nerves, Graeme noted. But why? Did he fear something? "Have you reason to suspect anything might go wrong?" he demanded. "Sabotage, perhaps?"

Sir Francis stiffened. For a long moment he said nothing, then he swallowed and shook his head. "Terrible thought, terrible. The chaos—"

"Precisely," Graeme said smoothly. "Have you reason to fear some such thing?"

"No! Of course not! The idea is—is ludicrous!" Matlock twisted his pen between his fingers. "Just nerves, old boy. My first big assignment, you know. Need to prove myself and all that. Don't want anything to go wrong."

"Neither do I." Graeme kept his steady gaze on the man's face. "There's a great deal at stake."

Matlock cast an anxious glance toward the window. "Think I'll just go and have a chat with that Reed fellow. Make sure he's doing his job." He hurried out.

Graeme's brow lowered. He wasn't sure what to make of his assistant. If the man knew of any potential threat to the conference, he would tell someone, wouldn't he? Uxbridge, even if not Graeme? Sir Francis must know as well as the rest of them the potential disaster if something went wrong. Ill-will, justification for war—anything up to and including total economic chaos in Europe could result.

Graeme strode to the window and glared out. Probably they were all just jittery—and with good cause. At least only a few more days remained before the conference would begin, then he would have something definite to occupy his time instead of all this worry.

For him, this was little more than a waiting period. All his planning was complete, the event not yet here. No wonder he made too much of Matlock's nerves. He suffered from his own.

He closed his eyes and tried to clear his mind of all the details that clamored for his attention. He needed to relax, find a diversion. . . . What was Miss Sayre doing, he wondered?

An image flashed through his mind of a painting—not one of his aunt, but a vibrant, strange concoction of colors in blocked shapes. Before he could identify it, the image faded. She was in the conservatory. Without questioning how he knew, he set forth.

He wanted to see her. Not her painting, not to demand if she were up to something, not to learn anything about her—just to see her, watch the smile tugging at her lips and the laughter sparkling in her eyes.

He was a fool, he told himself, and limped down the hall, swinging his cane to thud it on the floor with every step. A damned fool who was too fascinated by a lovely face for his own good.

His anticipation rising, he entered the conservatory. She was there, standing before the long wall of windows that flooded the cheery room with late afternoon light. A cover draped over her easel, and she wasn't at all surprised to see him. "You knew I was coming," he declared.

She looked up, appearing startled. "How could I?" She moved a step toward him—actually, she placed herself between him and the hidden canvas.

"You knew," he repeated. "You always know."

"Of course," she agreed. "I see you in my crystal ball."

"You might very well." He stared at her, his uncertainties about her fading as they always did in her presence.

She watched him with her steady regard. "What's disturbed you?"

"You cannot read everything in my mind, at least." He could only be glad she couldn't decipher the thoughts that lingered there, that the soft brown curls that clustered about her forehead gleamed with copper highlights, that her gown—and the apron she wore to protect the dress from paints—swayed in an enticing manner as she moved.

Soft color flooded her cheeks and her gaze met his. Her lips parted, and an awareness of her filled him, an awareness that went far beyond the merely physical. For one moment she seemed to merge with him, to become an extension of himself, and he of her. He felt stripped, naked, as if his soul had been laid bare—yet no humiliation or fear assailed him. It was only natural and right, the way it should be between them . . .

He blinked, the strange sensation gone, leaving him facing her, aware of her charms on a more normal level. With the return of sanity came wisdom. He turned on his heel and left as fast as his injured leg would carry him.

The night passed uneasily for Graeme. Waking worry blended into hideous dreams, all centering around the robbery at the Crystal Palace. Images filled his mind of Prince Albert bursting into Durham Court, carrying a bomb and abducting Henri-Phillipe de Loire.

He bolted upright in his bed, sweat beading his brow, to see only the familiar dark shapes of his bedchamber. No real dangers, only imaginary ones. And questions.

A gentle touch brushed his mind, as if someone stroked soothing fingers over the dull ache of his uncertainties. *Nightmares,* the answer filled his thoughts, but who—or what—did he answer? Only his own mind, he told himself. Some part of him questioned the cause of his disturbed slumber and sought reassurance.

He lay back against the pillows, fully awake now, allowing his thoughts to drift freely. They found their way to the most intriguing of his visitors, an impulsive creature, so very alive, who filled every empty space within him with her laughter—a laughter that could not quite break from him, but which he buried deep beneath the scars on his soul.

His hands clenched. He could feel her now, and—damn it, his body responded with a will of its own. She had no place in his life, he reminded himself. Such a vibrant, loving creature could never bear to tie herself to a crippled husk of a man. That she might come to him out of pity revolted him—but she wouldn't.

Again, a gentle calm soothed his troubled mind. For

some reason, he knew she didn't pity him. Instead, a sensation of admiration puffed him up, a conviction of his own worth. Lord, he must be set up in his own conceit—except the sensations felt alien to him, strange and not at all in harmony with his own views. He'd overreacted to his injuries—or perhaps to the betrayal of his regiment.

Only he hadn't overreacted. He'd behaved like a sensible, intelligent man, accepting his limitations . . . *afraid of stretching those limitations, of experiencing so much pain again.* No, that was as nonsensical as the concept of his being admirable. He still served his country, he was still a man . . . *half a man, for he kept the part that was himself locked safely away where it need take no more risks.* She was there, in his mind, laughing at him . . . *no, encouraging him to live again.* . . . Only she couldn't be there. That was impossible.

Without really knowing why, he threw back the bedclothes, found his slippers with a searching foot, and rose. Still dragging on his dressing gown, he caught up his cane and strode with his uneven gait from his chamber.

Would she be in the hall outside her room? Would she be awaiting this confrontation? Did she even *know* they had had one? He forged ahead, confused yet determined. It wasn't as if he heard her voice in his head. He merely experienced sensations, images and convictions.

He reached the corridor leading to her wing and slowed his pace. No movement disturbed the deep shadows. No one came forward to meet him. He hesitated outside her door, glaring into the darkness. Nothing.

Had those thoughts come from deep within himself? Did he question the life to which he had resigned himself because of her vibrant presence—because he wanted her life and vitality to surround and fill him? But that would be to cage a lovely, free dove, to clip her wings and force her to pursue a circumspect, dull existence.

He turned away, not at all sure why he had come, knowing only he wanted to be anywhere else. He headed back to the main corridor, where gas lights burned low, illuminating the stairs. He didn't want to return to his room to toss on his bed, sleep far from him. He—

A slow smile tugged at the corners of his mouth. He wanted to go exploring. Perhaps he might discover a painting that a certain young lady kept hidden from his sight.

With a definite purpose in mind, his steps quickened. He descended the stairs with care, found the lamp that awaited on the table at their base and turned it up. Guided by its glow, he made his way along the halls to the conservatory.

He entered the room redolent with lush greenery, and experienced a touch of pleasure all his own. He adjusted the wall lamp, and shadows danced backward and away as the rich terra cotta of the Italian tile came into focus. He crossed this slowly, making for the wall of windows where he could just distinguish the lumpy shape of a covered canvas. For a moment he stood before it, then he carefully lifted the sheet.

Before him, against a background of deep green grass and brilliant blue sky, rose a rainbow balloon with the still-sketchy shape of Aunt Clementina in her ludicrous new trousers hovering over the valves.

The wrong painting.

Sympathetic amusement filled him—amusement he did not agree with in the least. Had she known he would come like this, and deliberately switched the paintings? No, she never left her secret work where it might be discovered. She had it hidden away even now, as she always did. More fool he to think he could catch a march on that clever young lady. Awarding that round to her, he limped to the door, extinguished the room's light, and made his way back to his chamber.

The clock, he noted as he entered, showed the time to be a little before four. He had the conference organized down to the last minute. He had more than enough schemes on hand to occupy the de Loires until the arrival of the other delegates in London, when he could escort his charges to Sevington House. Nothing demanded his attention. He could return to his bed with a clear conscience. If only he could sleep.

An impulse to try touched him, and he cast aside cane, slippers and dressing gown. As he eased between sheets, an image flickered in his mind of tousled brown curls spread across a pillow . . . his pillow . . . and a certain lovely face turned toward him as he eased down beside her . . .

Oh, damn. He'd never sleep now with the wanting of her—and the certainty she would never be his.

His next groggy thoughts concerned the subtle sounds of movement about his chamber. He dragged open heavy eyelids and noted he could see within the curtained tent of his bed. The lamps must be turned up fully, which could only mean trouble. He dragged back the hangings and blinked into the sunlight that filled his chamber.

At the wardrobe, his valet turned from the coat he examined. "Good morning, sir. Never known you to sleep so late." He set the garment aside and crossed with stately tred to the table where a covered tray rested. Walters removed the lid, and the welcome aroma of coffee and cinnamon wafted through the chamber.

Graeme rose, and Walters helped him into the dressing gown he had discarded—he checked the clock— yes, a good five hours ago. He had slept late. "What is happening downstairs?" he demanded as he reached for the coffee.

"Very little, sir. Mister and Miss Sayre and her ladyship are at work on the portrait. And a very fine painting it is, sir, if I may say so. One her ladyship will be proud to hang amongst her ancestors, even though she is wearing that unusual garment. The young lady has impressive talent for a female."

"She has impressive talent for anyone." Graeme set down the drained cup and turned his attention to the cinnamon-filled roll that awaited his pleasure. "What of Sir Francis and Ellesmere?"

"His lordship has sent his apologies, sir." Newcombe's face betrayed nothing. "He is keeping to his bed with a head cold. A result, I fear, of his evening in London."

"Sick, is he?" And of no use to anyone—again. "What of Matlock and the de Loires?"

"The valet of *Monsieur le delegate* has assured me his master is still asleep. *Madame* and Sir Francis have just finished breakfast and expressed a desire to New-combe to go for a walk."

That should be safe enough. Graeme relaxed and enjoyed the sweet bread. Had the beautiful Mme. de Loire's companion been Ellesmere, he might have worried about their destination and purpose in taking a long ramble about the estate.

Sir Francis, though, would make a mull of flirtation. The lady might try, out of habit, but no one could call Matlock a figure of romance. Too brusque by far, and finesse was not in his nature—even if he saw an opportunity to advance his position in the government. All bluster and ambition, but too young and inexperienced yet to possess cunning or discretion.

Ah, yes. The perfect government official. Graeme contemplated the last bite of his roll. In a few years—with a little seasoning such as he obtained on this assignment—Matlock might well become a considerable force in the department. Possibly even an asset, as well. Time, he supposed, would tell.

Dressed at last, he made his way down to the breakfast parlor. A number of dishes remained on the sideboard—in spite of the fact most of the others already seemed to have partaken of the meal. Graeme filled a plate, selected the front page of the *London Times,* and settled down for a few minutes of peace.

The swinging back of the door shattered his peace all too soon. He looked up to see Mme. de Loire pause on the threshold.

Her sulky expression brightened into a devastating smile as he rose. "Ah, *Capitaine* Warwick, but it is too delightful to find you here. *Voyons,* but I so feared I should be bored." She swept to the coffee urn and poured herself a steaming cup, all the while chattering. "That man, he talks, talks, talks, but he says nothing, *enfin!* Nothing of interest. *Tiens,* but I wish *Monsieur le viscomte* had not taken the cold. *Mon Capitaine,*" she turned and fluttered her long lashes at him, "will you not take me out on the lake in a little boat?"

In spite of himself, Graeme smiled. "Sir Francis would not?"

"Mais non! It is too bad of him. And it was his idea to go to the lake, then all he seemed to wish to do was stand there and look at his so silly watch! And when I ask to go out in the boat and be with the swans, he says he does not know if it is safe, and he talks and he talks, as I said. Then a groundsman comes over, but me, I cannot understand what this man says who speaks so strangely. Only it seems to me they argue, which is not at all *comme il faut.* And then the man leaves, but still Sir Francis will not take me out, he says we must wait for this man to return, and finally I grow bored and come back here, where I know you will amuse me." She peeked up at him through lowered lashes.

What the devil was Matlock about? He was possessed of more address than that, and he should not have allowed Mme. de Loire to return to the house without his escort. Frowning, Graeme rose. *"Madame,* I shall get to the bottom of this. In the meantime, will you not care to join Mr. Sayre by the balloon? I believe he is watching his daughter paint my aunt's portrait."

"Ah, *Monsieur* Sayre. He is not handsome, *du vrai,* but he is *forte amusante.* I will go."

Leaving the remains of his breakfast, Graeme escorted her to the lawn. Vivienne took his arm, but he didn't experience the same rush of satisfaction he did when Miss Sayre touched him. He buried that thought and led his companion toward where the balloon still rose high against the morning sky. They must have added more hydrogen.

Vivienne paused. "But it is a thing of beauty, *n'est-ce pas?*"

Miss Sayre looked up. Her thoughtful gaze rested on Graeme for a moment, and warmth seeped through him. She said something to her father, who left the tanks and strolled over to join him.

"*Madame,* you brighten the day." The old rogue took Vivienne's hand and carried it to his lips.

Graeme left her with Mr. Sayre—was that in safe hands? he wondered. She would grow tired of watching the painting very soon, he made no doubt, but that enterprising gentleman could be counted on to tell her some of his bizarre stories of gold mining which would fascinate her. He grinned as he turned toward the lake. An entertaining old gentleman; he could see where his daughter got her unconscious charm.

He moved at his accustomed slow pace, but somehow today he didn't mind as much. It wasn't as if there were anything to hurry *to.* Still, he would like to know what Sir Francis thought he was about to neglect his charge of Vivienne de Loire—and why he should argue with a groundsman. Could it have been Reed?

Two of the swans stood on the shore, preening glistening feathers. Three more paddled in the shallows near by. In the distance—He narrowed his gaze. That looked like the old row boat floating upside down not far from the pavilion.

He quickened his stride, leaning more heavily on his cane as he followed the gravel path. Where was Sir Francis? Had he tried to launch the little boat—but how could even such a bumbler as Sir Francis tip it over? Unless he'd tried to climb in and set it rocking. He probably took a dunking if that were the case. Even now, he must be making for his room, dripping water with every step, bent on changing into dry clothes.

The mental image cheered Graeme considerably. He ought to see the boat brought in before it sank, though. He continued around the lake, at last emerging from the shrubbery that edged the corner near the pavilion.

Something floated beside the rowboat, about fifty yards from shore. Had the fool lost his hat and coat? Only there seemed to be more than that. Ignoring his boots, he waded onto the shallow ledge, stopping before the ground fell away into the deeper portion.

That bundle of clothes possessed too much shape. Someone—a man—lay face down in the water.

Chapter Twelve

Graeme looked about and spotted the other boat beached halfway round the lake. It would take him too long to reach it, then row out. Unless that man turned over in the next few seconds . . .

Graeme cast his cane aside and stripped off his coat, tossing it onto the bushes. His boots came off with more difficulty, but at last he pushed forward through the chill water and struck forth with long, even strokes. His left knee moved more easily in the liquid environment, paining him less, but he found it of little use for kicking. He concentrated on his arms, on reaching that still figure—hoping all the while he was in time.

His muscles ached in the icy cold, straining as they had not done since before his injury. Why could he not be strong, be in better condition, be a whole man, unencumbered with a disabling injury? Because he'd surrendered to it, he realized. He hadn't fought back hard enough to reclaim as much of his life as he could. He struck out harder, drawing closer. Another stroke, another . . .

He grasped an ankle, feeling his fingers fasten about the solid flesh. The body drifted, making no move of its own, only shifting with the wavelets caused by Graeme's efforts. Graeme tred water and, with an effort that thrust himself under the surface, he rolled the body.

Sir Francis Matlock lay in the water as if asleep, eyes shut, mouth slightly open. No movement, no sign, no struggle of returning consciousness. Graeme searched for a pulse but couldn't find one.

The accident couldn't have happened long ago, no more than minutes. Perhaps if he got him to shore he could revive him. Grabbing the man's shoulder, struggling to keep his head above water, Graeme struck out with a long sweep of his arm, gliding with care so as to disturb the water—and his charge—as little as possible.

Had Sir Francis stopped breathing? They used to store an old barrel behind the gazebo for emergencies. He refused to consider the possibility it might have been moved. It had never yet been needed to revive a drowning victim, but it had always been there. If it weren't—

A sensation of concern filled him, surprisingly tinged with calm. There were other, easier—more successful—ways to revive a drowning man—if they were not too late. A vision filled his mind of kneeling over an inert body, mouth covering mouth—only it wasn't him, but Miss Sayre who performed this mysterious task. He'd have her help—and she had ways he'd never heard of. If anything could be done, she'd do it. How he knew, he couldn't say. He simply did. The same way he knew other things about her.

Another image flickered before his eyes, of grass flying beneath running feet, of a flapping muslin apron over floral printed skirts. . . . It vanished at once, and before him stretched only water and more water.

His legs had gone numb from the cold—except for the throbbing ache in his knee. He lengthened his stroke, putting every ounce of his remaining energy into reaching solid ground. If he were a whole man, he could kick, drive them forward faster. He could have reached Sir Francis sooner; it would not have taken so long to walk from the house; he could have swum quicker.

If only.

What an empty phrase. He forced it from his thoughts and concentrated on doing what he could.

The shore seemed closer now, and from the corner of his eye he saw movement. He turned his head and saw a man running—an unfamiliar man—no, he'd met him the day before. Uxbridge's security man, who posed as a laborer and gardener. Reed.

Graeme threw the last ounce of his energy into bringing Sir Francis within reach of this unexpected help. "The barrel," he shouted as he came closer. "Behind the gazebo."

"Right 'o," the man called back and veered off in that direction.

Graeme pulled on, his left arm aching, the other wrapped about Sir Francis's limp shoulders. He'd have help lifting him. That knowledge renewed his strength.

He didn't look up again until his knee brushed the bottom of the lake. He'd made it. He dragged himself to his feet, still bent to support Sir Francis, and there came Reed, rolling the barrel before him around the corner. Thank God it had been there. Graeme slogged out of the water, still gripping his inert assistant, as Reed joined him.

The man panted heavily from his exertion, his ruddy complexion now scarlet. He grabbed Sir Francis's arms and hauled him over the barrel. "If you'll hold him, sir, I'll get this rolling."

Graeme nodded, too spent to speak, and gripped his assistant about the waist. Were they too late? He'd seen death—far too many times—but never by drowning.

Running footsteps sounded on the gravel behind him, but he didn't look up. He didn't need to. She'd come.

Miss Sayre dropped to her knees beside the barrel and cried, "Are you all right?"

Reed snorted. "That's a demmed fool question. O'-course 'e ain't."

Miss Sayre ignored him. She dragged back Sir Francis's eyelids, then pressed her ear to his chest. "Get him off this and let me try," she commanded.

Graeme released Sir Francis at once, but Reed hesitated. "Now, Missy, this ain't no—"

"I said let me try!" She shoved him aside and dragged Sir Francis to the grassy slope. She caught the man behind the neck, tilted his head back, and fastened her mouth to his.

"What the devil—" Reed muttered.

Graeme watched her, his gaze narrowed. He'd seen her do this in his mind, had felt her desperation as he did now.

She released Sir Francis, then settled the heel of one

hand against the left side of his chest and, using the other for leverage, pressed hard. She kept this up for perhaps fifteen seconds, then switched, once more blowing air into his mouth.

His aunt had joined them, Graeme realized, and Adam Sayre. They stood about in a circle, helpless, watching Miss Sayre, her father nodding as she switched from one effort to the other, then back again, relentless.

At last, after what felt like hours but must have been no more than thirty minutes, Adam Sayre stepped forward and laid a hand on his daughter's shoulder. "It's not working, Kat. It's too late."

She sat back on her heels, tears filling her eyes, her shoulders trembling with exhaustion and distress. It shot through Graeme like a physical pang, adding to the strain he already felt.

"I did it right," came her choking voice.

Adam patted her shoulder, then drew her to her feet. "You did fine, Kat. He was probably dead and long past reviving before you got here."

She nodded and turned away, and her pain enveloped Graeme, diminishing his own. No, it went beyond mere pain. Her horror over this death registered in his mind as a tangible force. She cared, so deeply.

He stepped forward, offering comfort, needing it himself. He touched her arm and with a stifled cry, she buried her face against his drenched shoulder, leaning into his embrace. He couldn't possess her but he could give her this support, ease her distress. His hand cupped about the nape of her neck, his fingers entangling in the thick, silken waves of her hair.

"It's all right, Kat," he murmured, and realized that somehow his cheek had come to rest against the top of her head. With an effort, he kept his lips from brushing the curl that tickled the corner of his mouth. There were others watching—his innate reserve struggled in distaste at being observed at such a moment, but Kat's need for his presence filled him, making him for once ignore the proprieties.

Slowly, she raised her face to look up into his. Her concern and caring filled him, easing into the crevices of his mind, calming his strained nerves. He gazed deep into her eyes as her warmth and vitality seeped through him, healing. . . . In her, he realized, he found a part of himself that had always been missing—and for which he had always longed. And he was no fit man to claim her for his own.

As if sensing his sudden withdrawal, she pulled slightly away. "You're drenched," she said. "You'd best get back to the house and dry off, or we'll have you laid up as well as Ellesmere."

She was wet too, now, from where he'd held her, but she didn't seem to mind. Her expression remained solemn, the laughing lights in her green eyes extinguished. She watched him in sober concern. "I wish I had a towel to offer you."

"I'll get one soon enough." He turned to regard the lifeless remains of the man who had been his assistant. He hadn't liked Matlock—had frequently found him insufferable and inept—he'd even, at times, longed to be rid of him. But not like this. No one deserved to die in such a pointless accident. "Let's take him back to the house."

For the first time, he looked about him at the small

crowd that had gathered. Besides his aunt, Sayre, Kat and Reed, two grooms had appeared, their expressions shocked and wide-eyed. There'd be a rare evening of tale-telling at whatever inn they frequented that night unless he put a stop to it. Grim, he sent them for a plank to make a stretcher.

Reed cleared his throat. "I'll see to this, sir. And to the lads. See there's no talking, like. You go back to the 'ouse."

Graeme turned to regard the man. He stood in a relaxed manner, thumbs hooked in the waistband of his trousers. He disentangled one and mopped the back of a callused hand across his forehead, catching a drip from his damp, stringy hair. "We should take him to London," Graeme said.

Reed nodded. "Aye, that we should. Won't be a pleasant job, it won't, but not one as needs to fall to your lot, sir. I'll do it, soon as I gets dried off. 'Is lordship will be wanting a full report from me, I makes no doubt, so's I might as well go and get it over with, like."

"What did happen?" Graeme asked.

"That *Madame* de Loire, she wanted to go out on the lake, but Sir Francis 'ere told 'er as it might not be safe. Seemed dead-set—sorry, sir, could 'ave phrased that better, I could. Sir Francis didn't want no one goin' out on that lake, it seemed. Called me over to talk about it, told me 'e wanted them boats gone over from stem to stern to make sure there wasn't no leaks nor nothin'. Sent me off for some tools, and when I come back, like, the *madame* was gone. Sir Francis and I, we went over them boats together, and they looked safe enough to me. Then 'e sent me off to fetch towels to 'ave on 'and down 'ere."

Graeme glanced about. "Where are they?"

" 'Ousekeeper said as she'd gather some together and send one of the maids out with 'em. Then I come back and see you swimmin' and 'im lyin' there and that boat all upside down." He nodded toward where the hull now listed badly to one side. He clucked his tongue. "Best fetch that back. 'Ere, you, lad." He waved at the elder of the two grooms, who had just returned with the board. "Take the other boat and fetch that 'un back in. And no argle-bargle, mind, you just do as you're told."

The groom, who had opened his mouth, shut it again and cast him a resentful look.

"I'd rather you brought it in, Reed," Graeme said. "You know something about boats, I gather?"

"Aye," the man said, though he frowned.

Graeme nodded. "Have a look at it. See if you can see why it capsized."

Reed snorted. "Don't take much. If'n 'e tried to stand, like—"

"But why would he? Just see if there's anything obviously amiss. Something that wasn't there when you checked it before."

The man's gaze narrowed, then he gave a short nod. "Aye, I'll do that, sir. I'll do that right now, I will. Then I'll come up and see you in your study, if'n that's all right."

Graeme agreed. Then, while Adam Sayre oversaw the transfer of Sir Francis's body from the ground to the board, Graeme dragged on his discarded boots.

Gravely, Kat retrieved his cane and handed it to him.

The two stable lads picked up their burden and set forth toward the house. The others fell into step behind, first Lady Clementina and Mr. Sayre, then Kat at Graeme's side. She carried his coat, clutching it to her.

What, he wondered, had made him ask Reed to personally bring in and check the rowboat? Did he suspect something? That Sir Francis's death was no accident, perhaps?

That thought took a firmer root in his mind. Why had Matlock sent Reed back to the house? Towels could have been brought later, when someone actually took the boats out. Had he wanted to be rid of Reed? If so, why? Was he meeting someone there?

Or *had* he sent Reed away? Graeme slowed his steps and turned to watch where the man now rowed the other little boat through the water. Reed had no trouble handling the vessel. Why did Graeme have the impression his clothes had been damp *before* he'd helped drag Matlock's body from the water?

Because they had been, Graeme realized. He'd noticed it but been too busy at the time to question it. Then both of them became drenched as they'd struggled to bring Sir Francis ashore. There was something not quite right about this whole business.

"Could he have hit his head when the boat went over?" Kat asked, as if she had been following his thoughts.

Graeme looked down at her. "We'll check to see if there's any sign of it. You don't believe this is an accident, do you?"

She hesitated. "No more than do you," she said at last. "Though I don't know why. Maybe it's just because *you're* suspicious."

He let that—and the uncanny link between them it implied—pass. "He could swim," he said, "but he made no attempt. He was right beside the boat."

"Then he had to have been knocked unconscious. Could he have taken the boat out to test it? He was so cocksure of himself all the time, he would never have doubted his ability to handle it."

Graeme studied the decorative knob of his cane. "I had the impression from *Madame* de Loire that he disliked boats. It would have been far more like him to order Reed to test it while he sat in a chair by the dock and shouted orders."

She walked in silence for several moments, and her gaze strayed to the grooms and their burden. "Murder," she breathed, voicing the thought that had hovered about the fringes of his mind, refusing to be named.

He cast her a sharp glance. "Don't so much as hint that to anyone."

"Of course not. We're rather jumping to unjustified conclusions, anyway. Except I can't get it out of my mind."

Nor could he. "I think," he said slowly, "we shall have to investigate Sir Francis's movements for the last several days."

She nodded. "And find out if anyone came here this morning."

He opened his mouth to say the murderer might have been here already, but stopped himself in time.

As soon as he'd changed into dry clothing, they would ask.

The grooms, though, when questioned, could provide no definite information. No one had come to the stables, but that didn't mean any number of people might not have entered the grounds at any number of places and no one the wiser. It was even possible, Graeme realized, that Mme. de Loire might not have come directly to see him after leaving Sir Francis. She might have waited until after he'd spoken to Reed, then returned, fluttering those lashes and flattering him until he took out a boat . . .

He was being fanciful beyond permission. Undoubtedly due to Miss Sayre's influence. If someone had killed Sir Francis Matlock, that person had taken a tremendous chance of being caught in the act. Which meant, most likely, this had been an accident. He'd do what had to be done; he'd examine the body for signs of a head injury.

The grooms had laid Sir Francis's body, still resting on the plank, between two chairs in the library—near the terrace doors for easy conveyance to the stables. Water pooled underneath, dripping from the sodden clothes. For a long moment Graeme looked down on the lifeless form, fighting back images of his comrades massacred in that mountain pass. He'd seen death too often—been too near it himself—to let one more corpse bother him.

Yet it did. Because Sir Francis had not been a soldier. Sudden death should not have been his lot. And Kat Sayre had been distraught at not being able to save him.

He shoved his feelings aside and bent to run his

fingers through Matlock's thick black hair which was now drying. He'd had experience in the past with broken heads—everything from gunshot grazes to subalterns taking a tumble from their mounts. In a minute or two he'd find the tell-tale dent, and this death could be labeled the unfortunate accident it undoubtedly was.

Only he didn't find anything.

Frowning, he sat back on the sofa behind him and studied Matlock's lifeless forehead, trying to will into being the mark he had been unable to detect. What did that leave? There had to be a reason Sir Francis had not simply swum to shore when the boat went over. He could find nothing to indicate the man had been unconscious. Unless . . .

With grim determination, he loosened the man's collar and eased it away from his neck, then bent to scrutinize the area with care. Nothing. His dawning relief checked, then faded as he focused on the faintest of blue marks.

A bruise—and damningly thumbprint shaped.

Sir Francis had been throttled, probably only into unconsciousness, then thrown into the lake face down to let the water finish the job. The verdict would be death by drowning. Except for that one tiny mark and his own misgivings, there would be no reason to suspect anything other than a tragic accident.

A light tapping sounded on the door, but he ignored it. He needed to think. He needed—The thought broke off as the door opened.

"He was murdered," Kat's voice said.

He didn't bother to question how she knew for certain. In fact, he'd have been surprised if she hadn't.

She came farther into the room and stood staring at the body.

"It will be best to leave him here until the authorities have seen him," Graeme said.

Kat nodded. "I wonder what Lord Uxbridge will make of this? You're going to London yourself, aren't you? May I go with you? No, you're quite right," she went on without his having to speak, "he would probably have me arrested at once. What *can* I do to help?"

Just be here, the thought flashed through his mind. Just be here with that irrepressible smile and that warmth and caring . . .

He stood. "I'll return as soon as I am able."

Kat watched Captain Warwick stride out of the library with a new sense of purpose in his uneven gait. Sir Francis's death had one grain of good in it; Captain Warwick rose to the challenge with a will that had been lacking even in his conference preparations. He was not a man to let another be murdered without demanding justice, she realized. His conference work had been to prove his abilities to himself; solving this murder was for the peace of another's soul.

Her impulsive smile tugged at her lips. "He won't let you down," she whispered to the man who was beyond hearing.

What did she do now? Stay here and guard the body? Against what—or whom? Yet it didn't seem right to just leave Sir Francis here alone.

A rumble of voices sounded without, the deep tones of the butler followed by another, trembling and

somewhat higher pitched. The door opened, and Newcombe entered, ushering in a slightly built man with a
narrow, pinched face of an unnatural pallor. The man
hesitated, shrinking within his loose fitting black garments, then strode quickly forward and fell on his
knees at Sir Francis's side. He shook his balding head
as if unable to accept what he saw.

Kat looked at the butler.

"This is Jenner, Miss Sayre." Newcombe remained
on the threshold. "Sir Francis's man."

"I'm sorry." Kat reached out to lay a sympathetic
hand on the man's shoulder.

He looked up at her, his expression blank except for
a misting in his eyes. "I'll sit with him until the doctor
comes," he said. At once, he looked away, back to his
master.

Which left her with nothing to do. Somehow, she
doubted the poor man wanted company in his sorrow.
That it was real shock and distress the valet displayed,
she could not doubt. She was glad, for Sir Francis's
sake.

She went to the door, which Newcombe held open
for her. "Get him some wine or brandy to drink," she
said softly, and went out into the hall, only to pause.

So what *did* she do now? She didn't feel like joining
the others—it would be too much like attending a
wake. Her father and Lady Clementina could divert
the de Loires better without her. Working on her
painting—at least the portrait of Lady Clementina—
didn't seem appropriate. She could try to see if she
could find anything strange in her other one, the one
she kept hidden from everyone, the one of the Crystal
Palace Exhibition Hall. But that didn't appeal to her,

either. Probably the only thing her subconscious would paint would be dead bodies floating in lakes.

She shuddered, suddenly chilled. What *had* brought poor Sir Francis to that waterlogged end? He'd gone to London only the day before. Had he quarreled with anyone? Or did this have to do with the upcoming conference?

Someone, she decided, should have a look in his room and among his papers to see if any clues could be gained or if anything were amiss. And the most likely someone, at the moment, seemed to be her. She should be able to make a fairly careful search without interruption. Sir Francis's man would not leave his side and none of the other servants would have any reason to enter his chamber. She might as well get on with it at once, and see if she couldn't have something to tell Captain Warwick when he returned.

She mounted the steps quickly, then hesitated, not sure which room he occupied. He'd be in the same wing with the rest of the visitors, she supposed. Near Ellesmere, perhaps? That gave her momentary pause. She didn't want him to hear her. But if he truly suffered as he claimed, he might well be asleep.

She tried the door on this side of Ellesmere's, found the room unoccupied, then tried the one on the other side. This chamber, decorated in shades of deep green, showed signs of habitation, for an array of brushes, combs and toiletry bottles stood on the dresser. The massive wardrobe held a selection of coats, trousers, waistcoats and shirts folded neatly in a pile. From the looks of the supply, it seemed their owner hadn't simply ridden down to tell Graeme about the robbery, but actually intended to make a very long stay. Or had intended.

She was here, she reminded herself, to discover why he would not now do so. She looked about the room, then headed for the writing desk on which a pile of papers lay. Seating charts, she noted, for dinners and meetings, each neatly labeled with the day, time and name of the event. Lady Clementina's precise handwriting.

She shuffled through more of these, then came to a list of the delegates' names, each with the name of a room or hotel following. The accommodation sheet, according to the lettering at the top of the page. This Sevington House mustn't be all that large, since only some would be staying beneath its roof. A nightmare for the security people, she supposed, having people coming and going.

She leafed through more sheets and came to a few in a different hand—Graeme's, she realized. These held topics for discussion, notes on how to encourage general agreement, lists of possible concessions. The last few pages contained a speech that rivaled any positive-thinking sales pitch she had heard on TV in her own time. Again, Graeme at his persuasive best.

She set the pile down and turned her attention to the drawers. The first two held nothing of any interest—only writing paper, ink and pens. Hadn't Sir Francis done any work of his own?

She dragged open the bottom drawer and froze, staring at the solitary item before her. A gun.

For a long moment she studied it, her hands thrust behind her back. It looked brand new, yet of old-fashioned design—well, of course it would. This was

1851, she reminded herself. And unless she was very much mistaken, it looked exactly like the Colt Repeating Pistol she had seen at the Crystal Palace Exhibition.

The one that just had been reported stolen.

Chapter Thirteen

Graeme sat stiffly in his curricle, holding his pair to a strict trot. They fidgeted, tossing their heads. Probably picking up the disquiet of his mood. Something had happened at Durham Court, something involving Miss Sayre. He'd felt it, felt her startlement, like a physical blow. He intended to get back to her as quickly as possible.

He had a few things on his own mind, things he would like to share with someone—with her—to get another opinion. His visit to London, though brief, had been highly informative, but not in the least pleasing. He cast a swift glance over his shoulder to where Lord Uxbridge tooled his own phaeton behind a pair of flashy black prads. He'd be glad to turn Sir Francis's body over to Uxbridge and those somber men who followed with the undertaker's cart for conveyance back to London.

They pulled through the iron gates at last, to be met by the westering sun casting its late afternoon glow over the gray stone facade of the Court. The beauty of the scene never failed to warm him, filling him with love for the old place.

Another warmth touched him, of relief ruffling the edges of his mind. Kat—he couldn't think of her as Miss Sayre anymore—would be waiting for him just inside the doors, glad to see him, full of news that she would barely be able to keep from tumbling out in deference to Uxbridge's presence. He truly was coming home—to her.

He checked that thought but found it refused to be banished. Somehow, in spite of all logic, some strange force linked them together so each shared what the other felt. But that didn't mean she'd want to share the life of an invalid, as well as his emotions. Yet he couldn't remain depressed, not with her excitement filling him.

He urged his grays forward, increasing their pace to reach her all the sooner. With a neat loop of his wrist, he guided his pair through the ancient hedged archway leading into the stableyard. A groom ran out to take charge of the equipage, and a younger lad followed as Uxbridge pulled up beside him. Graeme swung down, retrieved his cane, and crossed the few feet to join his superior.

"I won't be long," Uxbridge informed the groom. "Have them ready for the return journey within the hour."

The great black hearse, Graeme noted, had stopped before the front door. The undertaker and his minion remained on the seat, having received their instructions from Lord Uxbridge not to enter until he sent for them.

Uxbridge glanced at the somber carriage, nodded to himself, then turned to Graeme. "Where is he?"

Graeme led the way along the hedge-lined gravel path to the terrace leading into the library. As they reached it, Kat rose in a graceful swirl of flowered muslin skirts from a wooden chair near the house.

She hurried forward. "Lady Clementina has set me to welcome you," she said, a breathless note in her voice. "She and my father are tending to the de Loires."

"How are they taking this?" Uxbridge demanded.

"Monsieur de Loire is very grim." Kat cast a sideways glance at Graeme. *"Madame* is lamenting that viscount Ellesmere is not well enough to come down and bear them company. But I believe my father has managed to calm her."

Uxbridge snorted. "Ellesmere is a damned flirt."

"But extremely useful," Kat pointed out. "Sir Francis is—just inside. His valet is sitting with him." She stepped aside, allowing Uxbridge to enter through the long French windows, but caught Graeme's arm as he passed. "I have something to tell you," she whispered.

He laid his hand over hers for a brief moment, disturbed by how much he enjoyed the contact. He broke it. "I've learned a few things, too. Let's meet in the study as soon as we can."

She nodded and allowed him to precede her into the library. Somewhat to his surprise, she made no move to follow. Instead, she closed the doors from the terrace and strolled off across the paving stones toward the rose garden.

He couldn't blame her. A creature as full of life as

she should not be cooped up in a room with a dead man. Or even one half dead, as was he. He thrust that thought from him lest she should sense it, and turned to see Uxbridge standing by the chairs where Sir Francis lay. Jenner, the valet, sat on the sofa near his master's head, his gaze fixed on them with a blank, uncomprehending stare.

Slowly, Uxbridge removed his hat and stood for a long moment of silence. Then he shook his head. "I don't suppose there is really much I can do here. We should start the return journey with him as quickly as possible." Graeme glanced at the clock. "It lacks but twenty minutes before five, and Lady Matlock is not expected to return until almost eight."

"To change before going on to an evening party," Uxbridge stuck in dryly. "I fear Lady Matlock will not be pleased at having to forego her entertainment."

Graeme frowned. "I gathered there was little regard between husband and wife."

A half-smile, not at all pleasant, played about the corners of Uxbridge's mouth. "She will not treat me to a fit of the vapors. She is a—reasonable lady."

"Reasonable over murder?" Graeme raised skeptical eyebrows.

"You have yet to show me the evidence," Uxbridge reminded him mildly. "I am by no means convinced this is aught but the accident it appears."

Graeme started forward, but Jenner, who had been watching them in silence, stopped him. "If you will permit me, sir? I—I had the young lady show me." The valet rose with the stiffness of one who had remained immobile for too long and took up a position beside his master's head. With hands that trembled, he removed the collar, revealing the area of the neck where the faint bruising still showed.

Uxbridge bent close, examining the spot in tight-mouthed silence. "I see where you might have made that assumption. It is by no means conclusive, however. There might well be other explanations which we had best consider." He looked up. "This is not the time for alarmist behavior, Warwick. This is most likely an accident."

"And if it isn't?" Graeme watched his superior narrowly.

Uxbridge grimaced. "We will increase our security about His Highness. Now, though, is not the time to make any public declarations that might destroy the conference before it even begins. If—and I do mean *if*—Sir Francis were murdered, there will have been a reason for it. I will make discreet inquiries in White-hall."

"I did this noon," Graeme informed him. "And I found the results not at all to my liking."

"What did you discover?" Uxbridge demanded. "And why the devil didn't you inform me at once?"

"Because you already possessed more information about this rumored plot against Prince Albert than anyone else I spoke to."

"You dared ask about that?" Uxbridge straightened up and glowered at Graeme. "Did it not occur to you that your curiosity might be indiscreet—and that you might approach the wrong person?"

"Do you believe someone involved in such a dastardly treason is to be found within your own department?"

Uxbridge drew a ragged breath. "No—thank God! At least I can trust my own men." He sank onto an armchair and covered his face with his hands.

After a long minute of silence, Graeme asked, "Do you think Sir Francis's death is related to this plot against His Highness, then?"

"If this is murder, then what else?" Uxbridge demanded. "I had asked him to look into the matter— quietly, of course—in case the plot might extend to the conference. He found no evidence that it does, however. But there is a chance he betrayed his knowledge to the wrong person. There were times when he could be less than subtle. Perhaps I should not have used him, but everyone else in the department was already over busy, and you appeared to have the conference under control. So I thought you could spare him to make a few discreet inquiries and surveillances."

"Yet it was here he was killed," Graeme pointed out.

"Or died by accident," Uxbridge stuck in. "I doubt we will ever be certain which it was."

"Or if he were silenced to prevent him from telling you something."

"How does Ellesmere go on?" Uxbridge ran a hand through his hair. "He is needed here—doubly, now that you are deprived of Sir Francis's assistance. I am only sorry there is no one else I can spare you until he is recovered."

"We will manage quite well." Graeme straightened, but his gaze returned to that tell-tale bruise on Matlock's neck. "But I think we had best determine why Sir Francis died."

"You persist in thinking it foul play." Uxbridge made it a statement.

"Let us say rather that I will be glad if we could rule that out."

Uxbridge inclined his head. "If he had discovered anything, or if he were involved in anything—shall we say illicit?—he might have left evidence of it in his room." He straightened. "His things must be packed, anyway. I will accompany his man and see if anything turns up. Come," he added to the distraught valet, who dragged himself out of his morose reverie. Together the two left the room.

Graeme stared for a long moment at the bluish mark on Matlock's throat, and his jaw tightened. There might well be other explanations than murder. So why did he cling so stubbornly to that belief? Because Kat shared it? Irritated that he might be permitting someone else's views to influence him, he strode out after the other two.

In the corridor he looked about for her, but she hadn't yet returned. He wanted to talk to her—but that could wait. If there were any clues or revelations in Sir Francis's room, he wanted to know what they were. Kat, he felt certain, had found something. Had it been up there?

Uxbridge had paused in the main hall to send a footman for the undertaker, and now mounted the stairs after Jenner. Graeme followed in their wake. Uxbridge, he noted, moved with unaccustomed tension. He couldn't blame the man for not wanting to believe one of his men could have been murdered. He had enough worries at the moment. But the Foreign Office under Lord Palmerston's ministry ran itself very well, and Uxbridge, as Palmerston's assistant, enjoyed an excellent reputation for capability in Whitehall. If anyone could juggle so many problems, it was he.

Newcombe, it seemed, had already sent Sir Francis's trunk to his room. It stood just inside the door. Jenner's face crumpled as he gazed at it, then the next moment he pulled himself together, crossed to the great wardrobe and began the careful removal and folding of each of the elegant garments within.

Lord Uxbridge watched him for a minute in silence. "If you see anything unusual, let me know at once," he said at last, then turned to the bureau and pulled out the top drawer. Jenner spun about, opened his mouth in obvious protest, then shut it again.

Graeme went to the desk, located the papers and leafed through them. Uxbridge joined him, looking over his shoulder, as he pulled open the bottom drawer. The dark metal of a gun glinted at him. Graeme took it out, turned it over, and studied it with growing unease.

Uxbridge drew in a sharp breath. "What the devil," he muttered.

"It's the one from the Exhibition, is it not?" Graeme looked over his shoulder. "Is there any way of knowing for certain?"

Uxbridge sank onto the bed, holding the revolver, his expression grim. Graeme took it from his hand. This was what Kat had found, he realized. What connections had she made from it? He couldn't determine that. It would have to wait until he could speak with her.

"How came it into his possession?" Uxbridge

breathed, asking the question of no one in particular. He looked up slowly, focusing glazed eyes on Graeme. *"Why* did he have it?"

"At the moment," Graeme said, "I think we should worry about the whereabouts of the bombs."

Uxbridge waved a distracted hand. "All in good time. What can *this* mean? Is it possible—*could* Sir Francis have been working with the conspirators in the plot against the Prince Consort?"

Graeme's brow creased. "If he were, would he not have been trying to divert our attention from it? Instead, he has told me more of it than anyone else."

"He could never hold his tongue." Uxbridge sounded somewhat bitter. "A very poor choice for a companion in conspiracy."

"Yet fortunate for us, if we have learned enough from him to foil the plot."

"Let us hope we have." Uxbridge came to his feet with a decisive motion. "I can think of nothing more certain to ruin the economic conference than the abducting of His Royal Highness."

Graeme turned the repeating pistol over slowly in his hands. "I can see the purpose of stealing such a weapon. But why bombs?"

"To create a disturbance, I should think. A distraction that would leave the Prince Consort vulnerable. We must find those bombs."

But though they searched diligently through Sir Francis's belongings, not so much as a fuse did they find. At last, satisfied they could learn nothing more from the contents of the chamber, they allowed Jenner to finish packing his master's effects.

They returned downstairs to find the undertaker had completed his task; Sir Francis's body now lay in the back of the hearse, and they were ready to set forth for London. Uxbridge declined Graeme's suggestion he remain for dinner, and the funereal party set forth. Graeme remained on the front steps until Sir Francis's cabriolet, driven by his groom and bearing Jenner and his baggage, pulled through the wrought iron gates onto the road.

He turned back into the house, feeling unutterably exhausted—and as if a million questions hung over him, all demanding instant answers. He wanted to see Kat, but she would be dressing now for dinner. Dressing in that one green silk gown that hung so alluringly from her rounded curves. He enjoyed watching her at meals, trying so hard to resist the pastries and sweetmeats, instead selecting the fruit from the succession houses which he knew she found no where nearly as satisfying. He forced her from his mind and went to make himself presentable for the meal. It would not do, in his role as host, to be late.

The others had already gathered in the drawing room when he joined them. He accepted the glass of sherry handed him by Adam Sayre and looked about the assembled company. All wore solemn expressions, as befitting the circumstances of a death in the house, but in Kat's huge green eyes he also read a repressed eagerness. It washed over him like a wave, and prudently he took up a position on the opposite side of the room from her. He would seek her out after the meal, leave the de Loires once more in the charge of his aunt and Mr. Sayre. He would have Kat to himself—in the study, to discuss this problem, and for no other reason.

The meal itself passed with irritating slowness. No witty conversation enlivened the table. All seemed subdued by the day's tragic event. Graeme greeted with relief his aunt's rising, signaling the ladies' departure from the dining room. The butler brought out port and brandy, Mr. Sayre and M. de Loire moved their seats to join him, and the decanters made their rounds.

Adam drained his glass in one swallow. "Why do we not join the ladies?" he said abruptly.

Even de Loire brightened. "Perhaps *Mademoiselle* Sayre would favor us with one of her so very amusing stories."

"Actually, I have business to discuss with Miss Sayre," Graeme said. "My aunt's portrait."

"True, true." Adam rose and waved for de Loire to join him. "Have I told you yet about the time I was on a stagecoach that got held up? No? Come, let's go into the drawing room."

Graeme watched the two leave, and smiled at Adam Sayre's adroitness. Useful, that man. Far more so than either Ellesmere or Sir Francis. He rose and made his way to the study to wait.

He didn't have long. Less than five minutes later the door opened and Kat slipped in, her face alight with eagerness. He rose.

"What did Uxbridge have to say?" she demanded.

Why did the mere sight of her make him want to drag her into his arms? Because it was more than sight, he realized. Her personality, her spirit, everything that made her *her,* enveloped him.

He settled once more in his chair, mostly to prevent himself from crossing the room to be near to her. "He pointed out that there could be any number of causes for that bruise on Matlock's throat, and murder is the least likely."

Kat perched on the edge of the desk, thoughtfully swinging one foot that didn't reach the floor. "He's right, of course," she said after a moment. "It's just all so peculiar."

"I take it you found the pistol in his desk?"

She nodded. "What did he make of that? Is it the one stolen from the Exhibition?"

"He never said so, but it probably is." He folded his hands together in his lap and studied the glittering emerald in the heavy gold band on his little finger. In a few words, he summed up his discussion with his superior.

Kat listened, frowning, nodding from time to time as if he confirmed her own thoughts. When he finished, she cocked her head to one side and pursed her lips. "He's so certain it all has to do with this plot against Prince Albert."

Graeme ran a finger through his bushy side whiskers, considering his answer. "Hardly anyone knows of the conference except the planners and participants," he said at last. "That does make Albert a more likely target."

"And others at Whitehall had heard the rumors about his abduction?" Kat pursued.

Graeme nodded. "Uxbridge had the most information about it, of course—but then he'd been gathering it from everyone. Two of the other officials I spoke to had also heard the rumors—and were deeply perturbed. But it's no more than rumors!" Graeme sprang to his feet and with the aid of his cane took several restless steps.

"Could you find nothing tangible?" She watched him steadily.

Graeme gave a short, derisive laugh. "Uxbridge didn't think I needed to know his sources." His superior had in fact informed him it was none of Graeme's damned business. That still rankled. "He told me to let Whitehall concentrate on that, that I should concentrate on keeping the conference safe. He didn't seem to think I ever should have been bothered with those rumors in the first place."

"In short, you spent a frustrating day." She shifted on the desk. "Look, there's—there's something I really should tell you."

He stiffened, but waited in silence.

She drew a shaky breath. "I think your conference is in real danger. Uxbridge thinks the bombs are meant for the plot against Prince Albert. I'm afraid they're not."

"What do you mean?" He kept his voice steady with a palpable effort.

"I don't know if this is connected with the Albert business or not." She looked up, troubled. "But I do know something is going to happen to disrupt your meetings—and possibly something catastrophic."

"What the devil are you talking about?" He strode up to her, one hand gripping her shoulder. "What do you know?"

"Come with me. It's time you saw this." Somber, Kat slid from her perch and led the way out the door.

Graeme followed her across the main hall and up the stairs. At the next floor, she crossed the picture gallery and headed toward the wing where her room stood. Not the conservatory, after all. He'd expected her to show him her secret painting. At the door to her chamber he hesitated outside, alive to the impropriety of entering, but something about her tension and the uneasy set of her shoulders lured him inside.

"Close the door," she directed, and turned to the long draperies at her window. From behind them she pulled a medium-sized canvas, still covered by its concealing cloth.

So it was to be her painting, he realized, and came forward. Her tension, which he realized he must have been sensing for several minutes, now vibrated through him. It was all he could do to keep from tearing the cover aside to see what she had kept so secret.

She positioned the canvas on a chair and pulled back the cloth. For a long moment he stared at it, frowning, seeing only an array of brilliantly colored balloons dangling wicker baskets, floating across a sky filled with puffy silvered clouds. Except . . .

He blinked, and brought a hazy outline into focus. Disguised in the design of cloud and balloon, another picture emerged, a very different image. Now the balloons slid out of focus for him, leaving the outline of a large, transparent structure—the Crystal Palace. Reflected in its glass walls, he could just make out the image of a townhouse engulfed by explosion and fire.

He swallowed, his throat uncomfortably dry. He knew that facade. Sevington House.

There could be no doubt. The building being destroyed by flames could be no other than the one where the conference would be held.

Chapter Fourteen

"The connection," Graeme breathed. "There it is, the connection between the stolen bombs and the conference. But how—?" He turned to her, half accusing, half in awe. "How could you paint this?"

She turned away, hugging herself as if chilled. "This isn't the first time. Graeme—" She broke off, looking at him, her distress patent.

That was the first time she'd used his name, the thought shot through his mind, only to be replaced by the more urgent issue at hand. "What else?" He pressed her gently into a chair, his hands lingering on her bare shoulders, her skin soft beneath his touch.

"Before I came here—" She swallowed. "I also painted a scene of balloons . . ."

"What did you include that time?" With an effort, he stopped his thumb's caressing strokes.

"An outline of a map—of a united Europe beneath a French flag."

"French." He straightened, his brow snapping down. French. Not for a moment did he doubt her, nor did he question the accuracy of this uncanny prediction. She believed it, and her conviction convinced him. "France taking over all of Europe," he said slowly. "That's been tried before, by—" His eyes widened.

"Napoleon." She spoke the name aloud.

"And this time, Louis Napoleon." He spun away and took several unsteady striding steps about her chamber. Louis Napoleon. "He's already president of the Second French Republic. Do you think he plans to follow in his uncle's footsteps?"

She nodded. "I know he becomes emperor."

"Emperor! Good God, but—*how* do you know? Emperor!" He rubbed a hand over his forehead. "Another painting, I suppose?" He crossed to her once more and bent to grasp her hands within his own. "Kat, do your paintings come true?"

"I don't know. No, they don't *have* to. I think the paintings are a—a warning of some sort. We have history in our hands. Oh, damn, that sounds corny, but you know what I mean."

"Do I?" He watched her intently.

She drew an unsteady breath. "I think that if we allow things to go on, as planned, the predictions in the paintings will come true. If that's a future we want to prevent, we'd better get doing something."

A quick smile tugged at his lips at her turn of phrase, but it faded at once. He faced the painting once more and studied every line, every impression to be gained from the hazy rendition of the explosion. "That is Sevington House," he said, "and the connection between this one and your earlier prediction is all too obvious."

She came to stand just behind him, her shoulder

brushing against the arm of his coat. "Perhaps Louis Napoleon plans to destroy the economic leaders of the other European nations."

"The resulting distrust and accusations would throw Europe into chaos—paving the way for him to seize power and create for himself the empire his uncle failed to hold. Dear God, we can't allow him to succeed."

Kat stared at her painting. "And so it all hinges on your conference," she said. "If we can save that, we can save Europe. Or can we?" She looked up at him.

The horror in her expression sent a wrenching ache through him. "We can," he said with more conviction than he felt.

She shook her head. "Won't Louis Napoleon try something else? Graeme, what if it never ends? What if I'm stuck here for the rest of my life, painting these horrible predictions so we can keep history following the right path?"

He cupped her face between his hands, allowing his cane to slide to the chair behind him. His fingers stroked her cheek as he tried to calm her growing agitation. "Who's to say what history should become? Kat, it doesn't all lie on your shoulders. This one incident, yes, but that's enough for any person to deal with. You are here, with me now, and we can prevent this one thing from happening. But that is all there is. All."

Somehow, it seemed reasonable to kiss her forehead—just to soothe her—and when she turned her face toward his, he closed her eyes with the gentle caress of his lips. A half-sob, half-moan escaped her and she buried her face against his shoulder, her arms sliding about him. One of his own wrapped tightly about her shoulders, the other held her close about her waist.

"Oh, my Kitten," he breathed against her hair. It smelled of violets, of sunshine, of laughter. Of love.

Emotion, too long held in check, surged within, filling every part of him. Only it wasn't his alone. Awareness pulsated back and forth between them as tangible as a shock wave, as all-encompassing as being burned at the stake. Caution, prudence, common-sense—all the tenets by which he lived his life—melted beneath the raging need building between them.

Desire flared like a torch thrust into oiled rags, un-deniable in its rightness, in its inevitability. It wasn't only him; need enveloped her as well, flooding from her being, wrapping about him, and heightened by his own tide of passion . . . and love.

Love. Nothing mattered anymore but that one thought, that one certainty, that he held in his arms the one woman he truly loved, who truly loved him. That certainty spiraled between them, intensifying the ur-gency with which he sought her mouth. The kiss over-whelmed his senses. Nothing mattered but here, now, what they shared, what he had tried so foolishly to deny before.

She drew him backward, pulling him with her, until she sank onto the bed. He knelt at her side, his mouth exploring the pulse that raced at her throat. He had no need to ask, to question, to doubt. He simply knew, even before he caught the sharp intake of her breath and her gentle moan as she melted against him once more. Behind him, the flames flickered in the hearth, a mere semblance of the fire that consumed them.

* * *

Graeme stirred in the great bed, his cheek rubbing against an unfamiliar pillow, his body molding to an unfamiliar softness in the mattress. The scent of violets hovered about him, stirring him back to consciousness even before he became aware of the weight pressed against his arm and chest.

Kat. His beloved Kitten. His fingers stroked her bare arm and she snuggled against him in her sleep, so sweet and trusting. And so giving, as vibrant in her love as she was in everything else.

His lips brushed her hair and he settled back, fully awake and filled with awe at the depth and power of what they had shared. He hadn't been himself—he *couldn't* have been himself. Never had he experienced such complete abandonment, such a wildly sensual and all-encompassing communion.

Because it wasn't him. At least, it wasn't him *alone*. It had been Kat awakening in him desires and an unrestrained spirit, things he had not dared let himself experience since the ambusher's bullet lodged in his knee.

He sobered. Now, in the early hours of the morning, chilling reality began to return. What he had experienced last night in her bed, in her arms, had nothing to do with the day to day life he was forced to lead. Last night . . . last night had been special, something he would always remember and treasure—but it was not something he dared repeat. Kat could—and did— live her life fully with no physical limitations. He had no right to try to hold her, to subject her to the dull,

ordered routine that enabled him to manage his life.
He had no right to love her.

Her thoughts and feelings weren't influencing him at
the moment, he realized. Coolly, logically, he looked
back over his complete abandonment of the night
before, and panic set in. He felt out of control, vulnerable. This link between them defied the logic he relied
on to keep his world safe. He was a cripple, he reminded himself. He could never hope to make happy
a woman of Kat's passionate and impulsive nature.

He turned his head to study her shadowed face in
the darkness, both longing for her and fearing her. She
still slept in blissful peace—

An image sprang into his mind, startling, nightmar-
ish, of a low, box-like carriage that whisked along on
wide black wheels, rather like a tiny train without a
track. Thousands of these creations in a multitude of
hues maneuvered among each other at break-neck
speed in a narrow road . . .

The vision vanished, and he forced his tensed muscles to relax as he drew a deep, steadying breath. What
hellish turmoil caused her to create such monstrosities
in her sleep? Yet she didn't seem disturbed; she rested
against him in peace, not tossing and turning as she
ought. What else lurked in this mind so atuned to his,
yet still so alien?

He studied her, cautiously opening himself to receive other images. A dark room with lights that re-
volved in the ceiling, setting out brilliant colored
flashes, impressed itself in his thoughts. Beneath, bodies gyrated and thrashed about. Was this a view of
hell? But the faces that flickered before him laughed, as
if they enjoyed their unrestrained jerking about.

The scene faded—had been there, in fact, for scarcely a single second, yet it haunted his memory. And the clothing those people had worn. . . . He rolled his head against the pillow, confused, then realizing even this emotion emanated from the lady in his arms. Involuntarily, he tightened his grip, seeking to protect her yet knowing if he truly wished to do so, he would put her far from him.

She stirred, rubbing her cheek against his shoulder, and her eyelids fluttered open. For a long moment she lay staring through the darkness at him, then a slow smile tugged at her lips. "Is it morning?" she whispered.

Her voice rolled over him like velvet, reminding him forcibly of the wonders of their night. "It's long before dawn, still." He shouldn't be here, torn by the temptation of the silken body pressed against his. He wanted her again.

Her fingers trailed along the hairs of his chest, and his muscles tightened in anticipation. Only he couldn't let it happen, he couldn't risk losing control. He had to maintain some semblance of sanity. She would regret it when this glorious union they shared faded to insignificance in the face of endless days of dull, circumscribed activity suited to a man with a lame leg. Her fingers drew tantalizing circles along his flesh, and with reluctance he captured them, holding them away so they could not continue their sensual assault.

She sat up, crossing her legs, holding the coverlet to hide her exquisite curves even in the heavy darkness. "What's wrong?" Her voice held concern and gentleness.

"Your dreams."

"Oh." She sounded rueful. "Pretty strange, were they? It gets worse."

He pulled himself up, arranging the pillows behind him for support. He studied her features, barely discernible in the dark, then tried to recreate the vision he had experienced. "What—" he began, then broke off.

A shaky sigh escaped her. "I suppose it's time." She sounded uneasy. "All right, take a deep breath and clear your mind. Now just . . . wait."

He inhaled deeply, but nothing happened. He tried again, this time making an effort to quiet the questions and thoughts that bombarded him. Still nothing. Then a presence filled him, *her* presence, warm and loving and—

A jumble of impressions exploded within him, wilder even than her dreams, only to fade at once. Yet not completely. Something remained, something not quite tangible. He stared at her in complete incomprehension that slowly gave way to disbelief as her sense of time and reality solidified in his mind.

He shook his head. "Oh, my God," he breathed. He reached out a shaking hand to touch her arm. "You're real, you're here, but—"

She nodded. "But I won't even be born yet for more than a hundred years."

He pulled away, rejecting her words even as he knew in his heart they were true. He swung his legs out of the bed, wincing as he moved his left knee, and reached for the dressing gown that wasn't there. In fact, he didn't know where any of his clothes were. There'd been considerable abandon as they discarded one another's garments last night—an abandon fueled by an intensity of emotion that refused to be safely banished even now. He groped for anything to cover his scarred body.

"Graeme." Her soft voice stopped him.

Slowly, he forced himself to look at her, to see the silhouette of her hair tumbling about her shoulders, to remember how it felt beneath his searching hands. He shook his head and rose, putting as much distance as he could between them. He stepped behind the bedpost, gripping it for support as he sought his clothes.

The future. No, that was too much, more than he could deal with. He had a conference—perhaps the fate of all Europe—hanging over his head. How could he begin to cope with the impossibility that he had made passionate, unrestrained love last night to a woman who couldn't possibly exist for him?

"I know," came her gentle voice with a touch of dry humor. "It hasn't been easy for me to believe it, either."

"How?" he asked at last. The pain in his leg increased, and he sank down on the bed once more. "How can you be here?" He heard her unsteady intake of breath.

"That first painting I told you about? I did it in my own time. Here, at Durham Court. I'd come with my father for a balloon ascension. Then I started having visions."

He listened in a disbelief that refused to solidify as she described the images that had come to her. How could he deny her words when he had glimpsed the world through her eyes himself?

"My dragon," he said when she finished her tale of their arrival. "No wonder we could find no trace of your basket in the lake. And your clothing, everything that seemed so very odd about you—" And that now seemed so perfectly a part of this unique and tantalizing lady. "The future," he repeated once more, growing accustomed to the concept. "What is it like? What wonders—or nightmares," he added, remembering her dream, "does it hold?"

"Maybe very different ones, if the time-line as I know it is disrupted."

That sharpened his attention once more to the matter at hand, and with relief he turned to this. "Europe remains separate nations, as it is now?"

She hesitated. "Things change, but it doesn't become united under France."

He let her caveat pass. "So the uniting you predicted in your own time must be tied to the explosion you painted here?" He stirred and became vividly aware of the fact he had not a stitch on except the cover he had thrown across his lap. And that thought reminded him of why and what they had shared—and what he wanted once more.

The conference. He had to concentrate on the conference. As if reading his mind—she did, as far as his emotions went, he realized—she drew the comforter closer to her chin.

"We know there's a threat to the conference—and what that threat is," she said. "That should help us avoid it."

"Your painting shows an explosion at Sevington House," he said slowly, turning to look through the darkness to where the dim shape of her canvas rested on the chair. "I believe the best plan will be to move the venue—but not let it be known until the last minute."

"Where—" She broke off. "Of course. Here. But will that be fair to your aunt?" She turned her head to stare toward the window, where only the moon and starlight illuminated the grounds beyond. "It's such a beautiful old house. What if someone tries to blow *it* up?"

"I won't allow it!" Rage filled him, knotting his muscles, and he drew a deep breath to steady himself. He hadn't expected so violent a reaction to the mere thought of someone damaging his beloved Court.

"Having second thoughts?" Kat asked. She watched him now, as he struggled to solve his dilemma.

The Court—or the delegates, the conference, the strength that might be brought to the individual European countries through redefined trade agreements and good will. "Where else could I move it?" he asked, then realized he'd spoken the words aloud.

"Some place where you can have complete control—and where you can make all the arrangements without anyone realizing what you're about. That's a hard one. I assume anywhere at Whitehall is out?"

He grimaced. "Most definitely out. There is nowhere suitable—and even if there were, the arrangements would be so complex, there wouldn't be anyone working anywhere in the building who wouldn't realize something untoward was occurring."

"Bureaucracy." She sounded disgusted. "That's something that doesn't improve over the next hundred and fifty years, I'm afraid."

The next hundred and fifty years. The possibilities stretched before him, of marvelous wonders, of advances beyond his dreams. So much had changed in the world in just the last twenty or thirty years. Trains, telegraphs, machinery, medicine, even the hot water pipes that ran to the main bedrooms and bathrooms. That was what the Crystal Palace Exhibition was all about, to show these marvels to the world.

And that was what the conference was about, to promote a world in which more explorations and inventions could take place and benefit more people.

And that was what someone—Louis Napoleon, perhaps?—tried to destroy for the sake of his own blinding ambition.

"I don't know if I should tell you about the future." Kat spoke softly, her voice tinged with regret. "It might help you understand—"

He straightened. "I don't want to know. It would take away the joy of discovery for each new invention, and I'd regret missing the things I'd never live to see myself." And since when had he once again experienced that delight in the marvels of modern technology? Certainly not when he'd seen the Exhibition the first several times. He'd still been wrapped in that protective cocoon that prevented him from feeling pain, from facing his limitations. From living.

"There's another reason I shouldn't tell you." She sounded, for her, unusually solemn. "If we fail here, so very much might never come to pass. It's scary how much could be destroyed with one little bomb."

"Then we won't let it. There has to be a way to prevent it, to keep the conference safe."

"I could try another painting," she suggested, though she sounded dubious. "If you've made the decision to move the conference?"

"I have."

"Then make it official as soon as you can. That should cancel my last prediction. Once that's finished, I'll try again and see what we get. I only wish there were more I could do to help."

"That's better than anything I can come up with." For a long moment he stared at her, trying to make out the details of her face through the darkness. Now, though, was not the time to let her enthrall him. Would she disappear from his life as abruptly as his dragon basket had dropped her into it? The possibility of her loss left him shaken. But even if she stayed and lived out the rest of her life so far from her own time, he had no right to tie her down to him. That, he reminded himself with painful force, was the one truth he could not permit himself to forget.

"Graeme—" She held out her hand to him.

He rose. "No." He stooped, groping on the floor for his discarded garments.

The rustle of the bedclothes warned him she had moved. He tensed, but she merely reached for her dressing gown. The filmy muslin floated about her, ghostlike, playing havoc with his senses. He gritted his teeth and continued his search, keeping his gaze prudently from her hazy form.

"Here."

He looked up to find her holding out his trousers. They'd be sufficient. She turned her back while he dragged them on. As he fastened them, she retrieved his cane and other scattered articles of clothing. Solemnly, she held them out.

"Graeme—?" She touched his bewhiskered cheek.

He could just make out her smile as she stood on tiptoe to brush his lips with hers. He caught her and set her aside. "You're too tempting," he said, and realized at once he'd admitted too much. But he couldn't keep his feelings from her, anyway, no matter how hard he tried.

She blinked, and there might have been tears in her eyes. "Don't underestimate yourself. Or me."

"No," he said softly. "I won't do that." And he left her, not trusting himself if he remained.

Chapter Fifteen

Kat listened to the gentle thud as the door closed behind Graeme, and she fought the tears that trembled on her lashes. Why did this crazy, irrational link have to exist? It must have been that which gave her the vision she unconsciously worked into her first painting. And that which dragged her through the ages to be with him.

She sank back into her bed, now cool and empty while such a short time ago her senses had exploded there in Graeme's arms. His injury had hampered him even there, but somehow they had managed. Oh, how gloriously they had managed. Yet he had retreated in fear, the fear that he was not a whole man, not enough for her. His pain and self-doubt must run very deep to survive the soul-searing experience of the union—both physical and emotional—they had shared.

She, she realized with a sense of panic—could never now be satisfied with anything less. A merely sexual encounter, no matter how much love she might feel, would seem petty and unfulfilling after the completeness of what she experienced with Graeme—and only with Graeme. With him, she had found a portion of herself, a—

Oh, rats! She rolled onto her stomach and slammed her fist into the pillows. His turmoil affected her, as hers must him. This, she supposed, was the down-side of this mysterious force that bound them together. Not all emotions were pleasurable. Yet they could use this knowledge to strengthen one another.

She closed her eyes, willing her love and caring to wrap about him, to soothe his worries—and blanked from her mind his returning feelings that a crippled man would never be able to keep up with her tumultuous existence. *You're not just any man,* she flared back at him, and wondered in what manner he would receive the emotions behind that message.

Sometime after dawn, when her room began to feel like a prison, she straggled down the stairs, depressed that the perfection of their night had been shaken. She paused in the main hall, a sense of determination tugging at her thoughts. Graeme.

He was down here, probably in his study, working out the details for moving the conference. He was not one to waste time—and he was eager for her to start her next painting in the hopes of detecting the next threat. She strode along the hall in search of him.

As she reached the door to the study, it opened and he stood on the threshold, waiting. He must have sensed her coming just as she had known where to find him. The expression in his gray eyes as his gaze rested on her tugged at her heart. No one was about, no one would know. Without saying a word, trying to mask her intention from him, she walked up, straight into the arms that opened for her as if against their will.

She pulled his face down to meet hers, and for a warm, wonderful moment, everything about her world glowed once more.

"Good morning," she whispered, and rested her forehead against his shoulder.

His arm encircled her and his lips brushed her curls. "Oh, my Kat. What am I going to do with you?"

She looked up at that, eyes sparkling with sudden laughter.

His own eyes clouded. "And how long before that won't be enough for you? My sweet Kitten, I would willingly make love to you day in and day out, but other activities must intrude. I will never be able to go for long rambling walks with you, or even lead you out on a dance floor. I no longer cut a dashing figure in a saddle, and as time goes by, my doctor tells me I will only get worse and have to restrict my meager activities even more."

"So what do doctors know?" Kat kissed his stubbled chin, the only part of him she could reach. "In my time we know that a lot of sickness and pain is in the mind."

He caught her hands, holding her away. "Not all."

"No." And in her time they also had wonder drugs and arthroscopic surgery and joint replacements. But this was his time. She banished that shadow from her mind. This was her time, now, as well. She'd just apply a little modern thinking to it.

"I believe," she said, sliding her arms about his waist, "you'll be amazed at how many things we'll find we can do—together."

"Until you grow tired of my constraints."

"What? Haven't you realized by now I thrive on

challenges?" She hesitated, reached up to kiss him quickly, then strode away. Let him think. Let him experience the longing that shot through her whenever her thoughts drifted to him. She'd invaded his world— she probably took a little getting used to. For that matter, so did his world.

At the main hall once more she paused. A cinnamon roll would go down rather well right now. She'd sworn off donuts, but the fat content in a blueberry muffin she could still rationalize away. So where was one when you needed it?

Driven by that desire, she set forth looking for any servant who might direct her toward a much-needed muffinfest. She found a footman in the breakfast parlor, but he did no more than set out the chafing dishes that would warm the plates later. He looked surprised to see her there so early.

She put on her most hopeful smile. "How long?" she asked, inserting a note of pleading into her words.

The young man flushed slightly, probably in embarrassment at being addressed by a guest. "Not for another hour, Miss." He looked as if he would like to slide out of the room.

"An hour?" Kat protested. "Any chance of anything sooner?"

The lad looked uncomfortable.

"How about in the kitchens?" Kat tried.

"But—you can't go there, Miss!" he exclaimed.

Her smile broadened. "Oh, can't I? In pursuit of breakfast, you'd be amazed where I'd go."

The lad's jaw dropped and he regarded her with a measure of awe. She smiled brightly, and without another protest he led the way out the door, down the hall and to the back premises. There they encountered an indignant housekeeper, but Kat begged her to forgive the boy.

"I'm hungry," she sighed, and at once won sympathy. The housekeeper dismissed the boy to be about his duties and herself took Kat in tow. Already, fragrances impossible to resist reached her. "Fresh bread!" Kat exclaimed, and followed her nose.

The kitchen proved to be a cavernous room with a large range, dominated by a huge table down the center. The door to the oven stood open, and a maid lifted out a gigantic loaf. Kat stopped on the threshold, inhaling the heavenly aroma, then wandered to the table where several apples stood, one already peeled. Kat selected one of the others, looked hopefully at the cook, who turned to stare at the housekeeper, nonplussed. Apparently, visitors rarely found their way to the servants' domain.

Armed with her apple, a couple of flaky rolls, and a cup of only slightly bitter chocolate, she retreated to the main portion of the house, then out to the terrace beyond the library where she could enjoy her hard-won meal in peace. It would be a beautiful day. The scent of roses hung heavy in the air, stirred by a cool breeze. The clouds puffed along the horizon with every sign of coming closer. She had better not waste the morning light much longer.

She finished her sketchy meal and carried her cup back into the house. Was it too early to start on the next painting of balloons to see if their plan worked? Did she hope too much in that? She had no guarantee she would ever again paint another prediction. Yet if not to keep things as they should be, why was she here, in this alien time?

To be with Graeme. The thought filled her, impossible to deny. This link with him went beyond anything she could comprehend. Being with Graeme. Warmed by that thought, she went to prepare another canvas.

Half an hour later, as she pounded the last nail fastening the material onto the stretcher bars she had made, a familiar rap sounded on her door. It opened at once and Adam strolled in.

"You're creating an awful racket this morning," he said cheerfully.

She looked up and grinned. "Wanted to get started on a little project. Is Lady Clementina ready for another pose-job?"

His eyes narrowed. "How should I know?"

She laughed. "I wasn't accusing you of anything, Dad. I just figured you'd probably popped down to say good morning."

He huffed. "Ready and eager," he admitted. "Though I think breakfast is in order, first. Coming?"

Kat considered her rolls—now the merest memory—and said yes. She shoved her tools away and followed her father.

She entered the breakfast parlor to find that same young footman now placing various dishes over the flames. He blinked as he saw her; she gave him a conspiratorial wink, and for a moment a bright grin flashed across his face. He replaced it at once with an expression far more appropriate for a young man who had aspirations as high as the rank of an under-butler.

Kat took a deep breath, enjoying the heady aromas of the spiced sauce on the fish, the fried potatoes, the rich coffee . . . the coffee. She poured herself a cup, weakened it liberally with cream and sugar, and settled down to enjoy her second repast.

Lady Clementina entered a few minutes later, gowned in her voluminous split skirt for her portrait. "Ready to get to work?" she asked as she headed for the plates.

"Whenever you are." And what, Kat wondered, did the woman enjoy the most? Gaining her ballooning portrait—though maintaining a pose for more than an hour was never enjoyable work—or the fact that Adam bore her company, relating wildly implausible tales to help pass the tedium of the time?

While Adam and Lady Clementina made their way out to the lawn, Kat hurried to the conservatory where she had left everything. She would be getting very close to finishing soon, she realized, looking at the canvas as she picked it up. Just as well. She wanted her mind as free as possible for when she started her next painting of balloons—and whatever dangerous secrets their lines might reveal.

As she grabbed her portable easel, a sound from behind startled her. She started to spin about, her easel slipping from her grasp as she found herself caught in a strong arm. A scent of bay rum just touched her as the assailant dragged her against himself. Graeme's bewhiskered cheek brushed across her face as his mouth sought hers.

Her senses overpowered her; for a moment she clung, mindless, aware only of the wild disruption he created in her. Then he relaxed his hold, his hands lightly clasped about her waist as he gazed down on her. A chuckle sounded in his throat, uncertain at first, then richening to that of a man who knew what he wanted.

His fingers caressed upward. "You're right," he said. "I can still be impulsive, can't I?" He bent, brushed her lips lingeringly, touched her cheek with one finger, and limped out of the room.

She stared after his retreating figure, even after the door closed blocking him from her view, while she tried to recover. "Not bad for a start," she said, and grinned. Joy welled in her, and she sensed at once that he shared it. "Life," she murmured, "goes on."

On. But from what point? Now—or the time to which she was born? She collected her easel from where it had fallen on the floor and redistributed the other things she carried. She was here for a purpose, to prevent whatever disaster reshaped history as she knew it. But what about *after* that? Would she and her father just hop back into the dragon basket and float away home? Or was *this* home, now?

She started for the door. Here. For the rest of her life. Everything she knew, gone, irrevocably. Her family, her apartment, her friends, the gallery where she showed her paintings, the park where she fed the migrating ducks . . .

She could feed swans here, a little voice whispered in her mind. And here she had Graeme.

He tied her to this time; this unfathomable link they shared held her. And she wanted, she realized, to stay with him. She loved him. And wherever—or *whenever*—he was, she'd make a life for herself.

Contentment filled her, the certainty of making the

right choice. She could be very happy in this time, in this place. As long as she had Graeme.

But what about her father? He hadn't lost all things aeronautical, but wouldn't the lack of familiar technology grate on him? Had she gained her happiness at the cost of his? She walked on, once more uncertain.

As she crossed the lawn, she became aware of Adam and Lady Clementina at the balloon already. She blinked, bringing herself back to her current surroundings, and noted their good-natured combative stances. Arguing again, she supposed. From the few words that reached her, it sounded as if the relative merits of hot air and hydrogen once again came under discussion. The volume of the disagreement dropped, but the way her father leaned forward, an unmistakable gleam in his eye, alerted Kat. She quickened her step.

". . . race across the Channel," Lady Clementina pronounced with triumph as Kat neared.

Kat glared at her father, whose delighted expression was all she needed for interpreting the cryptic words. "Unfair advantage for her," Kat pointed out. "Make the trip together, first, Dad. Remember, she's made the crossing before. You haven't."

He straightened, the picture of indignation except for the enjoyment in his eyes. "What, do you think I'd end up in Copenhagen instead of Calais?"

"I think you'd be flying minus a few things you're accustomed to. Remember what you used to tell me about experienced help?"

"You were ten at the time!" he protested.

"Remember what happened the last time we set off without our own instruments."

That sobered him. In silence—a rare occurrence for him—he helped her set up.

It wasn't easy, concentrating on the portrait that morning. Amusement kept rippling through her, as if she were astounded to find she were alive. Graeme, stretching his wings, discovering life could be more than the circumscribed prison in which he had been living.

Her own worries couldn't compete. Happiness filled her again, intensified at once by his sharing of it. Pity she couldn't send him actual worded messages; she'd tell him to leave her alone until she finished this, or she wouldn't answer for the consequences in the finished product. At the rate she went, Lady Clementina would develop a knowing smile that would put the *Mona Lisa* to shame.

They had barely finished the session when an all-too familiar phaeton bowled up the drive at an impressive rate. Lady Clementina, who had abandoned her pose by the basket to examine Kat's work, frowned. "Lord Uxbridge, if I'm not mistaken. That should put Graeme in a foul mood."

"Shall we head 'em off at the pass?" Adam slid his hand under Lady Clementina's elbow. "Let's get this posse rolling," he said and led her off.

Kat grinned and rinsed out her brush in the jar of paint thinner. Maybe she shouldn't worry about her old dad, after all. She'd never met anyone more capable of taking in his stride whatever came at him. If they stayed here much longer, he'd set up a workshop in a barn and start reinventing things.

Better she should worry about Uxbridge. He must be coming in response to Graeme's message about changing the venue for the conference. And from the looks of him, he was none too pleased.

She wiped the brush on a cloth, then set it on end in a jar. She should probably stay away and let Graeme handle this on his own. The sight of her had never yet been known to have any calming influence on the assistant Foreign Secretary. For a minute she contemplated barging in on this meeting—she'd enjoy it even if no one else did—but couldn't think of an excuse. If only—

Her grin widened into one of unholy glee. Abandoning her painting things, she ran for the house. Breathless and full of mischief, she located her father and Lady Clementina in the library. Graeme and Uxbridge were nowhere in sight.

"You missed them," Adam informed her. "Gone to the study." He sounded indignant.

Kat nodded. "Thought they would."

"We weren't invited," Lady Clementina informed her.

Adam studied Kat, and the corners of his eyes crinkled with amused anticipation. "What are you planning, Kitten?"

"A job. Lady Clementina, I hereby apply for the position of assistant hostess."

The lady, no slowtop, regarded her with enjoyment. "Certainly. I suppose you wish to start at once? But Uxbridge made it very clear he didn't want me party to their discussion."

Kat lowered her gaze with mock demureness. "He didn't make it plain to *me*. I can go in all innocence."

Her loving father snorted.

Kat threw him a mischievous glance. "You're just

jealous you didn't think of it. By the way, I haven't seen you, so you couldn't warn me to stay away." With that, she slipped from the room and hurried along the corridor to Graeme's private study.

At the closed door she paused, smoothed her gown over her numerous petticoats, adjusted her expression into one of serious concern, then berated herself for forgetting a notebook. Oh, well, she'd improvise. She knocked briskly, then entered at once.

Graeme stood with his back to the window behind the huge mahogany desk, his expression stony. Uxbridge stood at his side, his complexion darkened. Both glared at Kat.

She strode forward with a reassuring rustle of her skirts. It helped, when facing down a stuffed shirt, to be dressed to the nines. She stopped at the desk, selected a pencil and paper, then faced them with a confident smile. "I'm ready for your instructions." She directed a prim, professional smile at Uxbridge.

He glared at her. "Get out."

"Nonsense. Did Lady Clementina not tell you? I have accepted the post of her secretary, and it is her express wish that I assist you with this difficult task that has been thrust upon us all. Such a dreadful upheaval, having to change the location of the conference. But I admire you for putting the safety of the delegates above all." She even managed that last with an almost completely straight face.

Graeme's sudden repressed laughter rippled through her. She avoided looking at him—she would have collapsed in a fit of giggles if she'd caught his eye.

Uxbridge glowered at her, but his fury faded from

full boil to simmer. "My dear Miss Sayre—" he began stiffly.

She lowered her lashes in the merest hint of a flutter. "I assure you, we are every one of us taking this terrible rumor seriously."

He rounded on Graeme. "Yes, this 'rumor.' You have yet to tell me where you heard it. I told you I want explanations, and I meant it. This—this outrage had better be justified, Warwick, I warn you. The office has enough problems already without responding to wild tales. What you are suggesting is a—a complete overturning of everything we have arranged!"

"Not at all." Graeme's voice sounded soothing, confident. "Everything will take place exactly as planned. Except here there will be more scope for entertainment."

"Which is where Lady Clementina and I come in. We take charge of the ladies of the party. You know, picnics, teas, walks in the gardens—" She bit back mention of boating on the lake. After what happened to Sir Francis, it seemed hardly politic.

"There is a measure of informality and relaxation in the country," Graeme added, "that is not to be found in London."

Uxbridge still glowered at him from beneath bushy eyebrows. *"Where* did you hear this rumor about sabotaging the conference?"

For a moment, Graeme and Kat stared at one another while inspiration failed. Graeme recovered first. "It was something Sir Francis said when he heard of the theft of the bombs."

"Sir Francis." Uxbridge's hands clenched. "Sir Francis," he repeated, softer. "I see." He shot Graeme a suddenly suspicious glance. "Why didn't you mention it before?"

"It didn't make sense at the time. It does now, since I've had time to think about it and remember other things he said." Graeme limped to the small table that held the decanters and poured Uxbridge and himself brandies.

The assistant Foreign Secretary drained half of his in one gulp. "The bombs," he said slowly, "are part of the plot to abduct Prince Albert."

"Are they, sir?" Graeme swirled the deep amber liquid in his glass.

Lord Uxbridge's gaze flew to meet his. "He gave you reason to suspect otherwise? I see." His tone held a note of comprehension. He finished the brandy and stared at the empty glass for a moment. "Very well. We will change the venue. Miss Sayre—" he turned to her with a curt nod "—you will have your work cut out for you. These delegates must be kept safe at all costs—but they must never suspect the possibility of danger."

She met his gaze steadily. "I believe I can guess the enormity of what's at stake."

"Can you?" He regarded her skeptically. "Just bear it in mind." He turned back to Graeme. "We have already installed the Italian minister at Sevington House. I suggest you prepare rooms for his party at once." With a curt nod, he strode from the study.

"It would help," Kat commented, "if he would tell us how many."

Graeme shook his head. "Prepare every room," he advised, and started after his superior. At the door, he turned back. "Do you have any idea what you have just taken on?"

Her grin slipped awry. "About as much idea as Uxbridge has of the disaster hanging over us. None at all."

Chapter Sixteen

Fifteen minutes later, Kat sat in her chair, awed as Lady Clementina issued rapid orders to Mrs. Erling. The housekeeper merely listened without taking notes, hands clasped before her, her expression abstracted.

When Lady Clementina finished, Mrs. Erling nodded. "We'll need four more maids, three additional footmen for serving, two tweenies and—" she considered a moment "—three scullions and a pastry chef, m'lady."

"You may choose from the list Whitehall has provided." Lady Clementina handed her the sheaf of menus. "Have Cook look these over and let you know what she needs. And Newcombe," she rounded on the butler, who had remained quietly in the background, "a ball is scheduled for three days hence. You'd best begin preparations at once. I'll let you know when we've decided on a decor."

"Very good, m'lady." Newcombe bowed, then crossed to the door which he held open for the housekeeper to exit before him.

Kat blinked at her hostess. "As easy as that?"

Lady Clementina laughed. "The plans have all been made. We have only to move it all here. My staff can work wonders. Now we have only to await the first arrivals."

They didn't have long. By mid-afternoon, a formal procession of traveling carriages pulled up the drive. Kat, from her position by the conservatory windows where she set her newly primed canvas to dry, watched with interest as the three vehicles, each pulled by four horses despite the shortness of the journey from London, proceeded around the curve leading to the front door.

Whom had Lord Uxbridge said had arrived already at Sevington House? The Italian minister and his party? How many, she wondered, eyeing the baggage strapped on the vehicles, did that include?

Italy in 1851 . . . an uneasy sensation crept over her. Rats, she knew absolutely *nothing* about what was going on there either socially or politically. At least she could talk about art knowledgeably—provided the subject interested anyone in the party. If not, she was in trouble.

If only she'd gone back to Renaissance times. Now *that* was an era with which she could cope. But that would be a time without Graeme.

Graeme. She closed her eyes. He awaited his guests in the front salon, she realized. Determination seemed to be his prevailing mood. Determination touched by—could that be amusement?

Amusement. *Why?* Fascinated—delighted by this change in his outlook—she cleaned her painting supplies, put them away, then pulled off the makeshift smock she wore to protect her gown. Wrinkles everywhere, she noted in dismay. Again. At home, she wouldn't have minded that much. At home, she could have changed clothes. Here, she had only this one gown for day and one other for dinner.

She fought an impulse to run upstairs and drag on her jeans and sweater, to wear something familiar, something of her own. Something comfortable that didn't involve thirty pounds of petticoats. She'd look ridiculous and out of place if she did, though. Oh, rats, it was worse than that. She'd *feel* out of place.

There was no help for it, she needed more dresses. She drew a deep breath. She couldn't ask Lady Clementina for any money; the portrait was meant as a present, a thank you for room, board, and the clothes Kat and her father already wore. That—and friendship. Perhaps her hostess could recommend other people from whom she could get commissions.

She didn't need much, just enough to purchase some material. She'd always been good at sewing. She could piece different parts from different patterns together—provided she could get her hands on patterns.

She cast a considering glance at the wide bell of her skirts, the full material of her sleeves, the fancy tuckwork of the bodice. So many seams, so much fitting, so much everything. For a long moment she thought wistfully of the sewing machine she'd seen at the Exhibition—the first treadle model. She could use that—if she could get to it. But without it—

If she had money, she could hire a seamstress to help her, someone like the maid Middy. The copies the woman had made of Kat's bra and bikinis were almost perfect, considering the change in materials. Even major alterations hadn't daunted her.

A deep sigh escaped her. Just this once, she'd like to look fresh, beautiful. That seemed to be the principal job of ladies of leisure at this time. And here she was, looking more and more rumpled every day, not knowing how to make the best of her hair or her lack of makeup or shawls or gloves . . .

She frowned. That wasn't like her. What made her so aware of her appearance, as if—as if she saw herself through the eyes of someone else. Graeme.

The Italian delegate, she realized, had brought a very decorative female with his party.

Anger surged in her, that Graeme should be admiring this woman, whoever she was—and that apparently he compared Kat to her and found Kat wanting. And there would be a ball in three days' time, and she would have nothing suitable to wear, and he would see once more how far she came from fitting into his world, how unsuitable she was for a man in his position.

She closed her eyes. Right now, she just wanted to go *home*. Except home might be the one place she could never go again.

Leaving her paints where they were, she hurried along the hall, not stopping at the salon from which she could hear Graeme's deep tones. Did he talk with that Italian woman, whoever she was? Kat would meet her later—when she regained the confidence of knowing she looked her best. She mounted the steps two at a time, then ran along the hall to her bedroom. She went straight to her mirror and studied her reflection.

Definitely room for improvement. Still, not quite a hopeless case, either. Time to call in reinforcements. She pulled the bell rope, then set about unfastening the gown. She needed to indulge in a little ironing—and more importantly, in a bit of picking Middy's brains for ways to make herself look different—and maybe just a bit fashionable.

She didn't go downstairs again until the gong sounded to gather for dinner. She wore—once more—the green silk, though now white lace fell from the points of her shoulders almost to her elbows and came to a low point in the front. A bow in darker green pulled up the top skirt on one side, revealing a newly borrowed white silk underskirt. If only she could change the color of the dress.

She entered the sitting room with a certain amount of trepidation, and found several strangers turning to look at her. With ease, she identified the lovely black-haired woman Graeme must have been admiring earlier. Kat admired her, herself—though not willingly. Her gown, quite simply, was the most beautiful thing she had ever seen. Of pale blue, the skirt boasted a single deep flounce edged in wide lace. The same lace trimmed the neckline, falling over belled-sleeves that ended in lace cuffs. Her ivory complexion Kat would kill for—if she weren't above such petty thoughts, of course.

"Come in, Kat. Don't just stand in the doorway," her father called.

She flushed, her discomfiture complete. She threw him a fulminating glare, met the sparkle dancing in his eyes, and realized he had done it on purpose. Funny. Real funny.

"Come, my dear." Lady Clementina rose in a rustle of purple satin. "Let me introduce you. I have been telling everyone so much about you."

Not much that was true, Kat wagered. She pinned on her gallery-opening-meet-the-public smile and came forward.

The party, as she expected, were the Italians. She didn't catch everyone's names as she was introduced to the two men and the one woman. The Italian minister's daughter, she gathered. Antonia something. Di Fiorelli, maybe. She found it hard to concentrate.

Uxbridge, who sat beside Henri-Phillipe de Loire, kept his steady gaze on her, driving her slowly up the wall. Was he concocting a new scheme to get rid of her? And why—and how—did Graeme hold himself aloof from her?

Then his mind touched hers in the gentlest of caresses and she turned to gaze directly into his eyes. She could lose herself in their smoky depths. Awareness tingled through her, a spark that fanned to a flame of desire, of longing to run her fingers through his waves of dark blond hair, to feel his hands touching her, eliciting the wild response that only he evoked . . .

She looked away at once, not daring to continue the contact. It became too intense, too all-consuming. She played with wildfire, and in another moment, if she weren't careful, everyone in the room would see the blaze.

"Miss Sayre." A grudging note sounded in Lord Uxbridge's voice. "I have seen the portrait you are doing of Lady Clementina. I must say I am impressed."

Kat looked at him, startled. "Thank you," she managed. What did he want? She sensed, again, Graeme's amusement, and her curiosity increased.

Uxbridge cleared his throat. "Our conference, as

you know," he began in pompous style, "will be a turning point in history. It has long been on my mind that we should commemorate the event for the sake of posterity. Never before has the world witnessed such a coming together of nations for mutual benefit. The occasion calls for—nay, demands!—a memorial worthy of it." He nodded his head. "You, my dear Miss Sayre, will paint this masterpiece."

"I will?" There was something about the inflection in his voice she didn't quite like.

Lord Uxbridge unbent enough to award her a condescending smile. "As you know, it is of the utmost importance to maintain secrecy surrounding the event until it is finished. To bring in an outsider at this stage, I fear, would be to threaten our security. You already know of the conference. You are here. And as you are an American with no other acquaintance in our country, no one unconnected with the conference is likely to ask you any questions you would not be able to answer. It is to be regretted, of course, that you are not an established artist with a prestigious reputation, but I suppose that cannot be helped."

She fought back a laugh at his tone, and realized Graeme's amusement enhanced her own. She managed a solemn expression. "I am honored to be chosen." Though in a field of one, the competition hadn't been very stiff.

Uxbridge inclined his head, as if he hadn't for a moment expected any other answer. "I believe the best pose will be of the delegates seated about a long table, pens in hand, awaiting their turns to sign the treaties."

Kat nodded. "Very appropriate for the situation." And very unimaginative.

"You will be releasing funds at once, I believe you said," Graeme interjected.

His expression remained serious, but Kat sensed his continued amusement. He'd planned this! she realized. He must have picked up her concern over money that afternoon, her need for a commission, and arranged it.

She looked toward him, but he refused to meet her gaze. Warmth enveloped her, as gentle and comforting as a cashmere shawl. Or the down comforter under which they had lain entangled together last night— heat flamed in her cheeks as she experienced his reaction to that memory.

Abruptly he strode to the sideboard and poured a glass of pale yellow liquid. He handed it to her, avoiding so much as touching her fingers as she took it from him. Just as well; it would be too easy to revel in the sensations caused by any physical contact with him. That was best kept for private, for later, when they could be alone to explore this new dimension of the bond that joined them so completely.

The Italians, Kat soon discovered, spoke excellent English. Aside from a measure of rivalry that appeared to exist between *Madame* de Loire and *Signorina* di Fiorelli, dinner passed smoothly. Kat noticed little of it as her thoughts flitted between Graeme and her future.

A government commission sounded like an excellent way to establish herself in this time. For a woman, it was unheard of. But it gave her a chance, a *real* chance, to earn a living. She and her father would have to find somewhere to live—they couldn't keep imposing on Lady Clementina. But perhaps there might be a cottage on or near the estate they could rent. She wouldn't mind an excuse to remain near Graeme.

She avoided any thoughts on where their relationship might lead. He'd sense it and might feel pursued. For that matter, she wasn't ready to think beyond the next few days herself. With the advance she'd receive, she could buy both herself and her father some clothes.

Her thoughts drifted happily. She might well be on her way to starting a new life—except she'd been very happy in her old one. She'd had everything—except Graeme.

Kat awoke from her reverie to realize the Italian delegate, who sat on her left, had addressed her.

He watched her, his precise little mustache atwitch. "Do you not think so?" he asked. "That a ball at Durham Court will be most delightful?"

Kat smiled. "I hope all the necessary preparations won't disturb you. I'm afraid the servants will have their hands full."

He waved that aside. "My daughter will be in her element, we will have to hold a tight rein on her."

"Pappa," the *signorina* protested with a laughing shake of her smooth dark hair. "You will not speak of me in such a way. You will enjoy this ball very much."

He inclined his head, his eyes gleaming. "If the *Signorina* Sayre will honor me with a dance, how can this ball be anything but perfect?"

Antonia di Fiorelli eyed Kat, then shrugged expressive shoulders.

Henri-Phillipe de Loire's smile slipped away. "A ball is but naturally of the most delightful for the ladies, *cela va sans dire.* One must do one's duty."

Lady Clementina raised one arched eyebrow.

"Never fear, we shall provide something more to your liking, as well. Outdoor entertainment," she promised.

His eyes brightened. "Perhaps you might show me that so-delightful balloon?"

Lady Clementina stared at him, then spun to face Adam. "Mr. Sayre, do you think we might organize a balloon ascension? Nothing extravagant, of course, but perhaps we could take up any of the delegates who might like to try it?"

"An idea of the most inspired!" De Loire beamed at her. *"Madame,* I kiss my fingers to you."

Delighted anticipation surged through Kat, only to be dimmed the next moment by a sharp pang of disappointment. For a moment the conflicting sensations buffeted her, then she looked directly at Graeme, at his expression of longing, and pinned down the unhappiness. He'd have to act as host, stay on the ground, when all he wanted was to float away in freedom . . .

"Pappa, you will not go up in this contraption," Antonia di Fiorelli announced. "It is not a thing you would enjoy."

"I would." Henri-Phillipe inclined his head toward Kat. *"Mademoiselle,* will you do me the honor of taking me up with you?"

Kat glanced down the table. "And your wife?"

Mme. de Loire shrugged her shoulders. "Balloons—they are of no interest. Me, I shall find something else to do, something *forte amusant."* Her glance slid sideways beneath half-lowered lids, and she eyed the young gentleman who served as assistant to the Italian delegate. The next moment it moved on to Graeme in a blatant invitation.

Kat stiffened, and to her outrage a sense of amusement rippled through her. Graeme enjoyed the French woman's flirtation, did he? More, she realized the next moment, than he enjoyed watching the woman's husband's advances toward herself.

Hot color touched her cheeks as she met Graeme's burning gaze. A wave of pure desire flooded through her, intense, pounding back and forth between them until she couldn't differentiate between his need and hers. She wrenched her gaze away. Not now, not with so many other people about. Not until they could be alone to talk . . . and so much more.

The rest of the evening strained her acting abilities to the fullest. She only wanted to escape, to be alone to think, to plan, to dream just a little. Instead, she had to sit in feigned appreciation as the *signorina* pounded out sonata after prelude after waltz on the piano.

The gentlemen, she noted in irritation, sat in low-voiced conversation on the opposite side of the room, ostensibly discussing the upcoming conference. An occasional hastily concealed laugh assured Kat they were having much more fun than she. At least it kept Graeme away, kept him from playing havoc with her senses.

She excused herself early and sought the solitude of her room. For a long moment she stood in the center of the chamber, unsure what to do next. She wasn't really tired. She should probably make out a list of what she'd need for her commissioned painting. Canvas, wood—and she'd better get some of those powdered paints. Why couldn't she have landed in a time when oils already came in neat little tubes?

The list complete, she set about making another,

itemizing in one column the various garments she would have to purchase and in another the ones she would rather make. The jokes she'd heard in her own time about Victorian women not needing closets because they wore the entire contents every day didn't seem so funny any more. With a sigh, she turned down the gas lamp at her writing desk and went to enjoy the pleasures offered by the enormous bathroom across the hall.

After a relaxing soak in steaming, scented water, she donned her borrowed dressing gown and returned to her room. Snuggled beneath her down comforter, she drifted between waking and sleeping, half-hearing the sounds of the others settling down for the night. The closing of the door next to hers brought her momentarily alert, but thanks to the thick walls, no sounds of the occupant's moving about disturbed her. Only the murmur of voices saying good night in the hall, the soft shutting of doors, hushed footsteps along the thick carpeting of the corridor. . .

She stirred, rising back toward consciousness as longing and desire seeped through her. Graeme. The soft shushing sound of fabric against fabric reached her, followed by the rubbing of a slippered sole on the rug, announcing his presence. Satin whispered as it slid away, and Kat pulled back the covers, welcoming him with a need that overpowered her.

"I couldn't keep away," he murmured as he drew her into his arms.

She buried her face in his shoulder; a faint scent of bay rum clung to his skin, familiar and welcome. It was part of him, like those bristly side whiskers or the heavy emerald ring, or . . .

Conscious thought ebbed as sensation took over, and she abandoned herself to the all-encompassing love that only he could provide.

It didn't seem possible Kat could feel so damned vulnerable. She huddled in the pre-dawn darkness amid the disordered covers, empty and alone as the door closed softly behind Graeme's retreating figure. He'd slipped away as if their being together were cheap and tawdry and something of which to be ashamed.

Wretched, longing for his presence, she cradled the pillow that still smelled faintly of bay rum. She wanted Graeme with her in the morning light, to see his lazy smile as he awakened and remembered what they had shared hours before. She wanted him to reach for her again—just to jog his memory, of course—and know herself loved and cherished.

A touch of caring caressed her mind, a promise of togetherness, of love, melting the ache from her heart. Their link.

Not alone. Never alone. Always loved.

The next day passed with the arrival of the delegates and their entourages—the translators, the secretaries, the assistants, the personal servants. Kat watched from a distance as carriage after carriage pulled into the drive and the passengers descended. Luggage piled high by the door, waiting to be carried into the main hall for sorting.

Idly, from her bench on the lawn, Kat sketched a caricature of the scene, complete with swaggering dele-

gates, sycophantic assistants, *grande dames,* and footmen bent double under their loads of trunks. A far
more appropriate memorial of the conference than the
formal treaty-signing piece Lord Uxbridge envisioned.
For a moment she contemplated giving it to him, then
grinned. It had better go into a fire as soon as possible,
before anyone saw it.

Her father, she noted with surprise, had abandoned
his watch over the filling balloons. Four of the mon-
sters there would be for the morrow—provided they
could generate enough hydrogen gas by then to get
them all into the air. They'd been at it since last
night—and Lady Clementina's had never been fully
deflated. Graeme's though, would probably remain
tethered to the ground while his duties as host kept
him earth-bound as well.

Now, Adam seemed to have appointed himself the
welcoming committee. He stood at the door like a
proud host, beaming on each new arrival, undoubtedly charming the ladies even if he couldn't speak a
word of their language. Kat added him to the sketch.
Of Graeme she'd seen a great deal—and all too little.
He seemed to be everywhere, managing everything,
redirecting servants with no more than a gesture of
hand or head.

Vivienne de Loire and the *Signorina* di Fiorelli
emerged from the library onto the terrace. Kat's eyebrows rose in surprise at these unlikely companions.
Then Ellesmere emerged after them, offering each an
arm. As a threesome they strolled toward the path—
toward her, Kat realized.

She ripped her satirical sketch from her pad, folded
it, and shoved it away out of site between the other

pages. By the time the party reached her, she worked diligently on a drawing of Bartholomew Reed ostensibly at work on a bed of roses. From where he knelt among the thorny bushes, he could keep the delegates under close observation and never draw anyone's attention. Graeme, she remembered, had suggested that position to him.

Her gaze narrowed, considering. Graeme didn't fully trust the man. But at the moment, Graeme didn't trust anyone. Sir Francis's death, viscount Ellesmere's so-called drugging—no, she couldn't blame him at all for being suspicious.

She sighed and rose. She had best work on her secret painting. By this time tomorrow, the last of the delegates should have arrived. Time might very well be running out.

She didn't see Graeme again until she entered the salon where the dignitaries gathered before dinner. He stood by the marble-topped table, decanter in hand, pouring drinks with a smile pinned to his tired features. Kat slipped into the back of the room, behind a knot of unfamiliar people who conversed in French—a language she could read but knew better than to try to speak.

After a minute wasted trying to catch any familiar word, she abandoned the attempt and instead concentrated on Graeme, sending him soothing images of tranquillity and love. He looked up, met her gaze, and the warmth of his expression assured her he'd gotten her message.

Dinner passed in a babble of foreign voices. Graeme, at the head of the table, kept up a constant flow of conversation. The gentleman on Kat's right—the delegate from Belgium, she knew, but his name escaped her—questioned her in labored English about every detail of the painting for which they would all pose. She maintained her smile as she answered, but as soon as Lady Clementina led the ladies from the room, Kat pleaded a headache and retired to her chamber.

Would Graeme even be able to come? she wondered as she prepared for bed. Probably he would be kept talking half the night. Unless her father heralded the early hour of the ascension scheduled for the morning and herded everyone to their rooms. Good old Dad, she reflected as she curled beneath her comforter with a book. She'd count on him.

She read until her eyes would no longer focus, then turned down her lamp and settled herself for sleep. It was well past midnight, she saw, and she hadn't heard anyone come upstairs yet. So much for her father's good efforts.

The creak of the mattress as someone sat on it awakened her some while later. She moved over, reaching for Graeme at the same time, drawing him down against her. "You're getting good at this," she whispered against his neck as she settled on his shoulder. "I didn't hear you come in."

He made no answer, merely rubbing his whiskered cheek on her hair. Or did he make himself comfortable on the pillow? She snuggled against him, warming him, but he made no response. She tilted her head back. "Graeme?" she tried.

Only his deeper breathing answered her. A smile, half regret and all love, tugged at the corners of her mouth, and she kissed his throat. He had come, as tired as he was, to be with her. That spoke for the closeness of their bond more surely than did their previous two nights.

Just before dawn, she stirred, realized the time, and kissed him until he stretched and muttered with returning consciousness. A protest at being disturbed, she reflected, and rubbed her hand across the satin chest of the dressing gown he hadn't removed the night before. "Time to get up." She kissed him again.

He reached for her, drawing her closer, and went back to sleep.

She held him, sensing only exhaustion. It was tempting to let him remain, sleep as long as he could—but he'd never forgive himself. Ruthlessly, she dragged back the covers.

He groaned, groped for them, then at last opened his eyes. "Unkind," he muttered.

She sat up, cross-legged, and wrapped her share about herself. "It's now or never if you want to get back to your own room without getting caught."

He hesitated, and longing seeped through her. She leaned forward, touched his cheek and kissed him lightly. "Go, while I'll still let you."

He caught her to him, then released her with reluctance. "I'll see you at breakfast."

"I'll be with the balloons."

"I'll join you if I can." And with that, he was gone.

An hour later, Kat stood on the grass and shivered in the fresh, chill morning. Her breath came out in puffs, hovered in the rose-scented air before her, then dissipated. Floating away, as she would in only a few minutes. She hugged herself, eager for the flight, wishing only that Graeme might escape with her. This morning, though, she would serve as pilot for Henri-

Phillipe de Loire and any other delegate brave enough
to commit his safety to a woman.

Adam strolled over and draped an arm about her
shoulders. "Where'd you get to last night?"

"Tired." She yawned, then grinned. "How many'd
you talk into going up?"

"Eleven. Four delegates, six assistants or secretaries
or whatever they are, and one wife."

"Not Madame de Loire, I'll wager."

Adam chuckled. "The mousy little one from
Austria. Can't remember her name. Promised her we'd
keep a tether to the ground."

"Oh, no." Kat glared at her father. "You're dump-
ing her on me, aren't you?"

He had the grace to look a trifle sheepish. "Couldn't
ask Lady Clemmy to stay tied up, could I?"

"And I suppose the men didn't trust themselves
flying free with me?" she demanded.

He ruffled her hair. "You still have de Loire, the old
goat."

"Gee, thanks. Do they know how early they have to
get up?"

He nodded. "That's why Ellesmere isn't coming."

She laughed. "Thank heavens for that. Here comes
Reed. Let's get everything rigged."

Preparations took less time than gathering their
eager—and somewhat nervous—passengers. At last,
Lady Clementina, resplendent in her split skirt,
climbed into her basket with three of the assistants.
Adam took the three delegates with him, and the language barriers seemed to be nonexistent. Kat watched
them loose their tethers and rise slowly into the air.

"Mon dieu." Vivienne de Loire moved forward, gaz-

ing upward as the baskets lifted above their heads, then climbed toward the sky. "You will entrust yourself to such a thing?" she demanded of her husband.

"So—so thrilling," a rather plain little woman breathed in a heavy German accent. She clasped her hands before her. *"Fraulein* Sayre, me you will take up—but still to the ground we are fastened?"

Kat roused herself and headed to the third balloon. It seemed a shame to leave the dragon crouching there all alone. She'd much rather take it—except last time she went for a short flight in it, it took a lot longer than she'd expected. Or did she mean a lot less time—like nearly a hundred and forty years less?

She checked with Reed who stood by the plain wicker basket, then climbed in and turned to assist the little Austrian woman and the two uncertain young men who would accompany her. "A hundred feet," she told Reed.

He nodded. "Raise your hand if you want more, Miss. Or lower it if you want to come down."

She didn't get a chance to raise her hand. As the basket lifted from the ground, her passengers clung to the side, one man white-faced, the other simply looking ill. The woman repeated something over and over in German, which Kat took to be a prayer. Even before they reached their allowed height, she gave up and signaled for a descent, and an audible sigh of relief sounded from one of her companions as they returned to earth.

They were met as they touched down by an eager crowd, led by Antonia di Fiorelli. The girl's eyes gleamed with determination. "I will go up," she announced. "And Pappa, you will come with me. Will no one else? No?"

"Vraiment, they are cowards." Vivienne de Loire swept forward. *"Mon* Henri-Phillipe, I shall test it for you, *n'est ce pas?"*

Another load of people who wanted to just hang in the sky. Kat's gaze drifted toward the rapidly disappearing balloons. Already the carriages followed in pursuit, ready to help the aeronauts when they finally returned to earth. Kat had hoped to be after them this trip, taking M. de Loire.

She stifled her disappointment. Not long. Not much longer.

These three proved braver than the last. At Antonia's demand, they rose an additional fifty feet, then stayed there for several minutes. Rather than looking over the edge, Vivienne de Loire explored the basket, exclaiming over everything. Antonia's father, at his most charming, joined in her examination of every valve and hook. It dawned on Kat that the two were less interested in ballooning than in dalliance.

So that explained the Frenchwoman's change of heart about going up. She signaled for a descent, and in a few minutes Antonia climbed out, proclaiming her own bravery in venturing so high into the sky. The other two, heads still close together, followed.

"And now, *ma cherie,* you are mine." Henri-Phillipe de Loire stepped forward and bowed over Kat's hand with an elegant grace. He seemed oblivious to his wife's flirtatious behavior—in fact, he seemed bent on emulating it.

Reed frowned. "You aren't really going to cut this loose, are you, Miss?"

"I'm not going to stay staked to the ground," Kat informed him. "And you needn't worry. I've been handling these things since I could walk." Of course, she preferred propane and had only flown hydrogen balloons a few times, but she'd gone over this antiquated equipment under her father's eagle eye. She'd manage—in spite of her cumbersome skirts.

Reed pursed his lips, then loosened the rope. At once the balloon lifted from the ground, and Henri-Phillipe hung over the side, waving smugly to the onlookers. Then Reed released his hold on them and they soared upward, higher, toward freedom.

She looked to where she had seen the other two balloons disappear, but they had vanished in the distance. They would drift alone—except for the carriage that headed for the road below them. About a hundred feet below them, she guessed.

She glanced at her passenger; he still leaned over the side, his expression one of childlike delight. She grinned, and felt the tension ease from her shoulders and arms. The others, she realized, had infected her with their nerves. It was sheer joy to fly with someone as thrilled as she.

She reached up and gave a testing tug on the release valve, and her smile faded. Stuck. She tried again, then a third time, harder. The sharpest tug on the rope produced no results. They continued to rise—with no way of controlling their progress.

She swallowed, watching the trees grow smaller and smaller, and fought back a rising panic. She'd figure this out. She'd had problems before. What was stuck could be unstuck—with a bit of effort. She had only to—

An eerie creak sounded, and the hook beside her—one of only four holding the basket to the bag—snapped. M. de Loire spun about, catching his balance as the corner sagged. He stared in speechless horror at it, then at Kat.

"It won't—" she began.

Another creak interrupted her, this time from the corner behind her passenger. She lunged toward him, grasping his arm as the hook pulled loose from the wicker. He caught the rim of the basket, clinging to it for his very life as the basket dangled, precariously supported by only one side.

Chapter Seventeen

Sabotage, the thought flashed through Kat's mind. Sabotage. This couldn't be a streak of uncanny accidents. Someone was out to kill de Loire—to destroy the conference.

She clung to the basket, fighting her panic. She had to think straight, she had to act swiftly, before a third hook broke free. She forced that thought from her mind. At the moment, de Loire's grip seemed to be holding. Keeping one arm wrapped about the wicker, Kat reached for the rope hanging from the balloon. Almost . . .

Her fingers brushed the rough fibers, then closed about them. "Got to . . . tie this," she gasped ". . . around you."

He stared at her, eyes blank with shock. She'd have to do it for him. Herself, first, though, to free her hands. She twisted, wrapping the line behind her, then she had the end in front again. Her arms ached, she needed both hands, the end was way too long to pull through to secure a knot. . . . She managed to form it into a loop, which gave her a short end.

Why had she never studied one-handed tying techniques? the hysterical thought rose in her mind. The best she could manage was a granny—but a very solid one. She eased her weight from her left arm, felt herself drop a few inches with a sickening lurch, then she swung free beneath the balloon, dangling in the air.

Now for M. de Loire. He watched her in fascinated horror, repeating something she couldn't quite make out under his breath, over and over. She needed another rope for him. Gritting her teeth, she swung herself like a pendulum until she caught the second loose hanging end. With amazing fortitude for a gentleman of his years—perhaps recognizing his only hope—M. de Loire inched himself along the wicker toward her. If a third hook gave way . . .

She forced herself to concentrate on reaching Henri-Phillipe before his strength deserted him. Right now, nothing else mattered. One task. One simple task. One—

They'd done it. She flung the end of the rope about him and secured it with a fireman's knot. Still, he gripped the side of the basket. She couldn't blame him. But at least if the basket fell away, they'd stay with the balloon instead of plunging to the ground.

Why did Victorian women wear such heavy clothes? The weight of so many layers of petticoats dragged her down so the rope pinched about her ribs. How long could they stay like this? M. de Loire looked ill. Somehow, she had to free the valve, release some hydrogen, stop their progress, allow them to settle gently to the earth before the poor man suffered a heart attack. No way could she administer CPR in their current position.

Desperation seized her, followed the next moment by grim determination. Graeme. His emotions filled her, so strong they squeezed out her own panic. She didn't even need to look to know the dragon basket rose to give chase.

"Rescue is coming," she called, elated—and still terrified.

M. de Loire opened the eyes he had squeezed shut. They stared at her, dull and dark in the ashen face.

"Graeme—Captain Warwick. He's coming. In his balloon." Only now did she dare a glance downward. So far away. How could he catch them—unless she could break that valve free?

She released her hold on the wicker and twisted, trying to control the arc of her swing. It *had* to be possible. She *would* do it. Every positive thinking litany she had ever tried played through her mind as she tried again. And again. And—

She caught the dangling end of the cord, then swung back to the side of the basket. Step one complete. Now, how to wrench it open? She'd already pulled as hard as she could. There was one force, though, she hadn't tried.

Life with her father, she reflected as she eyed the rope that supported her, certainly prepared one for the unexpected. She couldn't use her legs, but she'd climbed using only her arms before. She hadn't been wearing half a ton of useless petticoats, though. She'd dump them—but for what she planned, she needed as much weight as possible.

She draped the valve release cord over her shoulder, then dragged herself up her rope, hand over hand, until her muscles screamed their agonized protest. She had to go higher . . . another hand . . . she was slipping . . . another six inches upward . . . another . . . another . . . just one more . . .

She braced herself, let go with her bottom hand and caught the cord for the release valve, then grabbed it with her other hand as well. Her stomach collided with her heart as she fell, then the valve brought her up short, snapping her to a standstill. For a moment she hung there, then with an audible crack the valve broke open and she dropped another six inches, only to be strangled about the ribs as her safety line took over. Hydrogen seeped out of the balloon, reducing its lift power.

Kat held her breath, waiting, not daring to look down for fear she would find they still rose—or worse, that they now plummeted toward the ground with no way to check their descent. Where was Graeme?

His fear for her hit her like a palpable force. She looked down, searching—he was so far away. They sank lower, hit a cross-draft, and angled back at a tangent. If Graeme could only find one that would bear him on an intercepting course! She clung to her line, wishing she could maneuver her balloon.

Graeme rose higher, above them now, seeking the right air current. Kat glanced at Henri-Phillipe's gray face, his trembling hands as he gripped the basket, his knuckles white, his eyes closed. At least the rope that encircled him held tight. How fast did they drop? She looked down, and the ground seemed to be coming toward them at an alarming rate.

They shifted direction again, this time moving toward Graeme. Kat caught her breath. If only she could hold them here. If only Graeme could speed up his approach. He was so far above them, now, but if he came lower he'd be blown in a different direction.

He'd never reach them in time, they dropped faster and faster now. Surely she hadn't come back through time, defying all known laws of logic and science, only to be killed in a ballooning accident! That could have happened in her own time. Or was it merely Henri-Phillipe de Loire who must die, and she, as his pilot, with him? No, she had to think positive. And Graeme was closer—*much* closer—but still too far above them.

Something dropped over the wicker dragon's side—a rope! Was it long enough? For that matter, could he bring it close enough for her to reach it? The line dangled in the air, perhaps thirty feet away and a good twenty feet above her.

And the distance increased by the moment. Another air current buffeted them, and she drifted farther from rescue. Then the rope lowered, its speed increasing, now coming nearer. Graeme must be releasing hydrogen at a dangerous rate. He must have his valve fully open, like hers. Yet it all seemed to happen in slow motion.

The rope end was level with her—but too far away to reach. Perhaps if he came lower he could toss it toward her. And she could swing herself out by perhaps ten feet. If both their aims were good, they might have a chance.

"*Monsieur* de Loire," she called.

He made no acknowledgment. He remained still

except for his lips, which moved rapidly. In prayer, she realized. She didn't blame him.

"Monsieur," she tried again.

This time his eyelids opened and he stared at her with a serenity she found startling.

"Captain Warwick is almost here."

He nodded, as if taking personal credit for this miracle. "The *bon Dieu* is watching over us," he pronounced, and returned to his prayers.

Kat added a few of her own.

When she opened her eyes again, the dragon greeted her, now a mere ten feet above them but a good sixty feet away. Graeme, his expression as tense as the emotions that swept through Kat, leaned over the edge, the coiled rope in his hands. One end he had securely knotted about one of the hooks supporting his basket.

"Ready?" he called.

Kat nodded. She had to be.

He cast, but the line fell short of her by a good fifteen feet. Kat bit her lip until she tasted blood. It seemed to take an eternity for him to draw in the end, coil it once more and throw again. This time it went too far to the left but only a few feet short.

Grim, he retrieved the line again. He threw, Kat swung herself forward, and the rope brushed her fingers, slipping through them. With an anguished cry of frustration, she watched it drop away. Next time . . .

Confidence nudged at the edges of her mind, determined if not wholly real. Graeme, trying to make her feel better. He must have interpreted her last reaction as despair.

"This time," he called, making it a promise. He couldn't disguise the very real fear for her that drove him.

Emotion welled in her throat, choking her, and tears prickled against her eyes. If their positions were reversed, if it were Graeme in danger. . . . How was it possible to love someone so completely?

They had drifted below him, now. Graeme reached to adjust his valve, but a contrary air current seized her balloon, carrying it off on a tangent, farther from rescue. Graeme lunged, throwing his line once more while he still had a chance, and pain exploded in Kat's mind. For a moment it paralyzed her, and the rope snaked past, overshooting her by several feet. He'd hurt himself . . . he couldn't throw again . . . she *hurt* . . .

No! She rejected the pain and swung herself in the opposite direction. The backlash carried her into the path of the returning line. The rope landed on her arm, slid to her wrist, and she captured it firmly in both hands.

Exultation swept through her, and she found herself laughing with tears streaming down her cheeks. But Graeme—only pain reached her. His knee. What had that last, saving throw cost him?

She turned her attention to the more pressing matter of securing the two balloons together. If only she could pull them close enough so she and M. de Loire could transfer to the dragon basket—and she could be with Graeme—but she knew that to be hopeless. She would have to count on him, injured as he was, to land them both safely.

The rope jerked, setting her dangling and swaying,

as the line to the dragon basket pulled taut. They were under Graeme's control, now, their descent no longer a free-fall.

"We did it!" she called to de Loire.

The man managed a shaky smile which did nothing to relieve Kat's worries for him. His skin retained that sickly gray pallor that made her fear for his heart. If de Loire did not receive medical help soon—and competent help, at that—the saboteur might well achieve his end yet.

Kat shifted in her harness and managed to perch on the side of the basket that still remained attached to the balloon. Apparently, those hooks hadn't been tampered with. Taking infinite care, she inched herself around until she reached Henri-Phillipe. "Do you think you can get a leg up here if I help? You aren't hampered by skirts—you could straddle the side and probably be almost comfortable." She forced a grin, putting on a show of confidence.

"Mademoiselle." He drew a deep breath and let it out slowly. "You make of this a joke now, *enfin,* but me, I know that I owe to you my life."

"Actually, we both owe them to Captain Warwick. Now, if you can just hold onto the side—yes, I've got your ankle." She boosted gently, retaining her own balance with her other hand gripping the wicker. In another few moments of straining muscles, M. de Loire sat upright facing her, one leg bent across the wicker, the other hanging.

For several long minutes he sat very still, his breath steadying, a measure of color seeping back into his face. "This basket," he said slowly. "It was inspected, *n'est-ce-pas?"*

"Last night, thoroughly," she said. "And briefly this morning to make sure everything had been attached properly."

"And last night, there was no sign that those hooks, they had weakened?"

"None." She met his gaze steadily. "We won't be able to tell until we get to the ground, but that valve had to have been jammed. My dad and I went over it very carefully. We wouldn't have missed that—or the hooks."

"No, *mademoiselle*. I believe you. Especially when one considers the so tragic death of Sir Francis Matlock and the sudden moving of the conference to Durham Court, eh?"

Startled, she looked up quickly, meeting his gaze.

He managed a gentle smile. "You see, *mademoiselle*, me, I am not quite a fool. I know *sans doute* there are those in my country—and elsewhere in Europe, *du vrai*—who would be most glad to see us all in chaos and accusing one another of conduct of the most vile. *Non, mademoiselle,* I do not speak of this to the others—though now it is a thing that shall be much discussed, I fear."

"And a good thing, too." Kat eased her grip where her knuckles had whitened. "Everyone involved should know there might be danger."

De Loire tilted his head to one side. "Me, I do not know if that is wise. Might they not leave? And that would destroy the conference just as surely."

"But at least—" She broke off as a wave of pain tormented her. Graeme. How was he? She looked up, but could see only the multiple hues of her own collapsing envelope. They hung beneath him, now.

"You see, *mademoiselle?* We have diverted ourselves from our predicament, and quite soon we shall once more be upon the ground."

That was all too true. While only minutes before her sole hope had been to reach the earth, now she caught herself wishing that might be delayed. How hard they hit would depend completely on Graeme's ability to see where they were below him.

She couldn't detect any sign of pursuit vehicles yet. How far away were they? At least she no longer feared for de Loire—unless, of course, the landing proved bumpy, which would most likely be the case. Well, they'd find out any moment now.

They floated above a field—under full cultivation, naturally—and drifted toward trees. Oh, great, that's just what they needed, to get hung up in branches. They'd have to come down fast. There was no way they could lift above them, now. Nor could they pick their own spot. They'd have to land wherever they could.

"Hang on," she said, and stretched herself as flat as she could along the wicker, as far as her confining rope would allow. De Loire didn't hesitate. He copied her position as they dropped lower and lower.

A carriage, she saw, over the rim. Several people running. Probably the farm workers, coming for vengeance for any damage they did to their field. At least there'd be someone to help if they needed it.

The trees raced toward them—but they'd probably hit the hedge, first. They skimmed the top of the crop, then bumped and jarred against the ground. Why didn't she have a knife to cut them free? Their ropes secured them to the balloon. If they got caught in a draft, they'd be dragged with it.

Another bump, this time harder. Kat's fingers grappled with her make-shift knots. De Loire did the same. But she'd tied him so securely, and the knots had carried the full strain of their weight. The basket bounced again, then teetered, caught off balance, and toppled, landing on top of them.

A startled exclamation escaped de Loire, and Kat found herself lying in a well-irrigated furrow, the weight of the balloon pressing her down. She started to laugh, half in relief, half at her ludicrous position in the mud. The basket tilted, starting to pull at her, and she renewed her efforts to free herself, at last pulling the knot apart and crawling out from beneath the wicker.

Graeme's balloon hopped now along the ground, jarring him with every move, caught between the wind current and its anchor to their balloon. The wind won. Their equipage dragged after Graeme's, nearer and nearer the hedge as de Loire pulled himself free.

Kat scrambled to her feet and dove for the line to pull in Graeme. De Loire managed to stand, staggered a step, and collapsed to his knees. The dragon slammed into the hedge. Kat raced toward it as pain and frustration shot through her.

"Graeme!" His name tore from her, but no answer came. She scrambled into the basket and caught his valve release, allowing more hydrogen to escape. The balloon ceased its straining and settled where it lay, half-tilted against the thick shrubs. She dropped to her knees beside Graeme, who slumped in the bottom of the dragon.

Self-loathing flooded through her. His, that he should be so weak, so ineffectual, as to be harmed by what a whole man would take in stride—what he himself easily could have accomplished only a few short years ago. He couldn't even settle his own basket.

With a sob, Kat threw her arms about him, holding him close. For a moment he relaxed into her, and she could feel him gathering comfort from her love. Then he stiffened, and a door seemed to slam in her mind, cutting off the link.

"Graeme?" This time, she barely breathed his name.

He stared at her, and for a moment she glimpsed the longing, the love, the bond she knew existed between them. Then his expression set in hard, forbidding lines.

He shook his head. "No, Kitten."

"Why not? Graeme, one accident—"

"Don't you understand?" He spoke quietly, but that in no way diminished the determination behind his words. "For a little while I let myself forget—but I was only fooling myself." His hand touched her cheek, then dropped to his side. "I'm no suitable match for you."

"But—"

"Kat, you're vibrant, active, full of life. I have to lead too circumscribed an existence. That won't do for you. I could never make you happy. How long do you think it would be before you became bored and found someone who could climb mountains or explore jungles—or even mine for gold in that California your father is always talking about?"

"Graeme—"

"Damn it, Kat, I couldn't land my balloon because I couldn't stand up to reach the blasted valve rope!"

His self-disgust filled her, making her heart ache. "We'll—"

"*We* won't do anything." He looked away, over the side of the dragon's curved neck. "I want you to leave, at once. Get out of my time. Go back to wherever it is you came from."

"How?" She sat back on her heels, her heart aching, knowing he wouldn't let her touch him either physically or mentally. He'd retreated into himself, back to his safe, controlled way of life—away from her unpredictability. Away from her.

He glared at her. "What do you mean?"

"I don't know how to go back. I think I'm stuck here."

"Oh, God!" he breathed. He leaned his head against the wicker. "Don't torment me, Kitten. I'll give you whatever you need, just get out of the Court, find somewhere else to live. Keep away from me."

"That's a new one. You want to keep me as a non-mistress?"

"Kat!" His complexion darkened. "What little we have shared is over."

"*Little?*" She drew back, stung.

He kept his feelings blocked from her, as if he held a shield between them. As if they were two normal people who had never shared in one another's emotions. As if they were strangers. She shook her head.

He straightened. "A couple of days, a couple of

nights? My dear Kat, they might have been delightful, but no romantic interlude that short will make a lasting impression on someone as full of life as you, I promise you." He reached for his cane, grabbed the edge of the basket and hauled himself erect. He barely touched his injured leg to the ground. He stared out to where Henri-Phillipe de Loire now leaned against a tree some distance away. The farmers had almost reached him.

Kat stood, too, and tried to penetrate Graeme's mental armor. It held, keeping her out. "You can quit trying to treat this as a casual fling, Graeme. We both know the truth. What we've had—oh, damn, it sounds so trite to say it, but it's been earth-shattering! And I'll swear you've felt the same about it."

A muscle in his jaw twitched, but he refused to turn toward her.

"How dare you throw away this—this incredible gift we share, all for your antiquated ideals of machismo?"

"My what?" Still, he didn't look at her.

"For your damned male pride! You think you have to be tough and rugged. You're just like a little boy! If you can't be perfect, you won't play the game. Well, this isn't a game. This is our lives. And you're going to reject the most perfect union two people can have because of a physical challenge?"

He turned then and his steady, angry glare settled on her. "As far as you're concerned, I *am* antiquated. And as for this 'perfect union' of yours, for whom is it perfect? You're just enthralled by our mind link, like a child with a new toy. But understand this, Kat. I'm no one's plaything, to be discarded when something better comes along." He perched on the edge of the basket, swung himself over and turned to the first of the farmers who ran to support him.

Chapter Eighteen

Graeme leaned back in the overstuffed chair, the foot of his injured leg supported on a low stool. He kept his teeth gritted, his mind a blank. He wouldn't allow himself the self-indulgent luxury of sharing his feelings, of accepting the love and comfort that pressed against the fringes of his mind, seeking admittance.

Kat, perched on the arm of the opposite chair, sighed. "I wish we could pack your knee in ice."

He glared at her. "It sounds damnably uncomfortable."

She crossed her arms. "It would make it feel much better. It might even improve your temper."

He hunched a shoulder. "I suppose in *your* time you are able to keep ice conveniently at hand for emergencies—and in small enough pieces to use it, I suppose—even in the middle of summer?"

Her sudden smile flashed. "As a matter of fact, we are."

He looked away, fighting his curiosity to know more of her time—and struggling to prevent her from realizing that fact. The less he knew of her, the better. For that matter, the less he saw of her, the easier it would be for him. He stretched his leg, trying to ease it into a more comfortable position. There didn't seem to be one.

"I wish I had some ibuprofen," she said.

He glanced up at her, suspicious. "And what, may I ask, is that? No," he stopped her as she opened her mouth. "I doubt I'd understand. We're from different worlds. Will you please leave me?" For one determined moment, he dropped his mental shield and summoned every ounce of rejection he could manage.

Kat recoiled, her expression stark. For a moment her grief assailed him, then he gathered his defenses once more and turned his face away. She had nothing to do with him. She *couldn't* have anything to do with him.

"I'm going to work on my painting," she informed him with a formality far from her impulsive nature. Without another word, she strode from the chamber.

Strode, with swift, even steps he could never emulate. If she were tied to a cripple like him, it would destroy her liveliness, her impetuosity, all the things he loved most about her. He wouldn't let it happen.

He closed his eyes and pressed his head back into the cushions, trying to block out the throbbing in his leg. Exhaustion crept over him, the emptiness of loss, of pain—of knowing himself physically less than he needed to be.

But not mentally. He straightened. He was not defeated. He *had* saved Henri-Phillipe de Loire and Kat. The conference had not yet been destroyed.

Or was the target *not* the entire conference but merely the French delegate? The assassination of one man—the *right* man—could as easily throw Europe into chaos. France meant Louis Napoleon, and people's memories reached back thirty-five years to when the French president's uncle made his last bid for empire over all of the continent.

The door slammed back, jarring him out of his contemplation, and he looked up to see Lord Uxbridge, his thin frame drawn rigidly erect.

"What is this telegraph you sent me?" demanded the assistant Foreign Secretary. He stalked into the room to stand above Graeme.

Graeme made no attempt to rise. "I'm sorry I couldn't make the message clearer, but it didn't seem wise. An attempt was made this morning on the life of *Monsieur* de Loire."

"The devil," Uxbridge breathed. He took the chair opposite Graeme and frowned at him. "How? Did someone try to shoot him? Another repeating pistol?"

Graeme shook his head. "Someone sabotaged the balloon in which he was to ride."

"Sabotaged a balloon?" Incredulity marked his every feature. "Sabotaged—What the devil are you talking about, man? *How?*"

"Jammed the release valve so the balloon couldn't be lowered, and weakened the hooks so the basket would drop away."

Uxbridge's gaze narrowed. "Sabotage, you say. Are you certain? It sounds more like faulty equipment."

"It was checked thoroughly last night—and again this morning. There was no sign of wear."

Uxbridge surged to his feet and paced to the hearth, then spun back. "What, in the name of all that is holy,

was one of the delegates doing in anything as dangerous as a balloon?"

Graeme's jaw clenched. "He wanted to go up. So
did a number of the others."

"So you took him?" the question shot back.

"No. I stayed on the ground with those who only
wanted to watch."

"I see." A note of contempt crept into Uxbridge's
voice. "So you, who have been so busy seeing conspiracies against this conference, relegate the safety of its
participants to balloons—and balloons, for that matter, piloted by—by whom?"

"My aunt," he said levelly.

Uxbridge's head tilted to one side. "I will grant you
her undoubted competency. So Lady Clementina took
up—how many people?"

"Only three. Mr. Sayre took three more. It was the
equipage to be taken up by Miss Sayre that someone
tampered with."

"Miss Sayre." Scorn colored the words. "An esti-
mable young lady, I make no doubt. Certainly a fine
artist. But a balloonist? You actually entrusted the
safety of *Monsieur* de Loire to a female of questionable experience?"

"It was his choice. In fact, he insisted." Briefly,
Graeme described the decision to hold an ascension,
the French delegate's desire to accompany Kat, the
preparations and safety precautions, and finally Kat's
taking up several people while tethered. "The sabotage," he continued, "could have been done after the
final inspection, while everyone watched the other two
balloons rise. For that matter, one of the riders in Miss
Sayre's basket could have done the damage."

"And how was tragedy averted?" He listened, his expression clouded, while Graeme told him of the pursuit and landing. "And *Monsieur* de Loire? Is he recovered?"

"He is lying down in his chamber, at the insistence of his wife."

Uxbridge straightened. "I will go to him and apologize for what has occurred." With one last, contemptuous glance at Graeme, he left.

He returned twenty minutes later, his brow deeply furrowed. *"Monsieur* de Loire has nothing but praise for both you and Miss Sayre," he said with obvious reluctance. "And he shares your fears that someone is determined to destroy the conference. I am not satisfied, though."

"What is the alternative?" Graeme demanded. "An attempt at murder? That does not take into account the death of Sir Francis."

"Sir Francis," Uxbridge repeated. "That could have been an accident. Or he could have learned or seen something to alert him to *Monsieur* de Loire's danger. Warwick, I want a full accounting of what has occurred, who might be responsible. Who came near that balloon?"

Graeme tented his fingers and studied their tips. "Reed," he said after a moment. "He was supposed to check over the basket before they took off. He might have cut a few supports, instead."

Uxbridge stiffened. "He is an agent in the employ of Whitehall. You might as well suspect young Ellesmere!"

"I do," Graeme informed him. "He denies being at the Exhibition the afternoon before the bombs were stolen, yet Reed informed me just a little while ago that he himself saw him there. And as for his being found in the early hours of the morning drunk, claiming no memory of where he had been, it sounds highly suspect."

"Perhaps you might wish to implicate de Loire's wife, as well," Uxbridge suggested, his tone sarcastic. "On the grounds of her being so much younger than her husband and perhaps anxious to hurry along the natural course of events."

Graeme inclined his head. "That is a very definite possibility. She finds considerable enjoyment in the company of any personable gentleman. But if you really are going to be suspicious of her, your own reason—her reputed connection with Louis Napoleon—is far more likely. She also, I might add, went aloft on the tether with Miss Sayre just before her husband's disastrous journey. And, according to Miss Sayre, evinced much interest in the workings of the balloon."

Uxbridge watched him intently. "Is there anyone else you might wish to include on this list of suspects of yours?"

Graeme, paused, considering. "Anyone," he said at last, "outside of my aunt's immediate household. The potential for good—and the potential for disaster—from this conference is too great to be taken lightly."

"I suppose," Uxbridge said coldly, "that you include His Royal Highness Prince Albert in that broad, sweeping accusation of yours for divining the plan for the Crystal Palace Exhibition in the first place."

"I am accusing no one," Graeme said steadily. "But you must admit—"

"I don't know what is worse about you," Uxbridge broke in. "Your overwhelming, ungrounded fears or your blind faith in outsiders. You cannot possibly include those mysterious Sayres in your aunt's household, can you? Yet you have included them in everything. Who would have a better chance of sabotaging the balloon than those two who claim to know so much about them?"

Graeme raised an eyebrow. "I suppose you believe Miss Sayre deliberately placed herself in jeopardy?"

"She seems to have come out of it perfectly well," Uxbridge countered.

"And so did *Monsieur* de Loire," Graeme reminded him.

"Which might have been in spite of Miss Sayre's efforts and not because of them."

"This is ridiculous," Graeme slammed his fists in frustration on the arms of his chair. He couldn't explain. No one could possibly believe how he knew Miss Sayre innocent of any evil intent.

Uxbridge's eyes narrowed. "*Are* you taking this strange pair on faith? Or do you have something else in mind? Sir Francis conveniently drowning on your aunt's estate, when no one was by except you to find the body. You were seen swimming back to shore with him, but no one saw you swim out."

"Meaning, I suppose," Graeme said, keeping his voice even, "that I went out in the boat with him, drowned him, then brought the body back in a manner that made it appear I tried to rescue him?"

"As you say," Uxbridge said slowly. "A definite possibility. One I cannot overlook. And you were quite anxious to move the conference here. Why?"

"The bombs—" Graeme began.

"—could be used as easily here as at Sevington House. No, you wanted the conference here, for your own reasons. And you," he went on, "are an expert balloonist."

"May I point out that I did everything in my power to ensure they came down safely?"

The furrows in Uxbridge's brow deepened. "You certainly went up after them, but you could hardly do less when your balloon stood ready and waiting, with so many watching."

"I very nearly was not able to reach them."

"Perhaps your luck ran against you. Or perhaps you had qualms at the last moment about killing an innocent woman."

Graeme forced his fingers to unclench from the upholstered arm. "Are you accusing me?" he demanded.

Uxbridge drew a long, considering breath. "I wouldn't have thought it of you, Warwick. Your service record in India—" He frowned. "But the facts fit too well."

"*Why* would I want to sabotage the conference I have worked so hard to set up?"

Uxbridge shook his head. "I don't know. Perhaps you don't. But it's a chance, Warwick, I cannot afford to take. I want you to leave."

"Leave?" Graeme stared at him, incredulous.

"It's too late to switch the conference venue back to Sevington House. And if you are innocent, and your first guess was right and plans had been made to sabotage it there, then it would not be safe to do so. No.

The conference will remain here, and you will go back to London."

"I see," Graeme said. "And who will run everything?"

Uxbridge ran a harassed hand through his hair. "I'll stay as long as I can."

"And after that? Do you mean to send my aunt and her entire household away as well?"

"I have Ellesmere," Uxbridge said.

"If you think, for one moment, I will leave that incompetent fop—"

"You have no choice," Uxbridge snapped. "As of this moment, you are no longer involved in the conference. You will pack your things and depart within the hour." He turned on his heel and strode to the door. At the threshold he turned back. "I will so inform your aunt to instruct her servants to see your things packed, your carriage ready, and not to allow you back on the grounds until the conference has reached a successful conclusion."

Fury left Graeme speechless. Fury at Uxbridge's unfounded suspicion, fury at his own impotence in the situation. But in Uxbridge's place, would he have acted differently?

In fairness, the facts might be construed to stack against him. Even his positioning Adam Sayre and Kat at the conference to ultimately take the blame. He leaned his head back against the cushion and groaned. There was nothing for it. He couldn't stay in direct defiance of his orders. But did that leave the field open for anyone who might now sabotage to their heart's content with no one to prevent it?

No, Uxbridge knew. Uxbridge would take every

precaution. And Kat. Graeme could count on her, her father—even his aunt. He did not leave the place defenseless. But dear God, he would rather stay himself.

Sitting here being angry served no purpose. He had an hour before he would officially be thrown out. He would spend that time instructing the grooms, the footmen, the butler, even the maids. He would leave this place as protected as he possibly could. He eased his leg from the footstool and set it on the rug, gritting his teeth against the pain. Leaning heavily on his walking stick, he started for the door.

He knew she was coming before he heard the running footsteps in the hall beyond, knew her shock and puzzlement. He returned to the chair as she burst into the room, hair loose and tumbling about her shoulders, her huge painting smock covering most of her gown, her emotions battering down the barrier he had erected to protect himself. She paused long enough to close the door. When she turned back to him, her haggard expression tugged at him.

"You're going!" she cried, and it sounded almost a wail of despair.

"I have little choice." Unemotional, he reminded himself. Keep it plain, steady, simple. Don't let her in.

"You're just—going?"

He felt her confusion. He fought the impulse to reach out, to stroke the hair back from her face, to kiss her gently.

She came forward in a rush, dropping on her knees at his side. "How can he think you're guilty? After all you have done, after what you suffered today to save de Loire?"

"He has cause," Graeme said steadily. "We have

never gotten on well. Every questionable occurrence I saw, that I could accuse others of, I could be equally as guilty in the sight of someone else."

"That's absurd!" She sat back on her heels, her hands dropping to her sides. "Are you leaving so easily because it's a chance to get away from me?"

That aspect of it hadn't struck him. It should act as a palliative. Instead, it caused only further wretchedness.

"If you can't oust me from the Court, you'll oust yourself?"

The tremble in her voice cut like a razor in his already wounded soul. She leaned forward, suddenly contrite. He'd let her read him again.

"I'm sorry," she said. "And I promise, I won't let anything happen to the conference. My father, your aunt—"

He removed her hand gently. "I have much to do before I leave. Every servant in this household will know of the potential danger before I'm done."

She nodded. "Believe me, Graeme, we'll let nothing go wrong. That's why my father and I are here in your time. It must be."

And not, he thought as she rose and ran from the room, to be with him. Perhaps it hadn't been their link—their love—that brought her to him. Perhaps that bond only existed because of the role she would play in saving the conference, because he was unable to, because he had not been careful enough. He had let everyone down. He had let himself down.

When his slow, uneven steps at last took him to his room, he found his man there, already packing his things. "A short trip to London, I believe, sir," the valet said. "We will return as soon as this house is freed of its visitors."

Graeme's lips twitched. Leave it to Walters to put the best face on it for him. But the valet offered no further remarks as he stowed away shirts and trousers, then brushes and combs into the valise. He didn't need to take much, only the few things he had brought from his rooms in London. And he returned there to what was, after all, his real home. Leaving his valet to finish, he went in search of his aunt, only to encounter Uxbridge striding toward his room.

"I will see you to the stables," Uxbridge declared.

"I have first to—"

"I have already informed your aunt." Uxbridge blocked his way. "You need not take your leave of her. In fact, you need see no one."

Thus, neatly, he would be denied his chance to issue his warning. Furious at the man—all the more so because, had their positions been reversed, he would have done exactly the same—he dropped his mental barriers and sought Kat.

Surprise—or was it relief?—reached him. Words. If only he could use words. Instead, he sent all the frustration he possessed hammering toward her. Did she understand? Or would she think he meant only their relationship?

"This is nothing personal, Warwick," Uxbridge said cheerfully as they crossed the lawn toward the stable.

"Of course not," Graeme said. Like hell it wasn't.

"You'd do the same," Uxbridge went on.

Graeme remained silent. How did one ever really know whom one could trust? He could trust Kat, because he knew her soul.

Furious, he waited in the corner of the cobbled yard while his aunt's head groom himself hitched his grays to the shafts of the curricle. He climbed in, and to his surprise, Uxbridge swung up at his side.

"I'll just accompany you while you pick up your baggage," the man said, and smiled.

To make sure Graeme spoke to no one or slipped a message to a footman.

Walters stood waiting alone with the baggage at the front of the house. Uxbridge jumped down as Graeme pulled to a halt, then he stepped aside, watching while the valet hefted the bags into the back and secured them. Without acknowledging Uxbridge's presence, Walters climbed into the seat and Graeme gave his pair the office.

He turned through the circle, then headed down the short drive, away from Durham Court. Away, he realized, from his last work in government. That door would now be shut to him.

Nothing else appealed to him, nothing waited of excitement or interest. Nothing. He might as well retire to the insufferably boring life of a crippled country gentleman and be done with it.

His hands tightened on the reins, then he released his grip at once as his horses shook their heads in protest. He couldn't even indulge in any frenzied physical activity to ease his frustration.

Comfort wrapped about his mind. Kat. She was with him even now, her love as strong as ever. Even after all he had done to sever their connection, she wouldn't desert him. Faithful, loyal—wholly to be loved. For her own good, he would do all in his power to break that bond, never to touch her or be touched by her again.

A door slammed in Kat's mind with a finality that left her in no doubt. This time, Graeme meant it. He would accept no ease from his pain from her, no caring. No love. He had meant what he said.

But she was never one for taking answers she didn't like as final. He had not heard—or sensed—the last of her.

She turned away from the drawing room window, troubled. How could she overcome his ridiculous pride? That was all it was—wasn't it? Surely the strength of their emotional bond could overcome anything.

The problem wasn't so much with his knee as with his attitude toward it. There was so much they *could* do together, so much fun he could have—if only he'd let himself. He'd made a start, but at the first setback he'd closed up again.

For his own good, she'd just have to pry him open.

At the moment, though, she had to deal with his most immediate worry. The conference. And for that, her best hope seemed to be her painting.

She'd left her canvas in the conservatory, she realized—abandoned, brush tossed onto her rag instead of cleaned and put away, when Graeme's outrage assailed her. She should get back to work on it.

So far, it consisted of balloons. Everywhere balloons. And little else. If their outlines hid any secret messages, they eluded her still.

How much more time did she have? A sense of panic

assailed her as she hurried along the hall. She was on her own, with a conference to protect. Her reason for being in this particular here-and-now.

Longing gripped her, to see something familiar, to go to a mall, to telephone her brother Orville, even to heat up a TV dinner in a microwave. To be among people who took *baths*. Without Graeme, 1851 held no appeal. If only she could disappear in a puff of propane and go back to her own era.

She groped in a pocket for a handkerchief, couldn't find one, and with a muttered oath started for her room, trying not to sniff. *Damn* Graeme. She felt lonely without their contact. Why did he have to cut it off so completely? Of course, he'd always shielded himself from her a little, distrusting their link. Or had there been parts of his mind he hadn't wanted her to read?

She stopped dead.

Uxbridge had called him the most likely one to sabotage the conference. That was ridiculous—or was it? The conference sought to bring economic accord to Europe. Did he fear that might lead to economic unity—which, in turn, might bring about the political unity she sought to prevent?

Was that her *real* purpose here? Not to protect the conference but to prevent it? The possibilities staggered her. Graeme—

No! Had he attempted to sabotage the conference, he could never have hidden such treachery from her. He would never stoop to terrorizing poor Henri-Phillipe or anyone else. It was chaos, not accord, they had to fear.

In her room she found a fresh handkerchief, blew her nose, then took a deep breath. Painting time.

She started for her door, but it opened, and her father stuck in his head. "Ah, there you are, Kat. Been looking all over for you. What are we going to do about this?"

She twisted the handkerchief between her fingers. "Quite a bit. Looks like this is why we're here, Dad. I—" She broke off as she saw Lady Clementina peeking around her father's shoulder.

"You mean why you and Adam are here, in our time? Yes, he's told me." She marched forward. "And about your link with Graeme. But you really haven't any idea what, exactly, you are to do?"

"None."

"Nothing in your painting, yet?" Adam wrapped an arm about her shoulders and gave her a quick hug. "Keep going, my girl. That may be all the help we're going to get."

"I intend to. I'm not going to let Graeme down."

Adam quirked an eyebrow at her. "Not history?"

"Both!" She paced to the window, then spun about to face Lady Clementina. "Did Graeme get a chance to talk to the servants? All I could feel from him was frustration."

"Uxbridge, may he rot, bustled him out of here without letting him speak even to me."

Kat nodded. "Then you'll have to do it. Warn everyone."

Lady Clementina folded her arms before her. "Against what? To watch for suspicious men lurking about? That if they happen to see any bombs sticking out of drawers to please let the housekeeper know?"

"That'll do for a start. Oh, and if they happen to be straightening someone's room and notice any guns or daggers or vials of poison, they might just mention it to someone."

Adam chuckled, and Lady Clementina awarded this a grim smile. "We'll do our part, Kat." Her father patted her on the shoulder. "You do yours. We need to learn as much as possible—and fast!"

She nodded. "I was just heading down to do some painting. Want to come?"

"Have to talk to the servants," Lady Clementina informed her. "You go, Adam."

Adam, Kat reflected. At a time when formal address was the rule. She linked her arm through her father's. "Come on, Dad. Tell me what you've been up to." She led the way out the door.

"And just what are you implying by that?" he demanded when they were out of earshot of their hostess.

"Is there anything to imply?"

Adam grinned. "A remarkable woman, Clemmy. Haven't met such a one since your mother. Don't you worry. With her help, we'll keep this conference from blowing up all over us."

She cast him a deprecating look. "You could have chosen your words better."

"I think I said exactly what I mean." And for once, he sounded solemn.

In silence, they continued to the conservatory. Everything remained as she'd left it—no, she hadn't thrown that cover over the canvas. The paint was still wet. It would be smeared. She dropped her father's arm and ran forward, then saw the A-shape of the frame through the cloth, not the squared corners of a canvas. She dragged off the cover to reveal an empty easel.

The cloth fell from her fingers. "Dad—It's gone."

Adam chewed the ends of his mustache. "Graeme must have taken it."

She shook her head. "I saw him go. He couldn't have it—unless he saw it sitting here and put it somewhere else to keep it hidden? But—I don't see when he could have managed it. Or why he should."

"Unless he saw something in it he didn't want anyone else to see?" Adam shot back.

"He'd have let me know. We'd better search for it."

Kat took the rooms to the left, Adam the ones to the right. After an hour of thorough investigation, both reported failure. Worried, they made their way up the stairs where they checked those chambers not occupied by the delegates.

"Someone," Kat said as they at last returned downstairs, "has stolen it."

Adam nodded, grim. "You must have done it, Kitten. Painted another clue, I mean. And someone saw it and realized what it must represent and took away our only hope of stopping the saboteur."

Chapter Nineteen

Kat hesitated at the study door, then thrust it open and marched in. Lord Uxbridge, as impeccable as ever, sat behind Graeme's great desk, a sheaf of papers in his hands, his glasses perched low on his beak-like nose. He looked up, glowering from beneath his bushy eyebrows. She strode forward, and his eyes widened, the ferocity leaving his expression.

He spread the papers into neat piles before him. "Miss Sayre? To what do I owe the honor of this visit? Or need I ask?"

"I imagine you don't. How could you have sent Gr— Captain Warwick away like that? Don't you realize—"

He held up a hand, stopping her. He rose and came around the desk to stand before her. "Shall we sit down, Miss Sayre? You are agitated, understandably so. Would you care for a glass of sherry?"

"I'm not going to swoon or anything stupid like that. I just want to make you see how—how *disastrous* this might be. Captain Warwick has uncovered a plot to destroy the conference, and no one is taking it seriously."

"Now there you are wrong, Miss Sayre. I assure you, I take it very seriously. But you must understand how many so-called plots we hear of in connection with any major undertaking." He led her to the sofa and gently pressed her to take a seat. "You will find this hard to believe," he added, settling beside her, "but there is a certain element in our society which seems to enjoy raising alarms and spreading false rumors and threats. I believe that only one in every fifty proves to have any trace of truth in it."

Kat drew a deep breath and fixed her steady regard on him. "This one does. I can assure you of that."

"Can you?" His gaze narrowed on her face. "How?"

"It—" she began, then broke off.

"Because Captain Warwick is so convinced of it? My dear, it is for that very reason that I am giving credence to it, as well. His only source of information was Sir Francis Matlock, may he rest in peace. That poor gentleman's death is a double tragedy, for now we'll never be able to trace the source of his fears."

"Which might well be no coincidence," Kat pointed out.

Lord Uxbridge studied the hands he had clasped in his lap. "That could very possibly be true. And it is for that very reason I have deemed it necessary to remove Captain Warwick from all connection with the conference."

"But—"

Again, he held up his hand, silencing her. "I must ask you to put yourself in my position for a little while, Miss Sayre. I know Captain Warwick far better than do you. He has been my assistant for over two years—ever since he could get around on that knee of his. What I must say may come as a shock to you, but please bear with me. This is not easy for me, either."

He rose and strode to the hearth where he stared for a moment into the empty grate. "Captain Warwick is a driven man. An excellent officer, I make no doubt. He would have made his regiment proud had he not been forced to sell out. He was made for heroism. And I fear that since this has been denied him in his chosen profession, he may well have tried to create it in his adopted one."

Kat stared at him, open mouthed. "You mean you think he made up this plot so he could be the hero who prevents the tragedy?"

He spun back to face her. "It's possible. Far too possible. That ballooning accident—he had no intention of going aloft himself, yet there was his balloon, ready to fly to your rescue. And Sir Francis—surely, my dear, you see that Captain Warwick might have needed to silence—"

"No!" Kat sprang to her feet. "I *know* he didn't do any of it."

Uxbridge shook his head. "I wish I might be as certain. It is a chance I cannot take. If our positions were reversed, Warwick's and mine, do you not think he would send *me* away?"

Kat sank back onto the sofa, deflated. "Yes," she said, and her voice sounded hollow in her own ears. "Oh, yes. But that's the point! The safety of the delegates—of the conference—means everything to him."

"As it does to me."

She swallowed. "What will you do now?"

"Now? I must return to London, I fear. Young Ellesmere—"

"Oh, no," Kat broke in, "*not* Ellesmere."

Uxbridge raised his eyebrows. "Indeed, have you taken him in such dislike?"

"He drinks too much, and he spends far too much time flirting with the delegates' wives."

The smile he awarded her smacked of the condescending. "He has been playing a role, my dear, and very effectively, at that. His job has been to be an entertaining rattle, in which purpose he has succeeded to admiration. The ladies with whom he has flirted—and their husbands, I might add—are familiar with the game. It is expected at such functions as this. As for the rest, I have merely to tell him it is time to assume a more serious mien, and his behavior shall become as impeccable as you might wish."

"Will it? I don't see how—"

"It is his youth that troubles you, I make no doubt. Be assured, my dear, he will rise to this occasion. I will not be at all surprised if this challenge proves the making of him. An excellent young gentleman, I assure you."

"So you're going to leave him in charge?"

"Him, and Lady Clementina. Be of good cheer, Miss Sayre, all will work out for the best. And if Captain Warwick is indeed the innocent victim of circumstances you believe, why, then he, too, shall have cause to rejoice at the happy outcome. Now, I must speak with Ellesmere and then be off. There is much to set in motion before tomorrow. Rest assured, though, I shall return at the earliest possible moment."

Somehow, he had eased Kat toward the door, and

she realized she now stood before it. He opened it, still smiling, and she found herself maneuvered into the hall. Frustrated, she went to the conservatory where she paced, trying to think what to do next. Why couldn't she have some clear idea? Move the conference again, perhaps? But how?

She might be able to convince Lady Clementina to throw everyone out—or would that create the very chaos they had to prevent? No, it would have to be an orderly withdrawal, a decision made by the person in charge. And at the moment, that meant viscount Ellesmere.

She continued her pacing, trying to hit upon the right approach, the right argument, until noises from without announced the departure of a carriage. Uxbridge, returning to London. Ellesmere would be alone now, either gloating over his temporary promotion or panicking over it. She hoped for the latter.

She allowed a few more minutes to pass, then went to the study and knocked. The tenor voice that bid her to enter held a smugness that left her uneasy. She stepped inside and found the viscount lounging in the heavy chair behind Graeme's great desk, the papers still in the stacks where Uxbridge had placed them.

"Miss Sayre." He rose and came to join her. "How may I be of service to you?"

She eyed him critically. "Lord Uxbridge places a great deal of faith in your abilities."

He positively preened. "He is quite right to do so. I have long—far too long—awaited an opportunity to prove myself."

Might he have sabotaged Graeme—and the conference—to gain his chance? She thrust the thought aside.

"Do you take seriously the rumored threat to the conference?"

He leaned back against the desk, half-sitting on its edge, and fingered his neat little mustache. "My dear, I should be a fool not to give careful consideration to any threat that reached my ears—however ridiculous and impossible it might seem."

"Meaning you think Captain Warwick's fears ridiculous and impossible?" she shot back.

He took her hand and patted it. "My dear, my dear. We all know his consuming fear—his *bête noire,* as one might say—is ambush. Quite understandable, of course, but ludicrous when carried to extremes, is it not? Has he even managed to frighten you? There is no need, I assure you, to be alarmed. He sees hobgoblins hiding in every corner, where a less obsessed man sees only the normal shadows. Rest assured, I have taken the reins firmly into my own hands, now, and there shall be no more accidents, nothing more for you to fret your lovely head about. Very lovely, I might add."

She folded her arms. "I just heard a chauvinist pig oink."

"Did you?" He glanced at the window. "That's odd. I cannot imagine Lady Clementina allowing pigs near her house. But there, my dear Miss Sayre, it is no wonder you are feeling gloomy, lurking about within doors on such a beautiful day. Why do we not take a stroll down by the lake? A parasol to guard your perfect complexion, a light shawl to protect you against any chance breeze—a far more enjoyable way to spend the afternoon, do you not think?"

She forced a brittle smile to her lips. "I have been thinking about something you said the other night, about the conference being much safer at Sevington House. Now that you are in charge, I suppose you will move it back there?"

"Move it?" For a moment, alarm glittered in his dark eyes. "You mean re-organize *everything?* The work—"

She fluttered her lashes and peeped up at him. "It would only mean returning to the original plans. I thought your idea showed such—such wisdom."

For a moment he looked confused, as if unable to remember making any such remark—which in fact she knew he hadn't—then he beamed at her. "Wisdom is the art of being adaptable, my dear. It might distress the delegates to find themselves moved once more. No, you may trust in my judgment. The conference will remain here. And now, shall we take that stroll?"

"Another time, perhaps." She had trouble maintaining a friendly attitude. "I feel certain you must have a great deal of work to do, to familiarize yourself with so many details." To which he'd certainly paid no heed before.

The glance he directed toward the papers held nothing but distaste. "I believe Lady Clementina's staff to be quite capable."

Which was more than she could say for Ellesmere, himself. With a murmured excuse, she let herself out, then paced down the corridor. What now? She'd failed to get the conference moved—but was that step indeed necessary? Sabotage, of one kind or another, would occur wherever the event took place. Of that she felt certain.

What form would it take? A bomb, as had been planned at Sevington House? Or another "accident" like Sir Francis's or de Loire's? She had nothing tangible with which to work—or rather, against which to work. She didn't even have her painting that might have—*must* have—provided some clue. What she needed, she decided, would be a summit conference of her own, with the only people she could trust—her father and Lady Clementina.

As she crossed the entry hall, her father's deep voice reached her, using the rolling accents he adopted whenever relating one of his farfetched tales. She veered toward the first salon, whose door stood ajar. Adam stood by the fireplace, a glass of wine on the mantel beside him. His audience—one of the secretaries and five ladies, including Vivienne de Loire and Antonia di Fiorelli—sat entranced. Lady Clementina, she noted, was not of their number.

Adam glanced toward her, but if he recognized the urgency of her signal, he seemed in no hurry to act upon it. He awarded her the blandest of smiles, gave her an almost imperceptible nod and a slight jerk of his head upward, and continued his wholly fictional account of a mine cave-in.

Irritated, she hoped this time it would bury him alive. Serve him right. Could he never forego being in the limelight? At least he would meet her in her room as soon as he finished. She started toward the stairs, only to stop as Lady Clementina emerged from the back portions of the house.

"There you are." A worried frown creased the woman's brow. "Come, I have much to say to you." She caught Kat's arm and started up the steps.

"The servants—?" Kat hurried to keep pace with her.

"They'll keep watch as best they can, but everything is in chaos below stairs. Do you remember the help we needed to hire to carry us through the conference?"

Kat nodded. "They came from Whitehall's approved list."

Lady Clementina snorted. "Who's to say they're all who they say they are? Any one of them might be our saboteur. My own staff is busy keeping watch over them. Where has your father gone?"

"Digging enough mines in California to sink it into the ocean."

Lady Clementina stopped at the landing and stared at her. "He is—what?"

"Telling his stories. He'll be along as soon as he finishes." She followed her hostess to that woman's chamber, then cast herself into one of the chairs. "Uxbridge is being maddeningly reasonable about everything, with the result that I can't blame him for sending Graeme away. Only he's so *wrong*. And I can't even blame him for not listening to the truth, because it sounds preposterous even to me."

Lady Clementina paced to the window and back. "He left, did you know? Uxbridge, I mean?"

Kat nodded. "That *idiot* is in charge. How he can put his trust in Ellesmere and doubt Graeme—"

Lady Clementina touched Kat's shoulder as she passed in her perambulations. "We must come up with a plan."

"Sounds simple when you say it, doesn't it? After all, we only have to make sure no one is either hurt or frightened. That should be easy enough. Perhaps you'd like to—"

The door swung open and Adam stepped over the

hreshold. "Huddle time," he announced cheerfully.
"You want to be quarterback, Kitten?"

"I wouldn't mind a decent playbook. The only one
we've got was stolen."

Lady Clementina looked from one to the other of
them, frowning. "Is this more mining talk?" she asked
after a moment.

"Worse." Kat stretched her feet in front of her.
"Football. Don't worry, you won't ever have to deal
with it. But he's right, we need a game plan."

Adam perched on the arm of her chair. "What are
the most likely times for an attack?"

"Easy. Either when everyone's together, or when
everyone's separate."

"Which covers almost all the time," Lady Clementina pointed out.

"Not really." Adam rubbed his chin. "We can request that everyone remain in groups."

"The buddy system," murmured Kat.

Adam ruffled her hair, earning a glare from her.
"Exactly, Kitten. We'll assign people groups of four,
and tell them the truth. If we make a game of it, they
may not be as frightened, they'll think it a rare joke."

"Or panic," Kat objected. "We *can't* tell them, or
we'll have a mass exodus on our hands, and there goes
history."

"Well, we'll just keep 'em together, then. Ride herd
on 'em. Eh, pardner?"

Kat regarded him with a jaundiced eye. "What
about when it's time for them to go to bed?"

"I've already taken care of that." Lady Clementina
beamed on her. "Quite by chance, actually. We didn't
have sufficient rooms, so their servants will sleep on

truckle beds just inside their doors. No one will be alone."

Adam's eyebrows rose. "Madam, you have my congratulations. A fortuitous idea. That leaves us only with meals, the ball, and the conference itself."

"Not to mention all the times in between." Kat sighed. "Sounds simple enough, doesn't it? We'll just have the butler check for bombs in the dining room and the soup tureens before every meal, and—"

"That isn't as much of a joke as you think," Lady Clementina interrupted. "That is exactly what we'll have to do."

"Oh, great. As if poor Newcombe hasn't enough to do already. And what about the ball? There'll be caterers and musicians and who knows what all else coming in. I don't see how we can do it."

Adam leaned back. "That does sound like the best time to attack. Can we get more help from Whitehall?"

Lady Clementina tilted her head to one side. "Would we trust them if we did?"

Adam sighed. "Scratch that idea. Kat? What about you? Think you could manage another painting?"

"Before tomorrow night? I—" She broke off and drew a deep breath. "I'd better get to work, hadn't I?" She jumped to her feet and headed for the door. "It'll have to be small, all I have are a couple of canvas scraps I made up and primed. Could someone bring me some dinner on a tray?"

Without looking back, she exited, then ran lightly down the hall. How long would she have to get her impressions—and prediction—across? One day, perhaps, until the ball? No, they'd need to know sooner so they could avert whatever might happen. Tonight, then.

She retrieved her equipment from the conservatory and carried it to her room. It would smell to high heaven—she'd probably have to haul her mattress into the bathroom—if, of course, she managed to get to bed at all. She might be up until morning trying to capture something elusive in paint.

She set up her easel by the window and pushed open the casement. That should help with ventilation. Then she set out her jar of paint thinner and squeezed a variety of paints onto her palette. She could always smear colors on with her knife, but that would be too clumsy. Before, she'd found the tracery in the delicate outlines. It would have to be quick—with no chance for paints to dry before applying the next. Not if she wanted it down in time to do them any good.

She drew a chair into position, closed her eyes, took a deep breath and cleared her mind. With eyes still closed, she dabbed the brush into paint at random and prayed something would materialize from her subconscious or from wherever those images sprang. It took real effort to keep her thoughts from intruding.

She concentrated, allowing her mind to reach out, keeping herself open. Slowly, almost imperceptibly at first, awareness crept over her. Awareness of . . .

Graeme's presence filled her, tentative at first, then seeping through every segment of her being. Love, along with sensations of such longing as she had experienced only in his arms. It cut off abruptly.

She groped for him, straining for contact again, aching to close the distance, to be with him if only in spirit. Hazy images formed in her mind: a table containing a decanter and a glass, both containing the merest splash of amber liquid; a rumpled shirt sleeve; a wall of leatherbound books. They ebbed away like a retreating tide, receding from her grasp, until all that remained hummed in her inner ear like the vibrations echoing from a conch shell. Graeme . . . no, he was gone, beyond recall.

Shaken, bereft of his touch, she opened her eyes. The canvas stood propped before her, a rage of colors putting her vividly in mind of the wild French *Le Fauve* school. Or van Gogh, at his most dramatic. She studied it, frantic, seeking something . . .

An impressionistic representation of Graeme's features stared back at her. Graeme, who now filled her every thought, every part of her. No dire predictions of disaster to come. Only Graeme. She had failed.

This time.

She had the rest of the night, another small canvas, and several boards to go.

Chapter Twenty

Kat stood by the long French doors in the ballroom, staring out over the terrace. Behind her, Lord Uxbridge's voice droned on, as it had for the past twenty minutes with only brief respites.

"A most excellent job," he repeated for at least the fiftieth time in tones of immense satisfaction. "Ellesmere, Lady Clementina, you are both to be congratulated. I would defy any evil-doer to attempt any skullduggery this night."

Kat turned, frowning, to study the trio where they stood beneath the minstrels gallery. Uxbridge hadn't checked the locks on the windows by which she stood. Nor had he done more than cast the most cursory of glances behind the line of draperies that concealed the tiny alcoves lining the other side of the room. Her father, only an hour before Uxbridge's arrival, had checked the chains securing the chandeliers. His lordship hadn't thought of that.

For that matter, his lordship hadn't mounted the narrow steps leading to the balcony where the musicians would take their places that night. That van-tage—as she had discovered herself during their earlier inspection of the premises—offered an excellent view of everything and everyone on the dance floor below. One armed pseudomusician could wreak havoc from there.

She paced along the wall and wondered why her mind hadn't shut down yet. She'd been up all night, not finishing her last attempt at painting until breakfast. She had created nothing of use—nothing, even, of artistic merit. She hadn't even evoked Graeme's presence, again, to ease her troubled hours. A wasted effort, all around.

And now she was so tired she would probably miss anything of importance. What good would she be in this state? She had to be alert tonight, ready to spot trouble before it even *began* to happen. And Lord Uxbridge wasn't helping things in the least.

She blinked rapidly to ease the stinging of her tired eyes. Maybe she should slip off for a short nap before everything got under way. But the sabotage didn't necessarily have to happen at the ball. It might occur before, during the last-minute rush of preparations when the caterers carried in and arranged their platters of delicacies and the wine steward decanted his prize bottles. Or even during dinner in the great state dining room. So little time remained.

Oh, rats, what if the champagne or burgundy were poisoned? It would be so easy, just a few drops of something into each of the containers. Or what if—

"Miss Sayre?" Lady Clementina's precise voice hailed her, breaking across her racing thoughts.

Kat roused herself and hurried toward them. "Did

you inspect everything?" she demanded of Uxbridge. As a hint, she hoped it wouldn't be too subtle.

He bestowed his most condescending smile upon her. "My dear, for once I do honestly believe there to be no need. Young Ellesmere—" he inclined his head toward that gentleman, who beamed, "—has shown himself to be more than capable. I understand he and Lady Clementina have had the entire household inspecting for possible sabotage. What more could I possibly add to that?"

Kat opened her mouth, then closed it again. That hadn't been enough for her. She'd gone over everything with her father—including any number of places the servants overlooked. "Let's go on to the dining room," she suggested.

Irritation flashed across Uxbridge's face. Before he could speak, though, Ellesmere cleared his throat. "No need, no need, I assure you, sir. Unless you would wish to just glance inside?"

Uxbridge drew his watch from his pocket, and his expression cleared. "There, not as late as I feared. Very well, the dining room it is—though I mean this as no slight to your capabilities, my dear Ellesmere." He gestured for Kat and Lady Clementina to precede him.

Kat led the way with quick, determined steps. Almost, he made her want to plant something, just to give him a good shock. Maybe then he'd take a greater interest in the safety of this event that could mean so much for Europe—either good or evil.

She stalked along the corridor, fuming inwardly. Maybe he just didn't believe anything would happen at the ball. Or at dinner, apparently, or he'd be more concerned about the state apartments.

She reached the first of these, threw wide the great double doors, and found herself face-to-face with an uneasy—looking footman. The young man's sharp-featured face relaxed as his gaze swept over the party. Kat smiled at him and stepped within.

The long chamber still filled her with a sense of awe, with its white walls and gilt trim, the ten-foot square paintings of classical scenes, the muraled ceiling with its great crystal chandeliers. Muted blue draperies hung at the windows, tied back by thick, tasseled gold ropes. A perfect setting for a formal dinner, even for a momentous conference.

But not, she prayed, for murder or sabotage.

Nothing, she decided, had changed since her own inspection earlier in the day—at least, nothing that leapt to her attention.

Lord Uxbridge entered behind her. "Have you checked it yourselves?" he asked Lady Clementina.

"Several hours ago. We have had servants posted at each entrance since then."

Uxbridge smiled. "A more than adequate precaution, I make no doubt. Really, my dear lady, you and Ellesmere have done a superb job."

Lady Clementina's jaw set.

Kat stepped hastily forward to forestall any comment the woman might make about it being Graeme's work. "Don't you want to make your own inspection?"

"What? No, no need. You have posted a guard. What could possibly happen? No, I think our saboteur—if we ever had one—will not dare show his face. Now, I imagine we'd best remove ourselves. The staff will be needing to lay the covers. Lady Clementina?

Miss Sayre? I shall excuse myself now to prepare for the ball." With that he swept away, with Ellesmere hurrying in his wake.

"How are we going to get him to take any interest?" Kat muttered to her hostess as the men receded from earshot. "I would certainly have made my own search."

Lady Clementina frowned at the retreating backs. "Perhaps he really does have complete faith in Lord Ellesmere."

"Faith in that—that idiot!" Kat set off along the hall, keeping her steps controlled so as not to run the risk of overtaking the other two. "That just goes along with the rest of his carelessness. How did he ever get to his position, if this is his attitude?"

"He must have earned it," Lady Clementina said, but she sounded doubtful.

Kat sniffed. "No one could be that complacent unless he honestly *doesn't* care what happens." Her steps slowed even more. "Doesn't care—or perhaps he *does* care, very much."

"What do you—" Lady Clementina broke off and simply stared at her. "Oh, no, you *cannot* mean—"

"I don't know." Kat resumed her controlled steps. "It's ridiculous. I mean, it never would have occurred to me if it weren't for his not being more careful. But *why* would he want to sabotage his own conference?"

Lady Clementina adjusted the lace about her shoulders. "I know Palmerston—the Foreign Secretary—favors Louis Napoleon. And Uxbridge is his assistant."

Kat stopped in her tracks and stared at Lady Clementina. "You think Palmerston himself is behind this?" she demanded.

"N—no. This isn't his style. This is too under-handed, too ruthless."

Kat nodded. "I'm barely acquainted with Lord Ux-bridge, but my money's on him." She resumed her walking. "But are we right? What about Sir Francis's death? Uxbridge wasn't even here. Or could that have been just an accident, like he says?"

Lady Clementina pursed her lips. "We didn't see Uxbridge, but that doesn't conclusively mean he *wasn't* here. It would be interesting to know if anyone in London can confirm his whereabouts at that time."

"We could—" Kat broke off. "Damn, no phones. But you've got telegraph, haven't you? Let's cable Graeme. He could go to Whitehall and find out if anyone remembers being with him."

Lady Clementina's eyes gleamed. "I'll send one of the grooms at once." A frown took possession of her features. "It will be too late by the time he gets the message. Everyone will have gone home. And it would look so very particular should he knock on everyone's door, asking questions about their superior."

"Especially if we're wrong," Kat agreed. "Only think about the ballooning accident. How could Ux-bridge have managed that?"

"Young Ellesmere—" Lady Clementina broke off. "No, not likely. *I* wouldn't trust him not to make a mull of everything."

"That was why Sir Francis was killed, I suppose—he wasn't a very reliable assistant. I doubt Uxbridge—or whoever—would make the same mistake twice. No, the damage could have been done during the night and left natural-looking on the surface. We really only gave it the most cursory check in the morning. Uxbridge would have no way of knowing I'd take up the others on a tether. He probably figured by the time the hooks worked loose, *Monsieur* de Loire and I would be so far off, no one could help us. He was almost right as it was."

"What a horrid thought." Lady Clementina slowed to a stop. "If that man really tried to murder you—"

Kat caught her hand. "That's the worst of it. We can't be sure it *was* him. So what do we do now?"

"We could confront him with it," said Lady Clementina, but she sounded doubtful. "Or we might tell everyone we expect further sabotage."

Kat grimaced. "It might come to that, but only as an absolute last resort. A stampede to the door isn't going to help any."

Lady Clementina drew in a considering breath, then let it out on a decisive note. "We'll just have to keep a very close eye on his lordship, that's all."

"A careful eye," Kat countered. "If he realizes we've guessed, how long do you think it would take for *us* to become the victims of another 'accident?' " She repressed an involuntary shudder. She'd come close— far too close—already. And now Graeme wasn't around to help, to spread his protective wing over them all. "We've got to foul up his plans, and without his realizing what we're doing."

"It would help," Lady Clementina pointed out, "if we knew what his plans were."

With that sentiment, Kat found herself in complete agreement. She'd tried—and failed, over and over, last night. She must have painted some clue into that picture that vanished—but where could it be? Destroyed? Or in Uxbridge's possession?

Uxbridge. He must have it. *Could* he still have it? He must know she hadn't guessed its significance, yet. If he'd destroyed it, wouldn't she—or rather, the servants—have seen some trace in a hearth? Perhaps he took it away with him; he could have done that easily, with none of them the wiser. They were all too shaken after the ballooning incident and Graeme's abrupt banishment to notice much of anything. Uxbridge could have taken it away, and—and done what with it? Destroyed it, most likely. Unless its sheer peculiarity caused him to keep it.

Lady Clementina touched her shoulder. "I'll talk to your father. You go ahead and get ready."

Kat nodded, troubled, and made her way to her room to prepare for the ball. To her relief, Middy awaited her with her latest remodel job, a beautiful creation of dull rose-colored satin, all drooping lace and ruffles. "Is it ready?" Kat asked, quickly going to work on the buttons of the gown she wore. "I want to get down there first—to keep an eye on things."

A frown touched the woman's face. "It may need just a tuck here or there. I wish we'd had time for a proper fitting."

Kat grimaced. "Let's just hope it doesn't need letting back out." She'd been keeping herself awake all day with forays into the kitchen. The cook had obliged by baking a batch of something that resembled custard-filled croissants.

Kat scrambled out of her gown, then loosened the drawstring on the neckline of her camisole, pulling it off her shoulders. The maid tossed the yards of satin over her head, then twitched them deftly into place. Fastening, though, was not as easy. Kat stood very still, and Middy did her best, tugging at the fabric and muttering under her breath. It would be enough, Kat decided—provided she didn't move or breathe. Dancing was definitely out. But that didn't matter. Graeme wouldn't be present—nor would he take the floor if he were.

The maid had barely pinned a cluster of artificial roses at the decolletage and adjusted the lace that served as sleeves from the points of Kat's shoulders to where it fell just below her elbows, when a knock sounded on the door. "Come in," Kat called, and turned from studying her reflection in the mirror.

Outside, someone squawked, a baritone impersonation of a bird. Middy looked at Kat, uncertain.

For the first time that evening, a smile tugged at Kat's lips. "Come on in, Dad."

The door swung wide, and Adam waddled in.

"Penguin suit, right?" Kat asked.

He beamed at her. "Better than my butler rig, don't you think?" He turned about, allowing her to inspect. "Cut down from one of Warwick's old ones. And just look at you." A note of admiration crept into his voice. "Pity he isn't here."

Hot color flooded her cheeks. "Very funny, Dad. Did you talk to Lady Clementina?"

He perched on the edge of a chair. "I did. I can't decide if you two have vivid imaginations or if we've got one heap of trouble on our hands."

"Both, most likely. Are you ready to go down? Then why don't you go along to Uxbridge's room with some question and keep him company?"

Adam stood and shook out the tails of his coat. "Suppose there'll be fish for dinner?" he asked, squawked once more, and waddled out the door.

Kat turned back to her reflection, only to meet the maid's confused expression. "Ignore him," Kat recommended. "I always do."

"Yes, Miss." Middy gathered Kat's hair in her hands and set about pinning it into position.

As soon as Kat met with the maid's approval, she dismissed the woman to tend Lady Clementina. Kat paced to the window, knowing she should go down yet needing a few minutes to collect her thoughts. If it were Uxbridge—or rather, if it *weren't* Uxbridge—she needed to know for certain. Some good they would all do if they sat about all night keeping an eye on the wrong man. After all, Ellesmere might not be the idiot he appeared. Or it might be one of the other delegates or a member of their entourages who sought to destroy the good that might come of this meeting. It could be almost *anyone*. Except Graeme.

A fleeting touch caressed her mind, holding warmth and longing—and a measure of hopelessness. He'd come to her, sensing her distress. Kat closed her eyes, opening herself to it, needing him, wanting him near her. Even from London, he had sensed her troubled spirit.

Though it wasn't that far away, she supposed. Yet any distance from him seemed too much. At least he'd been able to go to his own rooms; he was not cut off from everything and everyone he knew. London—

Her mind clicked back into working order. If Uxbridge hadn't destroyed the picture, where else would he have taken it except home? And home—at least a close-at-hand home—meant London.

Her painting might well be in the city, within reach of Graeme.

If he could find it, see in it what Uxbridge must have seen, then perhaps he could send her the image, let her know what disaster awaited them. Uxbridge must think himself safe; he didn't know of her link with Graeme. If it worked, she would have the jump on him she needed to sabotage *his* sabotage.

Excitement flooded through her, hope for the first time since last night. She closed her eyes and concentrated hard on Graeme, on his face, then on just reaching him, touching his mind. Restraint hit her, as if she encountered a barrier. He had retreated, closing her out, refusing to accept the contact.

No. Her mental scream exploded from her, shattering his defenses. Puzzlement, concern, anxiety wrapped about her. Why, oh why, couldn't she send words? Would he be able to understand her message? She concentrated very hard on Lord Uxbridge, throwing every negative emotion she could muster into the image. Then she transferred to her unfinished painting, missing from the conservatory and perhaps present in his house? She emphasized the uncertainty, the need for the answer, the vitalness of uncovering the mysteries the canvas might reveal.

Stillness surrounded her. She opened her eyes to find herself slumped in a chair, exhausted by the effort of the communication, feeling . . . nothing. No response, no sign Graeme had received or understood.

She'd failed. She didn't have the strength to try

again, not when the first effort hadn't been enough.
Oh, Graeme—

A mish-mash of emotions swept over her, settling
into anger. He'd understood something, at least, but
enough? A conviction filled her of purpose, of something that must be accomplished. That much, he'd
gathered. But did he know what?

The contact faded too soon. She reached for him
once more, needing his reassurance, to know what he
would do. Everything could go wrong so easily. This
time her questing mind encountered only a vast noth-
ingness. He was gone.

Had she succeeded—or not?

Chapter Twenty-one

For a meal with so many people at the table, Kat decided, dinner passed with surprising ease. Everyone, even her father, seemed to be on his best behavior. The only element that grated on Kat's nerves was Lord Uxbridge's calm usurpation of the host's place—Graeme's place.

He sat at the head of the table, a considerable distance from Kat, with all the air of a king presiding over his court. As if *he* were responsible for the success of events so far. He certainly seemed pleased—as if not a single trouble or worry hung over him. Good acting?

Or was he innocent, and possessed of blind faith in the unreliable Ellesmere? What if she were wrong, and Uxbridge had nothing to do with sabotage? Then Graeme wasted his night—if indeed, he had ever understood her message—and she had no notion whatsoever where to look for danger.

They'd just have to keep everyone under observation, she decided. Guilty until proven innocent. Only there were far more of *them* than there were of the people she trusted. If only Graeme would find her painting at Uxbridge's house, then she'd know . . .

Frustration filled her, and it took a moment for her to realize she'd touched Graeme's mind. Yet was it his frustration or hers? It would be too early for him to attempt any housebreaking. He might, though, have paid a call at the house on the pretense of leaving some message.

Why couldn't they pass real words and thoughts back and forth? Emotions and images in this case might be disastrously insufficient. She forced herself to concentrate on the minted roast lamb before her, but found she had little appetite.

As they moved on to the ballroom, the scraping of strings and the muted tones of a flute announced that the musicians had taken up their positions. Had someone else slipped in with them? Kat paused by the door, her uneasy gaze sweeping the minstrels gallery, but she could see little. Nothing suspicious, at least. No masked men with guns or bombs, at any rate. A heartfelt sigh escaped her. This was going to be a long, tense evening.

She moved on, only to be hailed by Vivienne de Loire. Already the woman held a glass of champagne, and from the looks of her she had imbibed freely during dinner. She waved her hand gaily. *"Voyons,* but this is *merveilleuse.* But me, I think it is a great shame Captain Warwick is not here, *n'est-ce pas?* There are too few handsome men."

A middle-aged gentleman approached them, acknowledged Kat with a nod of his head, then bowed over the beautiful Vivienne's hand. An assistant or secretary or something. He sounded German—or did she mean Prussian? Kat was too tired to keep it straight. Vivienne, however, appeared more than up to the task. The woman fluttered her lashes, awarded the gentleman a languishing glance, and strolled off on his arm without another word to Kat.

Kat watched her departure with a frown. Vivienne's sole purpose appeared to be dalliance. Either the woman was far too preoccupied with affairs of the heart to ever have time to plan any sabotage, or she was an excellent actress. Kat wished she could be certain which it was.

Antonia di Fiorelli, looking as solid and determined as usual in spite of an ethereal gown of pale yellow silk, paused at her side. *"Madame* de Loire is correct," she pronounced. "These affairs, they are so very dull. The men, so serious."

Kat forced a smile to her lips. "They have a great deal to consider."

Antonia looked down her long straight nose at Kat. "It is not a good thing, the balloon ascension, that it should suffer an accident. The entertainments, they will be too quiet, now. Nothing of any excitement."

"Oh, we'll try not to let you get bored." Kat assumed her best recreation director manner. "We have a picnic planned for tomorrow, as soon as the delegates finish their first session."

The Italian girl shook her head. "Men. Their work, they will not forget it, not even while they eat. They will think only of treaties and trade."

"Don't worry," Kat said dryly. "There's always Viscount Ellesmere."

A slow, satisfied smile just touched Antonia's lips.

"That is so. And now, I will dance." She swept off, apparently to commandeer a partner.

Kat watched her for a moment, then looked about for Vivienne and her escort. From where she stood, she could no longer see either of them. Vexed, she glanced back for Antonia, but she had vanished, as well. How on earth was she to keep an eye on everyone?

Or did any of it matter? She looked around, wondering whose turn it was to shadow Uxbridge. Lady Clementina's, she supposed. Then would come her turn, then her father's. She searched among the various knots of people and spotted Lady Clementina and Uxbridge, somewhat to her surprise, together on the dance floor.

And what a dance. She fought back her wistfulness. She'd never seen such a wonderful waltz. She watched the rapid, swirling pace, the way the gowns made their wearers seem to float. How incredibly romantic, to be joined with the man you loved, moving in time with the music, meeting his gaze, sensing his lead, matching your steps with his. If only. . . .

But "if onlys" did no good whatsoever. She wasn't here to dream, she reminded herself sternly. She was here to—

Out of the corner of her eye, she caught a quick movement, a gentleman disappearing behind one of the long curtains into an alcove. Ellesmere. She'd recognize his swagger anywhere.

Her heart caught, pounding rapidly, making her giddy with sudden nerves. Was this it? That alcove, she knew, possessed a door leading onto the terrace. From there, a saboteur could slip around to any other door and gain access to anywhere else in the house.

She cast a rapid glance around, but the servants were all busy, her father nowhere to be seen—no, there he was on the far side of the ballroom, in conversation with de Loire. She didn't have time to go to him for help, not if she wanted to check up on Ellesmere's purpose in slipping out. Gathering her courage, she set off in pursuit.

Probably he just needed a breath of fresh air, she assured herself, yet she found her nerve quailing. What if he didn't, what if he planned more? The possibility of coming face to face with a saboteur bent on terror and destruction left her weak.

That, she reminded herself, was why she was here in this time—wasn't it? Didn't she have some destiny to fulfill? She groped for more rallying phrases for her pep-talk, but they eluded her.

She reached the draperies, hesitated, then plunged through. No one in the alcove. So far, safe—but that meant she had to go farther, to the terrace at least. She opened the door and peered out, to where lanterns festooned the stone flagging and part of the graveled garden walkway beyond.

Where? . . . There! She glimpsed movement, a lighter shadow against the darker shrubs, and heard the sudden, soft crunch of gravel beneath a shoe. Should she walk out boldly, as one taking the air? Or try to slip unnoticed after the viscount, who now hurried along the twisting path?

Only why would someone bent on sabotaging the ball be going *away* from it? Surely, if Ellesmere meant harm, he would be sneaking around to another window or door, not heading toward the rose arbor.

Emboldened by this thought, she stepped outside and hurried to the edge of the paved stones, then down the few steps to the garden below. Here she hesitated, not sure where to go next. As she stood there, a ghostly shape, a pale cloud gleaming in the moonlight, floated away from the side of the house. Kat caught her breath and drew back into the shadows as the figure drifted toward the steps farther along the terrace.

No ghost, Kat saw as the woman, her pale gown belling about her, paused by the fountain. Antonia di Fiorelli.

A snapping twig caught both their attentions. Antonia spun about to face the farther path, then swept forward with a soft exclamation of satisfaction.

Out of the darkness stepped viscount Ellesmere. He swept the girl into his arms—or was it the other way around? Kat, both relieved and annoyed at having been lured out for a mere tryst, retreated. Ellesmere would be occupied for awhile.

She'd wasted time on this dalliance; she'd better get back. A glance at the two by the fountain assured her they were oblivious to their surroundings. Still, she crept back up the steps, sticking to the shadows, and made her way some distance along the terrace before risking the creak of an opening door.

Once inside, she found herself emerging from beneath the minstrels gallery, where several tables of pastries, lobster cakes and other delicacies had been set out. The footman on duty did a double take as she came up behind him. She gave him a conspiratorial wink and, arming herself with a flaky shell stuffed to overflowing with salmon mayonnaise, strolled back into the ballroom. No one seemed to pay her any attention.

First things first, she decided. Where was Uxbridge? The waltz had long since ended, and another dance she didn't recognize had begun. She frowned, scanning the large chamber. Only the delegates and their entourages filled the area—not that many people, really. Uxbridge should be easy to spot.

There he was, speaking with some of the delegates. Why couldn't he just get on with his sabotage and get it over with? Frustration filled her, impatience, a feeling of inability. . . . It was Graeme.

She closed her eyes, willing him to take heart, willing him to share in the wonderful sensations his mental presence created in her mind and body. As she remained motionless, given over to the contact, she felt him touch her, as if he were there in the same room and had reached out with one finger to just brush her cheek. Her eyes flew open, but she stood alone, no one nearby. No Graeme. But the frustration faded from her.

Kat drew in a shaky breath, forcing her thoughts back to her current task. The saboteur. It had to be Uxbridge. That could be the only explanation for his too casual interest in their preparations. That meant as long as he were present, no harm would come to the conference. He didn't seem to her to be a fanatic who would gladly surrender his life to his cause. If she were correct, then she needn't worry until he tried to leave.

If she were correct.

She had to be.

Lady Clementina hurried past and gave her an al-

most imperceptible nod. Her turn on Uxbridge-watch.
Kat strolled forward, trying her best to look noncha-
lant. It wasn't easy keeping surveillance on someone
without being obvious about it.

Still, the nagging doubt haunted her; what if they
were wrong, and Uxbridge were innocent? She forced
that thought aside. No one escaped notice tonight.
The servants watched, her father watched, Lady Clementina watched.

Only not one of them seemed to have noticed Ellesmere and Antonia di Fiorelli slipping out to their tryst.

Her eyes ached from exhaustion, but her nerves kept
her alert. How long she could go on like this, though,
worried her. What if Uxbridge didn't try anything
during the ball? Then a long night—maybe several
long nights—lay ahead with no hope of sleep.

When her father finally relieved her of her watch
duty, he took one look at her and snorted. "You're not
going to be good for anything much longer. Go take
a nap. I'll drag you out when the ball's over."

"But—"

He pointed a finger upward. "Go to your room,
young lady, now! And if I hear one more argument out
of you, no TV for a week. Is that understood?"

"No bedtime story?" she asked. "Okay, okay. I'm
going. But it's only because I couldn't find any tooth-
picks to prop up my eyelids."

She watched him stroll over to Uxbridge and the
group that surrounded him, then join the conversation
with an ease she envied. She stayed only long enough
to promise Lady Clementina to awaken her during the
night if anything seemed about to happen, then made
her way up the stairs.

Music floated after her, and she found her thoughts drifting with the melody. She did need sleep. She stumbled up the last few steps, made it down the hall, then began the arduous task of taking off all those innumerable petticoats she'd had to put on.

She could trust her father and Lady Clementina, she reflected as she fell into her bed. They'd keep Uxbridge in sight . . . she could only hope he was the one . . . he had to be. . . . Frustration filled her as she drifted off, a sense of Graeme's presence she found soothing, welcome, wonderful, almost as if she awaited his coming and he would join her in her bed at any moment . . .

He had come. A hand rested on her shoulder and she rolled over, joy filling her. How—Her eyes flew open to meet the fluttering glare of a gas lamp.

Middy stood over her, her dressing gown wrapped about her, her features haggard with exhaustion. "Miss? I'm ever so sorry to disturb you, and that hard you was to waken. But Mr. Sayre says as you wanted to be called when the ball was over."

Kat yawned, rubbed her eyes, and forced herself to sit up. "What time is it?"

"Going on three, Miss. And we never thought as how they'd stay at it so late. It wasn't as if many of them was dancing, neither. They was just standing there talking. But the last of them's gone to their beds, now, and your father is down the hall, watching."

Kat nodded and reached for her borrowed dressing gown; she wasn't up to dragging on the layers of daytime clothes. Middy helped her into the garment and extinguished the light. Kat smothered a yawn, pulled herself together and eased open the door.

All lay quiet beyond, lit by the glowing gas lamps in their wall sconces. She listened a moment, then crept along toward the room allotted to Uxbridge. She turned a corner, a door beside her opened a crack, and a hand snaked out and grabbed her arm.

She jumped, spun about and glared at her father. "What are you trying to do," she demanded in a hoarse whisper, "make me scream?"

"That would put us in the suds, wouldn't it? Get in here before anyone sees you."

"What—?" She broke off as he dragged her into the spacious area. A bathroom. "Great hiding place. What if someone wants in here?"

He grinned. "Just pretend you're leaving, go around the corner, then come back. Now, Uxbridge hasn't emerged since brushing his teeth or whatever it is he does, and that's been a good half hour or so. He should be settling in for the night."

"And if he comes out again?"

He fixed a stern eye on her. "Then you send Middy for me. Confound it, where is the woman?"

The softest of taps sounded on the door, and it opened to admit the maid.

Kat sighed. "Great thinking, as always, Dad. How am I supposed to explain two of us in here?"

But that, it seemed, wouldn't be a problem. Middy, with a shy giggle, opened a huge wardrobe. "For towels, Miss. I can hide in here if someone wants in."

"Of course. Why didn't I think of that?" Kat shook her head. "It's the lack of sleep," she explained.

"No one blames you," her father patted her on the head. "Now, you two keep each other awake. I'm off for a nap." He ruffled her already tumbled hair and slipped out.

"Great," Kat muttered as the door closed. "Pity we didn't think to bring a deck of cards."

The maid stared at her, wide-eyed. "But you'll be needing to watch the hall, won't you, Miss?"

Kat settled on the floor, peering out the crack into the corridor. It was going to be a long night, she guessed. Behind her, Middy opened the wardrobe and moved towels, apparently preparing a hiding place. Kat contemplated crawling in there and making herself comfortable between the layers of linens. Perhaps she could—

A creak, from some distance away, snapped her back to full awareness. Her mind had been drifting for some time; she had no idea from which direction the sound had come. Uxbridge's room, perhaps?

Footsteps padded along the carpeting, and Kat gestured frantically to Middy before inching the door closed and locking it. She could still see through the keyhole, at least, though not very well. The sounds came closer.

Not Uxbridge. A very feminine form filled her limited view, all trailing clouds of frothy pale pink muslin with a multitude of ribbons and lace. Kat shifted her angle until she could look up and see the face, which was hidden partly behind a lacy nightcap. Vivienne de Loire.

The woman strolled up to the bathroom and Kat froze, preparing herself to climb silently to her feet. But no hand grasped the knob. Kat risked another peek, but could see only a pink haze which didn't move. It remained, blocking her view for several long moments, then it backed away. Vivienne slipped quietly down the corridor in the same direction she had been going before. At Uxbridge's room she glanced about, then eased the door open and vanished inside.

Kat sat back on her heels. Really, she'd have expected Vivienne to be making for Ellesmere's room—no, he'd been pursuing Antonia di Fiorelli—or vice versa. Well, another gentleman, at least. One younger and with more grace in his manner. Uxbridge seemed a very unlikely lover. Unless, of course, a night of illicit amorous activity was not—for once—on Vivienne's mind.

A night of sabotage, instead, perhaps?

Kat braced herself, then rose. As distasteful as the thought might be, she had to discover what those two might be about.

Chapter Twenty-two

Kat crept along the corridor, wishing all the while that someone would turn down the lights. Why did they have to keep the place lit up like a fair? She didn't want to be seen by anyone.

What would they think her, anyway? A peeping Tom? She wasn't into voyeurism. If Uxbridge and Vivienne de Loire were up to anything other than planning sabotage, she was going to feel incredibly stupid—not to mention being hideously embarrassed.

She slowed her steps, making as little noise as possible, resting her hand on the wall to maintain her balance. With infinite care she stooped to the keyhole. She couldn't see anything, where were—

She straightened, feeling the heat rushing to her cheeks. Uxbridge, of all men! Kat turned away. Oh, well, no accounting for taste. No sabotage would be planned for a little while yet, of that she could be sure. She returned to her bathroom, reassured the wide-eyed maid that no messages need yet be sent for reinforcements, and settled down to wait.

The night proved to be every bit as long as Kat had

feared. Pacing the spacious bathroom helped, but she didn't dare move far from the door in case anyone else wished admittance. And not for a moment could she rid herself of the fear they watched the wrong man.

Behind her, Middy slumped to the floor, leaning her head against the towel cabinet. Let the poor woman get a little sleep, Kat reflected. All would probably be still for awhile yet.

An hour passed, then two, before Uxbridge's door opened once more. Vivienne slipped out, then walked calmly down the hall, her expression betraying nothing. Kat sank to the floor, leaned her forehead against the door, and closed her eyes. Just for a few minutes, no longer . . .

Footsteps without startled her. She jerked back as fingers scratched the merest breath of sound on the panel. Who—? Kat peered through the keyhole and recognized Newcombe's imperturbable figure. She straightened, stiff, and stifled a yawn as she opened the door.

"The household is astir, Miss." From his calm air, he might have been announcing that luncheon was being served. Rather as if he carried messages to bathrooms every day.

Kat rubbed her eyes and yawned again. "Dad's turn," she muttered.

"Yes, Miss. I have already called him. He will be here shortly, I believe."

He was, complete with a makeshift tool kit and a faulty light to serve as his excuse for loitering in the corridor. Kat duly admired his ingenuity, then left Middy rearranging towels. She made her way to her bedroom, guiltily aware that she must have dozed off sometime during the last few hours. Surely, though, she awoke soon enough when Newcombe approached? She *must* have heard Uxbridge had he emerged. Clinging to that thought, she crawled once more into her bed, her eyes already closing.

She awoke with a start, instantly alert, awareness tingling through every part of her. A vision, vivid in its every detail, burned in her mind. Her painting. And through it all, clear, ringing, came Graeme's triumph. He was in Uxbridge's house . . . impressions of a surreptitious entry and search flickered through her mind, then faded. He had done it.

Love for him washed over her, and even at that great distance, she sensed his response—and his immediate withdrawal from it. Again, he let his injuries came between them.

She must deal with the sabotage first, she knew. After that . . . well, compromise could be a wonderful thing. A little less impetuosity would do her good. But now—

Now, she concentrated. The image of the soaring balloons she had painstakingly set on canvas filled her mind—but how long could he hold it? Long enough for her to discover the hidden clue? Then a hazy outline seemed to leap at her—Graeme, she realized, pointing it out to her. Pointing out . . . what?

It settled and cleared, revealing a rendition of a large manor house—of Durham Court. Fire exploded from a second story window.

Fire. Here. But *which* window? Where did it start?

She focused on her uncertainty, amplifying it, willing him to understand. *Where?* The question filled her.

Another image flashed in her mind, of the white and

gilt-trimmed walls of the State Dining Room, then focused on a small doorway and a long, narrow chamber. The servants' access. The bomb would be set in one of those two rooms, destroying the side of the house and the conference.

But *when?* Would it be there already? Had she missed it during their last search? Had it been put in place during the night while she slept instead of standing guard? Or would she tear the rooms apart now, frantic, only to discover it had not yet been hidden?

Urgency filled her. She couldn't take chances. She had to check, had to be sure, not waste a moment's time.

She glanced at the clock on her mantel and her throat tightened. Nine o'clock. The dignitaries would gather in the State Dining Room in just over two hours for the first of their formal meetings.

She clambered from bed and reached for her chemise, then balked. She didn't have time to don layer after layer of ridiculous petticoats this morning. She needed her jeans. She located them in the back of the wardrobe along with her sweater, then put on her heavy socks and tennies as well. Lord, it felt good to be herself again. She hurried out, ignoring the startled stare she received from the wife of one of the delegates.

She ran along the hall, then stumbled as the red carpeting shimmered into a cobbled road, and the walls with their neat floral wallpaper turned to buildings. Carriages jostled past, people strolled along the sidewalks, and frustration filled her at how very slow everything moved. A pair of grays trotted before her, and her hands—no, Graeme's hands—clutched the reins, guiding the animals.

Graeme. He was coming.

Only the corridor surrounded her once more. She had halted before the stairs, and now descended them at break-neck speed. He was setting out from London; that meant he would be with her—when? In a little more than an hour, perhaps. She ran on, hope surging through her. Everything would be all right, once he got here.

But until then, she had work to do.

She reached the State Dining Room, dragged open the door, and her heart sank. The footman who should have been on duty was nowhere to be seen. She closed her eyes in a moment of agony. How could anyone—? But of course, Uxbridge—or Ellesmere, following his superior's instructions—would simply tell the man he was needed elsewhere.

No one on guard, herself sleeping part of the night—a bomb might well have been hidden. She wouldn't know for sure, of course, until Uxbridge absented himself from the meeting, but by then it would be too late. She had to find—and defuse—it soon, before Uxbridge realized she knew and stopped her.

She scanned the room quickly, dismayed by how many hiding places she could see. The long table with its heavy carving, the numerous matching chairs—there must be sixty of them, both around the table and lining the wall. Then the sideboards, tables, covered bowls, paintings, draperies—and she had to search all this before anyone arrived and demanded to know what she was about!

The bomb could be anywhere—if there yet at all. She would have to go over everything with care. She could ask Lady Clementina to help—but no, the woman would be with the delegates, playing hostess at their breakfast table. She couldn't absent herself from them. Nor could Kat drag her father from his shadowing of Uxbridge. Knowledge of his lordship's movements was vital. If he left the house, under any pretext whatsoever, she could be sure they had run out of time.

She must be thorough. Now was not the time to impulsively dash about in her usual haphazard way. She had to think, be logical and precise, miss nothing.

She forced the panic from her mind. Concentrate on the task at hand, don't make everything worse. Work methodically. Approach this as Graeme would.

Thought of his steady nerve settled her. She drew a deep breath and, turning to the right of the door, found herself facing a massive sideboard. Fine, drawers first. She dragged them out one at a time, rummaging through them for anything odd, then shoved them back into place and went on to the next cabinet. Then the next. And the one after that. Nothing ticked or let off sulfurous odors or even remotely resembled her hazy concept of a nineteenth century bomb.

Finally, she was back at the door. Drawers all clear. Framework of the furniture next, she ordered herself, and got down on her hands and knees, grateful for the foresight that had made her put on her practical jeans. When the bottoms of each piece turned up nothing, she grabbed one of the chairs and dragged it about with her, searching the tops of mirrors, picture frames, and anything else large enough to conceal some object. Again, nothing except overlooked dust bunnies and an occasional feather from a duster, snagged in a large splinter.

She looked about once more, growing desperate. Dragging back the draperies revealed nothing but a startled moth. She squeezed the fabric, then checked along the sill, at last climbing onto a chair to check the rods. Nothing.

The clock on the mantel now showed the time to be nearly ten-fifteen. Less than an hour left . . . if only Graeme would hurry. He was coming closer, she knew, but she longed to have him with her, now! A wave of encouragement enveloped her, his confidence infusing her, and her flagging spirits revived.

With a will, she gave the room one last inspection, this time checking into every epergne, bowl and serving dish that stood at decorative attention. She even opened the clock, but no time bombs lurked within. At last she paused, reasonably sure no exploding devices could have been concealed in the dining room. That left the little adjoining apartment, and only half an hour before the delegates would start to file in. If she'd missed a bomb—

She refused to consider that possibility. She'd been careful and logical. She'd looked everywhere.

Resolutely moving on, she opened the door and considered the next chamber, which appeared to be little more than a widened corridor with a door at the far end. Its purpose was abundantly clear. Cabinets for holding linens and tableware lined one side of the narrow room. Several chairs stood against the opposite wall, where visiting servants could await their masters' summonses. The door at the end must lead to the kitchens.

She looked about, and fought the hopelessness that assailed her. The ideal place for hiding a bomb, with so many table items stowed away or stacked on shelves. The device needn't be in the meeting room at all; a large explosion right here would effectively destroy the entire wing of Durham Court, along with everything and everyone in that portion of the house.

Which meant she had better get to work—and fast.

She turned to the first cabinet, dragged open the doors, and groaned in dismay. Never had she beheld such quantities of linens, china pieces that defied identification, finger bowls, candles, snuffers, salt dishes and who knew what all else. She forged on, searching every one, driven by the conviction that somewhere lay some deadly trap.

Nothing in the next set of drawers, only napkins and the largest mass of tablecloth she had ever beheld, then a sideboard with a huge epergne. She lifted the lid and looked at the black ball within, then froze. With an unsteady hand, she reached in and touched it.

A black *iron* ball, about ten inches in diameter, with a long length of soft-fibered rope threaded through it, sticking out a couple of feet on each end, coiled neatly. An unpleasant smell drifted forth. Gunpowder.

She'd found it. For a long moment she simply stared in disbelief. She'd been looking for it, she *knew* it would be somewhere—but actually finding it, and in time . . .

Her trembling hand touched the fuse, uncoiling the loop. It's length would give Uxbridge plenty of time to light it, then escape from the house before it went off, blowing up the conference, the delegates, the hopes of Europe.

That wouldn't happen now. She had it safe, she could take it apart. The conference would continue without danger; history as she knew it in her time would remain the same. Triumph flashed through her as she gathered the bomb into her hands.

Behind her, a man cleared his throat. "Do you know, I believe you had best leave that where it is."

She spun about, startled—appalled—to find herself facing Uxbridge. He pointed a gun at her. A repeating pistol.

"I'm so sorry," he said, his expression purely apologetic. "Did I startle you? But you seemed quite absorbed in that. Now, my dear, if you will move away from that rather garish epergne? Yes, like that. Ah, and if you are hoping your father will creep up behind me and save you, I fear you will be disappointed. He's a very tiresome man, so very much like a hound on a scent. I was forced to knock him out to be free of his constant companionship."

Coldness gripped her heart. "Where is he?"

"Alas, not dead. At least, not yet. I have tied him up in my room. Not, of course, that you will ever get the chance to free him. I imagine he will be blown up with the rest. Pity, it's rather a beautiful old house, but there it is. Some sacrifices must always be made."

The dryness in her throat became unbearable. She swallowed, but it didn't help. "You can't shoot me," she managed. "It will bring the servants."

"That isn't what I have in mind." For a very long moment, he toyed with the pistol, running a finger along the barrel before grasping that end and swinging the butt at her head.

She lunged away, reaching for a cabinet to catch her balance, but his foot swept out directly in her path. She stumbled, flailed to catch hold of something, missed, and landed hard on the ground. She gasped for breath, rolling out of reach. If she failed she would be blown up along with the others.

He loomed over her, raised his arm, and for a fraction of a second she saw the carved handle of the gun swinging toward her before she twisted away. Pain flared from her temple, only to fade into the oblivion that engulfed her.

Chapter Twenty-three

A scraping noise sounded in her ears. Rats, her head hurt. She just wanted to lie here, undisturbed, oblivious. The noise grated louder, nearer, and memory surged back. The bomb—and Uxbridge.

Then fury welled within her, compounded by pain and determination. Graeme. He was here.

He was in trouble.

She dragged open her eyes to see him, locked in deadly struggle with Uxbridge. She had to help him. With his knee . . .

For once, he displayed no caution, no reticence. He fought with the reckless abandon of desperation. All impulse and instinct. So he did have it in him, after all.

She strained to move, to reach him, but her arms remained pinned behind her by something that bit into her wrists. What—He must have tied her. And gagged her, as well. A table cloth lay heaped on the floor, its end crammed into her mouth. Another cloth secured her ankles with large but utilitarian knots.

Graeme must have interrupted Uxbridge in the midst of this handiwork. If he hadn't finished, she might have a chance to work herself free. She had to, she realized the next moment. Graeme, hampered by his bad leg, showed signs of weakening already.

Uxbridge panted for breath, but could lunge, even run. He had the advantage. Graeme swung his fist, connecting with Uxbridge's jaw, then stumbled forward as his opponent staggered under the impact. Graeme fell to his knee, and pain exploded in Kat's mind. For a moment Graeme's head lowered, eyes shut.

Uxbridge wasted no time. He grabbed a chair, and Kat screamed her silent warning. Graeme rolled, instinctively reacting to Kat's mental alarm, swinging his body out of the way as the heavy wooden frame slammed into the floor.

Damn it, she had to get free! She renewed her struggles as the men closed on each other again. Pain throbbed through her, Graeme's pain, and she could do nothing to help him. Why hadn't Uxbridge just shot him?

Because, she realized as something hard dug into her hip, the gun lay beneath her. He must have set it down while he tied her. All she had to do was free herself, and she'd have a weapon. She'd kick it over to Graeme if only she could be sure Uxbridge wouldn't be able to reach it first.

Frantic, she tugged again, and an end of cloth fell loose in her hand. In another minute, she shook it off, rolled over, and grabbed the pistol. The fact she had no idea how to use it bothered her only a little.

"Get back!" she shouted to Uxbridge. Her voice quavered, as did the pistol, but she held tight and pointed.

Uxbridge didn't even glance at her. He lunged behind Graeme, pulling him between them. With a massive shove, Uxbridge hurled him against her, knocking her over so that Graeme's weight pinned her to the floor. As Graeme rolled free, she glimpsed Uxbridge diving out the door into the servants corridor. The next moment, it slammed in his wake.

Graeme muttered an oath as he grabbed the edge of the nearest cabinet and dragged himself to his feet. Kat, the gun still held gingerly in her hand, scrambled up, too.

"Here." She thrust the weapon into his hand.

He didn't so much as glance at it, but to her relief his fingers curved knowledgeably about the butt as he limped—badly—toward the far end of the narrow chamber. Kat, her legs stiff from her struggles to free herself, stumbled after him. He knew one end of a gun from another, thank heavens, which was more than could be said for her. The odds of her hitting Uxbridge by anything other than sheer accident were nonexistent.

Graeme reached the door first, his fingers closed on the handle, and his brow snapped down in a scowl. "Locked," he exclaimed.

"But—" Kat stared at the door—now a blockade. "How—"

"We'll have to go around." He ran unevenly halfway down the long chamber, then stopped abruptly before the cabinet with the epergne, the lid still lying beside it. He rammed the pistol into the waistband of his trousers, then grasped the bomb and yanked out the rope fuse. "In case he doubles back," he explained.

He tossed an end of the rope over his shoulder and headed into the State Dining Room.

Kat burst through after him into the echoing silence of the cavernous apartment. "Where—?" she managed to gasp as she drew abreast of him.

"Outside." He spared little breath on explanations.

It was enough, though. The delegates would be safe—for the moment, at least. Unless Uxbridge managed to outsmart them. "Where will he go?" she demanded, keeping pace at Graeme's side.

"Since we can't follow him, we'll have to guess." He led the way into the corridor and limped toward the back of the house. "He must not escape."

They continued in silence, dodging through doorways, across unused state apartments, then out into a tiny back hallway leading to a narrow servants stair.

"Do you think he has a backup plan?" she panted as Graeme, per force, slowed to negotiate the steps.

His features remained grim. "Another bomb, I'd wager."

Another bomb. Panic gripped at Kat, and she struggled to keep calm. "Where?" she managed to gasp. "In his room?" But they went down, not up.

"Not where a servant might find it." He made the sharp turn at the landing and forged on, lines of pain etched deep around his eyes and mouth. When he spoke again, his jaw remained tense. "He intended to be outside the house when the first bomb went off—"

"So most likely," Kat supplied for him, "he'd stash the second one somewhere within reach from wherever he intended to watch. But where?"

They emerged into a lower hall Kat had never seen before. But, Graeme knew every inch of his aunt's home. Without hesitation, he directed her to a door leading outside.

Where could Uxbridge have planned to watch in safety? Where might he have an excuse for being when the bomb exploded during a meeting at which he was supposed to be present? Her gaze traveled across the drive to the stable with its yard walled by the several buildings even as Graeme started toward it.

Kat caught up to him and wrapped an arm about his waist. "Lean on me," she gasped.

He made no protest, as she'd feared, but draped his arm about her shoulders, allowing her to carry some of his weight. With every step, pain seeped from his mind to hers. The damage he did to that knee—she forced down the thought. Later, she could regret and wish medical science had advanced far enough to help him and so many other sufferers. Now, Lord Uxbridge had to be caught, stopped, before he found another way to succeed in his self-appointed mission of destruction.

"There!" Kat cried, as a shape darted across the cobbled yard and into the carriage house. "Your instinct's serving you pretty well."

"Have to trust it more often." Graeme increased his pace.

His pain welled through Kat, and she strained with the control he exerted to keep his leg from buckling beneath him. Not much farther, only another thirty yards . . . twenty-five . . . now twenty. . . . They crossed the yard and Kat caught at the door of the barn, resting against it, as Graeme fought for mastery over his knee.

The darkness of the interior made it difficult to see— made them perfect targets as they stood silhouetted against the bright morning light behind them, she realized. She took a cautious step forward, her eyes adjusting.

A tall, slender shape stood about twenty feet away, next to one of the harness boxes. Uxbridge. He held something in his hands.

"Another bomb," Graeme muttered beneath his breath.

Kat winced at his words. Until that moment, she hadn't realized the hope existed within her that they were wrong, that Uxbridge sought only to escape. Horror filled her, dismay that Graeme had been right. Uxbridge had left nothing to chance; he was no coward to cut his losses and run. That made him a fanatic, the most dangerous enemy of all.

Graeme took an unsteady step forward. "It's over," he said, keeping his voice low and calm. "I removed the fuse from your bomb. The delegates are all outside, down by the lake. An explosion here will do them no harm." He took another step. "The one you're holding is useless. There's no rope in it, nothing to light." A third step.

"Stay where you are." Uxbridge's voice rose on a quavering note.

Madness? Kat wondered. He'd have to be on the verge, to have ever considered such a terrible plot, to have murdered Sir Francis, to have calmly planned the destruction of so many, of so much. Fanaticism carried too far.

Graeme paused. "There's no fuse," he repeated.

A sharp laugh escaped Uxbridge. "Do you think me incompetent? I wouldn't trust in only one kind of explosive device. This one doesn't need a fuse."

"That's nonsense." A smile actually touched Graeme's lips.

"Is it?" Uxbridge held the bomb before his face, turning it to examine it from more than one side. "This one," he looked at Graeme and grinned, "is filled with nitroglycerine."

Graeme froze. "You wouldn't be so mad," he breathed.

Nitroglycerine. Kat's heart lurched. The stuff was still unstable at this time. It wouldn't become "safe" for another ten or twenty years, not until Alfred Nobel perfected his experiments with dynamite. Nor did it need a fuse. Dropping it—or even just giving it a good, hard shake—could set it off, taking with it everything in its vicinity. She barely prevented herself from taking a few judicious steps backward.

Graeme held his ground, once more in calm control. "There's no point in that." He advanced a cautious pace forward. "Put it down."

Uxbridge retreated, both hands gripping the iron ball. "Why?" A shaky laugh escaped him. "Do you promise me safe escort to France? Do you think me fool enough to believe you if you did?" He backed farther, one foot after the other, until he bumped into an ancient bermline.

Kat cast a rapid glance about. If the nitroglycerine were set off, the entire carriage house would explode, she guessed. That stuff didn't go in for half measures. The whole structure, and everything and everyone in it, would blow.

Uxbridge looked to be at the limit of his nerves, ready to shake—or even drop—his deadly burden. He could, with her good will, if only she and Graeme weren't there to go up with it. But if she could just get Graeme outside, they could let Uxbridge blow himself up.

She sensed something—agreement?—from Graeme. Had he understood her idea? He'd probably reached the same conclusion himself. Then why didn't he begin backing toward the door? It stood open not that far behind them. Once outdoors, they could run—or limp—to safety.

He remained where he stood. Without taking his gaze from Uxbridge, he said softly, "Get out, Kat. Now."

He wouldn't go; he wouldn't leave anything to chance. The odds favored the explosion of the nitro-glycerin, but they didn't guarantee it. Graeme would never walk away, leaving Uxbridge free to work whatever devilment he could still manage.

Graeme's concern for her nudged at the edges of her mind. His fear for her hampered him, she realized. He wouldn't act, wouldn't force the issue, as long as she stood in any danger.

Yet how could he expect her to leave him in the same situation? If Uxbridge made a dash for it, Graeme hadn't a chance of catching him. That Uxbridge intended to use the bomb she knew, as a certainty, by the grim set of his face. What would he do, throw it at the house in frustration? Or head for the lake where the delegates gathered? That seemed most likely.

They'd have to keep him penned in here. They had to save the conference—and the independent futures of the European countries—even if it meant at the cost of their own lives.

Or did it have to be that way? If she could only

convince Graeme to get out of here—but for that, she'd need to assure him of some foolproof way to make Uxbridge shake the unstable bomb once they were gone.

Graeme still held the pistol. Perhaps he could shoot it . . .

Uxbridge stood tense, his hands trembling, his fingers lovingly clutching the black iron. Then he transferred the bomb to one hand, hefting it as if considering its weight—or its throwing potential. Graeme backed away, not hurrying but not lingering, either.

A slow grin spread across Uxbridge's wild countenance. He must believe he had them cowed. Perhaps he did, Kat admitted. She, for one, didn't feel like arguing with unstable nitroglycerin—or the patently unstable mind that held it.

Luring him outside might be best, she reflected. That way, if he did drop—or throw—it in the open, there would be no burning debris to fall on them. Just a straight explosion . . . and shrapnel. It didn't really matter, after all, where it happened.

The sooner they ended this standoff, the better. Her nerves couldn't stand much more. Graeme retreated another step, his hand going to the waist of his trousers. Inch by cautious inch, he eased the pistol free and held it close to himself.

A sense of Graeme's determination filled her. He wasn't going to wait or try any tricks. He intended to shoot the bomb and take the consequences to assure the safety of everyone else.

Uxbridge followed another step, then his gaze focused just over Graeme's shoulder and his face contorted with rage. Kat looked. Just outside the doorway stood her father with Lady Clementina. Behind them, pressing forward to peer over their shoulders, were the burly Bartholomew Reed and one of the grooms.

Uxbridge's mouth worked, and a rasping cry of fury tore from his throat. Kat froze. The man had realized, at last, he had no hope of reaching the delegates.

"Run!" Kat spun on the group clustering near. They had to move quickly, save as many of these people as possible before Uxbridge blew them all to bits.

Adam reacted first. With one hand he grabbed Lady Clementina's arm, with the other he shoved the groom, propelling them all away from the carriage house. Within a few steps they all ran.

Determination welled from Graeme. "Go!" he ordered.

She hesitated only a moment. He'd make no move while she remained; Uxbridge might regain the advantage. Torn, wanting to drag Graeme with her but knowing his stubbornness, she followed the others. Graeme brought up the pistol.

Across the yard, Adam threw Lady Clementina to the ground behind a line of shrubs. With a last backward glance, Kat broke into a run.

The explosion heaved her from her feet. She curled into a ball as she landed, throwing herself into a roll, her ears ringing, pain sparking on her hands, her legs. The fraction of her mind that still functioned screamed at her that Graeme hadn't fired the gun, the bomb had slipped from Uxbridge's shaking hands.

Graeme . . .

She sensed nothing from him. Then the faintest touches of pain, fading, slipping away . . .

She struggled to her feet. Flaming debris lay everywhere, smoking, shooting sparks that ignited patches of grass. The building itself . . . she was running without even realizing she had moved, dodging the rubble, desperate to reach the burning remains of the carriage house, screaming Graeme's name.

No answer, not even in her mind. Nothing but that vague prickle she couldn't lock onto, as if he were too weak to reach farther—or as if he clung to consciousness by an unraveling thread.

The back wall still stood, in part—though flames licked up the broken boards, threatening to complete the destruction. She slowed to a halt at what once had been the entrance, where flaming timbers and beams had fallen from the roof when their supports had been blown outward. A figure—she averted her gaze from what remained of Lord Uxbridge, as nausea left her ill and shaky kneed.

Graeme—

She stumbled forward, frantic, searching through the blazing destruction, seeking any sign. He wasn't dead—he couldn't be, or she wouldn't sense anything from him at all. But it was so weak, fading, as if his life ebbed away.

And she couldn't find him to prevent it.

Chapter Twenty-four

Where was Graeme? Kat stumbled amid the wreckage, grasping blackened fragments of lumber, not caring about the embers that burned her hands. Smoke filled the air, stinging her eyes, choking her as she tried to breathe. Where . . .

There! A boot, now charred and dusted with rubble, protruded from beneath a section of what must once have been a wall. Oh, God, it had landed fully on him . . . no, a thick beam stuck out its charred end nearby. It had protected him, at least partly. She fell to her knees, reaching for the first piece of wood.

"Easy, Kat." Her father leaned across her, grabbing one side. "Can't drag it or you'll crush him."

"I know." The words broke from her on a sob. "Dad, he's almost gone. I can barely feel him."

"We'll get him, don't worry, Kitten." With the wiry muscles in his arms bunching, he carefully raised the timber.

Then more hands reached to help, and Kat found herself shouldered aside by the brawny bulk of Bartholomew Reed. She could barely see Graeme over the men's shoulders, only the charred rags that had once been his elegant coat and trousers. And the burns, everywhere . . .

"He's dying," a high, trembling voice wailed. Lady Clementina, her tears causing rivulets of dust and soot to run down her lined cheeks, hovered on the fringes, reaching for Graeme's limp hand.

"No!" Kat yelled the word, and it echoed through her mind, her very being. She would not let Graeme die. She couldn't. She reached out through their link, seeking him, any part of him she could hold onto, strengthen with her will. He eluded her, fading farther, beyond her reach. "No!" she repeated, desperate, speaking only to Graeme. "Come back. Come back."

The last faded to silence, sounding over and over in her mind. *Where are you? Don't leave me, don't go.* Dizziness gripped her, sending her surroundings reeling as she pushed her way to where the men laid Graeme on the cobbled stones outside. Smoke hovered in the air; it hurt to breathe.

"Dad, your coat. Anything! Keep the air off his burns." She grabbed the garment her father held out, then gratefully accepted the petticoat Lady Clementina handed over. These she wrapped tenderly about Graeme. He needed antibiotics, something for shock, something to soothe the burns that covered so much of him.

She reached out again through the link, and a sob broke from her as she encountered nothing. Dear God, was she to lose everything? Her own time, her own people, and now Graeme, as well? How could she continue to exist, half a person, without this bond with him that made her whole? Without Graeme.

"I never wanted the paramedics more." Her father's voice broke on the last word.

An almost hysterical desire to laugh set Kat's shoulders shaking. The paramedics! They were more than a hundred years away.

Lady Clementina dropped to her knees at her side, the tears still slipping unheeded down her cheeks, and put her arms about Kat. "Oh, my dear—" She broke off, choking back a sob.

"Isn't there anything—anyone—?" Kat looked from Lady Clementina to her father, then to Reed, who stood helplessly beside them, watching.

"There is nothing we can do." Trembling, Lady Clementina touched a miraculously uninjured spot on Graeme's blistered cheek. "I've seen death before. He's already too close to it for a doctor to be able to save him, even if one were here."

Kat straightened, pulling away. "You can't give up! We've got to try something! I won't let him die."

Adam shook his head. "It's the wrong time, Kitten. The medical technology he needs just doesn't exist yet. Those burns—" He broke off, shaking his head. "Even if he survives the shock, blood poisoning will set in."

She swallowed. He'd die, because they were in the wrong time, because . . .

She caught her breath. Still staring at Graeme's face, not quite believing the idea that had occurred to her, she said, "If they can't save him here, then I'll take him where they can!"

Adam's eyes widened in comprehension. "There's no reason to think it'll work, Kitten. You may go nowhere but up. Or you may both be killed."

"But if it *does* work, he might live! And we could

heal his knee, as well. Dad, he'd have the chance for the life he wanted! Please, Dad."

Adam dropped to his knee and grasped Graeme's wrist. "His pulse is still there. He's no quitter." He chewed his lower lip. "Think you can reach him, Kat? I doubt he has more than a few hours left without help."

She touched his singed hair. "I'll reach him," she vowed, and closed her eyes. It had to work. She wouldn't let it *not* work. *Graeme* . . .

A stirring, as of a regaining consciousness barely acknowledged. He was there, she'd found him. With every ounce of her being, she enveloped that lone spark, nurturing it, sharing her strength, willing it to grow, hold on, not slip farther into the pit of darkness that lay just beyond. As eternity stretched past her, their link caught, weak but still viable. For how much longer, though, she didn't know. She could only pray it would be long enough.

Beyond her immediate focus, sounds of activity reached her, barely acknowledged. Only the acrid smoke stinging her lungs kept her aware of her surroundings.

"It's pretty burned," Adam's voice said.

"His dragon—" The rest of Lady Clementina's exclamation faded.

Vaguely, Kat realized the wicker dragon must have been in the carriage house or one of the stalls nearby. Damaged. Burned.

"Remember those metal plates?" Adam called. "Think I said at the time the repair job looked like something I'd have done myself. Looks like I did do it.

There are some thin ones right here waiting to fix up a carriage."

She opened her eyes. "Use your bag, Dad, not his. And the propane equipment. We haven't time for hydrogen, and everything's got to be as close as possible to the trip that brought us back here."

"I've already got Reed and the groom using bellows to inflate it," her father assured her.

Kat's eyes closed again as her concentration returned to Graeme. Had the link weakened? She shouldn't have risked speaking to her father; it hadn't even been necessary, he already had everything under control. Dear Dad.

His voice reached her, demanding a bolt, and Lady Clementina's softer tones answered. He'd repair the dragon, make it functional again. She focused her attention fully on Graeme.

Their link held, but he continued to weaken. "Blankets!" she shouted. She should have thought of that before. She had to get him warmer, lessen the effects of the shock. She might provide the will for him to survive, but the trauma inflicted on his body was so great.

"Carriage robes." Lady Clementina knelt at her side and spread first one blanket, then another over Graeme. "We're putting two in the bottom of the dragon for him to lie on."

"How much longer?" Kat managed to ask. She risked a glance at the balloon, which still lay limply in a heap. "How can we get it filled faster?" she cried. "Dad, isn't there some simple steam engine around here you can convert?"

"There's the forge, sir." A man's voice, doubtful. The groom.

"Lead me to it," Adam ordered.

The two disappeared, and Kat emptied her mind once more, melding her strength and will to Graeme. Behind her, the sounds of metal striking metal sounded for some time, but not until Lady Clementina gasped did Kat look up again.

A peculiar contraption, from which emitted a series of chugging noises, sat on the ground near the balloon, which now billowed with the air that surged into it. He'd done it.

Adam strode over and laid a hand on her shoulder, his smile grim but satisfied. "Trust your old Dad, Kitten. We'll get you aloft. You just hold on to your man, there."

She did, though her control faded moment by moment. Control. She'd learned that from Graeme. At least she had some.

Then miraculously the balloon rose. Adam fitted the nozzle of the propane tank into the dragon. Moments later he had it alight, and flames shot upward, heating the air.

"Help me lift him." Adam stooped at Graeme's head, and Reed took his feet.

Kat scrambled into the basket to assist with easing him to the blankets on the floor. At last he half-sat in the bottom, propped against a side. Adam stepped back, and Kat tore her gaze from Graeme's still face. "No time to go back to the house for anything, Dad. Get in."

He shook his head. "I'm not going, Kat."

"Not—"

Her father studied the woman who stood very still at his side, her gaze intent on his face. "Our time's gotten boring for me, Kat. You know that. Damn it, I've done everything but go up in a space shuttle."

"Maybe your old friends at NASA—" She felt the hopelessness of that comment even as she spoke it.

He gave a short laugh. "No, allow me my retirement here. This is the ultimate challenge, Kat, to fit into a different time. I can tinker and reinvent to my heart's content. And I've got someone who'll enjoy it all with me. If she will?" His arm slid around Lady Clementina's shoulders.

The woman reached up and touched his cheek with one tentative finger. "You did promise me a race across the Channel."

He grinned suddenly. "How about a train trip across America, too?"

"Dad—?" Kat reached out her hand.

Adam stepped forward and enveloped her in a bear hug. "Your filial blessing, Kitten?"

She nodded, fighting back the tears that stung her eyes. "You'll be happy."

"So will you, I promise you." He kissed her forehead. "We'll have an ambulance waiting for Graeme, don't you worry. You just leave everything to your old Dad."

He stepped back, and her hand slid from his as the basket, with a groaning creak, lifted from the ground. Charcoal smoke drifted from the smoldering remains of the carriage house, swirling about them, enveloping the dragon, obscuring from her view the beloved faces below. In the distance the figures gathered by the lake seemed to shimmer.

Kat sank to her knees, clinging to her link with Graeme. *Would* this work? She'd tried not to think about it, trusting that it would. But why should it? What guarantee was there? Time travel, of all impossible things. And she hadn't even the link with Graeme to draw her across the ages. He was here with her—for however long he could cling to his ebbing life.

She fought back the tears that threatened to overcome her again. They *had* to get back to her time, to a modern hospital with a trauma center and burn unit. She wouldn't, not for a moment, consider the damaged basket, patched so quickly by her father, that might give way at any moment and send them hurtling to the ground. If Graeme didn't reach medical help soon, it would make no difference to him. Or to her, without him.

She cast a quick glance over the side, but only a lingering haze greeted her. Had they risen far enough? She hadn't felt dizzy this time—or had she felt nothing *but* dizzy since the explosion?

Graeme couldn't wait any longer. With a sick sense of certainty, she knew she could maintain him for only minutes more. How many, she couldn't be sure, but he grew weaker, their link more tenuous, by the moment.

That settled it. She cut the flame, and moments later the tops of the trees crept up to welcome them. Then she had to tear her attention from Graeme, concentrate for a few vital minutes on their landing, easing them over a stone wall toward a stand of trees, gliding them toward a grassy knoll. She held her breath.

The basket touched down and she vaulted over the side, grabbing the tether lines as she rolled with her landing. The basket jerked against her, dragging her several steps, then she wrapped the loose end around the base of a shrub. The next minute, she grabbed the release valve and began deflating the balloon.

The air settled about her, calm. No wind, not even a gentle breeze. The heady smell of clover and wildflowers filled her, tinged with pollen—and acrid smoke. Kat looked about, searching for a clue as to where—or when—they were. The dragon basket remained before her feet, her fingers clutched its wicker side. Had it worked? Were they in her time—or his?

Which translated, she realized, to: would Graeme live—or die?

For that matter, could he survive the wait until she found out? Bees buzzed loudly somewhere nearby, and a bird sang out its challenge in the trees. In the distance—an odd noise reached her, barely audible at first, a two-tone beeping as of a horn, familiar yet foreign—an ambulance!

"They're coming!" She swung back into the basket and knelt at Graeme's side, afraid to touch him except with her mind. "They're coming," she whispered, then stood up to wave frantic arms as the siren grew louder and the vehicle swerved through a gate into the field.

As it pulled to a stop before her, the passenger door swung wide, and a small man tumbled out. "Mr. Jameson!" Kat cried in disbelief. "Quick," she turned to the uniformed ambulance driver who climbed out more slowly. "He's badly burned and in shock, he needs help!"

"Your father, Miss Sayre?" Mr. Jameson approached slowly, as if afraid to look inside the wicker dragon.

The ambulance driver, joined now by another attendant who must have been riding in back, ran up with a case in one hand. He vaulted the side, drew the blanket back from Graeme's face, and went to work. His companion opened another box, a crackling sound broke the quiet, and in moments they had a doctor on the radio, listening to the stats and vital signs they reported.

Kat hugged herself, trembling, as her link with Graeme faded a little more.

"Miss Sayre?" Mr. Jameson tugged at her elbow.

She shook her head, not sparing a thought for anything or anyone but Graeme. The two men had plugged a network of IVs into his veins. The second attendant scrambled out of the basket and took off at a run for the ambulance, only to return a minute later with a stretcher.

"Transporting," the attendant announced into the radio, and shut it off. Then somehow they transferred Graeme to the stretcher and moments later loaded him into the back of their van.

Kat started to clamber in after them, but stopped. Something . . . the dragon. As she looked back, the basket shimmered, then settled. Only now it looked different, older, and the wicker no longer smoldered. It had switched itself, she realized. This was now the one she and her father had found in the barn and repaired, and in which they set forth on their impossible journey. And the one that had carried her and Graeme to the present—that must have returned to the past, where Adam would store it for her.

Kat swung into the ambulance where the attendant hovered over Graeme. As the uniformed man reached out to close the door, Mr. Jameson, his face pinched, his thin nose aquiver beneath his thick glasses, thrust a letter yellowed with age, sealed with a gob of red wax, into her hands. "This is for you," he called, and stepped back.

Kat, perplexed, turned it over and stared at her name on the ancient sheet, inscribed in her father's familiar, sprawling hand.

Epilogue

Six months later

Graeme, seated in an overstuffed armchair, his feet propped on a footstool, finished the chapter he studied in the textbook on modern agriculture. He put a marker in it and set it aside, then contemplated instead the domestic holiday scene before him. The CD player—he still didn't fully understand that contraption—emitted the comfortable strains of Christmas carols, some familiar, most new to him.

Kat, her hair tied back with a festive plaid ribbon, knelt before the blazing fire, stirring the bowl of spiced cider set there to keep warm. Beside her, at the base of the Christmas tree, her hands folded across the front of her maternity smock, sat an older version of Kat, her dark hair a halo of curls about her laughing face. Kat's sister Tina. Clementina, rather.

A sad smile tugged at Graeme's lips. He missed his aunt, as Kat and her family must miss Adam. At least they hadn't been cut off completely. The past, thanks to Adam's penchant for meddling—bless him—would continue to intrude on their present and future for many long years to come.

"I wish they'd get back," Tina said, for at least the fifth time. She turned to look out the window at the snow-covered landscape and sighed.

"Customs." Kat rested the ladle in the bowl and stood. "And quit worrying about the trains, they run fine in the snow."

Tina grimaced, unconvinced. "Easy for you to say. Your husband isn't on one."

"No." Kat didn't look at Graeme—the man who couldn't be her husband.

His jaw tightened. With an effort, he forced a cheerful note into his voice and said, "The concept of being able to cross the Atlantic in a matter of hours instead of weeks still amazes me."

Tina, apparently oblivious of her *faux pas,* settled herself on the sofa. "Orville had just better be with them, that's all."

"Relax, he'd have called us if he had to cancel the flight." Kat paced to the window.

Graeme drew a steadying breath, trying to keep Kat from sensing his frustration. So many amazing things existed in this time. The machines, the conveniences, the medical knowledge. He could walk again, with only the slightest limp. So far, he'd only found one thing to be impossible in this new era of miracles. A man couldn't marry the woman of his choice unless he possessed some form of identification—which he lacked.

Kat might pretend not to care, she pointed out that other people of this era lived together all the time without benefit of clergy, and it never bothered them.

But he sensed a touch of regret in her, a knowledge that their relationship was less than perfect. He certainly felt that way. She called him old-fashioned—antiquated, in fact—but he couldn't help being a product of his time, as she called it. He wanted marriage.

Kat met his gaze for a fleeting moment. She always knew.

Tina picked up her knitting, then set it down again. "Isn't that Mr. Jameson of yours going to visit us today?"

A chuckle escaped Kat. "That poor man. He's gone through so much because of us. You really should have seen his face, Tina, when he showed up at the hospital with all those lawyers and Lady Clementina's will. What a tangle she created with that thing. Do you think she did it on purpose, Graeme?"

Graeme leaned his head against the cushioned back of the chair. "Every line of that document bore your father's stamp, and you know it. Only he could have dumped us in a quagmire like that."

"Good old Dad." Kat fell silent a moment. "You have to admit, though, it was pretty clever of him—of them both."

Tina looked up from the pattern with which she toyed. "You never told me how they worked it, just that they'd left everything to you. Which must have been some neat trick, since you didn't legally exist at the time they—died." She hesitated over the last word.

Kat hugged herself. "Damn, I miss him."

"According to that letter you showed me, he was perfectly happy. I can hardly wait to read the next installment." Tina's gaze drifted to the wicker basket that sat beneath the tree, in which rested a Christmas letter to them all, dated this year. Other letters—a whole large box of them—awaited other important occasions, each carefully labeled or dated. "He's not really gone, you know," she added. "Not as long as we can keep hearing from him like that."

"Only Dad could figure out how to keep on meddling. And that was our last visit from Mr. Jameson— at least, the last official one. The lawyers have finally transferred Durham Court out of the trusteeship and into my name."

Graeme smiled. "Which do you think astounded them more, my aunt's naming an heir yet to be born, or a letter almost a hundred and fifty years old addressed to Mr. Jameson personally, and demanding that ambulance for me?"

Kat perched on the arm of his chair. "You should have seen them, Tina. That poor man. Lady Clementina's will left instructions for him to open a sealed file as soon as Dad and I took off in the dragon basket. He said he nearly had a heart attack when his saw his name on the top sheet. And the cost of hiring an ambulance and crew to stand by every day until we showed up, like Dad ordered—! And trying to explain to those poor men *why* they had to sit there day after day, weekends too, doing nothing."

"You must have made their year for them, actually showing up and needing it," Tina commented.

Graeme leaned his head against Kat's arm. He didn't remember their arrival, or anything else, for that matter, until he'd been in this time for over a week. All he'd experienced had been a sensation of Kat's presence, holding on to him, forcing him to stay with her.

Outside, headlights swooped through the dusk as a car swung onto the long drive.

"They're here!" Tina eased herself to her feet. "No, Kat, I don't need a crane yet. Wait another month."

The car came to a stop before the front porch, doors slammed, and the sound of deep, cheerful male voices reached them. Graeme rose—it still pleased him he no longer needed a cane for such a simple maneuver—and went to throw open the door.

Three men stood in the great hall, dripping melting snow on the tiles as they dragged off their coats. Emily, their live-in housekeeper, collected overcoats. Graeme hesitated, his gaze brushing across the blond giant John, Tina's husband. The two shorter men, the twins, identical in every detail except dress, he had never seen together before. With a flash of surprise, though, he realized he knew which one was which. Kat's knowledge of them, conveyed to him through their link? He strode forward, noticing with pleasure his knee caused him only a twinge.

The twins looked up and both grinned. Identical smiles. One hurried forward, holding out his hand. "Good to see you again, Graeme."

"What, after only three hours? Good try, Wilbur, but I don't fool that easily. Hello, Orville." He moved past Wilbur, who stared at him with a touch of admiration, to greet his favorite of Kat's two brothers. "Good flight? Let's get your things upstairs."

Orville grinned as he hoisted a suitcase. "Gotten used to not having a battery of servants, I see. No, don't bother. Make Wilbur earn his keep. Same room I had last time? We'll be down in a few minutes, then. Have a hot drink ready for me, will you?"

Graeme returned to the drawing room where John now sat on the sofa, one arm about Tina, the other resting on her growing stomach. A child.

Wistfulness touched his mind and he glanced at Kat. That sensation had come from them both, but no child of hers—or of his—would ever be base-born. Somehow, he had to make Kat his legal wife.

Kat turned away and went to the fire. Graeme remained where he stood, wanting to comfort her, realizing he did without moving. She knew. Always.

The door opened and the two brothers strode in. Orville caught Kat in his arm and kissed her cheek, then went to the sofa to drop a kiss on Tina's hair.

"Thought you'd decided not to come." Tina caught his hand and squeezed it.

Orville grinned. "Sorry, I had a little bit of trouble getting something."

Graeme, with Wilbur's assistance, filled glasses with the steaming apple cider, and the scents of cinnamon and nutmeg filled the room.

Kat collected the basket. "Okay, everyone, time for the First Annual Reading of one of Dad's Christmas letters."

"This ought to be good." Wilbur settled cross-legged before the hearth. "Has it occurred to you, Kat, that Graeme's aunt is our step-mother?"

"A man didn't need papers to get married in my time," Graeme said, and wished his words hadn't sounded so short.

"That reminds me." Orville held up his hand. "My reason for being late. If you don't mind, Kat? I've spent five months trying to get Graeme his Christmas present, and I don't want to wait any longer to see if it's what he wants."

Kat frowned. "We were going to do presents later. Dad—"

"He wouldn't mind, believe me." Orville drew a small flat box from under his sweater and handed it to Graeme. "Open it."

Graeme glanced at Kat.

She shrugged. "You know Orville. He'll hound you until you do."

"Five months?" Tina asked. "Go on, Graeme, this we've got to see."

Graeme pulled the ribbon off, lifted the lid, and spread the snowman-printed tissue paper. A small folder lay inside. He opened it, and stared at a photograph of himself with typeset words beneath. He started to read, then froze as the meaning sank in.

"A passport," Orville announced to the others, smug. "Canadian, and made out in the name of Graeme Warwick. Congratulations, Graeme, you now officially exist."

Graeme transferred his gaze to Orville's grinning face. "How—?"

"Friends in the State Department who owed me a few favors. It's taken time, though. I started work on this as soon as Kat told me about you."

Papers. Graeme gazed at them for a moment, then looked up and met Kat's tear-filled eyes. He laid the passport aside—though perhaps he should lay it at her feet. "Kitten." He rose and took her hands in his. "I—"

"If you go down on your knee to propose to her,"

Wilbur announced from where he sprawled before the fire, "we're outta here. I'm warning you."

Graeme, who had been about to do just that, hesitated. "What do you suggest, then?"

A wicked grin spread across Wilbur's face. "Throw her over your shoulder and—"

"Don't you dare listen to him," Kat interrupted. Her fingers clung to Graeme's. "I like you old-fashioned."

"Antiquated?" Wilbur offered.

"Be polite to your elders," Graeme shot back at him.

"You're certainly taking long enough about this," John declared. "Or don't you plan to ask her after all? Kat, do you want the knave thrashed?"

"Wrong era," she shot back. "I don't think they had knaves in Victorian times."

"Of course we did," Graeme informed her. "Only we called them—"

"Get on with it," Tina urged. "The rest of these idiots need a lesson on being romantic from a *real* gentleman."

"Shall we just take the proposal as made and accepted?" Orville suggested.

"No!" Kat folded her arms, her chin sticking out stubbornly. "I've waited over a hundred and forty years for this, and I want it done properly."

"Talk about an old maid." Tina hefted herself to her feet and went to the large box of letters. "I know I saw one in here from Dad labeled for your wedding."

"Where?" Wilbur joined her.

Graeme grasped Kat's hand and dragged her out

the door. "Pity we can't lock them in," he muttered as he shut it behind him and pulled her into his arms.

She drew back. "Down on your knee."

"I had every intention of it." He complied, then possessed himself of her hand. "I'll have you know, a hundred and forty years ago I wouldn't have been able to do this. An old-fashioned proposal made possible by new-fashioned medicine. My dearest Kitten—"

The door opened, and Wilbur peered out. "He only wants you for your inheritance, Kat. He—"

"Back in here." Orville's voice interrupted him, and the next moment Wilbur was jerked back into the drawing room. The door shut with a reassuring bang.

Graeme sighed and fixed a stern eye on her. "Before we go any farther, I want you to promise me one thing, Kat."

Her sparkling eyes clouded. "That we not invite them back?"

"Oh, no. They're always welcome. Just promise me, beloved, our children will take after *my* side of the family."

Kat glanced toward the closed drawing room, then behind Graeme to where hung the portrait—her portrait—of Lady Clementina in her absurd, voluminous split-skirt, standing proudly with her balloon.

She burst out laughing.